经典回声 | Echoes from the Classics

呐喊 Call to Arms

鲁迅 著
杨宪益 戴乃迭 译
裘沙 王伟君 插图

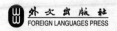
外文出版社
FOREIGN LANGUAGES PRESS

目　录
Contents

自序
Preface to *Call to Arms* [1]

　　我在年青时候也曾经做过许多梦，后来大半忘却了，但自己也并不以为可惜。所谓回忆者，虽说可以使人欢欣，有时也不免使人寂寞，使精神的丝缕还牵着已逝的寂寞的时光，又有什么意味呢，而我偏苦于不能全忘却，这不能全忘的一部分，到现在便成了《呐喊》的来由。

　　我有四年多，曾经常常，——几乎是每天，出入于质铺和药店里，年纪可是忘却了，总之是药店的柜台正和我一样高，质铺的是比我高一倍，我从一倍高的柜台外送上衣服或首饰去，在侮蔑里接了钱，再到一样高的柜台上给我久病的父亲去买药。回家之后，又须忙别的事了，因为开方的医生是最有名的，以此所用的药引也奇特：冬天的芦根，经霜三年的甘蔗，蟋蟀要原对的，结子的平地木，……多不是容易办到的东西。然而我的父亲终于日重一日的亡故了。

　　有谁从小康人家而坠入困顿的么，我以为在这途路中，大概可以看见世人的真面目；我要到N进K学堂去了，仿佛是想走异路，逃异地，去寻求别样的人们。我的母亲没有法，办了八元的川资，说是由我的自便；然而伊哭了，这正是情理中的事，因为那时读书应试是正路，所谓学洋务，社会上便以为是一种走投无路的人，只得将灵魂卖给鬼子，要加倍的奚落而且排斥的，而况伊又看不见自己的儿子了。然而我也顾不得这些事，终于到N去进了K学堂了，在这学堂里，我才知道世上还有所谓格致，算学，地理，历史，绘图和体操。生理学并不教，但我们却看到些木版的《全体新论》和《化学卫生论》之类了。我还记得先前的医生的议论和方药，和现在所知道的比较起来，便渐渐的悟得中医不过是一种有意的或无意的骗子，同时又很起了对于被骗的病人和他的家族的同情；而且从译出的历史上，又知道了日本维新是大半发端于西方医学的事实。

　　因为这些幼稚的知识，后来便使我的学籍列在日本一个乡间的医学专门学校里了。我的梦很美满，预备卒业回来，救治像我父亲似的被误的病人的疾苦，战争时候便去当军医，一面又促进了国人对于维新的信仰。我已不知

1. *Call to Arms*, Lu Xun's earliest collection of short stories,contains fourteen stories written between 1918 and 1922.

2. N— refers to Nanjing,and K— to the Kiangnan(Jiangnan) Naval Academy where the auther studied in 1898.

3. Two English books about physiology and nutrition, the former was translated into Chinese and published in 1851, the latter in 1879.

4. This refers to the Sendai Medical College where Lu Xun studied from 1904 to 1906.

When I was young I, too, had many dreams. Most of them I later forgot, but I see nothing in this to regret. For although recalling the past may bring happiness, at times it cannot but bring loneliness, and what is the point of clinging in spirit to lonely bygone days? However, my trouble is that I cannot forget completely, and these stories stem from those things which I have been unable to forget.

For more than four years I frequented, almost daily, a pawnshop and pharmacy. I cannot remember how old I was at the time, but the pharmacy counter was exactly my height and that in the pawnshop twice my height. I used to hand clothes and trinkets up to the counter twice my height, then take the money given me with contempt to the counter my own height to buy medicine for my father, a chronic invalid. On my return home I had other things to keep me busy, for our physician was so eminent that he prescribed unusual drugs and adjuvants: aloe roots dug up in winter, sugar-cane that had been three years exposed to frost, original pairs of crickets, and ardisia that had seeded... most of which were difficult to come by. But my father's illness went from bad to worse until finally he died.

It is my belief that those who come down in the world will probably learn in the process what society is really like. My eagerness to go to N — and study in the K — Academy[2] seems to have shown a desire to strike out for myself, escape, and find people of a different kind. My mother had no choice but to raise eight dollars for my travelling expenses and say I might do as I pleased. That she cried was only natural, for at that time the proper thing was to study the classics and take the official examinations. Anyone who studied "foreign subjects" was a social outcast regarded as someone who could find no way out and was forced to sell his soul to foreign devils. Besides, she was sorry to part with me. But in spite of all this, I went to N — and entered the K — Academy; and it was there that I learned of the existence of physics, arithmetic, geography, history, drawing and physical training. They had no physiology course, but we saw woodblock editions of such works as *A New Course on the Human Body* and *Essays on Chemistry and Hygiene*.[3] Recalling the talk and prescriptions of physicians I had known and comparing them with what I now knew, I came to the conclusion that those physicians must be either unwitting or deliberate charlatans; and I began to feel great sympathy for the invalids and families who suffered at their hands. From translated histories I also learned that the Japanese Reformation owed its rise, to a great extent, to the introduction of Western medical science to Japan.

These inklings took me to a medical college in the Japanese countryside.[4] It was my fine dream that on my return to China I would cure patients like my father who had suffered from the wrong treatment, while if war broke out I would serve as an army

道教授微生物学的方法，现在又有了怎样的进步了，总之那时是用了电影，来显示微生物的形状的，因此有时讲义的一段落已完，而时间还没有到，教师便映些风景或时事的画片给学生看，以用去这多余的光阴。其时正当日俄战争的时候，关于战事的画片自然也就比较的多了，我在这一个讲堂中，便须常常随喜我那同学们的拍手和喝采。有一回，我竟在画片上忽然会见我久违的许多中国人了，一个绑在中间，许多站在左右，一样是强壮的体格，而显出麻木的神情。据解说，则绑着的是替俄国做了军事上的侦探，正要被日军砍下头颅来示众，而围着的便是来赏鉴这示众的盛举的人们。

这一学年没有完毕，我已经到了东京了，因为从那一回以后，我便觉得医学并非一件紧要事，凡是愚弱的国民，即使体格如何健全，如何苗壮，也只能做毫无意义的示众的材料和看客，病死多少是不必以为不幸的。所以我们的第一要著，是在改变他们的精神，而善于改变精神的是，我那时以为当然要推文艺，于是想提倡文艺运动了。在东京的留学生很有学法政理化以至警察工业的，但没有人治文学和美术；可是在冷淡的空气中，也幸而寻到几个同志了，此外又邀集了必须的几个人，商量之后，第一步当然是出杂志，名目是取"新的生命"的意思，因为我们那时大抵带些复古的倾向，所以只谓之《新生》。

《新生》的出版之期接近了，但最先就隐去了若干担当文字的人，接着又逃走了资本，结果只剩下不名一钱的三个人。创始时候既已背时，失败时候当然无可告语，而其后却连这三个人也都为各自的运命所驱策，不能在一处纵谈将来的好梦了，这就是我们的并未产生的《新生》的结局。

我感到未尝经验的无聊，是自此以后的事。我当初是不知其所以然的；后来想，凡有一人的主张，得了赞和，是促其前进的，得了反对，是促其奋斗的，独有叫喊于生人中，而生人并无反应，既非赞同，也无反对，如置身毫无边际的荒原，无可措手的了，这是怎样的悲哀呵，我于

doctor, at the same time promoting my countrymen's faith in reform.

I have no idea what improved methods are now used to teach microbiology, but in those days we were shown lantern slides of microbes; and if the lecture ended early, the instructor might show slides of natural scenery or news to fill up the time. Since this was during the Russo-Japanese War, there were many war slides, and I had to join in the clapping and cheering in the lecture hall along with the other students. It was a long time since I had seen any compatriots, but one day I saw a newsreel slide of a number of Chinese, one of them bound and the rest standing around him. They were all sturdy fellows but appeared completely apathetic. According to the commentary, the one with his hands bound was a spy working for the Russians who was to be beheaded by the Japanese military as a warning to others, while the Chinese beside him had come to enjoy the spectacle.

Before the term was over I had left for Tokyo, because this slide convinced me that medical science was not so important after all. The people of a weak and backward country, however strong and healthy they might be, could only serve to be made examples of or as witnesses of such futile spectacles; and it was not necessarily deplorable if many of them died of illness. The most important thing, therefore, was to change their spirit; and since at that time I felt that literature was the best means to this end, I decided to promote a literary movement. There were many Chinese students in Tokyo studying law, political science, physics and chemistry, even police work and engineering, but not one studying literature and art. However, even in this uncongenial atmosphere I was fortunate enough to find some kindred spirits. We gathered the few others we needed and after discussion our first step, of course, was to publish a magazine, the title of which denoted that this was a new birth. As we were then rather classically inclined, we called it *Vita Nova* (*New Life*).

When the time for publication drew near, some of our contributors dropped out and then our funds ran out, until there were only three of us left and we were penniless. Since we had started our venture at an unlucky hour, there was naturally no one to whom we could complain when we failed; but later even we three were destined to part, and our discussions of a future dream world had to cease. So ended this abortive *Vita Nova*.

Only later did I feel the futility of it all. At that time I had not a clue. Later it seemed to me that if a man's proposals met with approval, that should encourage him to advance; if they met with opposition, that should make him fight back; but the real tragedy was for him to lift up his voice among the living and meet with no response,

是以我所感到者为寂寞。

这寂寞又一天一天的长大起来，如大毒蛇，缠住了我的灵魂了。

然而我虽然自有无端的悲哀，却也并不愤懑，因为这经验使我反省，看见自己了：就是我决不是一个振臂一呼应者云集的英雄。

只是我自己的寂寞是不可不驱除的，因为这于我太痛苦。我于是用了种种法，来麻醉自己的灵魂，使我沉入于国民中，使我回到古代去，后来也亲历或旁观过几样更寂寞更悲哀的事，都为我所不愿追怀，甘心使他们和我的脑一同消灭在泥土里的，但我的麻醉法却也似乎已经奏了功，再没有青年时候的慷慨激昂的意思了。

S会馆里有三间屋，相传是往昔曾在院子里的槐树上缢死过一个女人的，现在槐树已经高不可攀了，而这屋还没有人住；许多年，我便寓在这屋里钞古碑。客中少有人来，古碑中也遇不到什么问题和主义，而我的生命却居然暗暗的消去了，这也就是我惟一的愿望。夏夜，蚊子多了，便摇着蒲扇坐在槐树下，从密叶缝里看那一点一点的青天，晚出的槐蚕又每每冰冷的落在头颈上。

那时偶或来谈的是一个老朋友金心异，将手提的大皮夹放在破桌上，脱下长衫，对面坐下了，因为怕狗，似乎心房还在怦怦的跳动。

"你钞了这些有什么用？"有一夜，他翻着我那古碑的钞本，发了研究的质问了。

"没有什么用。"

"那么，你钞他是什么意思呢？"

"没有什么意思。"

"我想，你可以做点文章……"

我懂得他的意思了，他们正办《新青年》，然而那时仿佛不特没有人来赞同，并且也还没有人来反对，我想，他们许是感到寂寞了，但是说：

5. The Shaoxing Hostel where Lu Xun stayed in Beijing from 1912 to 1919.

6. This magazine played an important part in the May 4th Movement of 1919 by attacking feudalism, advocating the New Culture Movement and Spread Marxist ideas. Jin Xinyi is an alias for Qian Xuantong, one of the editors of *New Youth*. Lu Xun was an important contributor to the magazine.

neither approval nor opposition, just as if he were stranded in a boundless desert completely at a loss. That was when I became conscious of loneliness.

And this sense of loneliness grew from day to day, entwining itself about my soul like some huge poisonous snake.

But in spite of my groundless sadness, I felt no indignation; for this experience had made me reflect and see that I was definitely not the type of hero who could rally multitudes at his call.

However, my loneliness had to be dispelled because it was causing me agony. So I used various means to dull my senses, to immerse myself among my fellow nationals and to turn to the past. Later I experienced or witnessed even greater loneliness and sadness which I am unwilling to recall, preferring that it should perish with my mind in the dust. Still my attempt to deaden my senses was not unsuccessful — I lost the enthusiasm and fervour of my youth.

In S— Hostel[5] was a three-roomed house with a courtyard in which grew a locust tree, and it was said that a woman had hanged herself there. Although the tree had grown so tall that its branches were now out of reach, the rooms remained deserted. For some years I stayed here, copying ancient inscriptions. I had few visitors, the inscriptions raised no political problems or issues, and so the days slipped quietly away, which was all that I desired. On summer nights, when mosquitoes swarmed, I would sit under the locust tree waving my fan and looking at specks of blue sky through chinks in the thick foliage, while belated caterpillars would fall, icy-cold, on to my neck.

The only visitor to drop in occasionally for a talk was my old friend Jin Xinyi. Having put his big portfolio on the rickety table he would take off his long gown and sit down opposite me, looking as if his heart was still beating fast because he was afraid of dogs.

"What's the use of copying these?" One night, while leafing through the inscriptions I had copied, he asked me for enlightenment on this point.

"There isn't any use."

"What's the point, then, of copying them?"

"There isn't any point."

"Why don't you write something?..."

I understood. They were bringing out *New Youth*,[6] but since there did not seem to have been any reaction, favourable or otherwise, no doubt they felt lonely. However I said:

"Imagine an iron house having not a single window and virtually indestructible,

"假如一间铁屋子，是绝无窗户而万难破毁的，里面有许多熟睡的人们，不久都要闷死了，然而是从昏睡入死灭，并不感到就死的悲哀。现在你大嚷起来，惊起了较为清醒的几个人，使这不幸的少数者来受无可挽救的临终的苦楚，你倒以为对得起他们么？"

"然而几个人既然起来，你不能说决没有毁坏这铁屋的希望。"

是的，我虽然自有我的确信，然而说到希望，却是不能抹杀的，因为希望是在于将来，决不能以我之必无的证明，来折服了他之所谓可有，于是我终于答应他也做文章了，这便是最初的一篇《狂人日记》。从此以后，便一发而不可收，每写些小说模样的文章，以敷衍朋友们的嘱托，积久就有了十余篇。

在我自己，本以为现在是已经并非一个切迫而不能已于言的人了，但或者也还未能忘怀于当日自己的寂寞的悲哀罢，所以有时候仍不免呐喊几声，聊以慰藉那在寂寞里奔驰的猛士，使他不惮于前驱。至于我的喊声是勇猛或是悲哀，是可憎或是可笑，那倒是不暇顾及的；但既然是呐喊，则当然须听将令的了，所以我往往不恤用了曲笔，在《药》的瑜儿的坟上平空添上一个花环，在《明天》里也不叙单四嫂子竟没有做到看见儿子的梦，因为那时的主将是不主张消极的。至于自己，却也并不愿将自以为苦的寂寞，再来传染给也如我那年青时候似的正做着好梦的青年。

这样说来，我的小说和艺术的距离之远，也就可想而知了，然而到今日还能蒙着小说的名，甚而至于且有成集的机会，无论如何总不能不说是一件侥幸的事，但侥幸虽使我不安于心，而悬揣人间暂时还有读者，则究竟也仍然是高兴的。

所以我竟将我的短篇小说结集起来，而且付印了，又因为上面所说的缘由，便称之为《呐喊》。

一九二二年十二月三日，鲁迅记于北京。

with all its inmates sound asleep and about to die of suffocation. Dying in their sleep, they won't feel the pain of death. Now if you raise a shout to wake a few of the lighter sleepers, making these unfortunate few suffer the agony of irrevocable death, do you really think you are doing them a good turn?"

"But if a few wake up. You can't say there is no hope of destroying the iron house."

True, in spite of my own conviction, I could not blot out hope, for hope belongs to the future. I had no negative evidence able to refute his affirmation of faith. So I finally agreed to write, and the result was my first story "A Madman's Diary." And once started I could not give up but would write some sort of short story from time to time to humour my friends, until I had written more than a dozen of them.

As far as I am concerned, I no longer feel any great urge to express myself; yet, perhaps because I have not forgotten the grief of my past loneliness, I sometimes call out to encourage those fighters who are galloping on in loneliness, so that they do not lose heart. Whether my cry is brave or sad, repellent or ridiculous, I do not care. However, since this is a call to arms I must naturally obey my general's orders. This is why I often resort to innuendoes, as when I made a wreath appear from nowhere at the son's grave in "Medicine," while in "Tomorrow" I did not say that Fourth Shan's Wife never dreamed of her little boy. For our chiefs in those days were against pessimism. And I, for my part, did not want to infect with the loneliness which I had found so bitter those young people who were still dreaming pleasant dreams, just as I had done when young.

It is clear, then, that my stories fall far short of being works of art; hence I must at least count myself fortunate that they are still known as stories and are even being brought out in one volume. Although such good fortune makes me uneasy, it still pleases me to think that they have readers in the world of men, for the time being at any rate.

So now that these stories of mine are being reprinted in one collection, for the reasons given above I have chosen to entitle it *Call to Arms*.

Beijing
December 3, 1922

没有吃过人的孩子，或者还有？救救孩子……

Perhaps there are still children who haven't eaten men? Save the children....

狂人日记

A Madman's Diary

　　某君昆仲，今隐其名，皆余昔日在中学校时良友；
分隔多年，消息渐阙。日前偶闻其一大病；适归故乡，迂
道往访，则仅晤一人，言病者其弟也。劳君远道来视，然
已早愈，赴某地候补矣。因大笑，出示日记二册，谓可见
当日病状，不妨献诸旧友。持归阅一过，知所患盖"迫害
狂"之类。语颇错杂无伦次，又多荒唐之言；亦不著月
日，惟墨色字体不一，知非一时所书。间亦有略具联络
者，今撮录一篇，以供医家研究。记中语误，一字不易；
惟人名虽皆村人，不为世间所知，无关大体，然亦悉易
去。至于书名，则本人愈后所题，不复改也。七年四月二
日识。

　　一

　　今天晚上，很好的月光。

　　我不见他，已是三十多年；今天见了，精神分外爽
快。才知道以前的三十多年，全是发昏；然而须十分小
心。不然，那赵家的狗，何以看我两眼呢？

　　我怕得有理。

　　二

　　今天全没月光，我知道不妙。早上小心出门，赵贵翁
的眼色便怪：似乎怕我，似乎想害我。还有七八个人，交
头接耳的议论我，又怕我看见。一路上的人，都是如此。
其中最凶的一个人，张着嘴，对我笑了一笑；我便从头直
冷到脚跟，晓得他们布置，都已妥当了。

　　我可不怕，仍旧走我的路。前面一伙小孩子，也在那
里议论我；眼色也同赵贵翁一样，脸色也都铁青。我想我
同小孩子有什么仇，他也这样。忍不住大声说，"你告诉

Two brothers, whose names I need not mention here, were both good friends of mine in high school; but after a separation of many years we gradually lost touch. Some time ago I happened to hear that one of them was seriously ill, and since I was going back to my old home I broke my journey to call on them. I saw only one, however, who told me that the invalid was his younger brother.

"I appreciate your coming such a long way to see us," he said, "but my brother recovered some time ago and has gone elsewhere to take up an official post." Then, laughing, he produced two volumes of his brother's diary, saying that from these the nature of his past illness could be seen and there was no harm in showing them to an old friend. I took the diary away, read it through, and found that he had suffered from a form of persecution complex. The writing was most confused and incoherent, and he had made many wild statements; moreover he had omitted to give any dates, so that only by the colour of the ink and the differences in the writing could one tell that it was not all written at one time. Certain sections, however, were not altogether disconnected, and I have copied out a part to serve as a subject for medical research. I have not altered a single illogicality in the diary and have changed only the names, even though the people referred to are all country folk, unknown to the world and of no consequence. As for the title, it was chosen by the diarist himself after his recovery, and I did not change it.

I

Tonight the moon is very bright.

I have not seen it for over thirty years, so today when I saw it I felt in unusually high spirits. I begin to realize that during the past thirty-odd years I have been in the dark; but now I must be extremely careful. Otherwise why should the Zhaos' dog have looked at me twice?

I have reason for my fear.

II

Tonight there is no moon at all, I know that this is a bad omen. This morning when I went out cautiously, Mr. Zhao had a strange look in his eyes, as if he were afraid of me, as if he wanted to murder me. There were seven or eight others who discussed me in a whisper. And they were afraid of my seeing them. So, indeed, were all the people I passed. The fiercest among them grinned at me; whereupon I shivered from head to foot, knowing that their preparations were complete.

I was not afraid, however, but continued on my way. A group of children in front

我！”他们可就跑了。

我想：我同赵贵翁有什么仇，同路上的人又有什么仇；只有廿年以前，把古久先生的陈年流水簿子，踹了一脚，古久先生很不高兴。赵贵翁虽然不认识他，一定也听到风声，代抱不平；约定路上的人，同我作冤对。但是小孩子呢？那时候，他们还没有出世，何以今天也睁着怪眼睛，似乎怕我，似乎想害我。这真教我怕，教我纳罕而且伤心。

我明白了。这是他们娘老子教的！

三

晚上总是睡不着。凡事须得研究，才会明白。

他们——也有给知县打枷过的，也有给绅士掌过嘴的，也有衙役占了他妻子的，也有老子娘被债主逼死的；他们那时候的脸色，全没有昨天这么怕，也没有这么凶。

最奇怪的是昨天街上的那个女人，打他儿子，嘴里说道，“老子呀！我要咬你几口才出气！”他眼睛却看着我。我出了一惊，遮掩不住；那青面獠牙的一伙人，便都哄笑起来。陈老五赶上前，硬把我拖回家中了。

拖我回家，家里的人都装作不认识我；他们的眼色，也全同别人一样。进了书房，便反扣上门，宛然是关了一只鸡鸭。这一件事，越教我猜不出底细。

前几天，狼子村的佃户来告荒，对我大哥说，他们村里的一个大恶人，给大家打死了；几个人便挖出他的心肝来，用油煎炒了吃，可以壮壮胆子。我插了一句嘴，佃户和大哥便都看我几眼。今天才晓得他们的眼光，全同外面的那伙人一模一样。

想起来，我从顶上直冷到脚跟。

他们会吃人，就未必不会吃我。

你看那女人“咬你几口”的话，和一伙青面獠牙人

1. The characters Gu Jiu means "old." This refers to the age-old history of feudalism in China.

were also discussing me, and the look in their eyes was just like that in Mr. Zhao's while their faces too were ghastly pale. I wondered what grudge these children could have against me to make them behave like this. I could not help calling out, "Tell me!" But then they ran away.

I wonder what grudge Mr. Zhao has against me, what grudge the people on the road have against me. I can think of nothing except that twenty years ago I trod on Mr. Gu Jiu's[1] old ledgers, and Mr. Gu was most displeased. Although Mr. Zhao does not know him, he must have heard talk of this and decided to avenge him, thus he is conspiring against me with the people on the road. But then what of the children? At that time they were not yet born, so why should they eye me so strangely today, as if they were afraid of me, as if they wanted to murder me? This really frightens me, it is so bewildering and upsetting. I know. They must have learned this from their parents!

III

I can't sleep at night. Everything requires careful consideration if one is to understand it.

Those people, some of whom have been pilloried by the magistrate, slapped in the face by the local gentry, had their wives taken away by bailiffs or their parents driven to suicide by creditors, never looked as frightened and as fierce then as they did yesterday.

The most extraordinary thing was that woman on the street yesterday who was spanking her son. "Little devil!" she cried. "I'm so angry I could eat you!" Yet all the time it was me she was looking at. I gave a start, unable to hide my alarm. Then all those long-toothed people with livid faces began to hoot with laughter. Old Chen hurried forward and dragged me home.

He dragged me home. The folk at home all pretended not to know me; they had the same look in their eyes as all the others. When I went into the study, they locked me in as if cooping up a chicken or a duck. This incident left me even more bewildered.

A few days ago a tenant of ours from Wolf Cub Village came to report the failure of the crops and told my elder brother that a notorious character in their village had been beaten to death; then some people had taken out his heart and liver, fried them in oil, and eaten them as a means of increasing their courage. When I interrupted, the tenant and my brother both stared at me. Only today have I realized that they had exactly the same look in their eyes as those people outside.

Just to think of it sets me shivering from the crown of my head to the soles of my feet.

They eat human beings, so they may eat me.

I see that the woman's "eat you," the laughter of those long-toothed people with

的笑，和前天佃户的话，明明是暗号。我看出他话中全是毒，笑中全是刀。他们的牙齿，全是白厉厉的排着，这就是吃人的家伙。

照我自己想，虽然不是恶人，自从踹了古家的簿子，可就难说了。他们似乎别有心思，我全猜不出，况且他们一翻脸，便说人是恶人。我还记得大哥教我做论，无论怎样好人，翻他几句，他便打上几个圈；原谅坏人几句，他便说"翻天妙手，与众不同"。我那里猜得到他们的心思，究竟怎样；况且是要吃的时候。

凡事总须研究，才会明白。古来时常吃人，我也还记得，可是不甚清楚。我翻开历史一查，这历史没有年代，歪歪斜斜的每叶上都写着"仁义道德"几个字。我横竖睡不着，仔细看了半夜，才从字缝里看出字来，满本都写着两个字是"吃人"！

书上写着这许多字，佃户说了这许多话，却都笑吟吟的睁着怪眼睛看我。

我也是人，他们想要吃我了！

四

早上，我静坐了一会。陈老五送进饭来，一碗菜，一碗蒸鱼；这鱼的眼睛，白而且硬，张着嘴，同那一伙想吃人的人一样。吃了几筷，滑溜溜的不知是鱼是人，便把他兜肚连肠的吐出。

我说"老五，对大哥说，我闷得慌，想到园里走走。"老五不答应，走了；停一会，可就来开了门。

我也不动，研究他们如何摆布我；知道他们一定不肯放松。果然！我大哥引了一个老头子，慢慢走来；他满眼凶光，怕我看出，只是低头向着地，从眼镜横边暗暗看我。大哥说，"今天你仿佛很好。"我说"是的。"大哥说，"今天请何先生来，给你诊一诊。"我说"可以！"其实我岂不

livid faces, and the tenant's story the other day are obviously secret signs. I realize all the poison in their speech, all the daggers in their laughter. Their teeth are white and glistening: they use these teeth to eat men.

Evidently, although I am not a bad man, ever since I trod on Mr. Gu's ledgers it has been touch-and-go with me. They seem to have secrets which I cannot guess, and once they are angry they will call anyone a bad character. I remember when my elder brother taught me to write compositions, no matter how good a man was, if I produced arguments to the contrary he would mark that passage to show his approval; while if I excused evildoers he would say, "Good for you, that shows originality." How can I possibly guess their secret thoughts — especially when they are ready to eat people?

Everything requires careful consideration if one is to understand it. In ancient times, as I recollect, people often ate human beings, but I am rather hazy about it. I tried to look this up, but my history has no chronology and scrawled all over each page are the words: "Confucian Virtue and Morality." Since I could not sleep anyway, I read intently half the night until I began to see words between the lines. The whole book was filled with the two words — "Eat people."

All these words written in the book, all the words spoken by our tenant, eye me quizzically with an enigmatic smile.

I too am a man, and they want to eat me!

IV

In the morning I sat quietly for some time. Old Chen brought in lunch: one bowl of vegetables, one bowl of steamed fish. The eyes of the fish were white and hard, and its mouth was open just like those people who want to eat human beings. After a few mouthfuls I could not tell whether the slippery morsels were fish or human flesh, so I brought it all up.

I said, "Old Chen, tell my brother that I feel quite suffocated and want to have a stroll in the garden." Old Chen said nothing but went out, and presently he came back and opened the gate.

I did not move, but watched to see how they would treat me, feeling certain that they would not let me go. Sure enough! My elder brother came slowly out, leading an old man. There was a murderous gleam in his eyes, and fearing that I would see it he lowered his head, stealing side-glances at me from behind his glasses.

"You seem very well today," said my brother.

"Yes," said I.

知道这老头子是刽子手扮的！无非借了看脉这名目，揣一揣肥瘠：因这功劳，也分一片肉吃。我也不怕；虽然不吃人，胆子却比他们还壮。伸出两个拳头，看他如何下手。老头子坐着，闭了眼睛，摸了好一会，呆了好一会；便张开他鬼眼睛说，"不要乱想。静静的养几天，就好了。"

不要乱想，静静的养！养肥了，他们是自然可以多吃；我有什么好处，怎么会"好了"？他们这群人，又想吃人，又是鬼鬼祟祟，想法子遮掩，不敢直捷下手，真要令我笑死。我忍不住，便放声大笑起来，十分快活。自己晓得这笑声里面，有的是义勇和正气。老头子和大哥，都失了色，被我这勇气正气镇压住了。

但是我有勇气，他们便越想吃我，沾光一点这勇气。老头子跨出门，走不多远，便低声对大哥说道，"赶紧吃罢！"大哥点点头。原来也有你！这一件大发见，虽似意外，也在意中：合伙吃我的人，便是我的哥哥！

吃人的是我哥哥！

我是吃人的人的兄弟！

我自己被人吃了，可仍然是吃人的人的兄弟！

五

这几天是退一步想：假使那老头子不是刽子手扮的，真是医生，也仍然是吃人的人。他们的祖师李时珍做的"本草什么"上，明明写着人肉可以煎吃；他还能说自己不吃人么？

至于我家大哥，也毫不冤枉他。他对我讲书的时候，亲口说过可以"易子而食"；又一回偶然议论起一个不好的人，他便说不但该杀，还当"食肉寝皮"。我那时年纪还小，心跳了好半天。前天狼子村佃户来说吃心肝的事，他也毫不奇怪，不住的点头。可见心思是同从前一样狠。既然可以"易子而食"，便什么都易得，什么人都吃得。我从前单

2. (1518-93), famous pharmacologist. It is not stated in his *Compendium of Materia Medica* that human flesh could be used as a medicine; this was one of the delusions of the madman.

3. The ancient historial record Zuo Zhuan states that during a siege in 488 B.C. the besieged were so famished that they "exchanged their sons to eat."

"I have invited Mr. He here today to examine you."

"All right," I replied. Actually I knew quite well that this old man was the executioner in disguise! Feeling my pulse was simply a pretext for him to see how fat I was; for this would entitle him to a share of my flesh. Still I was not afraid. Although I do not eat men my courage is greater than theirs. I held out my two fists to see what he would do. The old man sat down, closed his eyes, fumbled for some time, remained motionless for a while; then opened his shifty eyes and said, "Don't let your imagination run away with you. Rest quietly for a few days, and you will be better."

Don't let your imagination run away with you! Rest quietly for a few days! By fattening me of course they'll have more to eat. But what good will it do me? How can it be "better"? The whole lot of them wanting to eat people yet stealthily trying to keep up appearances, not daring to do it outright, was really enough to make me die of laughter. I couldn't help it, I nearly split my sides, I was so amused. I knew that this laughter voiced courage and integrity. Both the old man and my brother turned pale, awed by my courage and integrity.

But my courage just makes them all the more eager to eat me, to acquire some of my courage for themselves. The old man went out of the gate, but before he had gone far he said to my brother in a low voice, "To be eaten at once!" My brother nodded. So you are in it too! This stupendous discovery, though it came as a shock, is no more than I might expect: the accomplice in eating me is my elder brother!

The eater of human flesh is my elder brother!

I am the younger brother of an eater of human flesh!

I, who will be eaten by others, am the younger brother of an eater of human flesh!

V

These few days I have been thinking again: suppose that old man were not an executioner in disguise, but a real doctor; he would be nonetheless an eater of human flesh. That book on herbs by his predecessor Li Shizhen[2] states explicitly that men's flesh can be boiled and eaten; how then can he still deny that he eats men?

As for my elder brother, I have also good reason to suspect him. When he was teaching me, he told me himself, "People exchange their sons to eat."[3] And once in discussing a bad man he said that not only did the fellow deserve to be killed, he should "have his flesh eaten and his hide slept on." I was still young at the time, and for quite a while my heart beat faster. That story our tenant from Wolf Cub Village told the other day about eating a man's heart and liver didn't surprise him at all — he kept nodding

听他讲道理，也胡涂过去；现在晓得他讲道理的时候，不但唇边还抹着人油，而且心里满装着吃人的意思。

六

黑漆漆的，不知是日是夜。赵家的狗又叫起来了。

狮子似的凶心，兔子的怯弱，狐狸的狡猾，……

七

我晓得他们的方法，直捷杀了，是不肯的，而且也不敢，怕有祸祟。所以他们大家连络，布满了罗网，逼我自戕。试看前几天街上男女的样子，和这几天我大哥的作为，便足可悟出八九分了。最好是解下腰带，挂在梁上，自己紧紧勒死；他们没有杀人的罪名，又偿了心愿，自然都欢天喜地的发出一种呜呜咽咽的笑声。否则惊吓忧愁死了，虽则略瘦，也还可以首肯几下。

他们是只会吃死肉的！——记得什么书上说，有一种东西，叫"海乙那"的，眼光和样子都很难看；时常吃死肉，连极大的骨头，都细细嚼烂，咽下肚子去，想起来也教人害怕。"海乙那"是狼的亲眷，狼是狗的本家。前天赵家的狗，看我几眼，可见他也同谋，早已接洽。老头子眼看着地，岂能瞒得我过。

最可怜的是我的大哥，他也是人，何以毫不害怕；而且合伙吃我呢？还是历来惯了，不以为非呢？还是丧了良心，明知故犯呢？

我诅咒吃人的人，先从他起头；要劝转吃人的人，也先从他下手。

his head. He is evidently just as cruel as before. Since it is possible to "exchange sons to eat," then anything can be exchanged, anyone can be eaten. In the past I simply listened to his explanations and let it go at that; now I know that when he gave me these explanations, not only was there human fat at the corner of his lips, but his whole heart was set on eating men.

VI

Pitch dark. I don't know whether it is day or night. The Zhaos' dog has started barking again.

The fierceness of a lion, the timidity of a rabbit, the craftiness of a fox....

VII

I know their way: they are not prepared to kill outright, nor would they dare, for fear of the consequences. Instead they have banded together and set traps everywhere, to force me to kill myself. The behaviour of the men and women in the street a few days ago and my elder brother's attitude these last few days make it quite obvious. What they like best is for a man to take off his belt and hang himself from a beam; for then they can enjoy their hearts' desire without being blamed for murder. Naturally that delights them and sets them roaring with laughter. On the other hand, if a man is frightened or worried to death, though that makes him rather thin, they still nod in approval.

They only eat dead flesh! I remember reading somewhere of a hideous beast with an ugly look in its eye called "hyena," which often eats dead flesh. Even the largest bones it crunches into fragments and swallows; the mere thought of this makes your hair stand on end. Hyenas are related to wolves, wolves belong to the canine species. The other day the Zhaos' dog eyed me several times: it is obviously in the plot too as their accomplice. The old man's eyes were cast down, but that did not deceive me.

The most deplorable is my elder brother. He's a man too, so why isn't he afraid, why is he plotting with others to eat me? Does force of habit blind a man to what's wrong? Or is he so heartless that he will knowingly commit a crime?

In cursing man-eaters, I shall start with my brother. In dissuading man-eaters, I shall start with him too.

八

其实这种道理，到了现在，他们也该早已懂得，……

忽然来了一个人；年纪不过二十左右，相貌是不很看得清楚，满面笑容，对了我点头，他的笑也不像真笑。我便问他，"吃人的事，对么？"他仍然笑着说，"不是荒年，怎么会吃人。"我立刻就晓得，他也是一伙，喜欢吃人的；便自勇气百倍，偏要问他。

"对么？"

"这等事问他什么。你真会……说笑话。……今天天气很好。"

天气是好，月色也很亮了。可是我要问你，"对么？"

他不以为然了。含含胡胡的答道，"不……"

"不对？他们何以竟吃？！"

"没有的事……"

"没有的事？狼子村现吃；还有书上都写着，通红斩新！"

他便变了脸，铁一般青。睁着眼说，"有许有的，这是从来如此……"

"从来如此，便对么？"

"我不同你讲这些道理；总之你不该说，你说便是你错！"

我直跳起来，张开眼，这人便不见了。全身出了一大片汗。他的年纪，比我大哥小得远，居然也是一伙；这一定是他娘老子先教的。还怕已经教给他儿子了；所以连小孩子，也都恶狠狠的看我。

九

自己想吃人，又怕被别人吃了，都用着疑心极深的眼光，面面相觑。……

去了这心思，放心做事走路吃饭睡觉，何等舒服。这只是一条门槛，一个关头。他们可是父子兄弟夫妇朋友师

VIII

Actually such arguments should have convinced them long ago....

Suddenly someone came in. He was only about twenty years old and I did not see his features very clearly. His face was wreathed in smiles, but when he nodded to me his smile didn't seem genuine. I asked him. "Is it right to eat human beings?"

Still smiling, he replied, "When there is no famine how can one eat human beings?"

I realized at once he was one of them; but still I summoned up courage to repeat my question:

"Is it right?"

"What makes you ask such a thing? You really are... fond of a joke.... It is very fine today."

"It is fine, and the moon is very bright. But I want to ask you: is it right?"

He looked disconcerted and muttered, "No...."

"No? Then why do they still do it?"

"What are you talking about?"

"What am I talking about? They are eating men now in Wolf Cub Village, and you can see it written all over the books, in fresh red ink."

His expression changed. He grew ghastly pale. "It may be so," he said staring at me. "That's the way it's always been...."

"Does that make it right?"

"I refuse to discuss it with you. Anyway, you shouldn't talk about it. It's wrong for anyone to talk about it."

I leaped up and opened my eyes wide, but the man had vanished. I was soaked with sweat. He was much younger than my elder brother, but even so he was in it. He must have been taught by his parents. And I am afraid he has already taught his son; that is why even the children look at me so fiercely.

IX

Wanting to eat men, at the same time afraid of being eaten themselves, they all eye each other with the deepest suspicion.

How comfortable life would be for them if they could rid themselves of such obsessions and go to work, walk, eat and sleep at ease. They have only this one step to take. Yet fathers and sons, husbands and wives, brothers, friends, teachers and students,

生仇敌和各不相识的人，都结成一伙，互相劝勉，互相牵掣，死也不肯跨过这一步。

十

大清早，去寻我大哥；他立在堂门外看天，我便走到他背后，拦住门，格外沉静，格外和气的对他说，

"大哥，我有话告诉你。"

"你说就是，"他赶紧回过脸来，点点头。

"我只有几句话，可是说不出来。大哥，大约当初野蛮的人，都吃过一点人。后来因为心思不同，有的不吃人了，一味要好，便变了人，变了真的人。有的却还吃，——也同虫子一样，有的变了鱼鸟猴子，一直变到人。有的不要好，至今还是虫子。这吃人的人比不吃人的人，何等惭愧。怕比虫子的惭愧猴子，还差得很远很远。

"易牙蒸了他儿子，给桀纣吃，还是一直从前的事。谁晓得从盘古开辟天地以后，一直吃到易牙的儿子；从易牙的儿子，一直吃到徐锡林；从徐锡林，又一直吃到狼子村捉住的人。去年城里杀了犯人，还有一个生痨病的人，用馒头蘸血舐。

"他们要吃我，你一个人，原也无法可想；然而又何必去入伙。吃人的人，什么事做不出；他们会吃我，也会吃你，一伙里面，也会自吃。但只要转一步，只要立刻改了，也就人人太平。虽然从来如此，我们今天也可以格外要好，说是不能！大哥，我相信你能说，前天佃户要减租，你说过不能。"

当初，他还只是冷笑，随后眼光便凶狠起来，一到说破他们的隐情，那就满脸都变成青色了。大门外立着一伙人，赵贵翁和他的狗，也在里面，都探头探脑的挨进来。有的是看不出面貌，似乎用布蒙着；有的是仍旧青面獠牙，抿着嘴笑。我认识他们是一伙，都是吃人的人。可

4. Yi Ya, a favourite of Duke Huan of Qi in the seventh century B.C., was a good cook and sycophant. When the duke remarked that he had never tasted the flesh of children, Yi Ya cooked his own son for him to eat. Jie and Zhou were kings of earlier periods. This misstatement is presented as a sign of mental derangement.

5. A mythological figure.

6. A revolutionary executed in 1907 for assassinating a Qing official. His heart and liver were eaten.

sworn enemies and even strangers, have all joined in this conspiracy, discouraging and preventing each other from taking this step.

X

Early this morning I went to find my elder brother. He was standing outside the hall door looking at the sky when I walked up behind him, standing between him and the door, and addressed him with exceptional poise and politeness:

"Brother, I have something to say to you."

"Go ahead then." He turned quickly towards me, nodding,

"It's nothing much, but I find it hard to say. Brother, probably all primitive people ate a little human flesh to begin with. Later, because their views altered some of them stopped and tried so hard to do what was right that they changed into men, into real men. But some are still eating people — just like reptiles. Some have changed into fish, birds, monkeys, and finally men; but those who make no effort to do what's right are still reptiles. When those who eat men compare themselves with those who don't, how ashamed they must be. Probably much more ashamed than the reptiles are before monkeys.

"In ancient times Yi Ya boiled his son for Jie and Zhou[4] to eat; that is the old story. But actually since the creation of heaven and earth by Pan Gu[5] men have been eating each other, from the time of Yi Ya's son to the time of Xu Xilin,[6] and from the time of Xu Xilin down to the man caught in Wolf Cub Village. Last year they executed a criminal in the city, and a consumptive soaked a piece of bread in his blood and sucked it.

"They want to eat me, and of course you can do nothing about it single-handed; but why must you join them? As man-eaters they are capable of anything. If they eat me, they can eat you as well; members of the same group can still eat each other. But if you will just change your ways, change right away, then everyone will have peace. Although this has been going on since time immemorial, today we could make a special effort to do what is right, and say this can't be done! I'm sure you can say that, Brother. The other day when the tenant wanted the rent reduced, you said it couldn't be done."

At first he only smiled cynically, then a murderous gleam came into his eyes, and when I spoke of their secret he turned pale. Outside the gate quite a crowd had gathered, among them Mr. Zhao and his dog, all craning their necks to peer in. I could not see all their faces, some of them seemed to be masked; others were the old lot, long-toothed with livid faces, concealing their laughter. I knew they were one gang, all eaters of human flesh. But I also knew that they did not all think alike by any means. Some

是也晓得他们心思很不一样，一种是以为从来如此，应该吃的；一种是知道不该吃，可是仍然要吃，又怕别人说破他，所以听了我的话，越发气愤不过，可是抿着嘴冷笑。

这时候，大哥也忽然显出凶相，高声喝道，

"都出去！疯子有什么好看！"

这时候，我又懂得一件他们的巧妙了。他们岂但不肯改，而且早已布置；预备下一个疯子的名目罩上我。将来吃了，不但太平无事，怕还会有人见情。佃户说的大家吃了一个恶人，正是这方法。这是他们的老谱！

陈老五也气愤愤的直走进来。如何按得住我的口，我偏要对这伙人说，

"你们可以改了，从真心改起！要晓得将来容不得吃人的人，活在世上。

"你们要不改，自己也会吃尽。即使生得多，也会给真的人除灭了，同猎人打完狼子一样！——同虫子一样！"

那一伙人，都被陈老五赶走了。大哥也不知那里去了。陈老五劝我回屋子里去。屋里面全是黑沉沉的。横梁和椽子都在头上发抖；抖了一会，就大起来，堆在我身上。

万分沉重，动弹不得；他的意思是要我死。我晓得他的沉重是假的，便挣扎出来，出了一身汗。可是偏要说，

"你们立刻改了，从真心改起！你们要晓得将来是容不得吃人的人，……"

十一

太阳也不出，门也不开，日日是两顿饭。

我捏起筷子，便想起我大哥；晓得妹子死掉的缘故，也全在他。那时我妹子才五岁，可爱可怜的样子，还在眼前。母亲哭个不住，他却劝母亲不要哭；大约因为自己吃了，哭起来不免有点过意不去。如果还能过意不去，……

of them thought that since it had always been so, men should be eaten. Others knew they shouldn't eat men but still wanted to, and were afraid people might discover their secret; so although what I said made them angry they still smiled their cynical, tight-lipped smiles.

Suddenly my brother's face darkened.

"Clear off, the whole lot of you!" He reared. "What's the point of looking at a madman?"

Then I realized part of their cunning. They would never be willing to change their stand, and their plans were all laid: they had labelled me a madman. In future when I was eaten, not only would there be no trouble but people would probably be grateful to them. When our tenant spoke of the villagers eating a bad character, it was exactly the same device. This is their old trick.

Old Chen came in too in a towering temper. But they could not stop my mouth, I had to warn those people:

"You should change, change from the bottom of your hearts. You must realize that there will be no place for man-eaters in the world in future.

"If you don't change, you may all be eaten by each other. However many of you there are, you will be wiped out by the real men, just as wolves are killed by hunter — just like reptiles!"

Old Chen drove everybody away. My brother had disappeared, Old Chen advised me to go back to my room. It was pitch dark in there. The beams and rafters shook above my head. After shaking for a while they grew bigger and bigger. They piled on top of me.

The weight was so great, I couldn't move. They meant that I should die. However, knowing that the weight was false I struggled out, dripping with sweat. But I had to warn them:

"You must change at once, change from the bottom of your hearts! You must know that there'll be no place for man-eaters in future...."

XI

The sun has stopped shining, the door is never opened. Just two meals day after day.

Picking up my chopsticks, I thought of my elder brother. I know now how my little sister died: it was all through him. My sister was only five at the time. I can still remember how sweet she looked, poor thing. Mother wept as if she would never stop, but he begged her not to cry, probably because he had eaten our sister himself and so this weeping made him rather ashamed. If he had any sense of shame....

妹子是被大哥吃了，母亲知道没有，我可不得而知。

母亲想也知道；不过哭的时候，却并没有说明，大约也以为应当的了。记得我四五岁时，坐在堂前乘凉，大哥说爷娘生病，做儿子的须割下一片肉来，煮熟了请他吃，才算好人；母亲也没有说不行。一片吃得，整个的自然也吃得。但是那天的哭法，现在想起来，实在还教人伤心，这真是奇极的事！

十二

不能想了。

四千年来时时吃人的地方，今天才明白，我也在其中混了多年；大哥正管着家务，妹子恰恰死了，他未必不和在饭菜里，暗暗给我们吃。

我未必无意之中，不吃了我妹子的几片肉，现在也轮到我自己，……

有了四千年吃人履历的我，当初虽然不知道，现在明白，难见真的人！

十三

没有吃过人的孩子，或者还有？

救救孩子……

一九一八年四月。

7. The doctrine of filial piety used by the feudal ruling class to poison the people preached that a son should, if necessary, cut off his own flesh to feed his parents.

My sister was eaten by my brother, but I don't know whether Mother realized it or not.

I think Mother must have known, but when she wept she didn't say so outright, probably because she also thought it proper. I remember when I was four or five, sitting in the cool of the hall, my brother told me that if a man's parents were ill he should cut off a piece of his flesh and boil it for them,[7] if he wanted to be considered a good son; and Mother didn't contradict him. If one piece could be eaten, obviously so could the whole. And yet just to think of the weeping then still makes my heart bleed; that is the extraordinary thing about it!

XII

I can't bear to think of it.

It has only just dawned on me that all these years I have been living in a place where for four thousand years human flesh has been eaten. My brother had just taken over the charge of the house when our sister died, and he may well have used her flesh in our food, making us eat it unwittingly.

I may have eaten several pieces of my sister's flesh unwittingly, and now it is my turn....

How can a man like myself, after four thousand years of man-eating history — even though I knew nothing about it at first — ever hope to face real men?

XIII

Perhaps there are still children who haven't eaten men?
Save the children....

April 2, 1918

争辩道："窃书！读书人的事，能算偷么？"
引得众人都哄笑起来。

He protested, "Taking books can't be counted as stealing..."
which soon had everybody roaring with laughter.

孔乙己
Kong Yiji

　　鲁镇的酒店的格局，是和别处不同的：都是当街一个曲尺形的大柜台，柜里面预备着热水，可以随时温酒。做工的人，傍午傍晚散了工，每每花四文铜钱，买一碗酒，——这是二十多年前的事，现在每碗要涨到十文，——靠柜外站着，热热的喝了休息；倘肯多花一文，便可以买一碟盐煮笋，或者茴香豆，做下酒物了，如果出到十几文，那就能买一样荤菜，但这些顾客，多是短衣帮，大抵没有这样阔绰。只有穿长衫的，才踱进店面隔壁的房子里，要酒要菜，慢慢地坐喝。

　　我从十二岁起，便在镇口的咸亨酒店里当伙计，掌柜说，样子太傻，怕侍候不了长衫主顾，就在外面做点事罢。外面的短衣主顾，虽然容易说话，但唠唠叨叨缠夹不清的也很不少。他们往往要亲眼看着黄酒从坛子里舀出，看过壶子底里有水没有，又亲看将壶子放在热水里，然后放心：在这严重监督之下，羼水也很为难。所以过了几天，掌柜又说我干不了这事。幸亏荐头的情面大，辞退不得，便改为专管温酒的一种无聊职务了。

　　我从此便整天的站在柜台里，专管我的职务。虽然没有什么失职，但总觉有些单调，有些无聊。掌柜是一副凶脸孔，主顾也没有好声气，教人活泼不得；只有孔乙己到店，才可以笑几声，所以至今还记得。

　　孔乙己是站着喝酒而穿长衫的唯一的人。他身材很高大；青白脸色，皱纹间时常夹些伤痕；一部乱蓬蓬的花白的胡子。穿的虽然是长衫，可是又脏又破，似乎十多年没有补，也没有洗。他对人说话，总是满口之乎者也，教人半懂不懂的。因为他姓孔，别人便从描红纸上的"上大人孔乙己"这半懂不懂的话里，替他取下一个绰号，叫作孔乙己。孔乙己一到店，所有喝酒的人便都看着他笑，有的叫道，"孔乙己，你脸上又添上新伤疤了！"他不回答，对柜里说，"温两碗酒，要一碟茴香豆。"便排出九文大钱。他们又故意的高声嚷道，"你一定又偷了人家的东西了！"孔乙己睁大眼睛说，"你

The layout of Luzhen's taverns is unique. In each, facing you as you enter, is a bar in the shape of a carpenter's square where hot water is kept ready for warming rice wine. When men come off work at midday and in the evening they spend four coppers on a bowl of wine — or so they did twenty years ago; now it costs ten — and drink this warm, standing by the bar, taking it easy. Another copper will buy a plate of salted bamboo shoots or peas flavoured with aniseed to go with the wine, while a dozen will buy a meat dish; but most of the customers here belong to the short-coated class, few of whom can afford this. As for those in long gowns, they go into the inner room to order wine and dishes and sit drinking at their leisure.

At the age of twelve I started work as a pot-boy in Prosperity Tavern at the edge of the town. The boss put me to work in the outer room, saying that I looked too much of a fool to serve long-gowned customers. The short-coated customers there were easier to deal with, it is true, but among them were quite a few pernickety ones who insisted on watching for themselves while the yellow wine was ladled from the keg, looked for water at the bottom of the wine-pot, and personally inspected the pot's immersion into the hot water. Under such strict surveillance, diluting the wine was very hard indeed. Thus it did not take my boss many days to decide that this job too was beyond me. Luckily I had been recommended by somebody influential, so he could not sack me. Instead I was transferred to the dull task of simply warming wine.

After that I stood all day behind the bar attending to my duties. Although I gave satisfaction at this post, I found it somewhat boring and monotonous. Our boss was a grim-faced man, nor were the customers much pleasanter, which made the atmosphere a gloomy one. The only times when there was any laughter were when Kong Yiji came to the tavern. That is why I remember him.

Kong Yiji was the only long-gowned customer who used to drink his wine standing. A big, pallid man whose wrinkled face often bore scars, he had a large, unkempt and grizzled beard. And although he wore a long grown it was dirty and tattered. It had not by the look of it been washed or mended for ten years or more. He used so many archaisms in his speech that half of it was barely intelligible. And as his surname was Kong, he was given the nickname Kong Yiji from *kong, yi, ji*, the first three characters in the old-fashioned children's copybook. Whenever he came in, everyone there would look at him and chuckle. And someone was sure to call out:

"Kong Yiji! What are those fresh scars on your face?"

Ignoring this, he would lay nine coppers on the bar and order two bowls of heated wine with a dish of aniseed-peas. Then someone else would bawl:

"You must have been stealing again!"

"Why sully a man's good name for no reason at all?" Kong Yiji would ask, raising his eyebrows.

"Good name? Why, the day before yesterday you were trussed up and beaten for stealing books from the He family. I saw you!"

怎么这样凭空污人清白……""什么清白？我前天亲眼见你偷了何家的书，吊着打。"孔乙己便涨红了脸，额上的青筋条条绽出，争辩道，"窃书不能算偷……窃书！……读书人的事，能算偷么？"接连便是难懂的话，什么"君子固穷"，什么"者乎"之类，引得众人都哄笑起来：店内外充满了快活的空气。

听人家背地里谈论，孔乙己原来也读过书，但终于没有进学，又不会营生；于是愈过愈穷，弄到将要讨饭了。幸而写得一笔好字，便替人家钞钞书，换一碗饭吃。可惜他又有一样坏脾气，便是好喝懒做。坐不到几天，便连人和书籍纸张笔砚，一齐失踪。如是几次，叫他钞书的人也没有了。孔乙己没有法，便免不了偶然做些偷窃的事。但他在我们店里，品行却比别人都好，就是从不拖欠；虽然间或没有现钱，暂时记在粉板上，但不出一月，定然还清，从粉板上拭去了孔乙己的名字。

孔乙己喝过半碗酒，涨红的脸色渐渐复了原，旁人便又问道，"孔乙己，你当真认识字么？"孔乙己看着问他的人，显出不屑置辩的神气。他们便接着说道，"你怎的连半个秀才也捞不到呢？"孔乙己立刻显出颓唐不安模样，脸上笼上了一层灰色，嘴里说些话；这回可是全是之乎者也之类，一些不懂了。在这时候，众人也都哄笑起来：店内外充满了快活的空气。

在这些时候，我可以附和着笑，掌柜是决不责备的。而且掌柜见了孔乙己，也每每这样问他，引人发笑。孔乙己自己知道不能和他们谈天，便只好向孩子说话。有一回对我说道，"你读过书么？"我略略点一点头。他说，"读过书，……我便考你一考。茴香豆的茴字，怎样写的？"我想，讨饭一样的人，也配考我么？便回过脸去，不再理会。孔乙己等了许久，很恳切的说道，"不能写罢？……我教给你，记着！这些字应该记着。将来做掌柜的时候，写账要用。"我暗想我和掌柜的等级还很远呢，而且我们掌柜也从不将茴香豆上账；又好笑，又不耐烦，

1. A Chinese character meaning "aniseed."

At that Kong Yiji would flush, the veins on his forehead standing out as he protested, "Taking books can't be counted as stealing.... Taking books... for a scholar... can't be counted as stealing." Then followed such quotations from the classics as "A gentlemen keeps his integrity even in poverty," together with a spate of archaisms which soon had everybody roaring with laughter, enlivening the whole tavern.

From the gossip that I heard, it seemed that Kong Yiji had studied the classics but never passed the official examinations and, not knowing any way to make a living, he had grown steadily poorer until he was almost reduced to beggary. Luckily he was a good calligrapher and could find enough copying work to fill his rice bowl. But unfortunately he had his failings too: laziness and a love of tippling. So after a few days he would disappear, taking with him books, paper, brushes and inkstone. And after this had happened several times, people stopped employing him as a copyist. Then all he could do was resort to occasional pilfering. In our tavern, though, he was a model customer who never failed to pay up. Sometimes, it is true, when he had no ready money, his name would be chalked up on our tally-board; but in less than a month he invariably settled the bill, and the name Kong Yiji would be wiped off the board again.

After Kong Yiji had drunk half a bowl of wine, his flushed cheeks would stop burning. But then someone would ask:

"Kong Yiji, can you really read?"

When he glanced back as if such a question were not worth answering, they would continue, "How is it you never passed even the lowest official examination?"

At once a grey tinge would overspread Kong Yiji's dejected, discomfited face, and he would mumble more of those unintelligible archaisms. Then everyone there would laugh heartily again, enlivening the whole tavern.

At such times I could join in the laughter with no danger of a dressing-down from my boss. In fact he always put such questions to Kong Yiji himself, to raise a laugh. Knowing that it was no use talking to the men, Kong Yiji would chat with us boys. Once he asked me:

"Have you had any schooling?"

When I nodded curtly he said, "Well then, I'll test you. How do you write the *hui*[1] in aniseed-peas?"

Who did this beggar think he was, testing me! I turned away and ignored him. After waiting for some time he said earnestly:

"You can't write it, eh? I'll show you. Mind you remember. You ought to remember such characters, because you'll need them to write up your accounts when you have a shop of your own."

It seemed to me that I was still very far from having a shop of my own; in addition to which, our boss never entered aniseed-peas in his account-book. Half amused and half exasperated, I drawled, "I don't need you to show me. Isn't it the *hui* written with the element for grass?"

Kong Yiji's face lit up. Tapping two long finger-nails on the bar, he nodded. "Quite

懒懒的答他道，"谁要你教，不是草头底下一个来回的回字么？"孔乙己显出极高兴的样子，将两个指头的长指甲敲着柜台，点头说，"对呀对呀！……回字有四样写法，你知道么？"我愈不耐烦了，努着嘴走远。孔乙己刚用指甲蘸了酒，想在柜上写字，见我毫不热心，便又叹一口气，显出极惋惜的样子。

有几回，邻舍孩子听得笑声，也赶热闹，围住了孔乙己。他便给他们茴香豆吃，一人一颗。孩子吃完豆，仍然不散，眼睛都望着碟子。孔乙己着了慌，伸开五指将碟子罩住，弯腰下去说道，"不多了，我已经不多了。"直起身又看一看豆，自己摇头说，"不多不多！多乎哉？不多也。"于是这一群孩子都在笑声里走散了。

孔乙己是这样的使人快活，可是没有他，别人也便这么过。

有一天，大约是中秋前的两三天，掌柜正在慢慢的结账，取下粉板，忽然说，"孔乙己长久没有来了。还欠十九个钱呢！"我才也觉得他的确长久没有来了。一个喝酒的人说道，"他怎么会来？……他打折了腿了。"掌柜说，"哦！""他总仍旧是偷。这一回，是自己发昏，竟偷到丁举人家里去了。他家的东西，偷得的么？""后来怎么样？""怎么样？先写服辩，后来是打，打了大半夜，再打折了腿。""后来呢？""后来打折了腿了。""打折了怎样呢？""怎样？……谁晓得？许是死了。"掌柜也不再问，仍然慢慢的算他的账。

中秋过后，秋风是一天凉比一天，看看将近初冬；我整天的靠着火，也须穿上棉袄了。一天的下半天，没有一个顾客，我正合了眼坐着。忽然间听得一个声音，"温一碗酒。"这声音虽然极低，却很耳熟。看时又全没有人。站起来向外一望，那孔乙己便在柜台下对了门槛坐着。他脸上黑而且瘦，已经不成样子；穿一件破夹袄，盘着两腿，下面垫一个蒲包，用草绳在肩上挂住；见了我，又说道，"温一碗酒。"掌柜也伸出头去，一面说，"孔

correct!" He said. "There are four different ways of writing *hui*. Do you know them?"

But my patience exhausted, I scowled and moved away. Kong Yiji had dipped his finger in wine to trace the characters on the bar. When he saw my utter indifference his face fell and he sighed.

Sometimes children in the neighbourhood, hearing laughter, came in to join in the fun and surrounded Kong Yiji. Then he would give them aniseed-peas, one apiece. After eating the peas the children would still hang round, their eyes fixed on the dish. Growing flustered, he would cover it with his hand and bending forward from the waist would say, "There aren't many left, not many at all." Straightening up to look at the peas again, he would shake his head and reiterete, "Not many, I do assure you. Not many, nay, not many at all." Then the children would scamper off, shouting with laughter.

That was how Kong Yiji contributed to our enjoyment, but we got along all right without him too.

One day, shortly before the Mid-Autumn Festival I think it was, my boss who was slowly making out his accounts took down the tally-board. "Kong Yiji hasn't shown up for a long time," he remarked suddenly. "He still owes nineteen coppers." That made me realize how long it was since we had seen him.

"How could he?" rejoined one of the customers. "His legs were broken in that last beating up."

"Ah!" said my boss.

"He'd been stealing again. This time he was fool enough to steal from Mr. Ding, the provincial-grade scholar. As if anybody could get away with that!"

"So what happened?"

"What happened? First he wrote a confession, then he was beaten. The beating lasted nearly all night, and they broke both his legs."

"And then?"

"Well, his legs were broken."

"Yes, but after?"

"After?... Who knows? He may be dead."

My boss asked no further questions but went on slowly making up his accounts.

After the Mid-Autumn Festival the wind grew daily colder as winter approached, and even though I spent all my time by the stove I had to wear a padded jacket. One afternoon, when the tavern was deserted, as I sat with my eyes closed I heard the words:

"Warm a bowl of wine."

It was said in a low but familiar voice. I opened my eyes. There was no one to be seen. I stood up to look out. There below the bar, facing the door, sat Kong Yiji. His face was thin and grimy — he looked a wreck. He had on a ragged lined jacket and was squatting cross-legged on a mat which was attached to his shoulders by a straw rope. When he saw me he repeated:

乙己么？你还欠十九个钱呢！"孔乙己很颓唐的仰面答道，"这……下回还清罢。这一回是现钱，酒要好。"掌柜仍然同平常一样，笑着对他说，"孔乙己，你又偷了东西了！"但他这回却不十分分辩，单说了一句"不要取笑！""取笑？要是不偷，怎么会打断腿？"孔乙己低声说道，"跌断，跌，跌……"他的眼色，很像恳求掌柜，不要再提，此时已经聚集了几个人，便和掌柜都笑了。我温了酒，端出去，放在门槛上。他从破衣袋里摸出四文大钱，放在我手里，见他满手是泥，原来他便用这手走来的。不一会，他喝完酒，便又在旁人的说笑声中，坐着用这手慢慢走去了。

　　自此以后，又长久没有看见孔乙己。到了年关，掌柜取下粉板说，"孔乙己还欠十九个钱呢！"到第二年的端午，又说"孔乙己还欠十九个钱呢！"到中秋可是没有说，再到年关也没有看见他。

　　我到现在终于没有见——大约孔乙己的确死了。

一九一九年三月。

"Warm a bowl of wine."

At this point my boss leaned over the bar to ask, "Is that Kong Yiji? You still owe nineteen coppers."

"That... I'll settle next time. He looked up dejectedly. Here's cash. Give me some good wine."

My boss, just as in the past, chuckled and said:

"Kong Yiji, you've been stealing again!"

But instead of stout denial, the answer simply was:

"Don't joke with me."

"Joke? How did your legs get broken if you hadn't been stealing?"

"I fell," whispered Kong Yiji. "Broke them in a fall." His eyes pleaded with the boss to let the matter drop. By now several people had gathered round, and they all laughed with the boss. I warmed the wine, carried it over, and set it on the threshold. He produced four coppers from his ragged coat pocket, and he placed them in my hand I saw that his own hands were covered with mud — he must have crawled there on them. Presently he finished the wine and, to the accompaniment of taunts and laughter, slowly pushed himself off with his hands.

A long time went by after that without our seeing Kong Yiji again. At the end of the year, when the boss took down the tally-board he said, "Kong Yiji still owes nineteen coppers." At the Dragon-Boat Festival the next year he said the same thing again. But when the Mid-Autumn Festival arrived he was silent on the subject, and another New Year came round without our seeing any more of Kong Yiji.

Nor have I ever seen him since — no doubt Kong Yiji really is dead.

March 1919

"喂！一手交钱，一手交货！"

"Hey! Give me the cash, and I'll give you the goods!"

药
Medicine

一

秋天的后半夜，月亮下去了，太阳还没有出，只剩下一片乌蓝的天；除了夜游的东西，什么都睡着。华老栓忽然坐起身，擦着火柴，点上遍身油腻的灯盏，茶馆的两间屋子里，便弥满了青白的光。

"小栓的爹，你就去么？"是一个老女人的声音。里边的小屋子里，也发出一阵咳嗽。

"唔。"老栓一面听，一面应，一面扣上衣服；伸手过去说，"你给我罢。"

华大妈在枕头底下掏了半天，掏出一包洋钱，交给老栓，老栓接了，抖抖的装入衣袋，又在外面按了两下；便点上灯笼，吹熄灯盏，走向里屋子去了。那屋子里面，正在窸窸窣窣的响，接着便是一通咳嗽。老栓候他平静下去，才低低的叫道，"小栓……你不要起来。……店么？你娘会安排的。"

老栓听得儿子不再说话，料他安心睡了；便出了门，走到街上。街上黑沉沉的一无所有，只有一条灰白的路，看得分明。灯光照着他的两脚，一前一后的走。有时也遇到几只狗，可是一只也没有叫。天气比屋子里冷得多了；老栓倒觉爽快，仿佛一旦变了少年，得了神通，有给人生命的本领似的，跨步格外高远。而且路也愈走愈分明，天也愈走愈亮了。

老栓正在专心走路，忽然吃了一惊，远远里看见一条丁字街，明明白白横着。他便退了几步，寻到一家关着门的铺子，蹩进檐下，靠门立住了。好一会，身上觉得有些发冷。

"哼，老头子。"

"倒高兴……。"

老栓又吃一惊，睁眼看时，几个人从他面前过去了。一个还回头看他，样子不甚分明，但很像久饿的人见了食物一般，眼里闪出一种攫取的光。老栓看看灯笼，已经熄了。按一按衣袋，硬硬的还在。仰起头两面一望，只见许

I

It was autumn, in the small hours of the morning. The moon had gone down, but the sun had not yet risen, and the sky appeared a sheet of darkling blue. Apart from night-prowlers, all was asleep. Old Shuan suddenly sat up in bed. He struck a match and lit the grease-covered oil-lamp, which shed a ghostly light over the two rooms of the teahouse.

"Are you going now, Dad?" queried an old woman's voice. And from the small inner room a fit of coughing was heard.

"H'm."

Old Shuan listened as he fastened his clothes, then stretching out his hand said, "Let's have it."

After some fumbling under the pillow his wife produced a packet of silver dollars which she handed over. Old Shuan pocketed it nervously, patted his pocket twice, then lighting a paper lantern and blowing out the lamp went into the inner room. A rustling was heard, and then more coughing. When all was quiet again, Old Shuan called softly, "Son!... Don't you get up!... Your mother will see to the shop."

Receiving no answer, Old Shuan assumed his son must be sound asleep again; so he went out into the street. In the darkness nothing could be seen but the grey roadway. The lantern light fell on his pacing feet. Here and there he came across dogs, but none of them barked. It was much colder than indoors, yet Old Shuan's spirits rose, as if he had grown suddenly younger and possessed some miraculous life-giving power. He had lengthened his stride. And the road became increasingly clear, the sky increasingly bright.

Absorbed in his walking, Old Shuan was startled when he saw the crossroad lying distinctly ahead of him. He walked back a few steps to stand under the eaves of a shop, in front of its closed door. After some time he began to feel chilly.

"Uh, an old chap."

"Seems rather cheerful...."

Old Shuan started again and, opening his eyes, saw several men passing. One of them even turned back to look at him, and although he could not see him clearly, the man's eyes shone with a lustful light, like a famished person's at the sight of food. Looking at his lantern, Old Shuan saw it had gone out. He patted his pocket — the hard packet was still there. Then he looked round and saw many strange people, in twos and threes, wandering about like lost souls. However, when he gazed steadily at them, he could not see anything else strange about them.

多古怪的人，三三两两，鬼似的在那里徘徊；定睛再看，却也看不出什么别的奇怪。

没有多久，又见几个兵，在那边走动；衣服前后的一个大白圆圈，远地里也看得清楚，走过面前的，并且看出号衣上暗红色的镶边。——一阵脚步声响，一眨眼，已经拥过了一大簇人。那三三两两的人，也忽然合作一堆，潮一般向前赶；将到丁字街口，便突然立住，簇成一个半圆。

老栓也向那边看，却只见一堆人的后背；颈项都伸得很长，仿佛许多鸭，被无形的手捏住了的，向上提着。静了一会，似乎有点声音，便又动摇起来，轰的一声，都向后退；一直散到老栓立着的地方，几乎将他挤倒了。

"喂！一手交钱，一手交货！"一个浑身黑色的人，站在老栓面前，眼光正像两把刀，刺得老栓缩小了一半。那人一只大手，向他摊着；一只手却撮着一个鲜红的馒头，那红的还是一点一点的往下滴。

老栓慌忙摸出洋钱，抖抖的想交给他，却又不敢去接他的东西。那人便焦急起来，嚷道，"怕什么？怎的不拿！"老栓还踌躇着；黑的人便抢过灯笼，一把扯下纸罩，裹了馒头，塞与老栓；一手抓过洋钱，捏一捏，转身去了。嘴里哼着说，"这老东西……。"

"这给谁治病的呀？"老栓也似乎听得有人问他，但他并不答应；他的精神，现在只在一个包上，仿佛抱着一个十世单传的婴儿，别的事情，都已置之度外了。他现在要将这包里的新的生命，移植到他家里，收获许多幸福。太阳也出来了；在他面前，显出一条大道，直到他家中，后面也照见丁字街头破匾上"古□亭口"这四个黯淡的金字。

二

老栓走到家，店面早经收拾干净，一排一排的茶桌，滑溜溜的发光。但是没有客人；只有小栓坐在里排的桌前

Presently he saw some soldiers strolling around. The large white circles on their uniforms, both in front and behind, were clear even at a distance; and as they drew nearer, the dark red border could be seen too. The next second, with a trampling of feet, a crowd rushed past. Thereupon the small groups which had arrived earlier suddenly converged and surged forward. Just before the crossroad, they came to a sudden stop and grouped themselves in a semi-circle.

Old Shuan looked in that direction too, but could only see people's backs. Craning their necks as far as they would go, they looked like so many ducks, held and lifted by some invisible hand. For a moment all was still; then a sound was heard, and a stir swept through the onlookers. There was a rumble as they pushed back, sweeping past Old Shuan and nearly knocking him down.

"Hey! Give me the cash, and I'll give you the goods!" A man clad entirely in black stood before him, his eyes like daggers, making Old Shuan shrink to half his normal size. This man was thrusting one huge extended hand towards him, while in the other he held a roll of steamed bread, from which crimson drops were dripping to the ground.

Hurriedly Old Shuan fumbled for his dollars, and trembling he was about to hand them over, but he dared not take the object. The other grew impatient, and shouted, "What are you afraid of? Why not take it?" When Old Shuan still hesitated, the man in black snatched his lantern and tore off its paper shade to wrap up the roll. This package he thrust into Old Shuan's hand, at the same time seizing the silver and giving it a cursory feel. Then he turned away, muttering, "Old fool...."

"Whose sickness is this for?" Old Shuan seemed to hear someone ask; but he made no reply. His whole mind was on the package, which he carried as carefully as if it were the sole heir to an ancient house. Nothing else mattered now. He was about to transplant this new life to his own home, and reap much happiness. The sun too had risen; lighting up the broad highway before him, which led straight home, and the worn tablet behind him at the crossroad with its faded gold inscription: "Ancient Pavilion."

II

When Old Shuan reached home, the shop had been cleaned, and the rows of tea-tables were shining brightly; but no customers had arrived. Only his son was sitting at a table by the wall, eating. Beads of sweat stood out on his forehead, his lined

吃饭，大粒的汗，从额上滚下，夹袄也帖住了脊心，两块肩胛骨高高凸出，印成一个阳文的"八"字。老栓见这样子，不免皱一皱展开的眉心。他的女人，从灶下急急走出，睁着眼睛，嘴唇有些发抖。

"得了么？"

"得了。"

两个人一齐走进灶下，商量了一会；华大妈便出去了，不多时，拿着一片老荷叶回来，摊在桌上。老栓也打开灯笼罩，用荷叶重新包了那红的馒头。小栓也吃完饭，他的母亲慌忙说：

"小栓——你坐着，不要到这里来。"一面整顿了灶火，老栓便把一个碧绿的包，一个红红白白的破灯笼，一同塞在灶里；一阵红黑的火焰过去时，店屋里散满了一种奇怪的香味。

"好香！你们吃什么点心呀？"这是驼背五少爷到了。这人每天总在茶馆里过日，来得最早，去得最迟，此时恰恰踅到临街的壁角的桌边，便坐下问话，然而没有人答应他。"炒米粥么？"仍然没有人应。老栓匆匆走出，给他泡上茶。

"小栓进来罢！"华大妈叫小栓进了里面的屋子，中间放好一条凳，小栓坐了。他的母亲端过一碟乌黑的圆东西，轻轻说：

"吃下去罢，——病便好了。"

小栓撮起这黑东西，看了一会，似乎拿着自己的性命一般，心里说不出的奇怪。十分小心的拗开了，焦皮里面窜出一道白气，白气散了，是两半个白面的馒头。——不多工夫，已经全在肚里了，却全忘了什么味；面前只剩下一张空盘。他的旁边，一面立着他的父亲，一面立着他的母亲，两人的眼光，都仿佛要在他身里注进什么又要取出什么似的；便禁不住心跳起来，按着胸膛，又是一阵咳嗽。

"睡一会罢，——便好了。"

小栓依他母亲的话，咳着睡了。华大妈候他喘气平静，才轻轻的给他盖上了满幅补钉的夹被。

jacket was sticking to his spine, and his shoulder blades stuck out so sharply, an inverted V seemed stamped there. At this sight, Old Shuan's brow, which had been clear, contracted again. His wife hurried in from the kitchen, with expectant eyes and a tremor to her lips.

"Get it?"

"Yes."

They went together into the kitchen, and conferred for a time. Then the old woman went out, to return shortly with a dried lotus leaf which she spread on the table. Old Shuan unwrapped the crimson-stained roll from the lantern paper and transferred it to the lotus leaf. Little Shuan had finished his meal, but his mother exclaimed hastily:

"Sit still, Little Shuan! Don't come over here."

Mending the fire in the stove, Old Shuan put the green package and the red and white lantern paper into the stove together. A red-black flame flared up, and a strange odour permeated the shop.

"Smells good! What are you eating?" The hunchback had arrived. He was one of those who spend all their time in teahouses, the first to come in the morning and the last to leave. Now he had just stumbled to a corner table facing the street, and sat down. But no one answered his question.

"Puffed rice gruel?"

Still no reply. Old Shuan hurried out to brew tea for him.

"Come here, little Shuan!" His mother called him into the inner room, set a stool in the middle, and sat the child down. Then, bringing him a round black object on a plate, she said gently:

"Eat it up... then you'll be better."

Little Shuan picked up the black object and looked at it. He had the oddest feeling, as if he were holding his own life in his hands. Presently he split it carefully open. From within the charred crust a jet of white vapour escaped, then scattered, leaving only two halves of a white flour steamed roll. Soon it was all eaten, the flavour completely forgotten, only the empty plate left. His father and mother were standing one on each side of him, their eyes apparently pouring something into him and at the same time extracting something. His small heart began to beat faster, and, putting his hands to his chest, he began to cough again.

"Have a sleep; then you'll be all right," said his mother.

Obediently, Little Shuan coughed himself to sleep. The woman waited till his breathing was regular, then covered him lightly with a much patched quilt.

三

店里坐着许多人，老栓也忙了，提着大铜壶，一趟一趟的给客人冲茶；两个眼眶，都围着一圈黑线。

"老栓，你有些不舒服么？——你生病么？"一个花白胡子的人说。

"没有。"

"没有？——我想笑嘻嘻的，原也不像……"花白胡子便取消了自己的话。

"老栓只是忙。要是他的儿子……"驼背五少爷话还未完，突然闯进了一个满脸横肉的人，披一件玄色布衫，散着纽扣，用很宽的玄色腰带，胡乱捆在腰间。刚进门，便对老栓嚷道：

"吃了么？好了么？老栓，就是运气了你！你运气，要不是我信息灵……。"

老栓一手提了茶壶，一手恭恭敬敬的垂着；笑嘻嘻的听。满座的人，也都恭恭敬敬的听。华大妈也黑着眼眶，笑嘻嘻的送出茶碗茶叶来，加上一个橄榄，老栓便去冲了水。

"这是包好！这是与众不同的。你想，趁热的拿来，趁热吃下。"横肉的人只是嚷。

"真的呢，要没有康大叔照顾，怎么会这样……"华大妈也很感激的谢他。

"包好，包好！这样的趁热吃下。这样的人血馒头，什么痨病都包好！"

华大妈听到"痨病"这两个字，变了一点脸色，似乎有些不高兴；但又立刻堆上笑，搭赸着走开了。这康大叔却没有觉察，仍然提高了喉咙只是嚷，嚷得里面睡着的小栓也合伙咳嗽起来。

"原来你家小栓碰到了这样的好运气了。这病自然一定全好；怪不得老栓整天的笑着呢。"花白胡子一面说，一面走到康大叔面前，低声下气的问道，"康大叔——听说今天结果的一个犯人，便是夏家的孩子，那是谁的孩

III

The shop was crowded, and Old Shuan was busy, carrying a big copper kettle to make tea for one customer after another. But there were dark circles under his eyes.

"Aren't you well, Old Shuan?... What's wrong with you?" asked one greybeard.

"Nothing."

"Nothing?... No, I suppose from your smile, there couldn't be," the old man corrected himself.

"It's just that Old Shuan's busy," said the hunchback. "If his son...." But before he could finish, a heavy-jowled man burst in. He had over his shoulders a dark brown shirt, unbuttoned and fastened carelessly by a broad dark brown girdle at his waist. As soon as he entered, he shouted to Old Shuan:

"Has he taken it? Any better? Luck's with you, Old Shuan. What luck! If not for my hearing of things so quickly...."

Holding the kettle in one hand, the other straight by his side in an attitude of respect, Old Shuan listened with a smile. In fact, all present were listening respectfully. The old woman, dark circles under her eyes too, came out smiling with a bowl containing tea-leaves and an added olive, over which Old Shuan poured boiling water for the newcomer.

"This is a guaranteed cure! Not like other things!" Declared the heavy-jowled man. "Just think, brought back warm, and eaten warm!"

"Yes indeed, we couldn't have managed it without Uncle Kang's help." The old woman thanked him very warmly.

"A guaranteed cure! Eaten warm like this. A roll dipped in human blood like this can cure any consumption!"

The old woman seemed a little disconcerted by the word "consumption," and turned a shade paler; however, she forced a smile again at once and found some pretext to leave. Meanwhile the man in brown was indiscreet enough to go on talking at the top of his voice until the child in the inner room was woken and started coughing.

"So you've had such a stroke of luck for your Little Shuan! Of course his sickness will be cured completely. No wonder Old Shuan keeps smiling." As he spoke, the greybeard walked up to the man in brown, and lowered his voice to ask:

"Mr. Kang, I heard the criminal executed today came from the Xia family. Who was it? And why was he executed?"

子？究竟是什么事？”

　　“谁的？不就是夏四奶奶的儿子么？那个小家伙！”康大叔见众人都耸起耳朵听他，便格外高兴，横肉块块饱绽，越发大声说，“这小东西不要命，不要就是了。我可是这一回一点没有得到好处；连剥下来的衣服，都给管牢的红眼睛阿义拿去了。——第一要算我们栓叔运气；第二是夏三爷赏了二十五两雪白的银子，独自落腰包，一文不花。”

　　小栓慢慢的从小屋子走出，两手按了胸口，不住的咳嗽；走到灶下，盛出一碗冷饭，泡上热水，坐下便吃。华大妈跟着他走，轻轻的问道，“小栓，你好些么？——你仍旧只是肚饿？……”

　　“包好，包好！”康大叔瞥了小栓一眼，仍然回过脸，对众人说，“夏三爷真是乖角儿，要是他不先告官，连他满门抄斩。现在怎样？银子！——这小东西也真不成东西！关在牢里，还要劝牢头造反。”

　　“阿呀，那还了得。”坐在后排的一个二十多岁的人，很现出气愤模样。

　　“你要晓得红眼睛阿义是去盘盘底细的，他却和他攀谈了。他说：这大清的天下是我们大家的。你想：这是人话么？红眼睛原知道他家里只有一个老娘，可是没有料到他竟会那么穷，榨不出一点油水，已经气破肚皮了。他还要老虎头上搔痒，便给他两个嘴巴！”

　　“义哥是一手好拳棒，这两下，一定够他受用了。”壁角的驼背忽然高兴起来。

　　“他这贱骨头打不怕，还要说可怜可怜哩。”

　　花白胡子的人说，“打了这种东西，有什么可怜呢？”

　　康大叔显出看他不上的样子，冷笑着说，“你没有听清我的话；看他神气，是说阿义可怜哩！”

　　听着的人的眼光，忽然有些板滞；话也停顿了。小栓已经吃完饭，吃得满身流汗，头上都冒出蒸气来。

　　“阿义可怜——疯话，简直是发了疯了。”花白胡子恍然大悟似的说。

"Who? Son of Widow Xia, of course! Young rascal!"

Seeing how they were all hanging on his words, Mr. Kang's spirits rose even higher. His jowls quivered, and he made his voice as loud as he could.

The rogue didn't want to live, simply didn't want to! There was nothing in it for me this time. Even the clothes stripped from him were taken by Red-eye, the jailer. Our Old Shuan was luckiest, and after him Third Uncle Xia. He pocketed the whole reward — twenty-five taels of bright silver — and didn't have to spend a cent!

Little Shuan walked slowly out of the inner room, his hands to his chest, coughing repeatedly. He went to the kitchen, filled a bowl with cold rice, added hot water to it, and sitting down started to eat. His mother, hovering over him, asked softly:

"Do you feel better, son? Still as hungry as ever."

"A guaranteed cure!" Kang glanced at the child, then turned back to address the company. "Third Uncle Xia is really smart. If he hadn't informed, even his family would have been executed, and their property confiscated. But instead? Silver! That young rogue was a real scoundrel! He even tried to incite the jailer to revolt!"

"No! The idea of it!" A man in his twenties, sitting in the back row, expressed indignation.

"You know, Red-eye went to sound him out, but he started chatting with him. He said the great Qing empire belongs to us. Just think: Is that kind of talk rational? Red-eye knew he had only an old mother at home, but had never imagined he was so poor. He couldn't squeeze anything out of him; he was already good and angry, and then the young fool would 'scratch the tiger's head', so he gave him a couple of slaps."

"Red-eye is a good boxer. Those slaps must have hurt!" The hunchback in the corner by the wall exulted.

"The rotter was not afraid of being beaten. He even said how sorry he was."

"Nothing to be sorry about in beating a wretch like that," said Greybeard.

Kang looked at him superciliously and said disdainfully, "You misunderstood. The way he said it, he was sorry for Red-eye."

His listeners' eyes took on a glazed look, and no one spoke. Little Shuan had finished his rice and was perspiring profusely, his head steaming.

"Sorry for Red-eye — crazy! He must have been crazy!" said Greybeard, as if suddenly he saw light.

"发了疯了。"二十多岁的人也恍然大悟的说。

店里的坐客，便又现出活气，谈笑起来。小栓也趁着热闹，拼命咳嗽；康大叔走上前，拍他肩膀说：

"包好！小栓——你不要这么咳。包好！"

"疯了。"驼背五少爷点着头说。

四

西关外靠着城根的地面，本是一块官地；中间歪歪斜斜一条细路，是贪走便道的人，用鞋底造成的，但却成了自然的界限。路的左边，都埋着死刑和瘐毙的人，右边是穷人的丛冢。两面都已埋到层层叠叠，宛然阔人家里祝寿时候的馒头。

这一年的清明，分外寒冷；杨柳才吐出半粒米大的新芽。天明未久，华大妈已在右边的一坐新坟前面，排出四碟菜，一碗饭，哭了一场。化过纸，呆呆的坐在地上；仿佛等候什么似的，但自己也说不出等候什么。微风起来，吹动他短发，确乎比去年白得多了。

小路上又来了一个女人，也是半白头发，褴褛的衣裙；提一个破旧的朱漆圆篮，外挂一串纸锭，三步一歇的走。忽然见华大妈坐在地上看他，便有些踌躇，惨白的脸上，现出些羞愧的颜色；但终于硬着头皮，走到左边的一坐坟前，放下了篮子。

那坟与小栓的坟，一字儿排着，中间只隔一条小路。华大妈看他排好四碟菜，一碗饭，立着哭了一通，化过纸锭；心里暗暗地想，"这坟里的也是儿子了。"那老女人徘徊观望了一回，忽然手脚有些发抖，跄跄踉踉退下几步，瞪着眼只是发怔。

华大妈见这样子，生怕他伤心到快要发狂了；便忍不住立起身，跨过小路，低声对他说，"你这位老奶奶不要伤心了，——我们还是回去罢。"

"He must have been crazy!" echoed the man in his twenties.

Once more the customers began to show animation, and conversation was resumed. Under cover of the noise, the child was seized by a paroxysm of coughing. Kang went up to him, clapped him on the shoulder, and said:

"A guaranteed cure! Don't cough like that, Little Shuan! A guaranteed cure!"

"Crazy!" agreed the hunchback, nodding his head.

IV

Originally, the land adjacent to the city wall outside the West Gate had been public land. The zigzag path slanting across it, trodden out by passers-by seeking a short cut, had become a natural boundary line. Left of the path, executed criminals or those who had died of neglect in prison were buried. Right of the path were paupers' graves. The serried ranks of grave mounds on both sides looked like the rolls laid out for a rich man's birthday.

The Qing Ming Festival that year was unusually cold. Willows were only beginning to put forth shoots no larger than grains. Shortly after daybreak, Old Shuan's wife brought four dishes and a bowl of rice to set before a new grave in the right section, and wailed before it. When she had burned paper money she sat on the ground in a stupor as if waiting for something; but for what, she herself did not know. A breeze sprang up and stirred her short hair, which was certainly whiter than in the previous year.

Another woman came down the path, grey-haired and in rags. She was carrying an old, round, red-lacquered basket, with a string of paper money hanging from it; and she walked haltingly. When she saw Old Shuan's wife sitting on the ground watching her, she hesitated, and a flush of shame spread over her pale face. However, she summoned up courage to cross over to a grave in the left section, where she set down her basket.

That grave was directly opposite Little Shuan's, separated only by the path. As Old Shuan's wife watched the other woman set out four dishes and a bowl of rice, then stand up to wail and burn paper money, she thought, "It must be her son in that grave too." The older woman took a few aimless steps and stared vacantly around, then suddenly she began to tremble and stagger backward: she felt giddy.

Fearing sorrow might send her out of her mind, Old Shuan's wife got up and stepped across the path, to say quietly, "Don't grieve, let's go home."

那人点一点头，眼睛仍然向上瞪着；也低声吃吃的说道，"你看，——看这是什么呢？"

华大妈跟了他指头看去，眼光便到了前面的坟，这坟上草根还没有全合，露出一块一块的黄土，煞是难看。再往上仔细看时，却不觉也吃一惊；——分明有一圈红白的花，围着那尖圆的坟顶。

他们的眼睛都已老花多年了，但望这红白的花，却还能明白看见。花也不很多，圆圆的排成一个圈，不很精神，倒也整齐。华大妈忙看他儿子和别人的坟，却只有不怕冷的几点青白小花，零星开着；便觉得心里忽然感到一种不足和空虚，不愿意根究。那老女人又走近几步，细看了一遍，自言自语的说，"这没有根，不像自己开的。——这地方有谁来呢？孩子不会来玩；——亲戚本家早不来了。——这是怎么一回事呢？"他想了又想，忽又流下泪来，大声说道：

"瑜儿，他们都冤枉了你，你还是忘不了，伤心不过，今天特意显点灵，要我知道么？"他四面一看，只见一只乌鸦，站在一株没有叶的树上，便接着说，"我知道了。——瑜儿，可怜他们坑了你，他们将来总有报应，天都知道；你闭了眼睛就是了。——你如果真在这里，听到我的话，——便教这乌鸦飞上你的坟顶，给我看罢。"

微风早经停息了；枯草支支直立，有如铜丝。一丝发抖的声音，在空气中愈颤愈细，细到没有，周围便都是死一般静。两人站在枯草丛里，仰面看那乌鸦；那乌鸦也在笔直的树枝间，缩着头，铁铸一般站着。

许多的工夫过去了；上坟的人渐渐增多，几个老的小的，在土坟间出没。

华大妈不知怎的，似乎卸下了一挑重担，便想到要走；一面劝着说，"我们还是回去罢。"

那老女人叹一口气，无精打采的收起饭菜；又迟疑了一刻，终于慢慢地走了。嘴里自言自语的说，"这是怎么一回事呢？……"

The other nodded, but her eyes were still fixed, and she muttered, "Look! What's that?"

Looking where she pointed, Old Shuan's wife saw that the grave in front had not yet been over-grown with grass. Ugly patches of soil still showed. But when she looked carefully, she was surprised to see at the top of the mound a wreath of red and white flowers.

Both of them suffered from failing eyesight, yet they could see these red and white flowers clearly. There were not many, but they were placed in a circle; and although not very fresh, were neatly set out. Little Shuan's mother looked round and found her own son's grave, like most of the rest, dotted with only a few little, pale flowers shivering in the cold. Suddenly she had a sense of futility and stopped feeling curious about the wreath.

Meantime the old woman had gone up to the grave to look more closely. "They have no roots," she said to herself. "They can't have grown here. Who could have been here? Children don't come here to play, and none of our relatives have ever been. What could have happened?" She puzzled over it, until suddenly her tears began to fall, and she cried aloud:

"Son, they all wronged you, and you do not forget. Is your grief still so great that today you worked this wonder to let me know?"

She looked all around, but could see only a crow perched on a leafless bough. "I know," she continued. "They murdered you. But a day of reckoning will come, Heaven will see to it. Close your eyes in peace.... If you are really here, and can hear me, make that crow fly on to your grave as a sign."

The breeze had long since dropped, and the dry grass stood stiff and straight as copper wires. A faint, tremulous sound vibrated in the air, then faded and died away. All around was deathly still. They stood in the dry grass, looking up at the crow; and the crow, on the rigid bough of the tree, its head drawn in, stood immobile as iron.

Time passed. More people, young and old, came to visit the graves.

Old Shuan's wife felt somehow as if a load had been lifted from her mind and, wanting to leave, she urged the other:

"Let's go."

The old woman sighed, and listlessly picked up the rice and dishes. After a moment's hesitation she started slowly off, still muttering to herself:

"What could it mean?"

他们走不上二三十步远，忽听得背后"哑——"的一声大叫；两个人都竦然的回过头，只见那乌鸦张开两翅，一挫身，直向着远处的天空，箭也似的飞去了。

一九一九年四月。

They had not gone thirty paces when they heard a loud caw behind them. Startled, they looked round and saw the crow stretch its wings, brace itself to take off, then fly like an arrow towards the far horizon.

April 1919

他昏昏的走去关上门，回来坐在床沿上，
纺车静静的立在地上。

She groped her way over to close the door, came back and sat on the bed,
while the loom stood silent on the floor.

明天

Tomorrow

"没有声音，——小东西怎了？"

红鼻子老拱手里擎了一碗黄酒，说着，向间壁努一努嘴。蓝皮阿五便放下酒碗，在他脊梁上用死劲的打了一掌，含含糊糊嚷道：

"你……你你又在想心思……。"

原来鲁镇是僻静地方，还有些古风：不上一更，大家便都关门睡觉。深更半夜没有睡的只有两家：一家是咸亨酒店，几个酒肉朋友围着柜台，吃喝得正高兴；一家便是间壁的单四嫂子，他自从前年守了寡，便须专靠着自己的一双手纺出棉纱来，养活他自己和他三岁的儿子，所以睡的也迟。

这几天，确凿没有纺纱的声音了。但夜深没有睡的既然只有两家，这单四嫂子家有声音，便自然只有老拱们听到，没有声音，也只有老拱们听到。

老拱挨了打，仿佛很舒服似的喝了一大口酒，呜呜的唱起小曲来。

这时候，单四嫂子正抱着他的宝儿，坐在床沿上，纺车静静的立在地上。黑沉沉的灯光，照着宝儿的脸，绯红里带一点青。单四嫂子心里计算：神签也求过了，愿心也许过了，单方也吃过了，要是还不见效，怎么好？——那只有去诊何小仙了。但宝儿也许是日轻夜重，到了明天，太阳一出，热也会退，气喘也会平的：这实在是病人常有的事。

单四嫂子是一个粗笨女人，不明白这"但"字的可怕：许多坏事固然幸亏有了他才变好，许多好事却也因为有了他都弄糟。夏天夜短，老拱们呜呜的唱完了不多时，东方已经发白；不一会，窗缝里透进了银白色的曙光。

单四嫂子等候天明，却不像别人这样容易，觉得非常之慢，宝儿的一呼吸，几乎长过一年。现在居然明亮了；天的明亮，压倒了灯光，——看见宝儿的鼻翼，已经一放一收的扇动。

单四嫂子知道不妙，暗暗叫一声"阿呀！"心里计

"Not a sound—what's wrong with the kid?"

A bowl of yellow wine in his hands, Red-nosed Gong jerked his head towards the next house as he spoke. Blue-skinned Awu set down his own bowl and punched the other hard in the back.

"Bah..." he growled thickly. "Going sentimental again!"

Being so out-of-the-way, Luzhen was rather old-fashioned. Folk closed their doors and went to bed before the first watch sounded. By midnight there were only two households awake: Prosperity Tavern where a few gluttons guzzled merrily round the bar, and the house next door where Fourth Shan's Wife lived. For, left a widow two years earlier, she had nothing but the cotton-yarn she spun to support herself and her three-year-old boy; this is why she also slept late.

It was a fact that for several days now there had been no sound of spinning. But since there were only two households awake at midnight, Old Gong and the others were naturally the only ones who could notice if there was any sound from Fourth Shan's Wife's house, and the only ones to notice if there was no sound.

After being punched, Old Gong — looking quite at his ease — took a great swig at his wine and piped up a folk tune.

Meanwhile Fourth Shan's Wife was sitting on the edge of her bed, Bao'er — her treasure — in her arms, while her loom stood silent on the floor. The murky lamplight fell on Bao'er's face, which showed livid beneath a feverish flush.

"I've drawn lots before the shrine," she was thinking. "I've made a vow to the gods, he's taken the guaranteed cure. If he still doesn't get better, what can I do ? I shall have to take him to Dr. He Xiaoxian. But maybe Bao'er's only bad at night; when the sun comes out tomorrow his fever may go and he may breathe more easily again. A lot of illnesses are like that."

Fourth Shan's Wife was a simple woman, who did not know what a fearful word "but" is. Thanks to this "but," many bad things turn out well, many good things turn out badly. A summer night is short. Soon after Old Gong and the others stopped singing the sky grew bright in the east; and presently through the cracks in the window filtered the silvery light of dawn.

Waiting for the dawn was not such a simple matter for Fourth Shan's Wife as for other people. The time dragged terribly slowly: each breath Bao'er took seemed to last at least a year. But now at last it was bright. Clear daylight swallowed up the lamplight. Bao'er's nostrils quivered as he gasped for breath.

Fourth Shan's Wife smothered a cry, for she knew that this boded ill. But what could

算：怎么好？只有去诊何小仙这一条路了。他虽然是粗笨
女人，心里却有决断，便站起身，从木柜子里掏出每天节
省下来的十三个小银元和一百八十铜钱，都装在衣袋里，
锁上门，抱着宝儿直向何家奔过去。

天气还早，何家已经坐着四个病人了。他摸出四角
银元，买了号签，第五个便轮到宝儿。何小仙伸开两个指
头按脉，指甲足有四寸多长，单四嫂子暗地纳罕，心里计
算：宝儿该有活命了。但总免不了着急，忍不住要问，便
局局促促的说：

"先生，——我家的宝儿什么病呀？"

"他中焦塞着。"

"不妨事么？他……"

"先去吃两帖。"

"他喘不过气来，鼻翅子都扇着呢。"

"这是火克金……"

何小仙说了半句话，便闭上眼睛；单四嫂子也不好意
思再问。在何小仙对面坐着的一个三十多岁的人，此时已
经开好一张药方，指着纸角上的几个字说道：

"这第一味保婴活命丸，须是贾家济世老店才有！"

单四嫂子接过药方，一面走，一面想。他虽是粗笨
女人，却知道何家与济世老店与自己的家，正是一个三角
点；自然是买了药回去便宜了。于是又径向济世老店奔过
去。店伙也翘了长指甲慢慢的看方，慢慢的包药。单四嫂
子抱了宝儿等着；宝儿忽然擎起小手来，用力拔他散乱着
的一绺头发，这是从来没有的举动，单四嫂子怕得发怔。

太阳早出了。单四嫂子抱了孩子，带着药包，越走觉
得越重；孩子又不住的挣扎，路也觉得越长。没奈何坐在
路旁一家公馆的门槛上，休息了一会，衣服渐渐的冰着肌
肤，才知道自己出了一身汗；宝儿却仿佛睡着了。他再起
来慢慢地走，仍然支撑不得，耳朵边忽然听得人说：

"单四嫂子，我替你抱勃罗！"似乎是蓝皮阿五的
声音。

1. The ancient Chinese believed that there were five elements: fire, wood, earth, metal and water. Fire could conquer metal. The traditional Chinese doctors also considered that the heart, lungs, liver, spleen and kidney corresponded to the five elements. Here, Dr. He is saying that heart trouble had affected the lungs.

she do? she wondered. Her only hope was to take him to Dr. He. She might be a simple woman, but she had a will of her own. She stood up, went to the cupboard, and took out her entire saving — thirteen small silver dollars and a hundred and eighty coppers in all. Having put the whole lot in her pocket, she locked the door and carried Bao'er as fast as she could to Dr. He's house.

Early as it was, there were already four patients sitting there. She produced forty silver cents for a registration slip, and Bao'er was the fifth to be seen. Dr. He stretched out two fingers to feel the child's pulses. His nails were a good four inches long, and Fourth Shan's Wife marvelled inwardly, thinking, "Surely my Bao'er must be fated to live!" She could not help feeling anxious all the same, and could not stop herself asking nervously:

"What's wrong with my Baro'er, doctor?"

"An obstruction of the digestive tract."

"Is it serious? Will he...?"

"Take these two prescriptions to start with."

"He can't breathe, his nostrils are twitching."

"The element of fire overpowers that of metal...."[1]

Leaving this sentence unfinished, Dr. He closed his eyes, and Fourth Shan's Wife did not like to say any more. Opposite the doctor sat a man in his thirties, who had now finished making out the prescription.

"The first is Infant Preserver Pills," he told her, pointing to the characters in one corner of the paper. "You can get those only at the Jia family's Salvation Shop."

Fourth Shan's Wife took the paper, and walked out thinking as she went. She might be a simple woman, but she knew Dr. He's house, Salvation Shop and her own home formed a triangle; so of course it would be simpler to buy the medicine first before going back. She hurried as fast as she could to Salvation Shop. The assistant raised his long finger-nails too as he slowly read the prescription, then slowly wrapped up the medicine. With Bao'er in her arms, Fourth Shan's Wife waited. Suddenly Bao'er stretched up a little hand and tugged at his loose tuft of hair. He had never done this before, and his mother was terrified.

The sun was fairly high now. With the child in her arms and the package of medicine to carry, the further she walked the heavier she found her load. The child kept struggling too, which made the way seem even longer. She had to sit down on the doorstep of a big house by the roadside to rest for a while; and presently her clothes lay so clammy against her skin that she realized she had been sweating. But Bao'er seemed fast asleep. When she stood up again to walk slowly on, she still found him too heavy. A voice beside her said:

"Let me take him for you, Fourth Shan's Wife!" It sounded like Blue-skinned Awu.

他抬头看时，正是蓝皮阿五，睡眼朦胧的跟着他走。

单四嫂子在这时候，虽然很希望降下一员天将，助他一臂之力，却不愿是阿五。但阿五有点侠气，无论如何，总是偏要帮忙，所以推让了一会，终于得了许可了。他便伸开臂膊，从单四嫂子的乳房和孩子中间，直伸下去，抱去了孩子。单四嫂子便觉乳房上发了一条热，刹时间直热到脸上和耳根。

他们两人离开了二尺五寸多地，一同走着。阿五说些话，单四嫂子却大半没有答。走了不多时候，阿五又将孩子还给他，说是昨天与朋友约定的吃饭时候到了；单四嫂子便接了孩子。幸而不远便是家，早看见对门的王九妈在街边坐着，远远地说话：

"单四嫂子，孩子怎了？——看过先生了么？"

"看是看了。——王九妈，你有年纪，见的多，不如请你老法眼看一看，怎样……"

"唔……"

"怎样……？"

"唔……"王九妈端详了一番，把头点了两点，摇了两摇。

宝儿吃下药，已经是午后了。单四嫂子留心看他神情，似乎仿佛平稳了不少；到得下午，忽然睁开眼叫一声"妈！"又仍然合上眼，像是睡去了。他睡了一刻，额上鼻尖都沁出一粒一粒的汗珠，单四嫂子轻轻一摸，胶水般粘着手；慌忙去摸胸口，便禁不住呜咽起来。

宝儿的呼吸从平稳变到没有，单四嫂子的声音也就从呜咽变成号咷。这时聚集了几堆人：门内是王九妈蓝皮阿五之类，门外是咸亨的掌柜和红鼻子老拱之类。王九妈便发命令，烧了一串纸钱；又将两条板凳和五件衣服作抵，替单四嫂子借了两块洋钱，给帮忙的人备饭。

第一个问题是棺木。单四嫂子还有一副银耳环和一支裹金的银簪，都交给了咸亨的掌柜，托他作一个保，半现半赊的买一具棺木。蓝皮阿五也伸出手来，很愿意自告奋

When she looked up, sure enough it was Ahu, who was following her with eyes still heavy from sleep.

Though Fourth Shan's Wife had been longing for an angel to come to her rescue, she had not wanted her champion to be Awu. But there was something of the gallant about Awu, for he absolutely insisted on helping her; and at last, after several refusals she gave way. As he stretched his arm between her breast and the child, then thrust it down to take over Bao'er, she felt a wave of heat along her breast. She flushed right up to her ears.

They walked along, two and a half feet apart. Awu made some remarks, most of which were left unanswered by Fourth Shan's Wife. They had not gone far when he gave the child back to her, saying he had arranged yesterday to have a meal at this time with a friend. Fourth Shan's Wife took Bao'er back. Luckily it wasn't far now: already she could see Ninth Aunt Wang sitting at the side of the street, calling out to her:

"Fourth Shan's Wife, how's the child?... Did you get to see the doctor?"

"We saw him.... Ninth Aunt Wang, you're old and you've seen a lot. Will you look him over for me, and say what you think?"

"Um."

"Well...?"

"Ummm...."

When Ninth Aunt Wang had examined Bao'er, she nodded her head twice, then shook it twice.

By the time Bao'er had taken his medicine it was after noon. Fourth Shan's Wife watched him closely, and he did seem a good deal quieter. In the afternoon he suddenly opened his eyes and called, "Ma!" Then he closed his eyes again and seemed to be sleeping. He had not slept long before his forehead and the tip of his nose were beaded with sweat, which, when his mother felt it, stuck to her fingers like glue. In a panic she felt his chest, then burst out sobbing.

After quieting down, his breathing had stopped completely. After sobbing, she started wailing. Soon groups of people gathered: inside the room Ninth Aunt Wang, Blue-skinned Awu and the like; outside others like the landlord of Prosperity Tavern and Red-nosed Gong. Ninth Aunt Wang decreed that a string of paper coins should be burnt; then, taking two stools and five articles of clothing as security, she borrowed two dollars for Fouth Shan's Wife to prepare a meal for all those who were helping.

The first problem was the coffin. Fourth Shan's Wife still had a pair of silver earrings and a silver hairpin plated with gold, which she gave to the landlord of Prosperity Tavern so that he would go surety for her and buy a coffin half for cash, half on credit.

勇；王九妈却不许他，只准他明天抬棺材的差使，阿五骂了一声"老畜生"，快快的努了嘴站着。掌柜便自去了；晚上回来，说棺木须得现做，后半夜才成功。

掌柜回来的时候，帮忙的人早吃过饭；因为鲁镇还有些古风，所以不上一更，便都回家睡觉了。只有阿五还靠着咸亨的柜台喝酒，老拱也呜呜的唱。

这时候，单四嫂子坐在床沿上哭着，宝儿在床上躺着，纺车静静的在地上立着。许多工夫，单四嫂子的眼泪宣告完结了，眼睛张得很大，看看四面的情形，觉得奇怪：所有的都是不会有的事。他心里计算：不过是梦罢了，这些事都是梦。明天醒过来，自己好好的睡在床上，宝儿也好好的睡在自己身边。他也醒过来，叫一声"妈"，生龙活虎似的跳去玩了。

老拱的歌声早经寂静，咸亨也熄了灯。单四嫂子张着眼，总不信所有的事。——鸡也叫了；东方渐渐发白，窗缝里透进了银白色的曙光。

银白的曙光又渐渐显出绯红，太阳光接着照到屋脊。单四嫂子张着眼，呆呆坐着；听得打门声音，才吃了一吓，跑出去开门。门外一个不认识的人，背了一件东西；后面站着王九妈。

哦，他们背了棺材来了。

下半天，棺木才合上盖：因为单四嫂子哭一回，看一回，总不肯死心塌地的盖上；幸亏王九妈等得不耐烦，气愤愤的跑上前，一把拖开他，才七手八脚的盖上了。

但单四嫂子待他的宝儿，实在已经尽了心，再没有什么缺陷。昨天烧过一串纸钱，上午又烧了四十九卷《大悲咒》；收敛的时候，给他穿上顶新的衣裳，平日喜欢的玩意儿，——一个泥人，两个小木碗，两个玻璃瓶，——都放在枕头旁边。后来王九妈掐着指头仔细推敲，也终于想不出一些什么缺陷。

这一日里，蓝皮阿五简直整天没有到；咸亨掌柜便替

2. This was a Buddhist chant, believed to help the soul of the deceased to reach heaven.

Bule-skinned Awu raised his hand to volunteer to help, but Ninth Aunt Wang would not hear of it. All she would let him do was carry the coffin the next day. "Old bitch!" He cursed, and stood there grumpily pursing his lips. The landlord left, coming back that evening to report that the coffin would have to be specially made, and would not be ready till nearly morning.

By the time the landlord came back the other helpers had finished their meal. And Luzhen being rather old-fashioned, they all went home to sleep before the first watch. Only Awu leant on the bar of Prosperity Tavern drinking, while Old Gong croaked a song.

Meanwhile Fourth Shan's Wife was sitting on the edge of the bed crying, Bao'er lay on the bed, and the loom stood silent on the floor. After a long time, when Fourth Shan's Wife had no more tears to shed, she opened wide her eyes, and looked around in amazement. All this was impossible! "This is only a dream," she thought. "It's all a dream. I shall wake up tomorrow lying snug in bed, with Bao'er sleeping snugly beside me. Then he'll wake and call, 'Ma!' and jump down like a young tiger to play."

Old Gong had long since stopped singing, and the light had gone out in Prosperity Tavern. Fourth Shan's Wife sat staring, but could not believe all that had happened. A cock crew, the sky grew bright in the east, and through the cracks in the window filtered the silvery light of dawn.

By degrees the silvery light of dawn turned copper, and the sun shone on the roof. Fourth Shan's Wife sat there staring till someone knocked, when she gave a start and ran to open the door. A stranger was there with something on his back, and behind him stood Ninth Aunt Wang.

Oh, it was the coffin he'd brought!

Not till that afternoon was the lid of the coffin put on, because Fourth Shan's Wife would keep crying, then taking a look, and could not bear to have the lid closed down. Luckily, Ninth Aunt Wang grew tired of waiting, hurried indignantly forward and pulled her aside. Then they hastily closed it up.

Fourth Shan's Wife had really done all she could for her Bao'er — nothing had been forgotten. The previous day she had burned a string of paper coins, this morning she had burned the forty-nine books of the *Incantation of Great Mercy*,[2] and before putting him in the coffin she had dressed him in his newest clothes and set by his pillow all the toys he liked best — a little clay figure, two small wooden bowls, two glass bottles. Though Ninth Aunt Wang reckoned carefully on her fingers, even then she could not think of anything they had forgotten.

Since Blue-skinned Awu did not turn up all day, the landlord of Prosperity Tavern

单四嫂子雇了两名脚夫，每名二百另十个大钱，抬棺木到义冢地上安放。王九妈又帮他煮了饭，凡是动过手开过口的人都吃了饭。太阳渐渐显出要落山的颜色；吃过饭的人也不觉都显出要回家的颜色，——于是他们终于都回了家。

单四嫂子很觉得头眩，歇息了一会，倒居然有点平稳了。但他接连着便觉得很异样：遇到了平生没有遇到过的事，不像会有的事，然而的确出现了。他越想越奇，又感到一件异样的事——这屋子忽然太静了。

他站起身，点上灯火，屋子越显得静。他昏昏的走去关上门，回来坐在床沿上，纺车静静的立在地上。他定一定神，四面一看，更觉得坐立不得，屋子不但太静，而且也太大了，东西也太空了。太大的屋子四面包围着他，太空的东西四面压着他，叫他喘气不得。

他现在知道他的宝儿确乎死了；不愿意见这屋子，吹熄了灯，躺着。他一面哭，一面想：想那时候，自己纺着棉纱，宝儿坐在身边吃茴香豆，瞪着一双小黑眼睛想了一刻，便说，"妈！爹卖馄饨，我大了也卖馄饨，卖许多许多钱，——我都给你。"那时候，真是连纺出的棉纱，也仿佛寸寸都有意思，寸寸都活着。但现在怎么了？现在的事，单四嫂子却实在没有想到什么。——我早经说过：他是粗笨女人。他能想出什么呢？他单觉得这屋子太静，太大，太空罢了。

但单四嫂子虽然粗笨，却知道还魂是不能有的事，他的宝儿也的确不能再见了。叹一口气，自言自语的说，"宝儿，你该还在这里，你给我梦里见见罢。"于是合上眼，想赶快睡去，会他的宝儿，苦苦的呼吸通过了静和大和空虚，自己听得明白。

单四嫂子终于朦朦胧胧的走入睡乡，全屋子都很静。这时红鼻子老拱的小曲，也早经唱完；跄跄踉踉出了咸亨，却又提尖了喉咙，唱道：

"我的冤家呀！——可怜你，——孤另另的……"

蓝皮阿五便伸手揪住了老拱的肩头，两个人七歪八斜

3. Dumplings stuffed with meat and boiled in soup.

hired two porters for Fourth Shan's Wife at 210 large coppers each, who carried the coffin to the public graveyard and dug a grave. Ninth Aunt Wang helped her prepare a meal to which everyone who had lifted a finger or opened his mouth was invited. Soon the sun made it clear that it was about to set, and the guests unwittingly made it clear that they were about to leave — home they all went.

Fourth Shan's Wife felt dizzy at first, but after a little rest she quietened down. At once, thought, she had the impression that things were rather strange. Something which had never happened to her before, and which she had thought never could happen, had happened. The more she thought, the more surprised she felt, and another thing that struck her as rather strange was the fact that the room had suddenly grown too silent.

She stood up and lit the lamp, and the room seemed even more silent. She groped her way over to close the door, came back and sat on the bed, while the loom stood silent on the floor. She pulled herself together and looked around, feeling unable either to sit or stand. The room was not only too silent, it was far too big as well, and the things in it were far too empty. This over-large room hemmed her in, and the emptiness all around her bore hard on her, till she could hardly breathe.

She knew now her Bao'er was really dead; and, not wanting to see this room, she blew out the light and lay down to cry and think. She remembered how Bao'er had sat by her said when she spun, eating peas flavoured with aniseed. He had watched her hard with his small black eyes and thought. "Ma!" He suddenly said. "Dad sold *hun dun.*[3] When I'm big I'll sell *hun dun* too, and make lots and lots of money — and I'll give it all to you."

At such times even every inch of yarn she spun seemed worthwhile and alive. But what now? Fourth Shan's Wife had not considered the present at all — as I have said, she was only a simple woman. What solution could she think of? All she knew was that this room was too silent, too large, too empty.

But even though Fourth Shan's Wife was a simple woman, she knew the dead cannot come to life again, and she would never see her Bao'er any more. She sighed and said, "Bao'er you must still be here. Let me see you in my dreams." Then she closed her eyes, hoping to fall asleep at once, so that she could see Bao'er. She heard her hard breathing clearly through the silence, the vastness and emptiness.

At last Fourth Shan's Wife dozed off, and the whole room was very still. Red-nosed Gong's folk song had long since ended, and he had staggered out of Prosperity Tavern to sing in a falsetto:

"I pity you — my darling — all alone...."

Blue-skinned Awu grabbed Old Gong's shoulder, and laughing tipsily they reeled

的笑着挤着走去。

单四嫂子早睡着了，老拱们也走了，咸亨也关上门了。这时的鲁镇，便完全落在寂静里。只有那暗夜为想变成明天，却仍在这寂静里奔波；另有几条狗，也躲在暗地里呜呜的叫。

一九二〇年六月。

away together.

Fourth Shan's Wife was asleep, Old Gong and the others had gone, the door of Prosperity Tavern was closed. Luzhen was sunk in utter silence. Only the night, eager to change into the morrow, was journeying on in the silence; and, hidden in the darkness, a few dogs were barking.

June 1920

独有这一件小事，却总是浮在我眼前，
有时反更分明，教我惭愧，催我自新，
并且增长我的勇气和希望。

Yet this small incident keeps coming back to me,
often more vivid than in actual life, teaching me shame,
spurring me on to reform,
and imbuing me with fresh courage and fresh hope.

一件小事

A Small Incident

我从乡下跑到京城里，一转眼已经六年了。其间耳闻目睹的所谓国家大事，算起来也很不少；但在我心里，都不留什么痕迹，倘要我寻出这些事的影响来说，便只是增长了我的坏脾气，——老实说，便是教我一天比一天的看不起人。

但有一件小事，却于我有意义，将我从坏脾气里拖开，使我至今忘记不得。

这是民国六年的冬天，大北风刮得正猛，我因为生计关系，不得不一早在路上走。一路几乎遇不见人，好容易才雇定了一辆人力车，教他拉到S门去。不一会，北风小了，路上浮尘早已刮净，剩下一条洁白的大道来，车夫也跑得更快。刚近S门，忽而车把上带着一个人，慢慢地倒了。

跌倒的是一个女人，花白头发，衣服都很破烂。伊从马路边上突然向车前横截过来；车夫已经让开道，但伊的破棉背心没有上扣，微风吹着，向外展开，所以终于兜着车把。幸而车夫早有点停步，否则伊定要栽一个大斤斗，跌到头破血出了。

伊伏在地上；车夫便也立住脚。我料定这老女人并没有伤，又没有别人看见，便很怪他多事，要自己惹出是非，也误了我的路。

我便对他说，"没有什么的。走你的罢！"

车夫毫不理会，——或者并没有听到，——却放下车子，扶那老女人慢慢起来，搀着臂膊立定，问伊说：

"你怎么啦？"

"我摔坏了。"

我想，我眼见你慢慢倒地，怎么会摔坏呢，装腔作势罢了，这真可憎恶。车夫多事，也正是自讨苦吃，现在你自己想法去。

车夫听了这老女人的话，却毫不踌躇，仍然搀着伊的臂膊，便一步一步的向前走。我有些诧异，忙看前面，是一所巡警分驻所，大风之后，外面也不见人。这车夫扶着那老女人，便正是向那大门走去。

我这时突然感到一种异样的感觉，觉得他满身灰尘的

Six years have slipped by since I came from the country to the capital. During that time the number of so-called affairs of state I have witnessed or heard about is far from small, but none of them made much impression. If asked to define their influence on me, I can only say they made my bad temper worse. Frankly speaking, they taught me to take a poorer view of people every day.

One small incident, however, which struck me as significant and jolted me out of my irritability, remains fixed even now in my memory.

It was the winter of 1917, a strong north wind was blustering, but the exigencies of earning my living forced me to be up and out early. I met scarcely a soul on the road, but eventually managed to hire a rickshaw to take me to S— Gate. Presently the wind dropped a little, having blown away the drifts of dust on the road to leave a clean broad highway, and the rickshaw man quickened his pace. We were just approaching S— Gate when we knocked into someone who slowly toppled over.

It was a grey-haired woman in ragged clothes. She had stepped out abruptly from the roadside in front of us, and although the rickshaw man had swerved, her tattered padded waistcoat, unbuttoned and billowing in the wind, had caught on the shaft. Luckily the rickshaw man had slowed down, otherwise she would certainly have had a bad fall and it might have been a serious accident.

She huddled there on the ground, and the rickshaw man stopped. As I did not believe the old woman was hurt and as no one else had seen us, I thought this halt of his uncalled for, liable to land him in trouble and hold me up.

"It's all right," I said. "Go on."

He paid no attention — he may not have heard — but set down the shafts, took the old woman's arm and gently helped her up.

"Are you all right?" He asked.

"I hurt myself falling."

I thought: I saw how slowly you fell, how could you be hurt? Putting on an act like this is simply disgusting. The rickshaw man asked for trouble, and now he's got it. He'll have to find his own way out.

But the rickshaw man did not hesitate for a minute after hearing the old woman's answer. Still holding her arm, he helped her slowly forward. Rather puzzled by this I looked ahead and saw a police-station. Because of the high wind, there was no one outside. It was there that the rickshaw man was taking the old woman.

Suddenly I had the strange sensation that his dusty retreating figure had in that

后影，刹时高大了，而且愈走愈大，须仰视才见。而且他对于我，渐渐的又几乎变成一种威压，甚而至于要榨出皮袍下面藏着的"小"来。

我的活力这时大约有些凝滞了，坐着没有动，也没有想，直到看见分驻所里走出一个巡警，才下了车。

巡警走近我说，"你自己雇车罢，他不能拉你了。"

我没有思索的从外套袋里抓出一大把铜元，交给巡警，说，"请你给他……"

风全住了，路上还很静。我走着，一面想，几乎怕敢想到我自己。以前的事姑且搁起，这一大把铜元又是什么意思？奖他么？我还能裁判车夫么？我不能回答自己。

这事到了现在，还是时时记起。我因此也时时熬了苦痛，努力的要想到我自己。几年来的文治武力，在我早如幼小时候所读过的"子曰诗云"一般，背不上半句了。独有这一件小事，却总是浮在我眼前，有时反更分明，教我惭愧，催我自新，并且增长我的勇气和希望。

一九二〇年七月。

instant grown larger. Indeed, the further he walked the larger he loomed, until I had to look up to him. At the same time he seemed gradually to be exerting a pressure on me which threatened to overpower the small self hidden under my fur-lined gown.

Almost paralysed at that juncture I sat there motionless, my mind a blank, until a policeman came out. Then I got down from the rickshaw.

The policeman came up to me and said, "Get another rickshaw. He can't take you any further."

On the spur of the moment I pulled a handful of coppers from my coat pocket and handed them to the policeman. "Please give him this," I said.

The wind had dropped completely, but the road was still quiet. As I walked along thinking, I hardly dared to think about myself. Quite apart from what had happened earlier, what had I meant by that handful of coppers? Was it a reward? Who was I to judge the rickshaw man? I could give myself no answer.

Even now, this incident keeps coming back to me. It keeps distressing me and makes me try to think about myself. The politics and the fighting of those years have slipped my mind as completely as the classics I read as a child. Yet this small incident keeps coming back to me, often more vivid than in actual life, teaching me shame, spurring me on to reform, and imbuing me with fresh courage and fresh hope.

July 1920

后来骂我的人也被警察剪去了辫子，
我就不再被人辱骂了……

Only after those who had cursed me had their queues cut off by
the police did I stop getting cursed...

头发的故事
The Story of Hair

星期日的早晨，我揭去一张隔夜的日历，向着新的那一张上看了又看的说：

"阿，十月十日，——今天原来正是双十节。这里却一点没有记载！"

我的一位前辈先生N，正走到我的寓里来谈闲天，一听这话，便很不高兴的对我说：

"他们对！他们不记得，你怎样他；你记得，又怎样呢？"

这位N先生本来脾气有点乖张，时常生些无谓的气，说些不通世故的话。当这时候，我大抵任他自言自语，不赞一辞；他独自发完议论，也就算了。

他说：

"我最佩服北京双十节的情形。早晨，警察到门，吩咐道'挂旗！''是，挂旗！'各家大半懒洋洋的踱出一个国民来，撅起一块斑驳陆离的洋布。这样一直到夜，——收了旗关门；几家偶然忘却的，便挂到第二天的上午。

"他们忘却了纪念，纪念也忘却了他们！

"我也是忘却了纪念的一个人。倘使纪念起来，那第一个双十节前后的事，便都上我的心头，使我坐立不稳了。

"多少故人的脸，都浮在我眼前。几个少年辛苦奔走了十多年，暗地里一颗弹丸要了他的性命；几个少年一击不中，在监牢里身受一个多月的苦刑；几个少年怀着远志，忽然踪影全无，连尸首也不知那里去了。——

"他们都在社会的冷笑恶骂迫害倾陷里过了一生；现在他们的坟墓也早在忘却里渐渐平塌下去了。

"我不堪纪念这些事。

"我们还是记起一点得意的事来谈谈罢。"

N忽然现出笑容，伸手在自己头上一摸，高声说：

"我最得意的是自从第一个双十节以后，我在路上走，不再被人笑骂了。

"老兄，你可知道头发是我们中国人的宝贝和冤家，古今来多少人在这上头吃些毫无价值的苦呵！

"我们的很古的古人，对于头发似乎也还看轻。据

1. October 10,1911 was the date of the Wuchang Uprising (the 1911 Revolution) led by Sun Yat-sen. October 10 became the National Day of the Republic of China ,and was also known as the Double Tenth Festival.

2. From 1911 to 1927 the Chinese national flag was of five colours — red, yellow, blue, white and black.

On Sunday morning, I turned over a page of my calendar and looked at the next one. Taking a second look I remarked, "Why, it's the tenth of October — so today is the Double Tenth Festival.[1] But there's no mention of it here!"

Mr. N, one of my seniors, had just dropped in for a chat. Hearing this, he retorted irately, "They're right. They've forgotten — so what? You remember — so what?"

This Mr. N is rather irascible. He often loses his temper for no reason and makes tactless remarks. At such times, I generally let him talk to himself, without putting in a word. After he has finished his monologue, that's that.

"The Double Tenth Festival in Beijing strikes me as admirable," he observed. "In the morning a policeman comes to your gate to order, 'Put up a flag.' 'A flag, right!' Most families lackadaisically bring out a national flag, and that cloth of many colours[2] is hung up till the evening, when they take it down and shut the gate. A few may forget and leave it up till the next morning.

"They have forgotten the anniversary, and the anniversary has forgotten them.

"I'm one of those who forget it. If I were to commemorate it, all that happened before and after the first Double Tenth would come back to my mind and upset me.

"Many faces from the past float before my eyes. Some young people kept on the go, hard as it was, for over ten years, till a bullet in the back ended their lives. Others, who weren't shot, were tortured for a month or more in jail. Yet others with high ideals suddenly vanished without a trace — no one knows where their corpses are.

"They were scoffed at, cursed, persecuted and betrayed all their lives by society. Now, little by little, their graves have crumbled away in oblivion.

"I can't bear to commemorate such things.

"Let's talk about more pleasant memories."

Suddenly N smiled. Reaching up to stroke his head he went on loudly, "What pleased me most was the fact that, after the first Double Tenth, people stopped laughing at me or cursing me in the street.

"You know, my friend, in China hair is our pride and our bane. How many people since ancient times have suffered because of it, all to no purpose!

"Our earliest ancestors don't seem to have taken hair too seriously. Judging by the criminal code, what counted most was naturally the head, so beheading was the worst

刑法看来，最要紧的自然是脑袋，所以大辟是上刑；次要便是生殖器了，所以宫刑和幽闭也是一件吓人的罚；至于髡，那是微乎其微了，然而推想起来，正不知道曾有多少人们因为光着头皮便被社会践踏了一生世。

"我们讲革命的时候，大谈什么扬州十日，嘉定屠城，其实也不过一种手段；老实说：那时中国人的反抗，何尝因为亡国，只是因为拖辫子。

"顽民杀尽了，遗老都寿终了，辫子早留定了，洪杨又闹起来了。我的祖母曾对我说，那时做百姓才难哩，全留着头发的被官兵杀，还是辫子的便被长毛杀！

"我不知道有多少中国人只因为这不痛不痒的头发而吃苦，受难，灭亡。"

N两眼望着屋梁，似乎想些事，仍然说：

"谁知道头发的苦轮到我了。

"我出去留学，便剪掉了辫子，这并没有别的奥妙，只为他太不便当罢了。不料有几位辫子盘在头顶上的同学们便很厌恶我；监督也大怒，说要停了我的官费，送回中国去。

"不几天，这位监督却自己被人剪去辫子逃走了。去剪的人们里面，一个便是做《革命军》的邹容，这人也因此不能再留学，回到上海来，后来死在西牢里。你也早已忘却了罢？

"过了几年，我的家景大不如前了，非谋点事做便要受饿，只得也回到中国来。我一到上海，便买定一条假辫子，那时是二元的市价，带着回家。我的母亲倒也不说什么，然而旁人一见面，便都首先研究这辫子，待到知道是假，就一声冷笑，将我拟为杀头的罪名；有一位本家，还预备去告官，但后来因为恐怕革命党的造反或者要成功，这才中止了。

"我想，假的不如真的直截爽快，我便索性废了假辫子，穿着西装在街上走。

"一路走去，一路便是笑骂的声音，有的还跟在后面骂：'这冒失鬼！''假洋鬼子！'

3. In 1645, Manchu troops stormed Yangzhou, then massacred the citizens for ten days. That same year, many massacres were carried out in Jiading, now part of Shanghai. Accounts of these massacres were circulated before the 1911 Revolution to arouse anti-Manchu feeling.

4. Manchu men shaved their heads above their temples and plaited their hair in a queue. After entering Beijing, they forced Han men to do the same.

5. Hong Xiuquan (1814-64) and Yang Xiuqing (1820?-56) were leaders of the Taiping Revolution (1851-64). The Qing Dynasty forced men to shave the hair over their temples and wear queues. The Taiping rebels who opposed feudal rule and national oppression refused to do this and let their hair hang to their shoulders, hence the name Long Hairs.

6. Zou Rong or Zou Weidan (1820?-56) from Baxian County in Sichuan went to Japan to study in 1902, and spread anti-Qing ideas. In 1903, after his return to China, he wrote *The Revolutionary Army*. In July that year, the Qing government in connivance with the authorities in the British Concession in Shanghai arrested and sentenced him to two years' imprisonment.

punishment. Next in importance was the sexual organ, so castration and sterilization was another fearful punishment. As for having one's hair cut off, that hardly counted; but when you come to think of it, goodness knows how many people must have been downtrodden all their lives because they had shaved heads.

"When we talked about revolution, a lot was said about the ten days in Yangzhou and the Jiading massacre,[3] but actually that was just a subterfuge. In fact, the Chinese people in those days revolted not because the country was on the verge of ruin, but because they had to wear queues.[4]

"By the time all refractory subjects had been killed off and the survivors had died of old age, the queue was here to stay. But then Hong and Yang[5] made trouble. My grandmother told me how hard it was in those days for common citizens: those who didn't shave off the hair over their temples were killed by government troops, those with queues were killed by the Long Hairs.

"Hair is insignificant, yet I've no idea how many Chinese suffered or died just on account of it."

N fixed his eyes, reflectively, on the rafter.

"Then, just fancy, it was my turn. Hair landed me in trouble.

"I went abroad to study, so cut off my queue. Not for any mysterious reason, just because it was too inconvenient. To my surprise, that made me an object of loathing to a few classmates who had coiled up their queues. Our supervisor was furious too. He threatened to stop my government grant and send me back to China.

"A few days later, though, that supervisor fled, as his queue had been cut off by other people. Among them was Zou Rong,[6] who wrote *The Revolutionary Army*. For this reason he was not allowed to go on studying abroad and went back to Shanghai, where he subsequently died in a western jail.

"A few years later, my family had become so badly off that unless I found a job I would have starved, so I had to go back to China too. As soon as I reached Shanghai I bought an artificial queue, which then cost two yuan, and took it home with me. My mother said nothing about it, but it was the first thing scrutinized by all the other people I met; and once they found out it was false, with a scornful laugh they adjudged me guilty of a capital offence. One of my own family planned to indict me, but he later refrained from doing this for fear the rebels of the revolutionary party might succeed.

"I thought, a sham is less straightforward than the truth so I discarded that artificial queue, and went out dressed in a Western suit.

"Wherever I went I heard jeers and abuse. Some people even tagged after me cursing, 'Lunatic!' 'Fake foreign devil!'

"我于是不穿洋服了，改了大衫，他们骂得更利害。

"在这日暮途穷的时候，我的手里才添出一支手杖来，拼命的打了几回，他们渐渐的不骂了。只是走到没有打过的生地方还是骂。

"这件事很使我悲哀，至今还时时记得哩。我在留学的时候，曾经看见日报上登载一个游历南洋和中国的本多博士[7]的事；这位博士是不懂中国和马来语的，人问他，你不懂话，怎么走路呢？他拿起手杖来说，这便是他们的话，他们都懂！我因此气愤了好几天，谁知道我竟不知不觉的自己也做了，而且那些人都懂了。……

"宣统初年，我在本地的中学校做监学，同事是避之惟恐不远，官僚是防之惟恐不严，我终日如坐在冰窖子里，如站在刑场旁边，其实并非别的，只因为缺少了一条辫子！

"有一日，几个学生忽然走到我的房里来，说，'先生，我们要剪辫子了。'我说，'不行！''有辫子好呢，没有辫子好呢？''没有辫子好……''你怎么说不行呢？''犯不上，你们还是不剪上算，——等一等罢。'他们不说什么，撅着嘴唇走出房去；然而终于剪掉了。

"呵！不得了了，人言啧啧了；我却只装作不知道，一任他们光着头皮，和许多辫子一齐上讲堂。

"然而这剪辫病传染了；第三天，师范学堂的学生忽然也剪下了六条辫子，晚上便开除了六个学生。这六个人，留校不能，回家不得，一直挨到第一个双十节[8]之后又一个多月，才消去了犯罪的火烙印。

"我呢？也一样，只是元年冬天到北京，还被人骂过几次，后来骂我的人也被警察剪去了辫子，我就不再被人辱骂了；但我没有到乡间去。"

N显出非常得意模样，忽而又沉下脸来：

"现在你们这些理想家，又在那里嚷什么女子剪发了，又要造出许多毫无所得而痛苦的人！

7. Seiroku Honda (1866-1952) studied forestry and wrote books on the subject.

8. 1908-11

"Then I stopped wearing a suit and wore a long gown, but they cursed me harder than ever.

"It was then, at a dead-end, that I took to carrying a cane, and after I had given several people a good trouncing, they gradually stopped cursing me. But if I went to some new place where I hadn't beaten anyone, I was still cursed.

"To this day, I keep remembering how wretched this made me. While studying in Japan, I read in some Japanese paper an account of Dr. Honda's[7] travels in the South Seas and China. Being unable to speak Chinese or Malaysian, or to understand the questions asked him, how could he travel? He expressed himself by brandishing a cane, for this was a language everyone understood! This had incensed me for days, yet here was I now unconsciously doing the same, and all those people understood....

"At the start of the Xuantong era,[8] when I was dean of our local middle school, my colleagues kept at a distance from me, officialdom mounted a strict watch over me. I felt as if sitting all day in an ice-house, or standing by an execution ground. And the sole reason for this was my lack of a queue!

"One day, without warning, some students came into my room. They said, 'Sir, we want to cut off our queues.'

"I told them 'Don't!'

"'Is it better to have queues or not?'

"'Better not.'

"'Then why tell us not to cut them?'

"'It's not worth it. Better not cut them off — wait a while.'

"They said nothing but marched out, pursing their lips. In the end, however, they cut them.

"Ha, what a to-do! What an uproar! But I simply turned a blind eye and let those shorn heads into the assembly hall together with all the queues.

"But this queue-cutting proved contagious. Three days later, six students in the normal school suddenly cut off their queues too, and that evening they were expelled. They could neither remain in the school nor go home. Not till a month or more after the first Double Tenth did they stop being branded as criminals.

"And I? It was the same. In the winter of 1912 I came to Beijing, and was still cursed several times. Only after those who had cursed me had their queues cut off by the police did I stop getting cursed; but I didn't go to the country."

N had been looking very smug. Now suddenly his face fell.

"Nowadays, idealists like you are calling on girls to cut their hair. You're going to make many more people suffer for nothing! Aren't there already girls who can't take the

"现在不是已经有剪掉头发的女人，因此考不进学校去，或者被学校除了名么？

"改革么，武器在那里？工读么，工厂在那里？

"仍然留起，嫁给人家做媳妇去：忘却了一切还是幸福，倘使伊记着些平等自由的话，便要苦痛一生世！

"我要借了阿尔志跋绥夫的话问你们：你们将黄金时代的出现豫约给这些人们的子孙了，但有什么给这些人们自己呢？

"阿，造物的皮鞭没有到中国的脊梁上时，中国便永远是这一样的中国，决不肯自己改变一支毫毛！

"你们的嘴里既然并无毒牙，何以偏要在额上帖起'蝮蛇'两个大字，引乞丐来打杀？……"

N愈说愈离奇了，但一见到我不很愿听的神情，便立刻闭了口，站起来取帽子。

我说，"回去么？"

他答道，"是的，天要下雨了。"

我默默的送他到门口。

他戴上帽子说：

"再见！请你恕我打搅，好在明天便不是双十节，我们统可以忘却了。"

一九二〇年十月。

9. M. P. Artzybashev (1878-1927) was a Russian novelist who fled the country after the October Revolution in 1917 and died in Warsaw. This quotation comes from one of his novels.

school entrance examinations, or who are expelled because they've bobbed their hair?

"Reform? Where are your weapons? Education for workers? Where are your factories?

"Let girls keep their long hair and marry, becoming daughters-in-law. Forgetting everything they can be happy. If you remind them of that talk of equality and freedom, they'll be wretched all their lives.

"Borrowing the words of Artzybashev,[9] let me ask you: You subscribe to a golden age for posterity, but what have you to give these people themselves?

"Ah, until lashed on the back by the Creator's whip, China will always remain the way she is, absolutely refusing to change a single hair on her body!

"Since you have no poisonous fangs, why paste that big sign 'Viper' on your forehead, inciting beggars to kill you?..."

N was talking more and more wildly. However, as soon as he noticed my lack of interest, he shut his mouth, stood up and picked up his hat.

"Going home?" I asked.

"Yes, it's going to rain," he answered.

I saw him out in silence.

As he put on his hat he said, "So long! Excuse me for disturbing you. Fortunately, tomorrow isn't the Double Tenth, so we can forget all about it."

October 1920

"他偏要死进城去，滚进城去，
进城便被人剪去了辫子。……"

"But go he would. Off he rolled, and in town they cut off his queue,
his glossy black queue."

风波

Storm in a Teacup

临河的土场上，太阳渐渐的收了他通黄的光线了。场边靠河的乌桕树叶，干巴巴的才喘过气来，几个花脚蚊子在下面哼着飞舞。面河的农家的烟突里，逐渐减少了炊烟，女人孩子们都在自己门口的土场上泼些水，放下小桌子和矮凳；人知道，这已经是晚饭时候了。

老人男人坐在矮凳上，摇着大芭蕉扇闲谈，孩子飞也似的跑，或者蹲在乌桕树下赌玩石子。女人端出乌黑的蒸干菜和松花黄的米饭，热蓬蓬冒烟。河里驶过文人的酒船，文豪见了，大发诗兴，说，"无思无虑，这真是田家乐呵！"

但文豪的话有些不合事实，就因为他们没有听到九斤老太的话。这时候，九斤老太正在大怒，拿破芭蕉扇敲着凳脚说：

"我活到七十九岁了，活够了，不愿意眼见这些败家相，——还是死的好。立刻就要吃饭了，还吃炒豆子，吃穷了一家子！"

伊的曾孙女儿六斤捏着一把豆，正从对面跑来，见这情形，便直奔河边，藏在乌桕树后，伸出双丫角的小头，大声说，"这老不死的！"

九斤老太虽然高寿，耳朵却还不很聋，但也没有听到孩子的话，仍旧自己说，"这真是一代不如一代！"

这村庄的习惯有点特别，女人生下孩子，多喜欢用秤称了轻重，便用斤数当作小名。九斤老太自从庆祝了五十大寿以后，便渐渐的变了不平家，常说伊年青的时候，天气没有现在这般热，豆子也没有现在这般硬：总之现在的时世是不对了。何况六斤比伊的曾祖，少了三斤，比伊父亲七斤，又少了一斤，这真是一条颠扑不破的实例，所以伊又用劲说，"这真是一代不如一代！"

伊的儿媳七斤嫂子正捧着饭篮走到桌边，便将饭篮在桌上一摔，愤愤的说，"你老人家又这么说了。六斤生下来的时候，不是六斤五两么？你家的秤又是私秤，加重称，十八两秤；用了准十六，我们的六斤该有七斤多哩。

On the mud flat by the river, the sun's bright yellow rays were gradually fading. The parched leaves of the tallow trees beside the river were at last able to take breath, while below them a few striped mosquitoes danced and droned. The smoke from the peasants' kitchen chimneys along the riverside dwindled, as the women and children sprinkled the ground before their doors with water and set out little tables and low stools. Everyone knew it was time for the evening meal.

The old folk and the men sat on the low stools, fanning themselves with plantain-leaf fans as they chatted. The children raced about or squatted under the tallow trees playing with pebbles. The women brought out steamed black dried rape and yellow rice, piping hot. Some literati passing in a pleasure boat waxed quite lyrical at the sight.

"Such carefree tranquillity!" They exclaimed. "How idyllic!"

However, these literati were wide of the mark, not having heard what Old Mrs. Ninepounder was saying. Old Mrs. Ninepounder was in a towering temper, whacking the legs of her stool with a tattered plantain fan.

"Seventy-nine years I've lived, that's enough," she declared. "I'm sick of watching this family go to the dogs.... Better die and be done with it. Just one minute to supper time, yet still eating roast beans — do you want to eat us out of house and home?"

Her great-granddaughter Sixpounder was just running towards her with a handful of beans, but seeing the situation she flew straight to the river bank and hid herself behind a tallow tree. Sticking out her small head with its twin tufts, she hooted, "Old Won't-die!"

Old Mrs. Ninepounder for all her great age was not deaf. She did not, however, catch what the child had called and went on muttering to herself, "Yes, indeed. Each generation is worse than the last."

It was the somewhat unusual custom in this village for mothers to weigh their children at birth and to call them the number of pounds they happened to weigh. Since Old Mrs. Ninepounder's celebration of her fiftieth birthday she had gradually become a fault-finder, for ever complaining that in her young days the summer had not been so hot nor the beans so tough as now. In a word, there was something wrong with the present-day world. Why else had Sixpounder weighed three pounds less than her great-grandfather and one pound less than her father, Sevenpounder? Surely this was irrefutable evidence. So she reiterated emphatically, "Yes, indeed. Each generation is worse than the last."

Her granddaughter-in-law, Mrs. Sevenpounder, had just brought out a basket of rice. Plonking this down on the table, she said crossly, "There you go again, granny! Sixpounder weighed six pounds five ounces at birth, didn't she? Your family scales weigh light: eighteen

我想便是太公和公公，也不见得正是九斤八斤十足，用的称也许是十四两……"

"一代不如一代！"

七斤嫂还没有答话，忽然看见七斤从小巷口转出，便移了方向，对他嚷道，"你这死尸怎么这时候才回来，死到那里去了！不管人家等着你开饭！"

七斤虽然住在农村，却早有些飞黄腾达的意思。从他的祖父到他，三代不捏锄头柄了；他也照例的帮人撑着航船，每日一回，早晨从鲁镇进城，傍晚又回到鲁镇，因此很知道些时事：例如什么地方，雷公劈死了蜈蚣精；什么地方，闺女生了一个夜叉之类。他在村人里面，的确已经是一名出场人物了。但夏天吃饭不点灯，却还守着农家习惯，所以回家太迟，是该骂的。

七斤一手捏着象牙嘴白铜斗六尺多长的湘妃竹烟管，低着头，慢慢地走来，坐在矮凳上。六斤也趁势溜出，坐在他身边，叫他爹爹。七斤没有应。

"一代不如一代！"九斤老太说。

七斤慢慢地抬起头来，叹一口气说，"皇帝坐了龙庭了。"

七斤嫂呆了一刻，忽而恍然大悟的道，"这可好了，这不是又要皇恩大赦了么！"

七斤又叹一口气，说，"我没有辫子。"

"皇帝要辫子么？"

"皇帝要辫子。"

"你怎么知道呢？"七斤嫂有些着急，赶忙的问。

"咸亨酒店里的人，都说要的。"

七斤嫂这时从直觉上觉得事情似乎有些不妙了，因为咸亨酒店是消息灵通的所在。伊一转眼瞥见七斤的光头，便忍不住动怒，怪他恨他怨他；忽然又绝望起来，装好一碗饭，搡在七斤的面前道，"还是赶快吃你的饭罢！哭丧着脸，就会长出辫子来么？"

ounces to the pound. With proper sixteen-ounce scales, Sixpounder would have weighed over seven pounds. I don't believe grandfather and father really weighed a full nine or eight pounds either. I daresay they were weighed with fourteen-ounce scales...."

"Each generation is worse than the last."

Before Mrs. Sevenpounder could answer, she saw her husband emerge from the top of the lane and rounded on him instead.

"Why so late back, you zombie? I thought you must be dead, keeping us waiting all this time for supper!"

Although a villager, Sevenpounder had always wanted to better himself. For three generations — grandfather, father and son — not a man in his family had handled a hoe. Like his father before him he worked on a boat which left Luzhen every morning for the town, returning to Luzhen in the evening. As a result he knew pretty well all that was going on; where, for instance, the thunder god had blasted a centipede spirit, or where a virgin had given birth to a demon. In the village he was quite a personage. Still he stuck to the country custom of not lighting a lamp for supper in the summer, so if he came home late he rated a scolding.

In one hand Sevenpounder held a speckled bamboo pipe over six feet long with an ivory mounthpiece and a pewter bowl. He walked slowly over, his head bent, and sat on one of the low stools. Sixpounder seized this chance to slip out and sit down beside him, calling "Dad!" But her father made no answer.

"Each generation is worse than the last," repeated Old Mrs. Ninepounder.

Sevenpounder slowly raised his head and sighed. "There's an emperor again on the Dragon Throne."

Mrs. Sevenpounder looked blank for a moment. Suddenly taking in the news she cried, "Good! That means another general amnesty, doesn't it?"

Sevenpounder sighed again. "I've no queue."

"Does the emperor insist on queues?"

"He does."

"How do you know?" she demanded in dismay.

"Everybody in Prosperity Tavern says so."

At that Mrs. Sevenpounder realized instinctively that things were in a bad way, because Prosperity Tavern was a place where you could pick up all the news. She threw a glance at Sevenpounder's shaved head, unable to hold back her anger, blaming him, hating him, resenting him. Then, abruptly reduced to despair, she filled a bowl with rice and slapped it down before him. "Hurry up and eat. Pulling a long face won't grow a queue for you, will it?"

太阳收尽了他最末的光线了，水面暗暗地回复过凉气来；土场上一片碗筷声响，人人的脊梁上又都吐出汗粒。七斤嫂吃完三碗饭，偶然抬起头，心坎里便禁不住突突地发跳。伊透过乌桕叶，看见又矮又胖的赵七爷正从独木桥上走来，而且穿着宝蓝色竹布的长衫。

赵七爷是邻村茂源酒店的主人，又是这三十里方圆以内的唯一的出色人物兼学问家；因为有学问，所以又有些遗老的臭味。他有十多本金圣叹批评的《三国志》，时常坐着一个字一个字的读；他不但能说出五虎将姓名，甚而至于还知道黄忠表字汉升和马超表字孟起。革命以后，他便将辫子盘在顶上，像道士一般；常常叹息说，倘若赵子龙在世，天下便不会乱到这地步了。七斤嫂眼睛好，早望见今天的赵七爷已经不是道士，却变成光滑头皮，乌黑发顶；伊便知道这一定是皇帝坐了龙庭，而且一定须有辫子，而且七斤一定是非常危险。因为赵七爷的这件竹布长衫，轻易是不常穿的，三年以来，只穿过两次：一次是和他呕气的麻子阿四病了的时候，一次是曾经砸烂他酒店的鲁大爷死了的时候；现在是第三次了，这一定又是于他有庆，于他的仇家有殃了。

七斤嫂记得，两年前七斤喝醉了酒，曾经骂过赵七爷是"贱胎"，所以这时便立刻直觉到七斤的危险，心坎里突突地发起跳来。

赵七爷一路走来，坐着吃饭的人都站起身，拿筷子点着自己的饭碗说，"七爷，请在我们这里用饭！"七爷也一路点头，说道"请请"，却一径走到七斤家的桌旁。七斤们连忙招呼，七爷也微笑着说"请请"，一面细细的研究他们的饭菜。

"好香的干菜，——听到了风声了么？"赵七爷站在七斤的后面七斤嫂的对面说。

"皇帝坐了龙庭了。"七斤说。

七斤嫂看着七爷的脸，竭力陪笑道，"皇帝已经坐了

1. A long historical novel by Luo Guanzhong of the fourteenth century based on the official history of the Three Kingdoms Period (A.D. 220-80).

2. A seventeenth-century scholar.

3. During the Three Kingdoms Period there were five famous generals in the Kingdom of Shu (A.D. 221-63), Guan Yu, Zhang Fei, Zhao Yun, Huang Zhong and Ma Chao, who figure in the *Romance of the Three Kingdoms*.

4. The Revolution of 1911 which overthrew the Qing Dynasty.

5. Zhao Yun had rescued his king's son in a battle, and hence was considered by some a hero who could save the empire.

The sun had withdrawn its last rays, the darkling water was cooling off again. From the mud flat rose a clatter of bowls and chopsticks, and the backs of all the diners were beaded with sweat. Mrs. Sevenpounder had finished three bowls of rice when she happened to look up. At once her heart started pounding. Through the tallow leaves she could see the short plump figure of Seventh Master Zhao approaching from the one-plank bridge. And he was wearing his long sapphire-blue glazed cotton gown.

Seventh Master Zhao was the owner of Abundance Tavern in the next village, the only notable within a radius of thirty li who also had some learning. And because of this learning there was about him a whiff of the musty odour of a departed age. He owned a dozen volumes of the *Romance of the Three Kingdoms*[1] annotated by Jin Shengtan,[2] which he would sit poring over character by character. Not only could he tell you the names of the Five Tiger Generals,[3] he even knew that Huang Zhong was also known as Hansheng, and Ma Chao as Mengqi. After the Revolution[4] he had coiled his queue on the top of his head like a Taoist priest, and he often remarked with a sigh that if only Zhao Yun were still alive the empire would not be in such a bad way.[5]

Mrs. Sevenpounder's eyesight was good. She had noticed at once that Seventh Master Zhao no longer looked like a Taoist. He had shaved the front of his head and let his queue down. From this she knew beyond a doubt that an emperor had ascended the throne, that queues were required again, and that Sevenpounder must be in great danger. For Seventh Master Zhao did not wear his long glazed cotton gown for nothing. During the last three years he had only worn it twice: once when his enemy Pock-marked Asi fell ill, once when First Master Lu who had wrecked his wineshop died. This was the third time, and it undoubtedly meant that something had happened to rejoice his heart and bode ill for his enemies.

Two years ago, Mrs. Sevenpounder remembered, her husband in a fit of drunkenness had cursed Seventh Master Zhao as a "bastard." Hence she at once realized instinctively the danger her husband was in, and her heart started pounding.

As Seventh Master Zhao passed them, all those sitting eating stood up and, pointing their chopsticks at their rice bowls, invited him to join them. He nodded greetings to them all, urging them to go on with their meal, while he made straight for Sevenpounder's table. Sevenpounder's family got up at once to greet him. Seventh Master Zhao urged them with a smile, "Go on with your meal, please!" At the same time he took a good look at the food on the table.

"That dried rape smells good — have you heard the news?" Seventh Master Zhao was standing behind Sevenpounder opposite Mrs. Sevenpounder.

"There's an emperor again on the Dragon Throne," said Sevenpounder.

Watching Seventh Master's expression, Mrs. Sevenpounder forced a smile. "Now

龙庭，几时皇恩大赦呢？"

"皇恩大赦？——大赦是慢慢的总要大赦罢。"七爷说到这里，声色忽然严厉起来，"但是你家七斤的辫子呢，辫子？这倒是要紧的事。你们知道：长毛时候，留发不留头，留头不留发，……"

七斤和他的女人没有读过书，不很懂得这古典的奥妙，但觉得有学问的七爷这么说，事情自然非常重大，无可挽回，便仿佛受了死刑宣告似的，耳朵里嗡的一声，再也说不出一句话。

"一代不如一代，——"九斤老太正在不平，趁这机会，便对赵七爷说，"现在的长毛，只是剪人家的辫子，僧不僧，道不道的。从前的长毛，这样的么？我活到七十九岁了，活够了。从前的长毛是——整匹的红缎子裹头，拖下去，拖下去，一直拖到脚跟；王爷是黄缎子，拖下去，黄缎子；红缎子，黄缎子，——我活够了，七十九岁了。"

七斤嫂站起身，自言自语的说，"这怎么好呢？这样的一班老小，都靠他养活的人，……"

赵七爷摇头道，"那也没法。没有辫子，该当何罪，书上都一条一条明明白白写着的。不管他家里有些什么人。"

七斤嫂听到书上写着，可真是完全绝望了；自己急得没法，便忽然又恨到七斤。伊用筷子指着他的鼻尖说，"这死尸自作自受！造反的时候，我本来说，不要撑船了，不要上城了。他偏要死进城去，滚进城去，进城便被人剪去了辫子。从前是绢光乌黑的辫子，现在弄得僧不僧道不道的。这囚徒自作自受，带累了我们又怎么说呢？这活死尸的囚徒……"

村人看见赵七爷到村，都赶紧吃完饭，聚在七斤家饭桌的周围。七斤自己知道是出场人物，被女人当大众这样辱骂，很不雅观，便只得抬起头，慢慢地说道：

"你今天说现成话，那时你……"

"你这活死尸的囚徒……"

6. "Keep your hair and lose your head" originally referred to the Qing rulers' decree on shaved temples at the beginning of the dynasty. Lu Xun made Seventh Master Zhao attribute this saying to the Taipings to ridicule his "learning."

that there's an emperor on the throne, when will there be a general amnesty?" she asked.

"A general amnesty?... All in good time." Suddenly Seventh Master spoke more sternly, "But what about Sevenpounder's queue, eh? That's the important thing. You know how it was in the time of the Long Hairs: keep your hair and lose your head; keep your head and lose your hair."[6]

Sevenpounder and his wife had never read any books, so this classical lore was lost on them; but this statement from a learned man like Seventh Master convinced them that the situation must be desperate, past saving. It was as if they had received their death sentence. Their ears buzzed, and they were unable to utter another word.

"Each generation is worse than the last." Old Mrs. Ninepounder, feeling put out, seized this chance to speak to Seventh Master Zhao. "The Long Hairs nowadays just cut off men's queues, leaving them looking neither Buddhist nor Taoist. The old Long Hairs never did that. Seventy-nine years I've lived and that's enough. The old Long Hairs wore red satin turbans with one end hanging down, right down to their heels. The prince wore a yellow satin turban with one end hanging down... yellow satin. Red satin, yellow satin... I've lived long enough... seventy-nine."

"What's to be done?" muttered Mrs. Sevenpounder, standing up. "Such a big family, old and young, and all dependent on him...."

"There's nothing you can do." Seventh Master Zhao shook his head. "The punishment for having no queue is written down clearly in a book, sentence by sentence. The size of a man's family makes no difference."

When Mrs. Sevenpounder heard that it was written in a book, she really gave way to despair. Beside herself with anxiety, she felt a sudden fresh hatred for Sevenpounder. Pointing her chopsticks at the tip of his nose, she cried. "As you make your bed, so you must lie on it! Didn't I say at the time of the revolt: Don't go out with the boat, don't go to town. But go he would. Off he rolled, and in town they cut off his queue, his glossy black queue. Now he looks neither Buddhist nor Taoist. He's made his own bed, he'll have to lie on it. But what right has the wretch to drag us into it? Jail-bird zombie...."

Seventh Master Zhao's arrival in the village made all the villagers finish their supper quickly and gather round Sevenpounder's table. Sevenpounder knew how unseemly it was for a prominent citizen to be cursed in public like this by his wife. So he raised his head to retort slowly:

"You've plenty to say today, but at the time...."

"Jail-bird zombie!..."

看客中间，八一嫂是心肠最好的人，抱着伊的两周岁的遗腹子，正在七斤嫂身边看热闹；这时过意不去，连忙解劝说，"七斤嫂，算了罢。人不是神仙，谁知道未来事呢？便是七斤嫂，那时不也说，没有辫子倒也没有什么丑么？况且衙门里的大老爷也还没有告示，……"

七斤嫂没有听完，两个耳朵早通红了；便将筷子转过向来，指着八一嫂的鼻子，说，"阿呀，这是什么话呵！八一嫂，我自己看来倒还是一个人，会说出这样昏诞胡涂话么？那时我是，整整哭了三天，谁都看见；连六斤这小鬼也都哭，……"六斤刚吃完一大碗饭，拿了空碗，伸手去嚷着要添。七斤嫂正没好气，便用筷子在伊的双丫角中间，直扎下去，大喝道，"谁要你来多嘴！你这偷汉的小寡妇！"

扑的一声，六斤手里的空碗落在地上了，恰巧又碰着一块砖角，立刻破成一个很大的缺口。七斤直跳起来，检起破碗，合上了检查一回，也喝道，"入娘的！"一巴掌打倒了六斤。六斤躺着哭，九斤老太拉了伊的手，连说着"一代不如一代"，一同走了。

八一嫂也发怒，大声说，"七斤嫂，你'恨棒打人'……"

赵七爷本来是笑着旁观的；但自从八一嫂说了"衙门里的大老爷没有告示"这话以后，却有些生气了。这时他已经绕出桌旁，接道说，"'恨棒打人'，算什么呢。大兵是就要到的。你可知道，这回保驾的是张大帅，张大帅就是燕人张翼德的后代，他一支丈八蛇矛，就有万夫不当之勇，谁能抵挡他，"他两手同时捏起空拳，仿佛握着无形的蛇矛模样，向八一嫂抢进几步道，"你能抵挡他！"

八一嫂正气得抱着孩子发抖，忽然见赵七爷满脸油汗，瞪着眼，准对伊冲过来，便十分害怕，不敢说完话，回身走了。赵七爷也跟着走去，众人一面怪八一嫂多事，一面让开路，几个剪过辫子重新留起的便赶快躲在人丛后面，怕他看见。赵七爷也不细心察访，通过人丛，忽然转

7. Zhang Xun (1854-1923), a reactionary officer of the Qing Dynasty. After the 1911 Revolution he kept his queue and ordered his soldiers to retain theirs as well, to show their loyalty to the overthrown dynasty. On July 1,1917, he and some others tried to restore the deposed emperor Pu Yi to the throne, but after only a fortnight their attempt failed. "There's an emperor again on the Dragon Throne" refers to this abortive restoration.

Widow Ba Yi had the kindest heart of all the onlookers there. Carrying her two-year-old, born after her husband's death, she was watching the fun at Mrs. Sevenpounder's side. Now she felt things had gone too far and hurriedly tried to make peace.

"Never mind, Mrs. Sevenpounder. People aren't spirits — who can foretell the future? Didn't you yourself say at the time there was nothing to be ashamed of in having no queue? Besides, no order's come down yet from the big mandarin in the yamen...."

Before she had finished, Mrs. Sevenpounder's ears were scarlet. She turned her chopsticks to point at the widow's nose. "Aiya, what a thing to say, Mrs. Ba Yi! I'm still a human being, ain't I — how could I have said anything so ridiculous? Why, at the time I cried for three whole days. Ask anyone you like. Even this little devil Sixpounder cried...." Sixpounder had just finished a big bowl of rice and was holding out her empty bowl clamouring to have it refilled. Mrs. Sevenpounder, being in a temper, smacked her chopsticks down between the twin tufts on the child's head. "Who wants you to barge in?" she yelled. "Little slut!"

Crack! The empty bowl in Sixpounder's hand thudded to the ground striking the corner of a brick so that a big piece broke off. Sevenpounder jumped to his feet and picked up the broken bowl. Having fitted the pieces together he examined it, swearing, "Mother's!" He gave Sixpounder a slap that knocked her over. Sixpounder lay there crying until Old Mrs. Ninepounder took her hand and led her away repeating, "Each generation is worse than the last."

Now it was Widow Ba Yi's turn to be angry. "How can you hit out at random like that, Mrs. Sevenpounder!" she shouted.

Seventh Master Zhao had been looking on with a smile, but after Widow Ba Yi's statement that no order had come down from "the big mandarin in the yamen" he began to lose his temper. Coming right up to the table, he declared, "Hitting out at random doesn't matter. The Imperial Army will be here any time now. I'd have you know the new Protector is General Zhang,[7] who's descended from Zhang Fei of the former state of Yan. With his huge lance eighteen feet long, he dares take on ten thousand men. Who can stand against him?" Raising both hands as if grasping a huge invisible lance, he took a few swift paces towards Widow Ba Yi. "Are you a match for him?"

Widow Ba Yi was trembling with rage as she held her child. But the sudden sight of Seventh Master Zhao bearing down on her with glaring eyes, his whole face oozing sweat, gave her the fright of her life. Not daring to say more, she turned and fled. Then Seventh Master Zhao left too. The villagers as they made way for him deplored Widow Ba Yi's interference, while a few men who had cut their queues and started growing them again hid hastily behind the rest for fear Seventh Master should see

入乌桕树后，说道"你能抵挡他么！"跨上独木桥，扬长去了。

村人们呆呆站着，心里计算，都觉得自己确乎抵不住张翼德，因此也决定七斤便要没有性命。七斤既然犯了皇法，想起他往常对人谈论城中的新闻的时候，就不该含着长烟管显出那般骄傲模样，所以对于七斤的犯法，也觉得有些畅快。他们也仿佛想发些议论，却又觉得没有什么议论可发。嗡嗡的一阵乱嚷，蚊子都撞过赤膊身子，闯到乌桕树下去做市；他们也就慢慢地走散回家，关上门去睡觉。七斤嫂咕哝着，也收了家伙和桌子矮凳回家，关上门睡觉了。

七斤将破碗拿回家里，坐在门槛上吸烟；但非常忧愁，忘却了吸烟，象牙嘴六尺多长湘妃竹烟管的白铜斗里的火光，渐渐发黑了。他心里但觉得事情似乎十分危急，也想想些方法，想些计画，但总是非常模糊，贯穿不得："辫子呢辫子？丈八蛇矛。一代不如一代！皇帝坐龙庭。破的碗须得上城去钉好。谁能抵挡他？书上一条一条写着。入娘的！……"

第二日清晨，七斤依旧从鲁镇撑航船进城，傍晚回到鲁镇，又拿着六尺多长的湘妃竹烟管和一个饭碗回村。他在晚饭席上，对九斤老太说，这碗是在城内钉合的，因为缺口大，所以要十六个铜钉，三文一个，一总用了四十八文小钱。

九斤老太很不高兴的说，"一代不如一代，我是活够了。三文钱一个钉；从前的钉，这样的么？从前的钉是……我活了七十九岁了，——"

此后七斤虽然是照例日日进城，但家景总有些黯淡，村人大抵回避着，不再来听他从城内得来的新闻。七斤嫂也没有好声气，还时常叫他"囚徒"。

过了十多日，七斤从城内回家，看见他的女人非常高兴，问他说，"你在城里可听到些什么？"

them. However, without making a careful inspection Seventh Master passed through the group, dived behind the tallow trees and with a parting "Think you're a match for him!" Strode on to the one-plank bridge and swaggered off.

The villagers stood there blankly, turning things over in their minds. All felt they were indeed no match for Zhang Fei, hence Sevenpounder's life was as good as lost. And since Sevenpounder had broken the imperial law he should not, they felt, have adopted that lordly air, smoking that long pipe of his, when he told them the news from town. So the thought that he had broken the law gave them a certain pleasure. They would have liked to air their views, but did not know what to say. Buzzing mosquitoes, brushing past their bare arms, zoomed back to swarm beneath the tallow trees; and the villagers too slowly scattered to their homes, shut their doors and went to bed. Grumbling to herself, Mrs. Sevenpounder also cleared away the dishes and took in the table and stools, then closed the door and went to bed.

Sevenpounder took the broken bowl inside, then sat on the doorstep smoking. He was so worried, however, that he forgot to inhale, and the light in the pewter bowl of his six-foot speckled bamboo pipe with the ivory mouthpiece gradually turned black. It struck him that matters had reached a most dangerous pass, and he tried to think of a way out, some plan of action. But his thoughts were in too much of a whirl for him to straighten them out. "Queues, eh, queues? An eighteen foot lance. Each generation is worse than the last! An emperor is on the Dragon Throne. The broken bowl will have to be taken to town to be riveted. Who's a match for him? It's written in a book. Mother's!..."

Early the next day, as usual, Sevenpounder went with the boat to town, coming back to Luzhen towards evening with his six-foot speckled bamboo pipe and the rice bowl. At supper he told Old Mrs. Ninepounder that he had had the bowl riveted in town. Because it was such a large break, sixteen copper clamps had been needed, each costing three cash, making the total cost forty-eight cash.

"Each generation is worse than the last," said Old Mrs. Ninepounder crossly. "I've lived long enough. Three cash for a clamp. Clamps didn't cost so much in the old days. The clamps we had.... Seventy-nine years I've lived...."

After this, though Sevenpounder continued making his daily trip to town, his house seemed to be under a cloud. Most of the villagers kept out of his way, no longer coming to ask him the news from town. Mrs. Sevenpounder was in a bad temper too, constantly addressing him as "Jail-bird."

A fortnight or so later, on his return from town Sevenpounder found his wife in a rare good humour. "Heard anything in town?" She asked him.

"没有听到些什么。"

"皇帝坐了龙庭没有呢？"

"他们没有说。"

"咸亨酒店里也没有人说么？"

"也没人说。"

"我想皇帝一定是不坐龙庭了。我今天走过赵七爷的店前，看见他又坐着念书了，辫子又盘在顶上了，也没有穿长衫。"

"…………"

"你想，不坐龙庭了罢？"

"我想，不坐了罢。"

现在的七斤，是七斤嫂和村人又都早给他相当的尊敬，相当的待遇了。到夏天，他们仍旧在自家门口的土场上吃饭；大家见了，都笑嘻嘻的招呼。九斤老太早已做过八十大寿，仍然不平而且康健。六斤的双丫角，已经变成一支大辫子了；伊虽然新近裹脚，却还能帮同七斤嫂做事，捧着十八个铜钉的饭碗，在土场上一瘸一拐的往来。

一九二〇年十月。

"No, nothing."

"Is there an emperor on the Dragon Throne?"

"They didn't say."

"Did no one in Prosperity Tavern say anything?"

"No, nothing."

"I don't believe there's an emperor again. I passed Seventh Master Zhao's wineshop today and he was sitting there reading, with his queue coiled on top of his head again. He wasn't wearing his long gown either."

"...."

"Do you think there's no emperor after all?"

"I think probably not."

Today Sevenpounder is once more respected and well treated by his wife and the villagers. In the summer his family still have their meals on the mud flat outside their door, and everyone greets them with smiles. Old Mrs. Ninepounder celebrated her eigthtieth birthday some time ago and is as full of complaints, as hale and hearty as ever. Sixpounder's twin tufts of hair have changed into a thick braid. Although recently they started binding her feet, she can still help Mrs. Sevenpounder with odd jobs. She hobbles to and fro on the mud flat carrying the rice bowl with sixteen copper rivets.

October 1920

"你夏天到我们这里来，我们到海边检贝壳去。"

"You must come to our place in summer,
we will go to the seashore to look for shells."

故 乡
My Old Home

我冒了严寒，回到相隔二千余里，别了二十余年的故乡去。

时候既然是深冬；渐近故乡时，天气又阴晦了，冷风吹进船舱中，呜呜的响，从篷隙向外一望，苍黄的天底下，远近横着几个萧索的荒村，没有一些活气。我的心禁不住悲凉起来了。

阿！这不是我二十年来时时记得的故乡？

我所记得的故乡全不如此。我的故乡好得多了。但要我记起他的美丽，说出他的佳处来，却又没有影像，没有言辞了。仿佛也就如此。于是我自己解释说：故乡本也如此，——虽然没有进步，也未必有如我所感的悲凉，这只是我自己心情的改变罢了，因为我这次回乡，本没有什么好心绪。

我这次是专为了别他而来的。我们多年聚族而居的老屋，已经公同卖给别姓了，交屋的期限，只在本年，所以必须赶在正月初一以前，永别了熟识的老屋，而且远离了熟识的故乡，搬家到我在谋食的异地去。

第二日清早晨我到了我家的门口了。瓦楞上许多枯草的断茎当风抖着，正在说明这老屋难免易主的原因。几房的本家大约已经搬走了，所以很寂静。我到了自家的房外，我的母亲早已迎着出来了，接着便飞出了八岁的侄儿宏儿。

我的母亲很高兴，但也藏着许多凄凉的神情，教我坐下，歇息，喝茶，且不谈搬家的事。宏儿没有见过我，远远的对面站着只是看。

但我们终于谈到搬家的事。我说外间的寓所已经租定了，又买了几件家具，此外须将家里所有的木器卖去，再去增添。母亲也说好，而且行李也略已齐集，木器不便搬运的，也小半卖去了，只是收不起钱来。

"你休息一两天，去拜望亲戚本家一回，我们便可以走了。"母亲说。

"是的。"

Braving the bitter cold, I travelled more than two thousand li back to the old home I had left over twenty years ago.

It was late winter. As we drew near my former home the day became overcast and a cold wind blew into the cabin of our boat, while all one could see through the chinks in our bamboo awning were a few desolate villages, void of any sign of life, scattered far and near under the sombre yellow sky. I could not help feeling depressed.

Ah! Surely this was not the old home I had been remembering for the past twenty years?

The old home I remembered was not in the least like this. My old home was much better. But if you asked me to recall its peculiar charm or describe its beauties, I had no clear impression, no words to describe it. And now it seemed this was all there was to it. Then I rationalized the matter to myself, saying: Home was always like this, and although it had not improved, still it is not so depressing as I imagine; it is only my mood that has changed, because I am coming back to the country this time with no illusions.

This time I had come with the sole object of saying goodbye. The old house our clan had lived in for so many years had already been sold to another family, and was to change hands before the end of the year. I had to hurry there before New Year's Day to say goodbye for ever to the familiar old house, and to move my family to another place where I was working, far from my old home town.

At dawn on the second day I reached the gateway of my home. Broken stems of withered grass on the roof, trembling in the wind, made very clear the reason why this old house could not avoid changing hands. Several branches of our clan had probably already moved away, so it was unusually quiet. By the time I reached the house my mother was already at the door to welcome me, and my eight-year-old nephew, Hong'er rushed out after her.

Though Mother was delighted, she was also trying to hide a certain feeling of sadness. She told me to sit down and rest and have some tea, letting the removal wait for the time being. Hong'er, who had never seen me before, stood watching me at a distance.

But finally we had to talk about the removal. I said that rooms had already been rented elsewhere, and I had bought a little furniture; in addition it would be necessary to sell all the furniture in the house in order to buy more things. Mother agreed, saying that the luggage was nearly all packed, and about half the furniture that could not be easily moved had already been sold. Only it was difficult to get people to pay up.

"You can rest for a day or two, and call on our relatives, and then we can go," said Mother.

"Yes."

"还有闰土，他每到我家来时，总问起你，很想见你一回面。我已经将你到家的大约日期通知他，他也许就要来了。"

这时候，我的脑里忽然闪出一幅神异的图画来：深蓝的天空中挂着一轮金黄的圆月，下面是海边的沙地，都种着一望无际的碧绿的西瓜，其间有一个十一二岁的少年，项带银圈，手捏一柄钢叉，向一匹猹尽力的刺去，那猹却将身一扭，反从他的胯下逃走了。

这少年便是闰土。我认识他时，也不过十多岁，离现在将有三十年了；那时我的父亲还在世，家景也好，我正是一个少爷。那一年，我家是一件大祭祀的值年。这祭祀，说是三十多年才能轮到一回，所以很郑重；正月里供祖像，供品很多，祭器很讲究，拜的人也很多，祭器也很要防偷去。我家只有一个忙月（我们这里给人做工的分三种：整年给一定人家做工的叫长年；按日给人做工的叫短工；自己也种地，只在过年过节以及收租时候来给一定的人家做工的称忙月），忙不过来，他便对父亲说，可以叫他的儿子闰土来管祭器的。

我的父亲允许了；我也很高兴，因为我早听到闰土这名字，而且知道他和我仿佛年纪，闰月生的，五行缺土，所以他的父亲叫他闰土。他是能装弶捉小鸟雀的。

我于是日日盼望新年，新年到，闰土也就到了。好容易到了年末，有一日，母亲告诉我，闰土来了，我便飞跑的去看。他正在厨房里，紫色的圆脸，头戴一顶小毡帽，颈上套一个明晃晃的银项圈，这可见他的父亲十分爱他，怕他死去，所以在神佛面前许下愿心，用圈子将他套住了。他见人很怕羞，只是不怕我，没有旁人的时候，便和我说话，于是不到半日，我们便熟识了。

我们那时候不知道谈些什么，只记得闰土很高兴，说是上城之后，见了许多没有见过的东西。

第二日，我便要他捕鸟。他说：

"这不能。须大雪下了才好。我们沙地上，下了雪，

1. Lu Xun explained in a letter of May 4, 1929 that *zha* was a word used by the local people in the Shaoxing countryside for badger.

2. The Chinese lunar calendar reckons 360 days to a year, and each month comprises 29 or 30 days, never 31. Hence every few years a 13th, or intercalary, month is inserted in the calender.

"Then there is Runtu. Each time he comes here he always asks after you, and wants very much to see you again. I told him the probable date of your return home, and he may be coming any time."

At this point a strange picture suddenly flashed into my mind: a golden moon suspended in a deep blue sky and beneath it the seashore, planted as far as the eye could see with jade-green watermelons, while in their midst a boy of eleven or twelve, wearing a silver necklet and grasping a steel pitchfork in his hand, was thrusting with all his might at a *zha*[1] which dodged the blow and escaped through his legs.

This boy was Runtu. When I first met him he was little more than ten — that was thirty years ago, and at that time my father was still alive and the family well off, so I was really a spoilt child. That year it was our family's turn to take charge of a big ancestral sacrifice, which came round only once in thirty years, and hence was an important one. In the first month the ancestral images were presented and offerings made, and since the sacrificial vessels were very fine and there was such a crowd of worshippers, it was necessary to guard against theft. Our family had only one part-time servant. (in our district we divide servants into three classes: those who work all the year for one family are called full-timers; those who are hired by the day are called dailies; and those who farm their own land and only work for one family at New Year, during festivals or when rents are being collected are called part-timers.) and since there was so much to be done, he told my father that he would send for his son Runtu to look after the sacrificial vessels.

When my father gave his consent I was overjoyed, because I had long since heard of Runtu and knew that he was about my own age, born in the intercalary month,[2] and when his horoscope was told it was found that of the five elements that of earth was lacking, so his father called him Runtu (Intercalary Earth). He could set traps and catch small birds.

I looked forward every day to New Year, for New Year would bring Runtu. At last the end of the year came, and one day Mother told me that Runtu had come, and I flew to see him. He was standing in the kitchen. He had a round, crimson face and wore a small felt cap on his head and a gleaming silver necklet on his neck, showing that his father doted on him and, fearing he might die, had made a pledge with the gods and Buddhas, using the necklet as a talisman. He was very shy, and I was the only person he was not afraid of. When there was no one else there, he would talk with me, so in a few hours we were fast friends.

I don't know what we talked of then, but I remember that Runtu was in high spirits, saying that since he had come to town he had seen many new things.

The next day I wanted him to catch birds.

"Can't be done," he said. "It's only possible after a heavy snowfall. On our sands,

我扫出一块空地来，用短棒支起一个大竹匾，撒下秕谷，看鸟雀来吃时，我远远地将缚在棒上的绳子只一拉，那鸟雀就罩在竹匾下了。什么都有：稻鸡，角鸡，鹁鸪，蓝背……"

我于是又很盼望下雪。

闰土又对我说：

"现在太冷，你夏天到我们这里来。我们日里到海边检贝壳去，红的绿的都有，鬼见怕也有，观音手也有。晚上我和爹管西瓜去，你也去。"

"管贼么？"

"不是。走路的人口渴了摘一个瓜吃，我们这里是不算偷的。要管的是獾猪，刺猬，猹。月亮地下，你听，啦啦的响了，猹在咬瓜了。你便捏了胡叉，轻轻地走去……"

我那时并不知道这所谓猹的是怎么一件东西——便是现在也没有知道——只是无端的觉得状如小狗而很凶猛。

"他不咬人么？"

"有胡叉呢。走到了，看见猹了，你便刺。这畜生很伶俐，倒向你奔来，反从胯下窜了。他的皮毛是油一般的滑……"

我素不知道天下有这许多新鲜事：海边有如许五色的贝壳；西瓜有这样危险的经历，我先前单知道他在水果店里出卖罢了。

"我们沙地里，潮汛要来的时候，就有许多跳鱼儿只是跳，都有青蛙似的两个脚……"

阿！闰土的心里有无穷无尽的希奇的事，都是我往常的朋友所不知道的。他们不知道一些事，闰土在海边时，他们都和我一样只看见院子里高墙上的四角的天空。

可惜正月过去了，闰土须回家里去，我急得大哭，他也躲到厨房里，哭着不肯出门，但终于被他父亲带走了。他后来还托他的父亲带给我一包贝壳和几支很好看的鸟毛，我也曾送他一两次东西，但从此没有再见面。

现在我的母亲提起了他，我这儿时的记忆，忽而全都

after it snows, I sweep clear a patch of ground, prop up a big threshing basket with a short stick, and scatter husks of grain beneath; then when I see the birds coming to eat, from a distance I give a tug to the string tied to the stick, and the birds are caught in the basket. There are all kinds: wild pheasants, woodcocks, woodpigeons, bluebacks...."

Accordingly I looked forward very eagerly to snow.

"Just now it is too cold," said Runtu another time, "but you must come to our place in summer. In the daytime we will go to the seashore to look for shells, there are green ones and red ones, besides 'scare-devil' shells and "Buddha's hands. In the evening when Dad and I go to see to the watermelons, you shall come too."

"Is it to look out for thieves?"

"No. If passers-by are thirsty and pick a watermelon, folk down our way don't consider it as stealing. What we have to look out for are stoats, hedgehogs and *zha*. When you hear a crunching sound under the moonlight, made by the *zha* biting the melons, then you take your pitchfork and creep stealthily over...."

I had no idea then what this thing called *zha* was — and I am not much clearer now, for that matter — but somehow I felt it was something like a small dog, and very fierce.

"Don't they bite people?"

"You have a pitchfork. You go across, and when you see it you strike. It's a very cunning creature and will rush towards you and get away between you legs. Its fur is as slippery as oil...."

I had never known that all these strange things existed: at the seashore were shells all the colours of the rainbow; watermelons had such a dangerous history, yet all I had known of them before was that they were sold in the greengrocer's.

"On our shore, when the tide comes in, there are lots of jumping fish, each with two legs like a frog...."

Runtu's mind was a treasure-house of such strange lore, all of it outside the ken of my former friends. They were ignorant of all these things and, while Runtu lived by the sea, they like me could see only the four corners of the sky above the high courtyard wall.

Unfortunately, a month after New Year Runtu had to go home. I burst into tears and he took refuge in the kitchen, crying and refusing to come out, until finally he was carried off by his father. Later he sent me by his father a packet of shells and a few very beautiful feathers, and I sent him presents once or twice, but we never saw each other again.

Now that my mother mentioned him, this childhood memory sprang into life like a

闪电似的苏生过来，似乎看到了我的美丽的故乡了。我应声说：

"这好极！他，——怎样？……"

"他？……他景况也很不如意……"母亲说着，便向房外看，"这些人又来了。说是买木器，顺手也就随便拿走的，我得去看看。"

母亲站起身，出去了。门外有几个女人的声音。我便招宏儿走近面前，和他闲话：问他可会写字，可愿意出门。

"我们坐火车去么？"

"我们坐火车去。"

"船呢？"

"先坐船，……"

"哈！这模样了！胡子这么长了！"一种尖利的怪声突然大叫起来。

我吃了一吓，赶忙抬起头，却见一个凸颧骨，薄嘴唇，五十岁上下的女人站在我面前，两手搭在髀间，没有系裙，张着两脚，正像一个画图仪器里细脚伶仃的圆规。

我愕然了。

"不认识了么？我还抱过你咧！"

我愈加愕然了。幸而我的母亲也就进来，从旁说：

"他多年出门，统忘却了。你该记得罢，"便向着我说，"这是斜对门的杨二嫂，……开豆腐店的。"

哦，我记得了。我孩子时候，在斜对门的豆腐店里确乎终日坐着一个杨二嫂，人都叫伊"豆腐西施"。但是擦着白粉，颧骨没有这么高，嘴唇也没有这么薄，而且终日坐着，我也从没有见过这圆规式的姿势。那时人说：因为伊，这豆腐店的买卖非常好。但这大约因为年龄的关系，我却并未蒙着一毫感化，所以竟完全忘却了。然而圆规很不平，显出鄙夷的神色，仿佛嗤笑法国人不知道拿破仑，美国人不知道华盛顿似的，冷笑说：

"忘了？这真是贵人眼高……"

"那有这事……我……"我惶恐着，站起来说。

flash of lightning, and I seemed to see my beautiful old home. So I answered:

"Fine! And he — how is he?"

"He?... He's not at all well off either," said Mother. And then, looking out of the door: "Here come those people again. They say they want to buy our furniture; but actually they just want to see what they can pick up. I must go and watch them."

Mother stood up and went out. Several women's voices could be heard outside. I called Hong'er to me and started talking to him, asking him whether he could write, and whether he was glad to be leaving.

"Shall we be going by train?"

"Yes, we shall go by train."

"And boat?"

"We shall take a boat first."

"Oh! Like this! With such a long moustache!" a strange shrill voice suddenly rang out.

I looked up with a start, and saw a woman of about fifty with prominent cheekbones and thin lips standing in front of me, her hands on her hips, not wearing a skirt but with trousered legs apart, just like the compass in a box of geometrical instruments.

I was flabbergasted.

"Don't you know me? And I have held you in my arms!"

I felt even more flabbergasted. Fortunately my mother came in just then and said, "He has been away so long, you must excuse him for forgetting."

"You should remember," she said to me, "this is Mrs. Yang from across the road.... She has a beancurd shop."

Then, to be sure, I remembered. When I was a child there was a Mrs. Yang who used to sit nearly all day long in the beancurd shop across the road, and everybody used to call her Beancurd Beauty. But she used to powder herself, and her cheekbones were not so prominent then nor her lips so thin; moreover she remained seated all the time, so that I had never noticed this resemblance to a compass. In those days people said that, thanks to her, that beancurd shop did very good business. But, probably on account of my age, she had made no impression on me, so that later I forgot her entirely. However, the Compass was extremely indignant and looked at me most contemptuously, just as one might look at a Frenchman who had never heard of Napoleon or an American who had never heard of Washington, and smiling sarcastically she said:

"You had forgotten? But naturally I must be beneath your notice...."

"Certainly not... I..." I answered nervously, getting to my feet.

"那么，我对你说。迅哥儿，你阔了，搬动又笨重，你还要什么这些破烂木器，让我拿去罢。我们小户人家，用得着。"

"我并没有阔哩。我须卖了这些，再去……"

"阿呀呀，你放了道台了，还说不阔？你现在有三房姨太太；出门便是八抬的大轿，还说不阔？吓，什么都瞒不过我。"

我知道无话可说了，便闭了口，默默的站着。

"阿呀阿呀，真是愈有钱，便愈是一毫不肯放松，愈是一毫不肯放松，便愈有钱……"圆规一面愤愤的回转身，一面絮絮的说，慢慢向外走，顺便将我母亲的一副手套塞在裤腰里，出去了。

此后又有近处的本家和亲戚来访问我。我一面应酬，偷空便收拾些行李，这样的过了三四天。

一日是天气很冷的午后，我吃过午饭，坐着喝茶，觉得外面有人进来了，便回头去看。我看时，不由的非常出惊，慌忙站起身，迎着走去。

这来的便是闰土。虽然我一见便知道是闰土，但又不是我这记忆上的闰土了。他身材增加了一倍；先前的紫色的圆脸，已经变作灰黄，而且加上了很深的皱纹；眼睛也像他父亲一样，周围都肿得通红，这我知道，在海边种地的人，终日吹着海风，大抵是这样的。他头上是一顶破毡帽，身上只一件极薄的棉衣，浑身瑟索着；手里提着一个纸包和一支长烟管，那手也不是我所记得的红活圆实的手，却又粗又笨而且开裂，像是松树皮了。

我这时很兴奋，但不知道怎么说才好，只是说：

"阿！闰土哥，——你来了？……"

我接着便有许多话，想要连珠一般涌出：角鸡，跳鱼儿，贝壳，猹，……但又总觉得被什么挡着似的，单在脑里面回旋，吐不出口外去。

他站住了，脸上现出欢喜和凄凉的神情；动着嘴唇，却没有作声。他的态度终于恭敬起来了，分明的叫道：

"Then you listen to me, Master Xun. You have grown rich, and they are too heavy to move, so you can't possibly want these old pieces of furniture any more. You had better let me take them away. Poor people like us can do with them."

"I haven't grown rich. I must sell these in order to buy...."

"Oh, come now, you have been made the intendant of a circuit, and do you still say you're not rich? You have three concubines now, and whenever you go out it is in a big sedan-chair with eight bearers, and do you still say you're not rich? Hah! You can't hide anything from me."

Knowing there was nothing I could say, I remained silent.

"Come now, really, the more money people have the more miserly they get, and the more miserly they are the more money they get," said the Compass, turning indignantly away and walking slowly off, casually picking up a pair of Mother's gloves and stuffing them into her pocket as she went out.

After this a number of relatives in the neighbourhood came to call. In the intervals between entertaining them I did some packing, and so three or four days passed.

One very cold afternoon, I was sitting drinking tea after lunch when I was aware of someone coming in, and turned my head to see who it was. At the first glance I gave an involuntary start, and hastily stood up and went over to welcome him.

The newcomer was Runtu. But although I knew at a glance that this was Runtu, it was not the Runtu I remembered. He had grown to twice his former size. His round face, crimson before, had become sallow and acquired deep lines and wrinkles; his eyes too had become like his father's with rims swollen and red, a feature common to most of the peasants who work by the sea and are exposed all day to the wind from the ocean. He wore a shabby felt cap and just one very thin padded jacket, with the result that he was shivering from head to foot. He was carrying a paper package and a long pipe, nor was his hand the plump red hand I remembered, but coarse and clumsy and chapped, like the bark of a pine tree.

Delighted as I was, I did not know how to express myself, and could only say:

"Oh! Runtu — so it's you?..."

After this there were so many things I wanted to talk about, they should have poured out like a string of beads: woodcocks, jumping fish, shells, *zha*....But I was tongue-tied, unable to put all I was thinking into words.

He stood there, mixed joy and sadness showing on his face. His lips moved, but not a sound did he utter. Finally, assuming a respectful attitude, he said clearly:

"老爷！……"

我似乎打了一个寒噤；我就知道，我们之间已经隔了一层可悲的厚障壁了。我也说不出话。

他回过头去说，"水生，给老爷磕头。"便拖出躲在背后的孩子来，这正是一个廿年前的闰土，只是黄瘦些，颈子上没有银圈罢了。"这是第五个孩子，没有见过世面，躲躲闪闪……"

母亲和宏儿下楼来了，他们大约也听到了声音。

"老太太。信是早收到了。我实在喜欢的了不得，知道老爷回来……"闰土说。

"阿，你怎的这样客气起来。你们先前不是哥弟称呼么？还是照旧：迅哥儿。"母亲高兴的说。

"阿呀，老太太真是……这成什么规矩。那时是孩子，不懂事……"闰土说着，又叫水生上来打拱，那孩子却害羞，紧紧的只贴在他背后。

"他就是水生？第五个？都是生人，怕生也难怪的；还是宏儿和他去走走。"母亲说。

宏儿听得这话，便来招水生，水生却松松爽爽同他一路出去了。母亲叫闰土坐，他迟疑了一回，终于就了坐，将长烟管靠在桌旁，递过纸包来，说：

"冬天没有什么东西了。这一点干青豆倒是自家晒在那里的，请老爷……"

我问问他的景况。他只是摇头。

"非常难。第六个孩子也会帮忙了，却总是吃不够……又不太平……什么地方都要钱，没有定规……收成又坏。种出东西来，挑去卖，总要捐几回钱，折了本；不去卖，又只能烂掉……"

他只是摇头；脸上虽然刻着许多皱纹，却全然不动，仿佛石像一般。他大约只是觉得苦，却又形容不出，沉默了片时，便拿起烟管来默默的吸烟了。

母亲问他，知道他的家里事务忙，明天便得回去；又没有吃过午饭，便叫他自己到厨下炒饭吃去。

"Master!..."

I felt a shiver run through me; for I knew then what a lamentably thick wall had grown up between us. Yet I could not say anything.

He turned his head to call:

"Shuisheng, bow to the master." Then he pulled forward a boy who had been hiding behind his back, and this was just the Runtu of twenty years before, only a little paler and thinner, and he had no silver necklet on his neck.

"This is my fifth," he said, "He has not seen any society, so he is shy and awkward."

Mother came downstairs with Hong'er, probably after hearing out voices.

"I got the letter some time ago, madam," said Runtu. "I was really so pleased to know that the master was coming back...."

"Now, why ever are you so polite? Weren't you playmates together in the past?" said Mother gaily. "You had better still call him Brother Xun as before."

"Oh, you are really too.... What bad manners that would be. I was a child then and didn't understand." As he was speaking Runtu motioned Shuisheng to come and bow, but the child was shy, and only stood stock-still behind his father.

"So he is Shuisheng? Your fifth?" asked Mother. "We are all strangers, you can't blame him for feeling shy. Hong'er had better take him to play."

When Hong'er heard this he went over to Shuisheng, and Shuisheng went out with him, entirely at his ease. Mother asked Runtu to sit down, and after a little hesitation he did so; then leaning his long pipe against the table he handed over the paper package, saying:

"In winter there is nothing worth bringing; but these few beans we dried ourselves there, if you will excuse the liberty, sir."

When I asked him how things were with him, he just shook his head.

"In a very bad way. Even my sixth can do a little work, but still we haven't enough to eat...and then there is no security.... All sorts of people want money, and there is no fixed rule...and the harvests are bad. You grow things, and when you take them to sell you always have to pay several taxes and lose money, while if you don't try to sell, the things may go bad.... "

He kept shaking his head; yet, although his face was lined with wrinkles, not one of them moved, just as if he were a stone statue. No doubt he felt intensely bitter, but could not express himself. After a pause he took up his pipe and began to smoke in silence.

From her chat with him, Mother learned that he was busy at home and had to go back the next day; and since he had had no lunch, she told him to go to the kitchen and fry some rice for himself.

他出去了；母亲和我都叹息他的景况：多子，饥荒，苛税，兵，匪，官，绅，都苦得他像一个木偶人了。母亲对我说，凡是不必搬走的东西，尽可以送他，可以听他自己去拣择。

下午，他拣好了几件东西：两条长桌，四个椅子，一副香炉和烛台，一杆抬秤。他又要所有的草灰（我们这里煮饭是烧稻草的，那灰，可以做沙地的肥料），待我们启程的时候，他用船来载去。

夜间，我们又谈些闲天，都是无关紧要的话；第二天早晨，他就领了水生回去了。

又过了九日，是我们启程的日期。闰土早晨便到了，水生没有同来，却只带着一个五岁的女儿管船只。我们终日很忙碌，再没有谈天的工夫。来客也不少，有送行的，有拿东西的，有送行兼拿东西的。待到傍晚我们上船的时候，这老屋里的所有破旧大小粗细东西，已经一扫而空了。

我们的船向前走，两岸的青山在黄昏中，都装成了深黛颜色，连着退向船后梢去。

宏儿和我靠着船窗，同看外面模糊的风景，他忽然问道：

"大伯！我们什么时候回来？"

"回来？你怎么还没有走就想回来了。"

"可是，水生约我到他家玩去咧……"他睁着大的黑眼睛，痴痴的想。

我和母亲也都有些惘然，于是又提起闰土来。母亲说，那豆腐西施的杨二嫂，自从我家收拾行李以来，本是每日必到的，前天伊在灰堆里，掏出十多个碗碟来，议论之后，便定说是闰土埋着的，他可以在运灰的时候，一齐搬回家里去；杨二嫂发见了这件事，自己很以为功，便拿了那狗气杀（这是我们这里养鸡的器具，木盘上面有着栅栏，内盛食料，鸡可以伸进颈子去啄，狗却不能，只能看着气死），飞也似的跑了，亏伊装着这么高底的小脚，竟跑得这样快。

After he had gone out, Mother and I both shook our heads over his hard life: many children, famines, taxes, soldiers, bandits, officials and landed gentry, all had squeezed him as dry as a mummy. Mother said that we should offer him all the things we were not going to take away, letting him choose for himself.

That afternoon he picked out a number of things: two long tables, four chairs, an incense-burner and candlesticks, and one balance. He also asked for all the ashes from the stove (in our part we cook over straw, and the ashes can be used to fertilize sandy soil), saying that when we left he would come to take them away by boat.

That night we talked again, but not of anything serious; and the next morning he went away with Shuisheng.

After another nine days it was time for us to leave. Runtu came in the morning. Shuisheng had not come with him — he had just brought a little girl of five to watch the boat. We were very busy all day, and had no time to talk. We also had quite a number of visitors, some to see us off, some to fetch things, and some to do both. It was nearly evening when we got on the boat, and by that time everything in the house, however old or shabby, large or small, fine or coarse, had been cleared away.

As we set off, the green mountains on either side of the river became deep blue in the dusk, receding towards the stern of the boat.

Hong'er and I, leaning against the cabin window, were looking out together at the indistinct scene outside, when suddenly he asked:

"Uncle, when shall we go back?"

"Go back? Do you mean that before you've left you want to go back?"

"Well, Shuisheng has invited me to his home...." He opened wide his black eyes in anxious thought.

Mother and I both felt rather sad, and so Runtu's name came up again. Mother said that ever since our family started packing up, Mrs. Yang from the beancurd shop had come over every day, and the day before in the ash-heap she had unearthed a dozen bowls and plates, which after some discussion she insisted must have been buried there by Runtu, so that when he came to remove the ashes he could take them home at the same time. After making this discovery Mrs. Yang was very pleased with herself, and flew off taking the dog-teaser with her. (The dog-teaser is used by poultry keepers in our part. It is a wooden cage inside which food is put, so that hens can stretch their necks in to eat but dogs can only look on furiously.) And it was a marvel, considering the size of her feet, how fast she could run.

老屋离我愈远了；故乡的山水也都渐渐远离了我，但我却并不感到怎样的留恋。我只觉得我四面有看不见的高墙，将我隔成孤身，使我非常气闷；那西瓜地上的银项圈的小英雄的影像，我本来十分清楚，现在却忽地模糊了，又使我非常的悲哀。

母亲和宏儿都睡着了。

我躺着，听船底潺潺的水声，知道我在走我的路。我想：我竟与闰土隔绝到这地步了，但我们的后辈还是一气，宏儿不是正在想念水生么。我希望他们不再像我，又大家隔膜起来……然而我又不愿意他们因为要一气，都如我的辛苦展转而生活，也不愿意他们都如闰土的辛苦麻木而生活，也不愿意都如别人的辛苦恣睢而生活。他们应该有新的生活，为我们所未经生活过的。

我想到希望，忽然害怕起来了。闰土要香炉和烛台的时候，我还暗地里笑他，以为他总是崇拜偶像，什么时候都不忘却。现在我所谓希望，不也是我自己手制的偶像么？只是他的愿望切近，我的愿望茫远罢了。

我在朦胧中，眼前展开一片海边碧绿的沙地来，上面深蓝的天空中挂着一轮金黄的圆月。我想：希望是本无所谓有，无所谓无的。这正如地上的路；其实地上本没有路，走的人多了，也便成了路。

一九二一年一月。

I was leaving the old house farther and farther behind, while the hills and rivers of my old home were also receding gradually ever farther in the distance. But I felt no regret. I only felt that all round me was an invisible high wall, cutting me off from my fellow, and this depressed me thoroughly. The vision of that small hero with the silver necklet among the watermelons had formerly been as clear as day, but now it had suddenly blurred, adding to depression.

Mother and Hong'er fell asleep.

I lay down, listening to the water rippling beneath the boat, and knew that I was going my way. I thought: although there is such a barrier between Runtu and myself, our children still have much in common, for wasn't Hong'er thinking of Shuisheng just now? I hope they will not be like us, that they will not allow a barrier to grow up between them. But again I would not like them, because they want to be one, to have a treadmill existence like mine, nor to suffer like Runtu until they become stupefied, nor yet, like others, to devote all their energies to dissipation. They should have a new life, a life we have never experienced.

The access of hope made me suddenly afraid. When Runtu had asked for the incense-burner and candlesticks I had laughed up my sleeve at him, to think that he was still worshipping idols and would never put them out of his mind. Yet what I now called hope was no more than an idol I had created myself. The only difference was that what he desired was close at hand, while what I desired was less easily realized.

As I dozed, a stretch of jade-green seashore spread itself before my eyes, and above a round golden moon hung from a deep blue sky. I thought: hope cannot be said to exist, nor can it be said not to exist. It is just like roads across the earth. For actually the earth had no roads to begin with, but when many men pass one way, a road is made.

January 1921

"你还不配⋯⋯" 这时候，
又仿佛在他头上的是一种高尚的光荣的癞头疮，
并非平常的癞头疮了；

"You don't even deserve...."
At this juncture it seemed as if the bald patches on his scalp were noble
and honourable, not just ordinary ringworm scars.

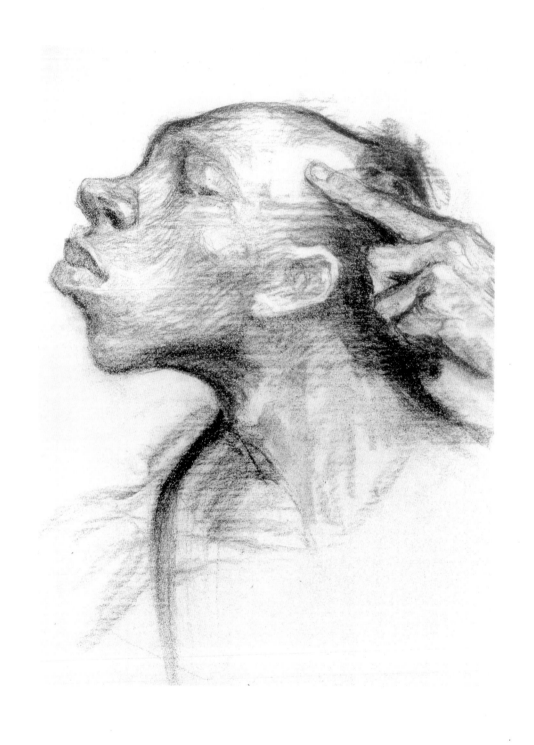

阿Q正传
The True Story of Ah Q

第一章 序

我要给阿Q做正传，已经不止一两年了。但一面要做，一面又往回想，这足见我不是一个"立言"的人，因为从来不朽之笔，须传不朽之人，于是人以文传，文以人传——究竟谁靠谁传，渐渐的不甚了然起来，而终于归结到传阿Q，仿佛思想里有鬼似的。

然而要做这一篇速朽的文章，才下笔，便感到万分的困难了。第一是文章的名目。孔子曰，"名不正则言不顺"。这原是应该极注意的。传的名目很繁多：列传，自传，内传，外传，别传，家传，小传……，而可惜都不合。"列传"么，这一篇并非和许多阔人排在"正史"里；"自传"么，我又并非就是阿Q。说是"外传"，"内传"在那里呢？倘用"内传"，阿Q又决不是神仙。"别传"呢，阿Q实在未曾有大总统上谕宣付国史馆立"本传"——虽说英国正史上并无"博徒列传"，而文豪迭更司也做过《博徒别传》这一部书，但文豪则可，在我辈却不可的。其次是"家传"，则我既不知与阿Q是否同宗，也未曾受他子孙的拜托；或"小传"，则阿Q又更无别的"大传"了。总而言之，这一篇也便是"本传"，但从我的文章着想，因为文体卑下，是"引车卖浆者流"所用的话，所以不敢僭称，便从不入三教九流的小说家所谓"闲话休题言归正传"这一句套话里，取出"正传"两个字来，作为名目，即使与古人所撰《书法正传》的"正传"字面上很相混，也顾不得了。

第二，立传的通例，开首大抵该是"某，字某，某地人也"，而我并不知道阿Q姓什么。有一回，他似乎是姓赵，但第二日便模糊了。那是赵太爷的儿子进了秀才的时候，锣声镗镗的报到村里来，阿Q正喝了两碗黄

1. In Chinese this title was translated as *Supplementary Biograpbies of the Gamblers.*

2. The Three Cults were Confucianism, Buddhism and Taoism. The Nine Schools included the Confucian, Taoist, Legalist, Mohist and other schools.

3. A book by Feng Wu of the Qing Dynasty (1644-1911).

Chapter 1 Introduction

For several years now I have been meaning to write the true story of Ah Q. But while wanting to write I was in some trepidation too, which goes to show that I am not one of those who achieve glory by writing; for an immortal pen has always been required to record the deeds of an immortal man, the man becoming known to posterity through the writing and the writing known to posterity through the man — until finally it is not clear who is making whom known. But in the end, as though possessed by some fiend, I always came back to the idea of writing the story of Ah Q.

And yet no sooner had I taken up my pen than I became conscious of tremendous difficulties in writing this far-from-immortal work. The first was the question of what to call it. Confucius said, "If the name is not correct, the words will not ring true"; and this axiom should be most scrupulously observed. There are many types of biography: official biographies, autobiographies, unauthorized biographies, legends, supplement biographies, family histories, sketches...but unfortunately none of these suited my purpose. "Official biography"? This account will obviously not be included with those of many eminent people in some authentic history. "Autobiography"? But I am obviously not Ah Q. If I were to call this an "unauthorized biography," then where is his "authenticated biography?" The use of "legend" is impossible because Ah Q was no legendary figure. "Supplementary biography"? But no president has ever ordered the National Historical Institute to write a "standard life" of Ah Q. It is true that although there are no "lives of gamblers" in authentic English history, the well-known author Conan Doyle nevertheless wrote *Rodney Stone*;[1] but while this is permissible for a well-known author it is not permissible for such as I. Then there is "family history"; but I do not know whether I belong to the same family as Ah Q or not, nor have his children or grandchildren ever entrusted me with such a task. If I were to use "sketch," it might be objected that Ah Q has no "complete account." In short, this is really a "life," but since I write in vulgar vein using the language of hucksters and pedlars, I dare not presume to give it so high-sounding a title. So I will take as my title the last two words of stock phrase of the novelist, who are not reckoned among the Three Cults and Nine Schools.[2] "Enough of this digression, and back to the *true story*"; and if this is reminiscent of the *True Story of Calligraphy*[3] of the ancients, it cannot be helped.

The second difficulty confronting me was that a biography of this type should start off something like this: "So-and-so, whose other name was so-and-so, was a native of such-and-such a place"; but I don't really know what Ah Q's surname was. Once, he seemed to be named Zhao, but the next day there was some confusion about the matter again. This was after Mr. Zhao's son had passed the county examination and, to the sound of gongs, his success was anounced in the village. Ah Q, who had just drunk two bowls of yellow wine,

144

酒，便手舞足蹈的说，这于他也很光彩，因为他和赵太
爷原来是本家，细细的排起来他还比秀才长三辈呢。其
时几个旁听人倒也肃然的有些起敬了。那知道第二天，
地保便叫阿Q到赵太爷家里去；太爷一见，满脸溅朱，
喝道：

"阿Q，你这浑小子！你说我是你的本家么？"

阿Q不开口。

赵太爷愈看愈生气了，抢进几步说："你敢胡说！我
怎么会有你这样的本家？你姓赵么？"

阿Q不开口，想往后退了；赵太爷跳过去，给了他一
个嘴巴。

"你怎么会姓赵！——你那里配姓赵！"

阿Q并没有抗辩他确凿姓赵，只用手摸着左颊，和地
保退出去了；外面又被地保训斥了一番，谢了地保二百文
酒钱。知道的人都说阿Q太荒唐，自己去招打；他大约未
必姓赵，即使真姓赵，有赵太爷在这里，也不该如此胡说
的。此后便再没有人提起他的氏族来，所以我终于不知道
阿Q究竟什么姓。

第三，我又不知道阿Q的名字是怎么写的。他活着
的时候，人都叫他阿Quei，死了以后，便没有一个人再
叫阿Quei了，那里还会有"著之竹帛"的事。若论"著
之竹帛"，这篇文章要算第一次，所以先遇着了这第一
个难关。我曾经仔细想：阿Quei，阿桂还是阿贵呢？倘
使他号叫月亭，或者在八月间做过生日，那一定是阿
桂了；而他既没有号——也许有号，只是没有人知道
他，——又未尝散过生日征文的贴子：写作阿桂，是武
断的。又倘若他有一位老兄或令弟叫阿富，那一定是阿
贵了；而他又只是一个人：写作阿贵，也没有佐证的。
其余音Quei的偏僻字样，更加凑不上了。先前，我也曾
问过赵太爷的儿子茂才先生，谁料博雅如此公，竟也茫
然，但据结论说，是因为陈独秀办了《新青年》提倡洋

4. A phrase used before paper was invented when bamboo and silk served as writing material in China.

5. The fragrant osmanthus blooms in the month of the Moon Festival. And according to Chinese folklore, the shadow on the moon is an osmanthus tree.

began to prance about declaring that this reflected credit on him too, since he belonged to the same clan as Mr. Zhao and by an exact reckoning was three generations senior to the successful candidate. At the time several bystanders even began to stand slightly in awe of Ah Q. but the next day the bailiff summoned him to Mr. Zhao's house. When the old gentleman set eyes on him his face turned crimson with fury and he roared:

"Ah Q, you miserable wretch! Did you say I belonged to the same clan as you?"

Ah Q made no reply.

The more he looked at him the angrier Mr. Zhao became. Advancing menacingly a few steps he said, "How dare you talk such nonsense! How could I have such a relative as you? Is your surname Zhao?"

Ah Q made no reply and was planning a retreat, when Mr. Zhao darted forward and gave him a slap on the face.

"How could *you* be named Zhao? Are you worthy of the name Zhao?"

Ah Q made no attempt to defend his right to the name Zhao but rubbing his left cheek went out with the bailiff from whom, once outside, he had to listen to another torrent of abuse. He then by way of atonement paid him two hundred cash. All who heard this said Ah Q was a great fool to ask for a beating like that. Even if his surname *were* Zhao — which wasn't likely — he should have known better than to boast like that when there was a Mr. Zhao living in the village. After this no further mention was made of Ah Q's ancestry, thus I still have no idea what his surname really was.

The third difficulty I encountered in writing this work was that I don't know how Ah Q personal name should be written either. During his lifetime everybody called him Ah Gui, but after his death not a soul mentioned Ah Gui again; for he was obviously not one of those whose name is" preserved on bamboo tablets and silk."[4] If there is any question of preserving his name, this essay must be the first attempt at doing so. Hence I am confronted with this difficulty at the outset. I have given the question careful thought. Ah Gui — would that be the "Gui" meaning fragrant osmanthus or the "Gui" meaning nobility? If his other name had been Moon Pavilion, or if he had celebrated his birthday in the month of the Moon Festival, then it would certainly be the "Gui" for fragrant osmanthus.[5] But since he had no other name — or if he had, no one knew it — and since he never sent out invitations on his birthday to secure complimentary verses, it would be arbitrary to write Ah Gui (fragrant osmanthus). Again, if he had had an elder or younger brother called Ah Fu (prosperity), then he would certainly be called Ah Gui (nobility). But he was all on his own; thus there is no justification for writing Ah Gui (nobility). All the other, unusual characters with the sound Gui are even less suitable. I once put this question to Mr. Zhao's son, the successful county candidate, but even such a learned man as he was baffled by it. According to him, however, the reason why this name could not be traced was that Chen

字，所以国粹沦亡，无可查考了。我的最后的手段，只有托一个同乡去查阿Q犯事的案卷，八个月之后才有回信，说案卷里并无与阿Quei的声音相近的人。我虽不知道是真没有，还是没有查，然而也再没有别的方法了。生怕注音字母还未通行，只好用了"洋字"，照英国流行的拼法写他为阿Quei，略作阿Q。这近于盲从《新青年》，自己也很抱歉，但茂才公尚且不知，我还有什么好办法呢。

第四，是阿Q的籍贯了。倘他姓赵，则据现在好称郡望的老例，可以照《郡名百家姓》上的注解，说是"陇西天水人也"，但可惜这姓是不甚可靠的，因此籍贯也就有些决不定。他虽然多住未庄，然而也常常宿在别处，不能说是未庄人，即使说是"未庄人也"，也仍然有乖史法的。

我所聊以自慰的，是还有一个"阿"字非常正确，绝无附会假借的缺点，颇可以就正于通人。至于其余，却都非浅学所能穿凿，只希望有"历史癖与考据癖"的胡适之先生的门人们，将来或者能够寻出许多新端绪来，但是我这《阿Q正传》到那时却又怕早经消灭了。

以上可以算是序。

第二章　优胜记略

阿Q不独是姓名籍贯有些渺茫，连他先前的"行状"也渺茫。因为未庄的人们之于阿Q，只要他帮忙，只拿他玩笑，从来没有留心他的"行状"的。而阿Q自己也不说，独有和别人口角的时候，间或瞪着眼睛道：

"我们先前——比你阔的多啦！你算是什么东西！"

阿Q没有家，住在未庄的土谷祠里；也没有固定的职

6. Chen Duxiu (1880-1942) was then chief editor of *New Youth*, the magazine which gave the lead in the movement for a new culture.

7. A school primer in which surnames were written into verse.

Duxiu[6] had brought out the magazine *New Youth* advocating the use of the Western alphabet, hence the national culture was going to the dogs. As a last resort, I asked someone from my district to go and look up the legal documents recording Ah Q's case, but after eight months he sent me a letter saying that there was no name anything like Ah Gui in those records. Although uncertain whether this was the truth or whether my friend had simply done nothing, after failing to trace the name this way I could think of no other means of finding it. Since I am afraid the new system of phonetics has not yet come into common use, there is nothing for it but to use the Western alphabet, writing the name according to the English spelling as Ah Gui and abbreviating it to Ah Q. This approximates to blindly following *New Youth*, and I am thoroughly ashamed of myself; but since even such a learned man as Mr. Zhao's son could not solve my problem, what else can I do?"

My fourth difficulty was with Ah Q's place of origin. If his surname were Zhao, then according to the old custom which still prevails of classifying people by their district, one might look up the commentary in *The Hundred Surnames*[7] and find "Native of Tianshui in Gansu." But unfortunately this surname is open to question, with the result that Ah Q's place of origin must also remain uncertain. Although he lived for the most part in Weizhuang, he often stayed in other places, so that it would be wrong to call him a native of Weizhuang. It would, in fact, amount to a distortion of history.

The only thing that consoles me is the fact that the character "Ah" is absolutely correct. This is definitely not the result of false analogy, and is well able to stand the test of scholarly criticism. As for the other problems. It is not for such unlearned people as myself to solve them, and I can only hope that disciples of Dr. Hu Shi, who has such "a passion for history and research," may be able in future to throw new light on them. I am afraid, however, that by that time my "True Story of Ah Q" will have long since passed into oblivion.

The foregoing may be considered as an introduction.

Chapter 2   A Brief Account of Ah Q's Victories

In addition to the uncertainty regarding Ah Q's surname, personal name, and place of origin, there is even some uncertainty regarding his "background." This is because the people of Weizhuang only made use of his services or treated him as a laughing-stock, without ever paying the slightest attention to his "background." Ah Q himself remained silent on this subject, except that when quarrelling with someone he might glare at him and say, "We used to be much better off than you! Who do you think you are?"

Ah Q had no family but lived in the Tutelary God's Temple at Weizhuang. He had no

业，只给人家做短工，割麦便割麦，舂米便舂米，撑船便撑船。工作略长久时，他也或住在临时主人的家里，但一完就走了。所以，人们忙碌的时候，也还记起阿Q来，然而记起的是做工，并不是"行状"；一闲空，连阿Q都早忘却，更不必说"行状"了。只是有一回，有一个老头子颂扬说："阿Q真能做！"这时阿Q赤着膊，懒洋洋的瘦伶仃的正在他面前，别人也摸不着这话是真心还是讥笑，然而阿Q很喜欢。

阿Q又很自尊，所有未庄的居民，全不在他眼睛里，甚而至于对于两位"文童"也有以为不值一笑的神情。夫文童者，将来恐怕要变秀才者也；赵太爷钱太爷大受居民的尊敬，除有钱之外，就因为都是文童的爹爹，而阿Q在精神上独不表格外的崇奉，他想：我的儿子会阔得多啦！加以进了几回城，阿Q自然更自负，然而他又很鄙薄城里人，譬如用三尺长三寸宽的木板做成的凳子，未庄叫"长凳"，他也叫"长凳"，城里人却叫"条凳"，他想：这是错的，可笑！油煎大头鱼，未庄都加上半寸长的葱叶，城里却加上切细的葱丝，他想：这也是错的，可笑！然而未庄人真是不见世面的可笑的乡下人呵，他们没有见过城里的煎鱼！

阿Q"先前阔"，见识高，而且"真能做"，本来几乎是一个"完人"了，但可惜他体质上还有一些缺点。最恼人的是在他头皮上，颇有几处不知起于何时的癞疮疤。这虽然也在他身上，而看阿Q的意思，倒也似乎以为不足贵的，因为他讳说"癞"以及一切近于"赖"的音，后来推而广之，"光"也讳，"亮"也讳，再后来，连"灯""烛"都讳了。一犯讳，不问有心与无心，阿Q便全疤通红的发起怒来，估量了对手，口讷的他便骂，气力小的他便打；然而不知怎么一回事，总还是阿Q吃亏的时候多。于是他渐渐的变换了方针，大抵改为怒目而视了。

谁知道阿Q采用怒目主义之后，未庄的闲人们便愈喜

regular work either, being simply an odd-job man for others: when there was wheat to be cut he would cut it, when there was rice to be hulled he would hull it, when there was a boat to be punted he would punt it. If the work lasted for any length of time he might stay in the house of his temporary employer, but as soon as it was finished he would leave. Thus whenever people had work to be done they would remember Ah Q, but what they remembered was his service and not his "background." By the time the job was done even Ah Q himself was forgotten, to say nothing of his "background." Once indeed an old man remarked, "What a worker Ah Q is!" Ah Q, bare-backed scrawny sluggard, was standing before him at the time, and others could not tell whether the remark was serious or derisive, but Ah Q was overjoyed.

Ah Q, again, had a very high opinion of himself. He looked down on all the inhabitants of Weizhuang, thinking even the two young "scholars" not worth a smile, though most young scholars were likely to pass the official examinations. Mr. Zhao and Mr. Qian were held in great respect by the villagers, for in addition to being rich they were both the fathers of young scholars. Ah Q alone showed them no exceptional deference, thinking to himself, "My sons may be much greater."

Moreover, after Ah Q had been to town several times he naturally became even more conceited, although at the same time he had the greatest contempt for townspeople. For instance, a bench made of a wooden plank three feet by three inches the Weizhuang villagers called a "long bench." Ah Q called it a "long bench" too; but the townspeople called it a "straight bench," and he thought, "This is wrong. Ridiculous!" Again, when they fried large-headed fish in oil the Weizhuang villagers all added shallots sliced half an inch thick, whereas the townspeople added finely shredded shallots, and he thought, "This is wrong too. Ridiculous!" But the Weizhuang villagers were really ignorant rustics who had never seen fish fried in town.

Ah Q who "used to be much better off," who was a man of the world and a "worker," would have been almost the perfect man had it not been for a few unfortunate physical blemishes. The most annoying were some patches on his scalp where at some uncertain date shiny ringworm scars had appeared. Although these were on his own head, apparently Ah Q did not consider them as altogether honourable, for he refrained from using the word "ringworm" or any words that sounded anything like it. Later he improved on this, making "bright" and "light" forbidden words, while later still even "lamp" and "candle" were taboo. Whenever this taboo was disregarded, whether intentionally or not, Ah Q would fly into a rage, his ringworm scars turning scarlet. He would look over the offender, and if it were someone weak in repartee he would curse him while if it were a poor fighter he would hit him. Yet, curiously enough, it was usually Ah Q who was worsted in these encounters, until finally he adopted new tactics, contenting himself in general with a furious glare.

It so happened, however, that after Ah Q had taken to using this furious glare, the

欢玩笑他。一见面，他们便假作吃惊的说：

"哙，亮起来了。"

阿Q照例的发了怒，他怒目而视了。

"原来有保险灯在这里！"他们并不怕。

阿Q没有法，只得另外想出报复的话来：

"你还不配……"这时候，又仿佛在他头上的是一种高尚的光荣的癞头疮，并非平常的癞头疮了；但上文说过，阿Q是有见识的，他立刻知道和"犯忌"有点抵触，便不再往底下说。

闲人还不完，只撩他，于是终而至于打。阿Q在形式上打败了，被人揪住黄辫子，在壁上碰了四五个响头，闲人这才心满意足的得胜的走了，阿Q站了一刻，心里想，"我总算被儿子打了，现在的世界真不像样……"于是也心满意足的得胜的走了。

阿Q想在心里的，后来每每说出口来，所以凡有和阿Q玩笑的人们，几乎全知道他有这一种精神上的胜利法，此后每逢揪住他黄辫子的时候，人就先一着对他说：

"阿Q，这不是儿子打老子，是人打畜生。自己说：人打畜生！"

阿Q两只手都捏住了自己的辫根，歪着头，说道：

"打虫豸，好不好？我是虫豸——还不放么？"

但虽然是虫豸，闲人也并不放，仍旧在就近什么地方给他碰了五六个响头，这才心满意足的得胜的走了，他以为阿Q这回可遭了瘟。然而不到十秒钟，阿Q也心满意足的得胜的走了，他觉得他是第一个能够自轻自贱的人，除了"自轻自贱"不算外，余下的就是"第一个"。状元不也是"第一个"么？"你算是什么东西"呢！？

阿Q以如是等等妙法克服怨敌之后，便愉快的跑到酒店里喝几碗酒，又和别人调笑一通，口角一通，又得了胜，愉快的回到土谷祠，放倒头睡着了。假使有钱，他便去押牌宝，一堆人蹲在地面上，阿Q即汗流满面的夹在这中间，声音他最响：

idlers in Weizhuang grew even more fond of making jokes at his expense. As soon as they saw him they would pretend to give a start and say:

"Look! It's lighting up."

Ah Q rising to the bait as usual would glare in fury.

"So there is a paraffin lamp here," they would continue, unafraid.

Ah Q could do nothing but rack his brains for some retort. "You don't even deserve...." At this juncture it seemed as if the bald patches on his scalp were noble and honourable, not just ordinary ringworm scars. However, as we said above, Ah Q was a man of the world: he knew at once that he had nearly broken the "taboo" and refrained from saying any more.

"If the idlers were still not satisfied but continued to pester him, they would in the end come to blows. Then only after Ah Q had to all appearances been defeated, had his brownish queue pulled and his head bumped against the wall four or five times, would the idlers walk away, satisfied at having won. And Ah Q would stand there for a second thinking to himself, "It's as if I were beaten by my son. What the world is coming to nowadays!...." Thereupon he too would walk away, satisfied at having won.

Whatever Ah Q thought he was sure to tell people later; thus almost all who made fun of Ah Q knew that he had this means of winning a psychological victory. So after this anyone who pulled or twisted his brown queue would forestall him by saying, "Ah Q, this is not a son beating his father, it is a man beating a beast. Let's hear you say it: A man beating a beast!"

Then Ah Q, clutching at the root of his queue, his head on one side, would say, "Beating an insect — how about that? I am an insect — now will you let me go?"

But although he was an insect the idlers would not let him go until they had knocked his head five or six times against something nearby, according to their custom, after which they would walk away satisfied that they had won, confident that this time Ah Q was done for. In less than ten seconds, however, Ah Q would walk away also satisfied that he had won, thinking that he was the "Number One self-belittler," and that after subtracting "self-belittler" what remained was "Number One." Was not the highest successful candidate in the official examination also "Numbeer One"? "And who do you think *you* are?"

After employing such cunning devices to get even with his enemies, Ah Q would make his way cheerfully to the tavern to drink a few bowls of wine, joke with the others again, quarrel with them again, come off victorious again, and return cheerfully to the Tutelary God's Temple, there to fall asleep as soon as his head touched the pillow. If he has money he would gamble. A group of men would squat on the ground, Ah Q sandwiched in their midst, his face streaming with sweat; and his voice would shout the

"青龙四百！"

"咳～～开～～啦！"桩家揭开盒子盖，也是汗流满面的唱。"天门啦～～角回啦～～！人和穿堂空在那里啦～～！阿Q的铜钱拿过来～～！"

"穿堂一百———一百五十！"

阿Q的钱便在这样的歌吟之下，渐渐的输入别个汗流满面的人物的腰间。他终于只好挤出堆外，站在后面看，替别人着急，一直到散场，然后恋恋的回到土谷祠，第二天，肿着眼睛去工作。

但真所谓"塞翁失马安知非福"罢，阿Q不幸而赢了一回，他倒几乎失败了。

这是未庄赛神的晚上。这晚上照例有一台戏，戏台左近，也照例有许多的赌摊。做戏的锣鼓，在阿Q耳朵里仿佛在十里之外；他只听得桩家的歌唱了。他赢而又赢，铜钱变成角洋，角洋变成大洋，大洋又成了叠。他兴高采烈得非常：

"天门两块！"

他不知道谁和谁为什么打起架来了。骂声打声脚步声，昏头昏脑的一大阵，他才爬起来，赌摊不见了，人们也不见了，身上有几处很似乎有些痛，似乎也挨了几拳几脚似的，几个人诧异的对他看。他如有所失的走进土谷祠，定一定神，知道他的一堆洋钱不见了。赶赛会的赌摊多不是本村人，还到那里去寻根柢呢？

很白很亮的一堆洋钱！而且是他的——现在不见了！说是算被儿子拿去了罢，总还是忽忽不乐；说自己是虫豸罢，也还是忽忽不乐：他这回才有些感到失败的苦痛了。

但他立刻转败为胜了。他擎起右手，用力的在自己脸上连打了两个嘴巴，热剌剌的有些痛；打完之后，便心平气和起来，似乎打的是自己，被打的是别一个自己，不久也就仿佛是自己打了别个一般，——虽然还有些热剌剌，——心满意足的得胜的躺下了。

他睡着了。

loudest: "Four hundred on the Green Dragon!"

"Hey — open there!"

The stake-holder, his face streaming with sweat too, would open the box and chant: "Heavenly Gate! — Nothing for the Corner!.... No stakes on Popularity Passage! Pass over Ah Q's coppers! "

"The Passage — one hundred — one hundred and fifty."

To the tune of his chanting, Ah Q's money would gradually vanish into the pockets of other sweating players. Finally he would be forced to squeeze his way out of the crowd and watch from the back, taking a vicarious interest in the game until it broke up, when he would return reluctantly to the Tutelary God's Temple. The next day he would go to work with swollen eyes.

However, the truth of the proverb "Misfortune may prove a blessing in disguise" was shown when Ah Q was unfortunate enough to win and almost suffered defeat in the end.

This was the evening of the Festival of the Gods in Weizhuang. According to custom there was an opera; and close to the stage, also according to custom, were numerous gambling tables, the drums and gongs of the stake-holder's chant. He staked successfully again and again, his coppers turning into silver coins, his silver coins into dollars, and his dollars mounting up. In his excitement he cried out, "Two dollars on Heavenly Gate!"

He never knew who started the fight, nor for what reason. Curses, blows and footsteps formed a a confused medley of sound in his head, and by the time he clambered to his feet the gambling tables had vanished and so had the gamblers. Several parts of his body seemed to be aching as if he had been kicked and knocked about, while a number of people were looking at him in astonishment. Feeling as if something were amiss he walked back to the Tutelary God's Temple, and by the time he had calmed down again he realized that his pile of dollars had gone. Since most of the people who ran gambling tables at the Festival were not natives of Weizhuang, where could he look for the culprits?

So white and glittering a pile of silver! All of it his...but now it had disappeared. Even to consider this tantamount to being robbed by his son did not comfort him. To consider himself as an insect did not comfort him either. This time he really tasted something of the bitterness of defeat.

But presently he changed defeat into victory. Raising his right hand he slapped his own face hard, twice, so that it tingled with pain. After this slapping his heart felt lighter, for it seemed as if the one who had given the slap was himself, the one slapped some other self, and soon it was just as if he had beaten someone else — in spite of the fact that his face was still tingling. He lay down satisfied that he had gained the victory.

Soon he was asleep.

第三章　续优胜记略

　　然而阿Q虽然常优胜，却直待蒙赵太爷打他嘴巴之后，这才出了名。

　　他付过地保二百文酒钱，愤愤的躺下了，后来想："现在的世界太不成话，儿子打老子……"于是忽而想到赵太爷的威风，而现在是他的儿子了，便自己也渐渐的得意起来，爬起身，唱着《小孤孀上坟》到酒店去。这时候，他又觉得赵太爷高人一等了。

　　说也奇怪，从此之后，果然大家也仿佛格外尊敬他。这在阿Q，或者以为因为他是赵太爷的父亲，而其实也不然。未庄通例，倘如阿七打阿八，或者李四打张三，向来本不算一件事，必须与一位名人如赵太爷者相关，这才载上他们的口碑。一上口碑，则打的既有名，被打的也就托庇有了名。至于错在阿Q，那自然是不必说。所以者何？就因为赵太爷是不会错的。但他既然错，为什么大家又仿佛格外尊敬他呢？这可难解，穿凿起来说，或者因为阿Q说是赵太爷的本家，虽然挨了打，大家也还怕有些真，总不如尊敬一些稳当。否则，也如孔庙里的太牢一般，虽然与猪羊一样，同是畜生，但既经圣人下箸，先儒们便不敢妄动了。

　　阿Q此后倒得意了许多年。

　　有一年的春天，他醉醺醺的在街上走，在墙根的日光下，看见王胡在那里赤着膊捉虱子，他忽然觉得身上也痒起来了。这王胡，又癞又胡，别人都叫他王癞胡，阿Q却删去了一个癞字，然而非常渺视他。阿Q的意思，以为癞是不足为奇的，只有这一部络腮胡子，实在太新奇，令人看不上眼。他于是并排坐下去了。倘是别的闲人们，阿Q本不敢大意坐下去。但这王胡旁边，他有什么怕呢？老实说：他肯坐下去，简直还是抬举他。

　　阿Q也脱下破夹袄来，翻检了一回，不知道因为新洗呢还是因为粗心，许多工夫，只捉到三四个。他看那王

8. A local opera popular in Shaoxing.

Chapter 3   A Further Account of Ah Q's Victories

Although Ah Q was always gaining victories, it was only after he was favoured with a slap in the face by Mr. Zhao that he became famous.

After paying the bailiff two hundred cash he lay down angrily. Then he said to himself, "What is the word coming to nowadays, with sons beating their fathers!" And then the thought of the prestige of Mr. Zhao, who was now his son, gradually raised his spirits. He scrambled up and made his way to the tavern singing *The Young Widow at Her Husband's Grave*.[8] At that time he did feel that Mr. Zhao was a cut above most people.

After this incident, strange to relate, it was true that everybody seemed to pay him unusual respect. He probably attributed this to the fact that he was Mr. Zhao's father, but actually such was not the case. In Weizhuang, as a rule, if the seventh child hit the eighth child or Li So-and-so hit Zhang So-and-so, it was not taken seriously. A beating had to be connected with some important personage like Mr. Zhao before the villagers thought it worth talking about. But once they thought it worth talking about, since the beater was famous the one beaten enjoyed some of his reflected fame. As for the fault being Ah Q's, that was naturally taken for granted, the reason being that Mr. Zhao could do no wrong. But if Ah Q were wrong, why did everybody seem to treat him with unusual respect? This is difficult to explain. We may put forward the hypothesis that it was because Ah Q had said he belonged to the same family as Mr. Zhao; thus, although he had been beaten, people were still afraid there might be some truth in his assertion and therefore thought it safer to treat him more respectfully. Or, alternatively, it may have been like the case of the sacrificial beef in the Confucian temple: although the beef was in the same category as the pork and mutton, being of animal origin just as they were, later Confucians did not dare touch it since the sage had enjoyed it.

After this Ah Q prospered for several years.

One spring, when he was walking along in a state of happy intoxication, he saw Whiskers Wang sitting stripped to the waist in the sunlight at the foot of a wall, catching lice; and at this sight his own body began to itch. Since Whiskers Wang was scabby and bewhiskered, everybody called him "Ringworm Whiskers Wang." Although Ah Q omitted the word "Ringworm," he had the greatest contempt for the man. To Ah Q, while scabs were nothing to take exception to, such hairy cheeks were really too outlandish and could excite nothing but scorn. So Ah Q sat down by his side. Had it been any other idler, Ah Q would never have dared sit down so casually; but what had he to fear by the side of Whiskers Wang? In fact, his willingness to sit down was doing the fellow an honour.

Ah Q took off his tattered lined jacket and turned it inside out; but either because he had

胡，却是一个又一个，两个又三个，只放在嘴里毕毕剥剥
的响。

阿Q最初是失望，后来却不平了：看不上眼的王胡尚
且那么多，自己倒反这样少，这是怎样的大失体统的事
呵！他很想寻一两个大的，然而竟没有，好容易才捉到一
个中的，恨恨的塞在厚嘴唇里，狠命一咬，劈的一声，又
不及王胡响。

他癞疮疤块块通红了，将衣服摔在地上，吐一口唾
沫，说：

"这毛虫！"

"癞皮狗，你骂谁？"王胡轻蔑的抬起眼来说。

阿Q近来虽然比较的受人尊敬，自己也更高傲些，但
和那些打惯的闲人们见面还胆怯，独有这回却非常武勇
了。这样满脸胡子的东西，也敢出言无状么？

"谁认便骂谁！"他站起来，两手叉在腰间说。

"你的骨头痒了么？"王胡也站起来，披上衣服说。

阿Q以为他要逃了，抢进去就是一拳。这拳头还未
达到身上，已经被他抓住了，只一拉，阿Q跄跄踉踉的
跌进去，立刻又被王胡扭住了辫子，要拉到墙上照例去
碰头。

"'君子动口不动手'！"阿Q歪着头说。

王胡似乎不是君子，并不理会，一连给他碰了五
下，又用力的一推，至于阿Q跌出六尺多远，这才满足的
去了。

在阿Q的记忆上，这大约要算是生平第一件的屈辱，
因为王胡以络腮胡子的缺点，向来只被他奚落，从没有奚
落他，更不必说动手了。而他现在竟动手，很意外，难道
真如市上所说，皇帝已经停了考，不要秀才和举人了，因
此赵家减了威风，因此他们也便小觑了他么？

阿Q无可适从的站着。

远远的走来了一个人，他的对头又到了。这也是阿Q
最厌恶的一个人，就是钱太爷的大儿子。他先前跑上城里

washed it recently or because he was too clumsy, a long search yielded only three or four lice. He saw that Whiskers Wang, on the other hand, was catching first on and then another in swift succession, cracking them between his teeth with a popping sound.

Ah Q felt first disappointed, then resentful: the despicable Whiskers Wang had so many, he himself so few — what a great loss of face! He longed to find one or two big ones, but there were none, and when at last he managed to catch a middle-sized one, stuffed it fiercely between his thick lips and bit hard, the resultant pop was again inferior to the noise made by Whiskers Wang.

All Ah Q's ringworm patches turned scarlet. He flung his jacket on the ground, spat, and swore, "Hairy worm!"

"Mangy dog, who are you calling names?" Whiskers Wang looked up contemptuously.

Although the relative respect accorded him in recent years had increased Ah Q's pride, he was still rather timid when confronted by those loafers accustomed to fighting. But today he was feeling exceptionally pugnacious. How dare a hairy-cheeked creature like this insult him?

"If the cap fits wear it," he retorted, standing up and putting his hands on his hips.

"Are your bones itching?" demanded Whiskers Wang, standing up too and draping his jacket over his shoulders.

Thinking that the fellow meant to run away, Ah Q lunged forward to punch him. But before his fist reached the target, his opponent seized him and gave him a tug which sent him staggering. Then Whiskers Wang seized his queue and started dragging him towards the wall to knock his head in the time-honoured manner.

"'A gentleman uses his tongue but not his hands!'" protested Ah Q, his head on one side.

Apparently Whiskers Wang was no gentleman, for without paying the slightest attention to what Ah Q said he knocked his head against the wall five times in succession, then with a great push shoved him two yards away, after which he walked off in triumph.

As far as Ah Q could remember, this was the first humiliation of his life, because he had always scoffed at Whiskers Wang on account of his ugly bewhiskered cheeks, but had never been scoffed at, much less beaten by him. And now, contrary to all expectations, Whiskers Wang had beaten him. Could it really be true, as they said in the market-place: "The Emperor has abolished the official examinations, so that scholars who have passed them are no longer in demand"? This must have undermined the Zhao family's prestige. Was this why people were treating him contemptuously too?

Ah Q stood there irresolutely.

From the distance approached another of Ah Q's enemies. This was Mr. Qian's eldest

去进洋学堂，不知怎么又跑到东洋去了，半年之后他回到家里来，腿也直了，辫子也不见了，他的母亲大哭了十几场，他的老婆跳了三回井。后来，他的母亲到处说，"这辫子是被坏人灌醉了酒剪去的。本来可以做大官，现在只好等留长再说了。"然而阿Q不肯信，偏称他"假洋鬼子"，也叫作"里通外国的人"，一见他，一定在肚子里暗暗的咒骂。

阿Q尤其"深恶而痛绝之"的，是他的一条假辫子。辫子而至于假，就是没有了做人的资格；他的老婆不跳第四回井，也不是好女人。

这"假洋鬼子"近来了。

"秃儿。驴……"阿Q历来本只在肚子里骂，没有出过声，这回因为正气忿，因为要报仇，便不由的轻轻的说出来了。

不料这秃儿却拿着一支黄漆的棍子——就是阿Q所谓哭丧棒——大踏步走了过来。阿Q在这刹那，便知道大约要打了，赶紧抽紧筋骨，耸了肩膀等候着，果然，拍的一声，似乎确凿打在自己头上了。

"我说他！"阿Q指着近旁的一个孩子，分辩说。

拍！拍拍！

在阿Q的记忆上，这大约要算是生平第二件的屈辱。幸而拍拍的响了之后，于他倒似乎完结了一件事，反而觉得轻松些，而且"忘却"这一件祖传的宝贝也发生了效力，他慢慢的走，将到酒店门口，早已有些高兴了。

但对面走来了静修庵里的小尼姑。阿Q便在平时，看见伊也一定要唾骂，而况在屈辱之后呢？他于是发生了回忆，又发生了敌忾了。

"我不知道我今天为什么这样晦气，原来就因为见了你！"他想。

他迎上去，大声的吐一口唾沫：

"咳，呸！"

小尼姑全不睬，低了头只是走。阿Q走近伊身旁，突

9. The stiff-legged stride of many foreigners led some Chinese to believe that their knees had no joints.

son whom Ah Q thoroughly despised. After studying in a foreign-style school in the city, it seemed he had gone to Japan. When he came home half a year later his legs were straight[9] and his queue had disappeared. His mother wept bitterly a dozen times, and his wife tried three times to jump into the well. Later his mother told everyone, "His queue was cut off by some scoundrel when he was drunk. By rights he ought to be a big official, but now he'll have to wait till it's grown again." Ah Q, however, did not believe this, and insisted on calling him a "Bogus Foreign Devil" or "Traitor in Foreign Pay." At sight of him he would start cursing under his breath.

What Ah Q despised and detested most in him was his false queue. When it came to having a false queue, a man could scarcely be considered human; and the fact that his wife had not attempted to jump into the well a fourth time showed that she was not a good woman either.

Now this "Bogus Foreign Devil" was approaching.

"Baldhead! Ass..." In the past Ah Q had just cursed under his breath, inaudibly; but today, because he was in a rage and itching for revenge, the words slipped out involuntarily.

Unfortunately this Baldhead was carrying a shiny brown cane which looked to Ah Q like the "staff carried by a mourner." With great strides he bore down on Ah Q who, guessing at once that a beating was in the offing, hastily flexed his muscles and hunched his shoulders in anticipation. Sure enough, *Thwack*! Something struck him on the head.

"I meant him!" explained Ah Q, pointing to a nearby child.

Thwack! Thwack! Thwack!

As far as Ah Q could remember, this was the second humiliation of his life. Fortunately after the thwacking stopped it seemed to him that the matter was closed, and he even felt somewhat relieved. Moreover, the precious "ability to forget" handed down by his ancestors stood him in good stead. He walked slowly away and by the time he approached the tavern door he was quite cheeful again.

Just then, however, a little nun from the Convent of Quiet Self-Improvement came walking towards him. The sight of a nun always made Ah Q swear; how much more so, then, after these humiliations? When he recalled what had happened, his anger flared up again.

"I couldn't think what made my luck so bad today — so it's meeting you that did it!" he fumed to himself.

Going towards her he spat noisily. "Ugh!... Pah!"

The little nun paid not the least attention but walked on with lowered head. Ah

然伸出手去摩着伊新剃的头皮，呆笑着，说：

"秃儿！快回去，和尚等着你……"

"你怎么动手动脚……"尼姑满脸通红的说，一面赶快走。

酒店里的人大笑了。阿Q看见自己的勋业得了赏识，便愈加兴高采烈起来：

"和尚动得，我动不得？"他扭住伊的面颊。

酒店里的人大笑了。阿Q更得意，而且为满足那些赏鉴家起见，再用力的一拧，才放手。

他这一战，早忘却了王胡，也忘却了假洋鬼子，似乎对于今天的一切"晦气"都报了仇；而且奇怪，又仿佛全身比拍拍的响了之后更轻松，飘飘然的似乎要飞去了。

"这断子绝孙的阿Q！"远远地听得小尼姑的带哭的声音。

"哈哈哈！"阿Q十分得意的笑。

"哈哈哈！"酒店里的人也九分得意的笑。

第四章　恋爱的悲剧

有人说：有些胜利者，愿意敌手如虎，如鹰，他才感得胜利的欢喜；假使如羊，如小鸡，他便反觉得胜利的无聊。又有些胜利者，当克服一切之后，看见死的死了，降的降了，"臣诚惶诚恐死罪死罪"，他于是没有了敌人，没有了对手，没有了朋友，只有自己在上，一个，孤另另，凄凉，寂寞，便反而感到了胜利的悲哀。然而我们的阿Q却没有这样乏，他是永远得意的：这或者也是中国精神文明冠于全球的一个证据了。

看哪，他飘飘然的似乎要飞去了！

然而这一次的胜利，却又使他有些异样。他飘飘然的飞了大半天，飘进土谷祠，照例应该躺下便打鼾。谁知道这一晚，他很不容易合眼，他觉得自己的大拇指和第二指有点古怪：仿佛比平常滑腻些。不知道是小尼姑的脸上有一点滑腻的东西粘在他指上，还是他的指头在小尼姑脸上

Q stepped up to her and shot out a hand to rub her newly shaved scalp, then with a guffaw cried, "Baldhead! Go back quick, your monk's waiting for you...."

"Who are you pawing?...."demanded the nun, flushing all over her face as she quickened her pace.

The men in the tavern roared with laughter. This appreciation of his feat added to Ah Q's elation.

"If the monk paws you, why can't I?" He pinched her cheek.

Again the men in the tavern roared with laughter. More bucked than ever, and eager to please his admirers, Ah Q pinched her hard again before letting her go.

This encounter had made him forget Whiskers Wang and the Bogus Foreign Devil, as if all the day's bad luck had been avenged. And strange to relate, even more completely relaxed than after the thwacking, he felt as if he were walking on air.

"Ah Q, may you die sonless!" wailed the little nun already some distance away.

Ah Q roared with delighted laugher.

The men in the tavern joined in, with only a shade less gusto in their laughter.

Chapter 4   The Tragedy of Love

There are said to be some victors who take no pleasure in a victory unless their opponents are as fierce as tigers or eagles: in the case of foes as timid as sheep or chickens they find their triumph empty. There are other victors who, having carried all before them, with the enemy slain or surrendered, utterly cowed, realize that now no foe, no rival, no friend is left — none but themselves, supreme, lonely, lost, and forlorn. Then they find their triumph a tragedy. But not so our hero: he was always exultant. This may be a proof of the moral supremacy of China over the rest of the world.

Look at Ah Q, elated as if he were walking on air!

This victory was not without strange consequences, though. For after walking on air for quite a time he floated into the Tutelary God's Temple, where he would normally have started snoring as soon as he lay down. This evening, however, he found it very hard to close his eyes, being struck by something odd about his thumb and first finger, which seemed to be smoother than usual. It is impossible to say whether something soft and smooth on the little nun's face had stuck to his fingers, or whether his fingers had been rubbed smooth against her cheek.

磨得滑腻了？……

　　"断子绝孙的阿Q！"

　　阿Q的耳朵里又听到这句话。他想：不错，应该有一个女人，断子绝孙便没有人供一碗饭，……应该有一个女人。夫"不孝有三无后为大"，而"若敖之鬼馁而"，也是一件人生的大哀，所以他那思想，其实是样样合于圣经贤传的，只可惜后来有些"不能收其放心"了。

　　"女人，女人！……"他想。

　　"……和尚动得……女人，女人！……女人！"他又想。

　　我们不能知道这晚上阿Q在什么时候才打鼾。但大约他从此总觉得指头有些滑腻，所以他从此总有些飘飘然；"女……"他想。

　　即此一端，我们便可以知道女人是害人的东西。

　　中国的男人，本来大半都可以做圣贤，可惜全被女人毁掉了。商是妲己闹亡的；周是褒姒弄坏的；秦……虽然史无明文，我们也假定他因为女人，大约未必十分错；而董卓可是的确给貂蝉害死了。

　　阿Q本来也是正人，我们虽然不知道他曾蒙什么明师指授过，但他对于"男女之大防"却历来非常严；也很有排斥异端——如小尼姑及假洋鬼子之类——的正气。他的学说是：凡尼姑，一定与和尚私通；一个女人在外面走，一定想引诱野男人；一男一女在那里讲话，一定要有勾当了。为惩治他们起见，所以他往往怒目而视，或者大声说几句"诛心"话，或者在冷僻处，便从后面掷一块小石头。

　　谁知道他将到"而立"之年，竟被小尼姑害得飘飘然了。这飘飘然的精神，在礼教上是不应该有的，——所以女人真可恶，假使小尼姑的脸上不滑腻，阿Q便不至于被蛊，又假使小尼姑的脸上盖一层布，阿Q便也不至于被蛊了，——他五六年前，曾在戏台下的人丛中拧过一个女人的大腿，但因为隔一层裤，所以此后并不飘飘然，——而小尼姑并不然，这也足见异端之可恶。

10. A quotation from *Mencius* (372-289 B.C.).

11. A quotation from the old classic *Zuo Zhuan*.

12. Da Ji, in the twelfth century B.C., was the concubine of last king of the Shang Dynasty. Bao Si, in the eight century B.C., was the concubine of the last king of the Western Zhou Dynasty. Diao Chan was the concubine of Dong Zhuo, a powerful warlord at the end of the Han Dynasty.

13. Confucius said that at thirty he "stood firm." The phrase was later used to indicate that a man was thirty years old.

"Ah Q, may you die sonless!"

These words sounded again in Ah Q's ears, and he thought, "Quite right, I should take a wife; for if a man dies sonless he has no one to sacrifice a bowl of rice to his spirit....I ought to have a wife." As the saying goes, "There are three forms of unfilial conduct, of which the worst is to have no descendants,[10]" and it is one of the tragedies of life that "spirits without descendants go hungry."[11] Thus his view was absolutely in accordance with the teachings of the saints and sages, and it is indeed a pity that later he should have run amok.

"Woman, woman!..." he thought.

"....The monk paws....Woman, woman!.... Woman!" He thought again."

We shall never know when Ah Q finally fell asleep that evening. After this, however, he probably always found his fingers rather soft and smooth, and always remained a little light-headed. "Woman..." he kept thinking.

From this we can see that woman is a menace to mankind.

The majority of Chinese men could become saints and sages, were it not for the unfortunate fact that they are ruined by women. The Shang Dynasty was destroyed by Da Ji, the Zhou Dynasty was undermined by Bao Si; as for the Qin Dynasty, although there is no historical evidence to that effect, if we assume that it fell no historical evidence to that effect, if we assume that it fell on account of some woman we shall probably not be far wrong. And it is a fact that Dong Zhuo's death was caused by Diao Chan.[12]

Ah Q, too, was a man of strict morals to begin with. Although we do not know whether he was guided by some good teacher, he had always shown himself most scrupulous in observing "strict segregation of the sexes," and was righteous enough to denounce such heretics as the little nun and the Bogus Foreign Devil. His view was, "All nuns must carry on in secret with monks. If a woman walks alone on the street, she must want to seduce bad men. When a man and a woman talk together, it must be to arrange to meet." In order to correct such people, he would glare furiously, pass loud, cutting remarks, or, if the place were deserted, throw a small stone from behind.

Who could tell that close on thirty, when a man should "stand firm,"[13] he would lose his head like this over a little nun? Such light-headedness, according to the classical canons, is most reprehensible; thus women certainly are hateful creature. For if the little nun's face had not been soft and smooth, Ah Q would not have been bewitched by her; nor would this have happened if the little nun's face had been covered by a cloth. Five or six years before, when watching an open-air opera, he had pinched the leg of a woman in the audience; but because it was separated from him by the cloth of her trousers he had not had this light-headed feeling afterwards. The little nun had not covered her face, however, and this is another proof of the odiousness of the heretic.

　　"女……"阿Q想。

　　他对于以为"一定想引诱野男人"的女人，时常留心看，然而伊并不对他笑。他对于和他讲话的女人，也时常留心听，然而伊又并不提起关于什么勾当的话来。哦，这也是女人可恶之一节：伊们全都要装"假正经"的。

　　这一天，阿Q在赵太爷家里春了一天米，吃过晚饭，便坐在厨房里吸旱烟。倘在别家，吃过晚饭本可以回去的了，但赵府上晚饭早，虽说定例不准掌灯，一吃完便睡觉，然而偶然也有一些例外：其一，是赵大爷未进秀才的时候，准其点灯读文章；其二，便是阿Q来做短工的时候，准其点灯春米。因为这一条例外，所以阿Q在动手春米之前，还坐在厨房里吸旱烟。

　　吴妈，是赵太爷家里唯一的女仆，洗完了碗碟，也就在长凳上坐下了，而且和阿Q谈闲天：

　　"太太两天没有吃饭哩，因为老爷要买一个小的……"

　　"女人……吴妈……这小孤孀……"阿Q想。

　　"我们的少奶奶是八月里要生孩子了……"

　　"女人……"阿Q想。

　　阿Q放下烟管，站了起来。

　　"我们的少奶奶……"吴妈还唠叨说。

　　"我和你困觉，我和你困觉！"阿Q忽然抢上去，对伊跪下了。

　　一刹时中很寂然。

　　"阿呀！"吴妈楞了一息，突然发抖，大叫着往外跑，且跑且嚷，似乎后来带哭了。

　　阿Q对了墙壁跪着也发楞，于是两手扶着空板凳，慢慢的站起来，仿佛觉得有些糟。他这时确也有些志忑了，慌张的将烟管插在裤带上，就想去春米。蓬的一声，头上着了很粗的一下，他急忙回转身去，那秀才便拿了一支大竹杠站在他面前。

　　"你反了，……你这……"

　　大竹杠又向他劈下来了。阿Q两手去抱头，拍的正打

"Woman...." thought Ah Q.

He kept a close watch on those women who he believed must "want to seduce men,"but they did not smile at him. He listened very carefully to those women who talked to him, but not one of them mentioned anything relevant to secret rendezvous. Ah! This was simply another example of the odiousness of women: they all assumed a false modesty.

One day when Ah Q was grinding rice in Mr. Zhao's house, he sat down in the kitchen after supper to smoke a pipe. If it had been anyone else's house, he could have gone home after supper, but they dined early in the Zhao family. Although it was the rule that you must not light a lamp but go to bed after eating, there were occasional exceptions to the rule. Before Mr. Zhao's son passed the county examination he was allowed to light a lamp to study the examination essays, and when Ah Q went to do odd jobs he was allowed to light a lamp to grind rice. Because of this latter exception to the rule. Ah Q still sat in the kitchen smoking before going on with his work.

When Amah Wu, the only maidservant in the Zhao household, had finished washing the dishes, she sat down on the long bench too and started chatting to Ah Q:

"Our mistress hasn't eaten anything for two days, because the master wants to get a concubine...."

"Woman....Amah Wu....this little widow," thought Ah Q.

"Our young mistress is going to have a baby in the eighth moon...."

"Woman...." thought Ah Q.

He put down his pipe and stood up.

"Our young mistress —" Amah Wu chattered on.

"Sleep with me!" Ah Q suddenly rushed forward and threw himself at her feet.

There was a moment of absolute silence.

"Aiya!" Dumbfounded for an instant, Amah Wu suddenly began to tremble, then rushed out shrieking and could soon be heard sobbing.

Ah Q kneeling opposite the wall was dumbfounded too. He grasped the empty bench with both hands and stood up slowly, dimly aware that something was wrong. In fact, by this time he was in rather a nervous state himself. In a flurry, he stuck his pipe into his belt and decided to go back to grind rice. But — *Bang*! — a heavy blow landed on his head, and he spun round to see the successful county candidate standing before him brandishing a big bamboo pole.

"How dare you...you...."

The big bamboo pole came down across Ah Q's shoulders. When he put up both hands

在指节上，这可很有一些痛。他冲出厨房门，仿佛背上又着了一下似的。

"忘八蛋！"秀才在后面用了官话这样骂。

阿Q奔入舂米场，一个人站着，还觉得指头痛，还记得"忘八蛋"，因为这话是未庄的乡下人从来不用，专是见过官府的阔人用的，所以格外怕，而印象也格外深。但这时，他那"女……"的思想却也没有了。而且打骂之后，似乎一件事也已经收束，倒反觉得一无挂碍似的，便动手去舂米。舂了一会，他热起来了，又歇了手脱衣服。

脱下衣服的时候，他听得外面很热闹，阿Q生平本来最爱看热闹，便即寻声走出去了。寻声渐渐的寻到赵太爷的内院里，虽然在昏黄中，却辨得出许多人，赵府一家连两日不吃饭的太太也在内，还有间壁的邹七嫂，真正本家的赵白眼，赵司晨。

少奶奶正拖着吴妈走出下房来，一面说：

"你到外面来，……不要躲在自己房里想……"

"谁不知道你正经，……短见是万万寻不得的。"邹七嫂也从旁说。

吴妈只是哭，夹些话，却不甚听得分明。

阿Q想："哼，有趣，这小孤孀不知道闹着什么玩意儿了？"他想打听，走近赵司晨的身边。这时他猛然间看见赵大爷向他奔来，而且手里捏着一支大竹杠。他看见这一支大竹杠，便猛然间悟到自己曾经被打，和这一场热闹似乎有点相关。他翻身便走，想逃回舂米场，不图这支竹杠阻了他的去路，于是他又翻身便走，自然而然的走出后门，不多工夫，已在土谷祠内了。

阿Q坐了一会，皮肤有些起粟，他觉得冷了，因为虽在春季，而夜间颇有余寒，尚不宜于赤膊。他也记得布衫留在赵家，但倘若去取，又深怕秀才的竹杠。然而地保进来了。

"阿Q，你的妈妈的！你连赵家的用人都调戏起来，简直是造反。害得我晚上没有觉睡，你的妈妈的！……"

to protect his head, the blow landed on his knuckles, causing him considerable pain. As he escaped through the kitchen door it seemed as if his back also received a blow.

"Turtle's egg!" shouted the successful candidate, cursing him in mandarin from behind.

Ah Q fled to the hulling-floor where he stood alone, his knuckles still aching and still remembering that "Turtle's egg!" because it was an expression never used by the Weizhuang villagers but only by the rich who had seen something of official life. This made it the more alarming, the more impressive. By now, however, all thought of "Woman...." had flown. After this cursing and beating it seemed as if something were done with, and quite light-heartedly he began to grind rice again. Soon this made him hot, and he stopped to take off his shirt.

While taking off his shirt he heard an uproar outside, and since Ah Q was all for excitement he went out in search of the sound. Step by step he traced it into Mr. Zhao's inner courtyard. Although it was dusk he could see many people there: all the Zhao family including the mistress who had not eaten for two days. In addition, their neighbour Mrs. Zou was there, as well as their relatives Zhao Baiyan and Zhao Sichen.

The young mistress was leading Amah Wu out of the servants' quarters, saying as she did so:

"Come outside...don't stay brooding in you own room."

"Everybody knows you are a good woman," put in Mrs. Zou from the side. "You mustn't think of committing suicide."

Amah Wu merely wailed, muttering something inaudible.

"This is interesting," thought Ah Q." What mischief can this little widow be up to?" Wanting to find out, he was approaching Zhao Sichen when suddenly he caught sight of Mr. Zhao's eldest son rushing towards him with, what was worse, the big bamboo pole in his hand. The sight of this big bamboo pole reminded him that he had been beaten by it, and he realized that apparently he was connected in some way with all this excitement. He turned and ran, hoping to escape to the hulling-floor, not foreseeing that the bamboo pole would cut off his retreat. When it did, he turned and ran in the other direction, leaving without further ado by the back gate. Soon he was back in the Tutelary God's Temple.

After Ah Q had been sitting down for a time, he broke out in goose-flesh and felt cold, because although it was spring the nights were still chilly and not suited to bare backs. He remembered that he had left his shirt in the Zhaos' house but was afraid that if he went to fetch it he might get another taste of the successful candidate's bamboo pole.

Then the bailiff came in.

"Curse you, Ah Q!" said the bailiff. "So you can't even keep your hands off the Zhao family servants, you rebel! You've made me lose my sleep, damn it!..."

如是云云的教训了一通，阿Q自然没有话。临末，因为在晚上，应该送地保加倍酒钱四百文，阿Q正没有现钱，便用一顶毡帽做抵押，并且订定了五条件：

一　明天用红烛——要一斤重的——一对，香一封，到赵府上去赔罪。

二　赵府上请道士祓除缢鬼，费用由阿Q负担。

三　阿Q从此不准踏进赵府的门槛。

四　吴妈此后倘有不测，惟阿Q是问。

五　阿Q不准再去索取工钱和布衫。

阿Q自然都答应了，可惜没有钱。幸而已经春天，棉被可以无用，便质了二千大钱，履行条约。赤膊磕头之后，居然还剩几文，他也不再赎毡帽，统统喝了酒。但赵家也并不烧香点烛，因为太太拜佛的时候可以用，留着了。那破布衫是大半做了少奶奶八月间生下来的孩子的衬尿布，那小半破烂的便都做了吴妈的鞋底。

第五章　生计问题

阿Q礼毕之后，仍旧回到土谷祠，太阳下去了，渐渐觉得世上有些古怪。他仔细一想，终于省悟过来：其原因盖在自己的赤膊。他记得破夹袄还在，便披在身上，躺倒了，待张开眼睛，原来太阳又已经照在西墙上头了。他坐起身，一面说道，"妈妈的……"

他起来之后，也仍旧在街上逛，虽然不比赤膊之有切肤之痛，却又渐渐的觉得世上有些古怪了。仿佛从这一天起，未庄的女人们忽然都怕了羞，伊们一见阿Q走来，便个个躲进门里去。甚而至于将近五十岁的邹七嫂，也跟着别人乱钻，而且将十一岁的女儿都叫进去了。阿Q很以为奇，而且想："这些东西忽然都学起小姐模样来了。这娼妇们……"

Under this torrent of abuse Ah Q naturally had nothing to say. Finally, since it was night-time, he had to pay the bailiff double: four hundred cash. Because he happened to have no ready money by him, he gave his felt hat as security, and agreed to the following five terms:

1. The next morning Ah Q must take a pair of red candles, weighing one pound each, and a bundle of incense sticks to the Zhao family to atone for his misdeeds.

2. Ah Q must pay for the Taoist priests whom the Zhao family had called to exorcize evil spirits.

3. Ah Q must never again set foot in the Zhao household.

4. If anything unfortunate should happen to Amah Wu, Ah Q must be held responsible.

5. Ah Q must not go back for his wages or shirt.

Ah Q naturally agreed to everything, but unfortunately he had no ready money. Luckily it was already spring, so it was possible to do without his padded quilt which he pawned for two thousand cash to comply with the terms stipulated. After kowtowing with bare back he still had a few cash left, but instead of using these to redeem his felt hat from the bailiff, he spent them all on drink.

Actually, the Zhao family burned neither the incense nor the candles, because these could be used when the mistress worshipped Buddha and were put aside for that purpose. Most of the ragged shirt was made into diapers for the baby which was born to the young mistress in the eighth moon, while the tattered remainder was used by Amah Wu to made shoe-soles.

Chapter 5   The Problem of Making a Living

After Ah Q had kowtowed and complied with the Zhao family's terms, he went back as ususl to the Tutelary God's Temple. The sun had gone down, and he began to feel that something was wrong. Careful thought led him to the conclusion that this was probably because his back was bare. Remembering that he still had a ragged lined jacket, he put it on and lay down, and when he opened his eyes again the sun was already shining on the top of the west wall. He sat up, saying, "Curse it!"

After getting up he loafed about the streets as usual, until he began to feel that something else was wrong, though this was not to be compared to the physical discomfort of a bare back. Apparently, from that day onwards all the women in Weizhuang fought shy of Ah Q: whenever they saw him coming they took refuge indoors. In fact, even Mrs. Zou who was nearing fifty retreated in confusion with the rest, calling her eleven-year-old daughter to go inside. This struck Ah Q as very strange.

但他更觉得世上有些古怪，却是许多日以后的事。其一，酒店不肯赊欠了；其二，管土谷祠的老头子说些废话，似乎叫他走；其三，他虽然记不清多少日，但确乎有许多日，没有一个人来叫他做短工。酒店不赊，熬着也罢了；老头子催他走，噜苏一通也就算了；只是没有人来叫他做短工，却使阿Q肚子饿：这委实是一件非常"妈妈的"的事情。

阿Q忍不下去了，他只好到老主顾的家里去探问，——但独不许踏进赵府的门槛，——然而情形也异样：一定走出一个男人来，现了十分烦厌的相貌，像回复乞丐一般的摇手道：

"没有没有！你出去！"

阿Q愈觉得稀奇了。他想，这些人家向来少不了要帮忙，不至于现在忽然都无事，这总该有些蹊跷在里面了。他留心打听，才知道他们有事都去叫小Don。这小D，是一个穷小子，又瘦又乏，在阿Q的眼睛里，位置是在王胡之下的，谁料这小子竟谋了他的饭碗去。所以阿Q这一气，更与平常不同，当气愤愤的走着的时候，忽然将手一扬，唱道：

"我手执钢鞭将你打！……"

几天之后，他竟在钱府的照壁前遇见了小D。"仇人相见分外眼明"，阿Q便迎上去，小D也站住了。

"畜生！"阿Q怒目而视的说，嘴角上飞出唾沫来。

"我是虫豸，好么？……"小D说。

这谦逊反使阿Q更加愤怒起来，但他手里没有钢鞭，于是只得扑上去，伸手去拔小D的辫子。小D一手护住了自己的辫根，一手也来拔阿Q的辫子，阿Q便也将空着的一只手护住了自己的辫根。从先前的阿Q看来，小D本来是不足齿数的，但他近来挨了饿，又瘦又乏已经不下于小D，所以便成了势均力敌的现象，四只手拔着两颗头，都弯了腰，在钱家粉墙上映出一个蓝色的虹形，至于半点钟之久了。

14. A line from *The Battle of the Dragon and the Tiger*, an opera popular in Shaoxing.

"The bitches!" he thought. "All of a sudden they're behaving like young ladies...."

A good many days later, however, he felt even more forcibly that something was wrong. First, the tavern refused him credit; secondly, the old man in charge of the Tutelary God's Temple made some uncalled-for remarks, as if he wanted Ah Q to leave; and thirdly, for many days — how many exactly he could not remember — not a soul had come to hire him. To be refused credit in the tavern he could put up with; if the old man kept urging him to leave, he could just ignore his complaints; but when no one came to hire him he had to go hungry, and this was really a "cursed" state to be in.

When Ah Q could stand it no longer he went to his former employers' homes to find out what was the matter — it was only Mr. Zhao's threshold that he was not allowed to cross. But he met with a strange reception. The one to appear was always a man looking thoroughly annoyed who waved him away as if he were a beggar, saying:

"There's nothing for you, get out!"

Ah Q found it more and more extraordinary. "These people always needed help in the past," he thought. "They can't suddenly have nothing to be done. This looks fishy." After making careful inquiries he found out that when they had any odd jobs they all called in Young D. Now this Young D was a thin and weakly pauper, even lower in Ah Q's eyes than Whiskers Wang. Who could have thought that this low fellow would steal his living from him? So this time Ah Q's indignation was greater than usual, and going on his way, fuming, he suddenly raised his arm and sang:

"*Steel mace in hand I shall trounce you....*"[14]

A few days later he did indeed meet Young D in front of Mr. Qian's house. "When two foes meet, there is no mistaking each other." As Ah Q advanced upon him, Young D stood his ground.

"Beast!" spluttered Ah Q, glaring.

"I'm an insect — will that do?" rejoined Young D.

Such modesty only enraged Ah Q even more, but since he had no steel mace in his hand all he could do was rush forward to grab at Young D's queue. Young D, protecting his own queue with one hand, grabbed at Ah Q's with the other, whereupon Ah Q also used his free hand to protect his own queue. In the past Ah Q had never considered Young D worth taking seriously, but owing to his recent privations he was now as thin and weak as his opponent, so that they presented a spectacle of evenly matched antagonists, four hands clutching at two heads, both men bending at the waist, casting a blue, rainbow-shaped shadow on the Qian family's white wall for over half an hour.

"好了，好了！"看的人们说，大约是解劝的。

"好，好！"看的人们说，不知道是解劝，是颂扬，还是煽动。

然而他们都不听。阿Q进三步，小D便退三步，都站着；小D进三步，阿Q便退三步，又都站着。大约半点钟，——未庄少有自鸣钟，所以很难说，或者二十分，——他们的头发里便都冒烟，额上便都流汗，阿Q的手放松了，在同一瞬间，小D的手也正放松了，同时直起，同时退开，都挤出人丛去。

"记着罢，妈妈的……"阿Q回过头去说。

"妈妈的，记着罢……"小D也回过头来说。

这一场"龙虎斗"似乎并无胜败，也不知道看的人可满足，都没有发什么议论，而阿Q却仍然没有人来叫他做短工。

有一日很温和，微风拂拂的颇有些夏意了，阿Q却觉得寒冷起来，但这还可担当，第一倒是肚子饿。棉被，毡帽，布衫，早已没有了，其次就卖了棉袄；现在有裤子，却万不可脱的；有破夹袄，又除了送人做鞋底之外，决定卖不出钱。他早想在路上拾得一注钱，但至今还没有见；他想在自己的破屋里忽然寻到一注钱，慌张的四顾，但屋内是空虚而且了然。于是他决计出门求食去了。

他在路上走着要"求食"，看见熟识的酒店，看见熟识的馒头，但他都走过了，不但没有暂停，而且并不想要。他所求的不是这类东西了；他求的是什么东西，他自己不知道。

未庄本不是大村镇，不多时便走尽了。村外多是水田，满眼是新秧的嫩绿，夹着几个圆形的活动的黑点，便是耕田的农夫。阿Q并不赏鉴这田家乐，却只是走，因为他直觉的知道这与他的"求食"之道是很辽远的。但他终于走到静修庵的墙外了。

"All right!" All right!" exclaimed some of the onlookers, probably by way of mediation.

"Good, good!" exclaimed others, but whether to mediate, applaud the fighters, or spur them on to further efforts, is not certain.

The two combatants turned deaf ears to them all, however. If Ah Q advanced three paces, Young D would recoil three paces, and there they would stand. If Young D advanced three paces, Ah Q would recoil three paces, and there they would stand again. After about half an hour — Weizhuang had few clocks, so it is difficult to tell the time; it may have been twenty minutes — when steam was rising from their heads and sweat pouring down their cheeks, Ah Q let fall his hands, and in the same second Young D's hands fell too. They straightened up simultaneously and stepped back simultaneously, pushing their way out through the crowd.

"Just you wait, curse you!" called Ah Q over his shoulder.

"Curse you!" Just you wait..." echoed Young D, also over his shoulder.

This epic struggle had apparently ended in neither victory nor defeat, and it is not known whether the spectators were satisfied or not, for none of them expressed any opinion. But still not a soul came to hire Ah Q for odd jobs.

One warm day, when a balmy breeze seemed to give some foretaste of summer, Ah Q actually felt cold; but he could put up with this — his greatest worry was an empty stomach. His cotton quilt, felt hat, and shirt had long since disappeared, and after that he had sold his padded jacket. Now nothing was left but his trousers, and these of course he could not take off. He had a ragged lined jacket, it is true; but this was certainly worthless, unless he gave it away to be made into shoe-soles. He had long been dreaming of finding some money on the road, but hitherto he had not come across any; he had also been hoping he might suddenly discover some money in his tumble-down room, and had frantically ransacked it, but the room was quite, quite empty. Then he made up his mind to go out in search of food.

As he walked along the road "in search of food" he saw the familiar tavern and the familiar steamed bread, but he passed them by without pausing for a second, without even hankering after them. It was not these he was looking for, although what exactly he was looking for he did not know himself.

Since Weizhuang was not a big place, he soon left it behind. Most of the country outside the village consisted of paddy fields, green as far as the eye could see with the tender shoots of young rice, dotted here and there with round black, moving objects — peasants cultivating their fields. But blind to the delights of country life, Ah Q simply went on his way, for he knew instinctively that this was far removed from his "search for food." Finally, however, he came to the walls of the Convent of Quiet Self-Improvement.

庵周围也是水田，粉墙突出在新绿里，后面的低土墙里是菜园。阿Q迟疑了一会，四面一看，并没有人。他便爬上这矮墙去，扯着何首乌藤，但泥土仍然簌簌的掉，阿Q的脚也索索的抖；终于攀着桑树枝，跳到里面了。里面真是郁郁葱葱，但似乎并没有黄酒馒头，以及此外可吃的之类。靠西墙是竹丛，下面许多笋，只可惜都是并未煮熟的，还有油菜早经结子，芥菜已将开花，小白菜也很老了。

阿Q仿佛文童落第似的觉得很冤屈，他慢慢走近园门去，忽而非常惊喜了，这分明是一畦老萝卜。他于是蹲下便拔，而门口突然伸出一个很圆的头来，又即缩回去了，这分明是小尼姑。小尼姑之流是阿Q本来视若草芥的，但世事须"退一步想"，所以他便赶紧拔起四个萝卜，拧下青叶，兜在大襟里。然而老尼姑已经出来了。

"阿弥陀佛，阿Q，你怎么跳进园里来偷萝卜！……阿呀，罪过呵，阿唷，阿弥陀佛！……"

"我什么时候跳进你的园里来偷萝卜？"阿Q且看且走的说。

"现在……这不是？"老尼姑指着他的衣兜。

"这是你的？你能叫得他答应你么？你……"

阿Q没有说完话，拔步便跑；追来的是一匹很肥大的黑狗。这本来在前门的，不知怎的到后园来了。黑狗哼而且追，已经要咬着阿Q的腿，幸而从衣兜里落下一个萝卜来，那狗给一吓，略略一停，阿Q已经爬上桑树，跨到土墙，连人和萝卜都滚出墙外面了。只剩着黑狗还在对着桑树嗥，老尼姑念着佛。

阿Q怕尼姑又放出黑狗来，拾起萝卜便走，沿路又检了几块小石头，但黑狗却并不再出现。阿Q于是抛了石块，一面走一面吃，而且想道，这里也没有什么东西寻，不如进城去……

待三个萝卜吃完时，他已经打定了进城的主意了。

The convent too was surrounded by paddy fields, its white walls standing out sharply in the fresh green, and inside the low earthen wall at the back was a vegetable garden. Ah Q hesitated for a time, looking around him. Since there was no one in sight he scrambled on to the low wall, holding on to some milkwort. The mud wall started crumbling, and Ah Q shook with fear; however, by clutching at the branch of a mulberry tree he managed to jump over it. Within was a wild profusion of vegetation, but no sign of yellow wine, steamed bread, or anything edible. A clump of bamboos by the west wall had put forth many young shoots, but unfortunately these were not cooked. There was also rape which had long since gone to seed, mustard already about to flower, and some tough old cabbages.

Resentful as a scholar who has failed the examinations Ah Q walked slowly towards the gate of the garden. Suddenly, however, he gave a start of joy, for what did he see there but a patch of turnips! He knelt down and had just begun pulling when a round head appeared from behind the gate, only to be promptly withdrawn. This was no other than the little nun. Now though Ah Q had always had the greatest contempt for such people as little nuns, there are times when "Discretion is the better part of valour." He hastily pulled up four turnips, tore off the leaves, and stuffed them under his jacket. By this time an old nun had already come out.

"May Buddha preserve us, Ah Q! How dare you climb into our garden to steal turnips!... Mercy on us, what a wicked thing to do! Aiya, Buddha preserve us!"

"When did I ever climb into your garden and steal turnips?" retorted Ah Q as he started off, keeping his eyes on her.

"Now — aren't you?" The old nun pointed at the bulge in his jacket.

"Are these yours? Will they come when you call? You...."

"Leaving his sentence unfinished, Ah Q took to his heels as fast as he could, followed by a huge fat black dog. Originally this dog had been at the front gate, and how it reached the back garden was a mystery. With a snarl the black dog gave chase and was just about to bite Ah Q's leg when most opportunely a turnip fell from his jacket, and the dog, taken by surprise, stopped for a second. During this time Ah Q scrambled up the mulberry tree, scaled the mud wall, and fell, turnips and all, outside the convent. He left the black dog still barking by the mulberry tree, and the old nun saying her prayers.

Fearing that the nun would let the black dog out again, Ah Q gathered together his turnips and ran, picking up a few small stones as he went. But the black dog did not reappear. Ah Q threw away the stones and walked on, eating as he went, thinking to himself, "There is nothing to be had here: better go to town...."

By the time the third turnip was finished he had made up his mind to go to town.

第六章　从中兴到末路

在未庄再看见阿Q出现的时候，是刚过了这年的中秋。人们都惊异，说是阿Q回来了，于是又回上去想道，他先前那里去了呢？阿Q前几回的上城，大抵早就兴高采烈的对人说，但这一次却并不，所以也没有一个人留心到。他或者也曾告诉过管土谷祠的老头子，然而未庄老例，只有赵太爷钱太爷和秀才大爷上城才算一件事。假洋鬼子尚且不足数，何况是阿Q：因此老头子也就不替他宣传，而未庄的社会上也就无从知道了。

但阿Q这回的回来，却与先前大不同，确乎很值得惊异。天色将黑，他睡眼蒙胧的在酒店门前出现了，他走近柜台，从腰间伸出手来，满把是银的和铜的，在柜上一扔说，"现钱！打酒来！"穿的是新夹袄，看去腰间还挂着一个大搭连，沉钿钿的将裤带坠成了很弯很弯的弧线。未庄老例，看见略有些醒目的人物，是与其慢也宁敬的，现在虽然明知道是阿Q，但因为和破夹袄的阿Q有些两样了，古人云，"士别三日便当刮目相待"，所以堂倌，掌柜，酒客，路人，便自然显出一种疑而且敬的形态来。掌柜既先之以点头，又继之以谈话：

"嚄，阿Q，你回来了！"

"回来了。"

"发财发财，你是——在……"

"上城去了！"

这一件新闻，第二天便传遍了全未庄。人人都愿意知道现钱和新夹袄的阿Q的中兴史，所以在酒店里，茶馆里，庙檐下，便渐渐的探听出来了。这结果，是阿Q得了新敬畏。

据阿Q说，他是在举人老爷家里帮忙。这一节，听的人都肃然了。这老爷本姓白，但因为合城里只有他一个举人，所以不必再冠姓，说起举人来就是他。这也不独在未庄是如此，便是一百里方圆之内也都如此，人们几乎多以

Chapter 6   From Resurgence to Decline

Weizhuang did not see Ah Q again till just after the Moon Festival that year. Everybody was surprised to hear of his return, and this made them think back and wonder where he had been all that time. In the past Ah Q had usually taken great pleasure in announcing his few visits to town; but since he had not done so this time, his going had passed unnoticed. He may have told the old man in charge of the Tutelary God's Temple, but according to the custom of Weizhuang only a trip to town counted as important. Even the Bogus Foreign Devil's going was not talked about, much less Ah Q's. This would explain why the old man had not spread the news for him, with the result that the villagers remained in the dark.

Ah Q's return this time was very different from before, and in fact quite enough to occasion astonishment. The day was growing dark when he showed up, bleary-eyed, at the tavern door, walked up to the counter, and tossed down on it a handful of silver and coppers produced from his belt."Cash! "he announced. "Bring the wine!" He was wearing a new lined jacket and at his waist hung a large purse, the great weight of which caused his belt to sharp in a sharp curve.

It was the custom in Weizhuang that anyone in any way unusual should be treated with respect rather than disregarded, and now, although they knew quite well that this was Ah Q, still he was very different from the Ah Q of the ragged coat. The ancients say, "A scholar who has been away three days must be looked at with new eyes." So the waiter, tavern-keeper, customers and passers-by all quite naturally expressed a kind of suspicion mingled with respect. The tavern-keeper started off by nodding, following this up with the words:

"So you're back, Ah Q!"

"Yes, I'm back."

"Made a pretty packet, eh?...where...?"

"I've been in town."

By the next day this piece of news had spread through Weizhuang. And since everybody wanted to hear the success story of this Ah Q of the ready money and the new lined jacket, in the tavern, teahouse, and under the temple eaves, the villagers gradually ferreted out the news. The result was that they began to treat Ah Q with a new deference.

According to Ah Q, he had been a servant in the house of a successful provincial candidate. This part of the story filled all who heard it with awe. This successful provincial candidate was named Bai, but because he was the only successful provincial candidate in the whole town there was no need to use his surname: Whenever anyone spoke of the successful provincial candidate, it meant him. And this was so not only in Weizhuang, for almost everyone within a radius of a hundred li imagined his name to be Mr. Successful Provincial

为他的姓名就叫举人老爷的了。在这人的府上帮忙，那当然是可敬的。但据阿Q又说，他却不高兴再帮忙了，因为这举人老爷实在太"妈妈的"了。这一节，听的人都叹息而且快意，因为阿Q本不配在举人老爷家里帮忙，而不帮忙是可惜的。

据阿Q说，他的回来，似乎也由于不满意城里人，这就在他们将长凳称为条凳，而且煎鱼用葱丝，加以最近观察所得的缺点，是女人的走路也扭得不很好。然而也偶有大可佩服的地方，即如未庄的乡下人不过打三十二张的竹牌，只有假洋鬼子能够叉"麻酱"，城里却连小乌龟子都叉得精熟的。什么假洋鬼子，只要放在城里的十几岁的小乌龟子的手里，也就立刻是"小鬼见阎王"。这一节，听的人都赧然了。

"你们可看见过杀头么？"阿Q说，"咳，好看。杀革命党。唉，好看好看，……"他摇摇头，将唾沫飞在正对面的赵司晨的脸上。这一节，听的人都凛然了。但阿Q又四面一看，忽然扬起右手，照着伸长脖子听得出神的王胡的后项窝上直劈下去道：

"嚓！"

王胡惊得一跳，同时电光石火似的赶快缩了头，而听的人又都悚然而且欣然了。从此王胡瘟头瘟脑的许多日，并且再不敢走近阿Q的身边；别的人也一样。

阿Q这时在未庄人眼睛里的地位，虽不敢说超过赵太爷，但谓之差不多，大约也就没有什么语病的了。

然而不多久，这阿Q的大名忽又传遍了未庄的闺中。虽然未庄只有钱赵两姓是大屋，此外十之九都是浅闺，但闺中究竟是闺中，所以也算得一件神异。女人们见面时一定说，邹七嫂在阿Q那里买了一条蓝绸裙，旧固然是旧的，但只化了九角钱。还有赵白眼的母亲，——说是赵司晨的母亲，待考，——也买了一件孩子穿的大红洋纱衫，七成新，只用三百大钱九二串。于是伊们都眼巴巴的

Candidate. To have worked in the household of such a man naturally called for respect; but according to Ah Q's further statements, he was unwilling to go on working there because this successful candidate was really too much of a "turtle's egg." This part of the story made all who heard it sigh, but with a sense of pleasure, because it showed that Ah Q was unworthy to work in the household of such a man, yet not to work there was a pity.

According to Ah Q, his return was also due to his dissatisfaction with the townspeople because they called a long bench a straight bench, used shredded shallots to fry fish, and — a defect he had recently discovered — the women did not sway in a very satisfactory manner as they walked. However, the town had its good points too; for instance, in Weizhuang everyone played with thirty-two bamboo counters and only the Bogus Foreign Devil could play mahjong, but in town even the street urchins excelled at mahjong. You had only to place the Bogus Foreign Devil in the hands of these young rascals in their teens for him straightway to become like "a small devil before the King of Hell." This part of the story made all who heard it blush.

"Have you seen an execution?" asked Ah Q. "Ah, that's a fine sight....When they execute the revolutionaries.... Ah, that's a fine sight, a fine sight...." He shook his head, sending his spittle flying onto the face of Zhao Sichen who was standing opposite him. This part of the story made all who heard it tremble. Then with a glance around, he suddenly raised his right hand and dropped it on the neck of Whiskers Wang who, craning forward, was listening with rapt attention

"Off with his head!" shouted Ah Q.

Whiskers Wang gave a start, and jerked back his head as fast as lightning or a spark struck from a flint, while the bystanders shivered with pleasurable apprehension. After this, Whiskers Wang went about in a daze for many days and dared not go near Ah Q, nor did the others.

Although we cannot say that in the eyes of the inhabitants of Weizhuang Ah Q's status at this time was suprior to that of Mr. Zhao, we can at least affirm without any danger of inaccuracy that it was approximately equivalent.

Not long after, Ah Q's fame suddenly spread into the women's apartments of Weizhuang too. Although the only two families of any pretensions in Weizhuang were those of Qian and Zhao, and nine-tenths of the rest were poor, still women's apartments are women's apartments, and the way Ah Q's fame spread into them was quite miraculous. When the womenfolk met they would say to each other, "Mrs. Zou bought a blue silk skirt from Ah Q. Although it was old, it only cost ninety cents. And Zhao Baiyan's mother (this has yet to be verified, because some say it was Zhao Sichen's mother) bought a child's costume of crimson foreign calico which was nearly new for

想见阿Q，缺绸裙的想问他买绸裙，要洋纱衫的想问他买洋纱衫，不但见了不逃避，有时阿Q已经走过了，也还要追上去叫住他，问道：

"阿Q，你还有绸裙么？没有？纱衫也要的，有罢？"

后来这终于从浅闺传进深闺里去了。因为邹七嫂得意之余，将伊的绸裙请赵太太去鉴赏，赵太太又告诉了赵太爷而且着实恭维了一番。赵太爷便在晚饭桌上，和秀才大爷讨论，以为阿Q实在有些古怪，我们门窗应该小心些；但他的东西，不知道可还有什么可买，也许有点好东西罢。加以赵太太也正想买一件价廉物美的皮背心。于是家族决议，便托邹七嫂即刻去寻阿Q，而且为此新辟了第三种的例外：这晚上也姑且特准点油灯。

油灯干了不少了，阿Q还不到。赵府的全眷都很焦急，打着呵欠，或恨阿Q太飘忽，或怨邹七嫂不上紧。赵太太还怕他因为春天的条件不敢来，而赵太爷以为不足虑：因为这是"我"去叫他的。果然，到底赵太爷有见识，阿Q终于跟着邹七嫂进来了。

"他只说没有没有，我说你自己当面说去，他还要说，我说……"邹七嫂气喘吁吁的走着说。

"太爷！"阿Q似笑非笑的叫了一声，在檐下站住了。

"阿Q，听说你在外面发财，"赵太爷踱开去，眼睛打量着他的全身，一面说。"那很好，那很好的。这个，……听说你有些旧东西，……可以都拿来看一看，……这也并不是别的，因为我倒要……"

"我对邹七嫂说过了。都完了。"

"完了？"赵太爷不觉失声的说，"那里会完得这样快呢？"

"那是朋友的，本来不多。他们买了些，……"

"总该还有一点罢。"

"现在，只剩了一张门幕了。"

"就拿门幕来看看罢。"赵太太慌忙说。

"那么，明天拿来就是，"赵太爷却不甚热心了。

only three hundred cash, less eight per cent discount."

Then those who had no silk skirt or needed foreign calico were most anxious to see Ah Q in order to buy from him. Far from avoiding him now, they sometimes followed him when he passed, calling to him to stop.

"Ah Q, have you any more silk skirts?" they would ask. "No? We want foreign calico too. Do you have any?"

This news later spread from the poor households to the rich ones, because Mrs. Zou was so pleased with her silk skirt that she took it to Mrs. Zhao for her approval, and Mrs. Zhao told Mr. Zhao, speaking very highly of it.

Mr. Zhao discussed the matter that evening at dinner with his son the successful county candidate, suggesting that there was certainly something strange about Ah Q and that they should be more careful about their doors and windows. They did not know, though, what if anything Ah Q had left — he might still have something good. Since Mrs. Zhao happened to want a good cheap fur jacket, after a family council it was decided to ask Mrs. Zou to find Ah Q for them at once. For this a third exception was made to the rule, special permission being given that evening for a lamp to be lit.

A considerable amount of oil had been burned, but still there was no sign of Ah Q. The whole Zhao household was yawning with impatience, some of them resenting Ah Q's casualness, others blaming Mrs. Zou for not making a greater effort. Mrs. Zhao was afraid that Ah Q dared not come because of the terms agreed upon that spring, but Mr. Zhao did not think this anything to worry about because, as he said, "This time I sent for him." Sure enough, Mr. Zhao proved himself a man of insight, for Ah Q finally arrived with Mrs. Zou.

"He keeps saying he has nothing left," panted Mrs. Zou as she came in. "When I told him to come and tell you so himself he kept talking back. I told him...."

"Sir!" cried Ah Q with an attempt at a smile, coming to a halt under the eaves.

"I hear you did well for yourself in town, Ah Q," said Mr. Zhao, going up to him and looking him over carefully. "Very good. Now...they say you have some old things....Bring them all here for us to look at. This is simply because I happen to want...."

"I told Mrs. Zou — there's nothing left."

"Nothing left?" Mr. Zhao could not help sounding disappointed. "How could they go so quickly?"

"They belonged to a friend, and there wasn't much to begin with. People bought some...."

"There must be something left."

"Only a door curtain."

"Then bring the door curtain for us to see," said Mrs. Zhao hurriedly.

"Well, tomorrow will do," said Mr. Zhao without much enthusiasm. "When you

“阿Q，你以后有什么东西的时候，你尽先送来给我们看，……”

“价钱决不会比别家出得少！”秀才说。秀才娘子忙一瞥阿Q的脸，看他感动了没有。

“我要一件皮背心。”赵太太说。

阿Q虽然答应着，却懒洋洋的出去了，也不知道他是否放在心上。这使赵太爷很失望，气愤而且担心，至于停止了打呵欠。秀才对于阿Q的态度也很不平，于是说，这忘八蛋要提防，或者竟不如吩咐地保，不许他住在未庄。但赵太爷以为不然，说这也怕要结怨，况且做这路生意的大概是“老鹰不吃窝下食”，本村倒不必担心的；只要自己夜里警醒点就是了。秀才听了这“庭训”，非常之以为然，便即刻撤消了驱逐阿Q的提议，而且叮嘱邹七嫂，请伊万不要向人提起这一段话。

但第二日，邹七嫂便将那蓝裙去染了皂，又将阿Q可疑之点传扬出去了，可是确没有提起秀才要驱逐他这一节。然而这已经于阿Q很不利。最先，地保寻上门了，取了他的门幕去，阿Q说是赵太太要看的，而地保也不还，并且要议定每月的孝敬钱。其次，是村人对于他的敬畏忽而变相了，虽然还不敢来放肆，却很有远避的神情，而这神情和先前的防他来“嚓”的时候又不同，颇混着“敬而远之”的分子了。

只有一班闲人们却还要寻根究底的去探阿Q的底细。阿Q也并不讳饰，傲然的说出他的经验来。从此他们才知道，他不过是一个小脚色，不但不能上墙，并且不能进洞，只站在洞外接东西。有一夜，他刚才接到一个包，正手再进去，不一会，只听得里面大嚷起来，他便赶紧跑，连夜爬出城，逃回未庄来了，从此不敢再去做。然而这故事却于阿Q更不利，村人对于阿Q的“敬而远之”者，本因为怕结怨，谁料他不过是一个不敢再偷的偷儿呢？这实在是“斯亦不足畏也矣”。

have anything in future, Ah Q, you must bring it us first...."

"We certainly won't pay less than other people!" said the successful county candidate. His wife shot a hasty glance at Ah Q to see his reaction.

"I need a fur jacket, " said Mrs. Zhao.

Althorgh Ah Q agreed, he slouched out so carelessly that they did not know whether he had taken their instructions to heart or not. This so disappointed, annoyed and worried Mr. Zhao that he even stopped yawning. The successful candidate was also far from satisfied with Ah Q's attitude. "People should be on their guard against such a turtle's egg," he said. "It might be best to order the bailiff to forbid him to live in Weizhuang."

Mr. Zhao did not agree, saying that then Ah Q might bear a grudge, and that in a business like this it was probably a case of "the eagle does not prey on its own nest": his own village need not worry so long as they were a little more watchful at night. The successful candidate, much impressed by this parental instruction, immediately withdrew his proposal for banishing Ah Q but cautioned Mrs. Zou on no account to repeat what had been said.

The next day, however, when Mrs. Zou took her blue skirt to be dyed black she repeated these insinuations about Ah Q, although not actually mentioning what the successful candidate had said about driving him away. Even so, it was most damaging to Ah Q. In the first place, the bailiff appeared at his door and took away the door curtain. Although Ah Q protested that Mrs. Zhao wanted to see it, the bailiff would not give it back and even demanded monthly hush money. In the second place, the villagers' respect for Ah Q suddenly changed. Although they still dared not take liberties, from their previous fear of his "Off with his head!" it closely resembled the attitude of the ancients to spirits: they kept a respectul distance.

Some idlers who wanted to get to the bottom of the business went to question Ah Q carefully. And with no attempt at concealment Ah Q told them proudly of his experiences. They learned that he had merely been a petty thief, not only unable to climb walls but even unable to go through openings: he simply stood outside an opening to receive the stolen goods.

One night he had just received a package and his chief had gone in again, when he heard a great uproar inside and took to his heels as fast as he could. He fled from the town that same night, back to Weizhuang; and after this he dared not return to do any more thieving. This story, however, was even more damaging to Ah Q, since the villagers had been keeping a respectful distance because they did not want to incur his enmity; for who could have guessed that he was only a thief who dared not steal again? Now they knew he was really too low to inspire fear.

第七章　革命

宣统三年九月十四日——即阿Q将搭连卖给赵白眼的这一天——三更四点，有一只大乌蓬船到了赵府上的河埠头。这船从黑魆魆中荡来，乡下人睡得熟，都没有知道；出去时将近黎明，却很有几个看见的了。据探头探脑的调查来的结果，知道那竟是举人老爷的船！

那船便将大不安载给了未庄，不到正午，全村的人心就很摇动。船的使命，赵家本来是很秘密的，但茶坊酒肆里却都说，革命党要进城，举人老爷到我们乡下来逃难了。惟有邹七嫂不以为然，说那不过是几口破衣箱，举人老爷想来寄存的，却已被赵太爷回复转去。其实举人老爷和赵秀才素不相能，在理本不能有"共患难"的情谊，况且邹七嫂又和赵家是邻居，见闻较为切近，所以大概该是伊对的。

然而谣言很旺盛，说举人老爷虽然似乎没有亲到，却有一封长信，和赵家排了"转折亲"。赵太爷肚里一轮，觉得于他总不会有坏处，便将箱子留下了，现就塞在太太的床底下。至于革命党，有的说是便在这一夜进了城，个个白盔白甲：穿着崇正皇帝的素。

阿Q的耳朵里，本来早听到过革命党这一句话，今年又亲眼见过杀掉革命党。但他有一种不知从那里来的意见，以为革命党便是造反，造反便是与他为难，所以一向是"深恶而痛绝之"的。殊不料这却使百里闻名的举人老爷有这样怕，于是他未免也有些"神往"了，况且未庄的一群鸟男女的慌张的神情，也使阿Q更快意。

"革命也好罢，"阿Q想，"革这伙妈妈的的命，太可恶！太可恨！……便是我，也要投降革命党了。"

阿Q近来用度窘，大约略略有些不平；加以午间喝了两碗空肚酒，愈加醉得快，一面想一面走，便又飘飘然起

15. Novermber 4, 1911, the day on which Shaoxing was freed in the 1911 Revolution.

16. Chong Zhen, the last emperor of the Ming Dynasty, reigned from 1628 to 1644. He hanged himself before the insurgent peasant army under Li Zicheng entered Beijing.

Chapter 7   The Revolution

On the fourteenth day of the ninth moon of the third year in the reign of Emperor Xuan Tong[15] — the day on which Ah Q sold his purse to Zhao Baiyan — at midnight, after the fourth stroke of the third watch, a large boat with a big black awning arrived at the Zhao family's landing-place. This boat floated up in the darkness while the villagers were sound asleep, so that they knew nothing about it; but it left again about dawn, when quite a number of people saw it. Investigation revealed that this boat actually belonged to the successful provincial candidate!

This incident caused great uneasiness in Weizhuang, and before midday the hearts of all the villagers were beating faster. The Zhao family kept very quiet about the errand of the boat, but according to gossip in the teahouse and tavern, the revolutionaries were going to enter the town and the successful provincial candidate had come to the country to take refuge. Mrs. Zou alone thought otherwise, maintaining that the successful candidate merely wanted to deposit a few battered cases in Weizhuang, but that Mrs. Zhao had sent them back. Actually the successful provincial candidate and the successful country dandidate in the Zhao family were not on good terms, so that it was scarcely logical to expect them to prove friends in adversity; moreover, since Mrs. Zou was a neighbour of the Zhao family and had a better idea of what was going on, she ought to have known.

Then a rumour spread to the effect that although the scholar had not come in person, he had sent a long letter tracing some distant relationship with the Zhao family; and since Mr. Zhao after thinking it over had decided it could after all do him no harm to keep the cases, they were now stowed under his wife's bed. As for the revolutionaries, some people said they had entered the town that night in white helments and white armour — in mourning for Emperor Chong Zhen.[16]

Ah Q had long since known of revolutionaries and this year with his own eyes had seen revolutionaries decapitated. But since it had occurred to him that the revolutionaries were rebels and that a rebellion would make things difficult for him, he had always detested and kept away from them. Who could have guessed that they could strike such fear into a successful provincial candidate renowned for a hundred li around? In consequence, Ah Q could not help feeling rather fascinated, the terror of all the villagers only adding to his delight.

"Revolution is not a bad thing," thought Ah Q. "Finish off the whole lot of them...curse them!... I'd like to go over to the revolutionaries myself."

Ah Q had been hard up recently, which no doubt made him rather dissatisfied; moreover he had drunk two bowls of wine at noon on an empty stomach. Consequently he became

来。不知怎么一来，忽而似乎革命党便是自己，未庄人却都是他的俘虏了。他得意之余，禁不住大声的嚷道：

"造反了！造反了！"

未庄人都用了惊惧的眼光对他看。这一种可怜的眼光，是阿Q从来没有见过的，一见之下，又使他舒服得如六月里喝了雪水。他更加高兴的走而且喊道：

"好，……我要什么就是什么，我欢喜谁就是谁。

得得，锵锵！

悔不该，酒醉错斩了郑贤弟，

悔不该，呀呀呀……

得得，锵锵，得，锵令锵！

我手执钢鞭将你打……"

赵府上的两位男人和两个真本家，也正站在大门口论革命。阿Q没有见，昂了头直唱过去。

"得得，……"

"老Q，"赵太爷怯怯的迎着低声的叫。

"锵锵，"阿Q料不到他的名字会和"老"字联结起来，以为是一句别的话，与己无干，只是唱。"得，锵，锵令锵，锵！"

"老Q。"

"悔不该……"

"阿Q！"秀才只得直呼其名了。

阿Q这才站住，歪着头问道，"什么？"

"老Q，……现在……"赵太爷却又没有话，"现在……发财么？"

"发财？自然。要什么就是什么……"

"阿……Q哥，像我们这样穷朋友是不要紧的……"赵白眼惴惴的说，似乎想探革命党的口风。

"穷朋友？你总比我有钱。"阿Q说着自去了。

大家都怃然，没有话。赵太爷父子回家，晚上商量到点灯。赵白眼回家，便从腰间扯下搭连来，交给他女人藏在箱底里。

drunk very quickly; and as he walked along thinking to himself, he seemed again to be treading on air. Suddenly, in some curious way, he felt as if he were a revolutionary and all the people in Weizhuang were his captives. Unable to contain himself for joy, he shouted at the top of his voice:

"Rebellion! Rebellion!"

All the villagers stared at him in consternation. Ah Q had never seen such pitiful looks before; they refreshed him as much as a drink of iced water in summer. So he walked on even more happily, shouting:

"Fine!...I shall take what I want! I shall like whom I please!

"*Tra la tra la*!

Alas, in my cups I have slain my sworn brother Zheng.

Alas, ya-ya-ya...

Tra la, tra la, tum ti tum tum!

Steel mace in hand I shall trounce you."

Mr. Zhao and his son were standing at their gate with two relatives discussing the revolution. Ah Q did not see them as he passed with his head thrown back, singing, "*Tra la la, tum ti tum!*"

"Q, old fellow!" called Mr. Zhao timidly in a low voice.

"*Tra la,*" sang Ah Q, unable to imagine that his name could be linked with those words "old fellow." Sure that he had heard wrongly and was in no way concerned, he simply went on singing, "*Tra la la, tum ti tum!*"

"Q, old fellow!"

"*Alas, in my cups....*"

"Ah, Q! The successful candidate had no choice but to name him outright.

Only then did Ah Q come to a stop. "Well?" he asked with his head on one side.

"Q, old fellow...now...." But Mr. Zhao was at a loss for words again. "Are you well off now?"

"Ah Q, old man, poor friends of yours like us are of no consequence..." faltered Zhao Baiyan, as if sounding out the revolutionaries' attitude.

"Poor friends? You're richer anyway than I am." With this Ah Q walked away.

This left them in speechless dismay. Back home that evening Mr. Zhao and his son discussed the question until it was time to light the lamps. And Zhao Baiyan once home took the purse from his waist and gave it to his wife to hide for him at the bottom of a chest.

阿Q飘飘然的飞了一通，回到土谷祠，酒已经醒透了。这晚上，管祠的老头子也意外的和气，请他喝茶；阿Q便向他要了两个饼，吃完之后，又要了一支点过的四两烛和一个树烛台，点起来，独自躺在自己的小屋里。他说不出的新鲜而且高兴，烛火像元夜似的闪闪的跳，他的思想也迸跳起来了：

"造反？有趣，……来了一阵白盔白甲的革命党，都拿着板刀，钢鞭，炸弹，洋炮，三尖两刃刀，钩镰枪，走过土谷祠，叫道，'阿Q！同去同去！'于是一同去。……

"这时未庄的一伙鸟男女才好笑哩，跪下叫道，'阿Q，饶命！'谁听他！第一个该死的是小D和赵太爷，还有秀才，还有假洋鬼子，……留几条么？王胡本来还可留，但也不要了。……

"东西，……直走进去打开箱子来：元宝，洋钱，洋纱衫，……秀才娘子的一张宁式床先搬到土谷祠，此外便摆了钱家的桌椅，——或者也就用赵家的罢。自己是不动手的了，叫小D来搬，要搬得快，搬得不快打嘴巴。……

"赵司晨的妹子真丑。邹七嫂的女儿过几年再说。假洋鬼子的老婆会和没有辫子的男人睡觉，吓，不是好东西！秀才的老婆是眼胞上有疤的。……吴妈长久不见了，不知道在那里，——可惜脚太大。"

阿Q没有想得十分停当，已经发了鼾声，四两烛还只点去了小半寸，红焰焰的光照着他张开的嘴。

"荷荷！"阿Q忽而大叫起来，抬了头仓皇的四顾，待到看见四两烛，却又倒头睡去了。

第二天他起得很迟，走出街上看时，样样都照旧。他也仍然肚饿，他想着，想不起什么来；但他忽而似乎有了主意了，慢慢的跨开步，有意无意的走到静修庵。

For a while Ah Q walked upon air, but by the time he reached the Tutelary God's Temple he had come down to earth again. That evening the old man in charge of the temple was also unexpectedly friendly and offered him tea. Then Ah Q asked him for two flat cakes, and after eating these damanded a four-ounce candle that had been lighted once and a candlestick. He lit the candle and lay down alone in his little room feeling inexpressibly refreshed and happy, while the candlelight leaped and flickered as if this were the Lantern Festival and his imagination soared with it.

"Revolt? It would be fine.... A troop of revolutionaries would come, all in white helmets and white armour, with swords, steel maces, bombs, foreign guns, sharp-pointed double-edged knives, and spears with hooks. When they passed this temple they would call out, 'Ah Q! Come along with us!' And then I would go with them....

"Then the fun would start. All the villagers, the whole lousy lot, would kneel down and plead, 'Ah Q! Spare us!' But who would listen to them! The first to die would be Young D and Mr. Zhao, then the successful country candidate and the Bogus Foreign Devil.... But perhaps I would spare a few. I would once have spared Whiskers Wang, but now I don't even want him....

"Things...I would go straight in and open the cases: silver ingots, foreign coins, foreign calico jackets....First I would move the Ningbo bed of the successful county candidate's wife to the temple, as well as the Qian family tables and chairs — or else just use the Zhao family's. I wouldn't lift a finger myself, but order Young D to move the things for me, and to look smart about it if he didn't want his face slapped....

"Zhao Sichen's younger sister is very ugly. In a few years Mrs. Zou's daughter might be worth considering. The Bogus Foreign Devil's wife is willing to sleep with a man without a queue, hah! She can't be a good woman! The successful county candidate's wife has scars on her eyelids.... I haven't seen Amah Wu for a long time and don't know where she is — what a pity her feet are so big."

Before Ah Q had reached a satisfactory conclusion, there was a sound of snoring. The four-ounce candle had burned down only half an inch, and its flickering red light lit up his open mouth.

"Ho, ho! Shouted Ah Q suddenly, raising his head and looking wildly around. But at sight of the four-ounce candle, he lay back and fell asleep again.

The next morning he got up very late, and when he went out into the street everything was the same as usual. He was still hungry, but though he racked his brains he did not seem able to think of anything. All of a sudden, however, an idea struck him and he walked slowly off until, either by design or accident, he reached the Convent of Quiet Self-Improvement.

庵和春天时节一样静，白的墙壁和漆黑的门。他想了一想，前去打门，一只狗在里面叫。他急急拾了几块断砖，再上去较为用力的打，打到黑门上生出许多麻点的时候，才听得有人来开门。

阿Q连忙捏好砖头，摆开马步，准备和黑狗来开战。但庵门只开了一条缝，并无黑狗从中冲出，望进去只有一个老尼姑。

"你又来什么事？"伊大吃一惊的说。

"革命了……你知道？……"阿Q说得很含胡。

"革命革命，革过一革的，……你们要革得我们怎么样呢？"老尼姑两眼通红的说。

"什么？……"阿Q诧异了。

"你不知道，他们已经来革过了！"

"谁？……"阿Q更其诧异了。

"那秀才和洋鬼子！"

阿Q很出意外，不由的一错愕；老尼姑见他失了锐气，便飞速的关了门，阿Q再推时，牢不可开，再打时，没有回答了。

那还是上午的事。赵秀才消息灵，一知道革命党已在夜间进城，便将辫子盘在顶上，一早去拜访那历来也不相能的钱洋鬼子。这是"咸与维新"的时候了，所以他们便谈得很投机，立刻成了情投意合的同志，也相约去革命。他们想而又想，才想出静修庵里有一块"皇帝万岁万万岁"的龙牌，是应该赶紧革掉的，于是又立刻同到庵里去革命。因为老尼姑来阻挡，说了三句话，他们便将伊当作满政府，在头上很给了不少的棍子和栗凿。尼姑待他们走后，定了神来检点，龙牌固然已经碎在地上了，而且又不见了观音娘娘座前的一个宣德炉。

这事阿Q后来才知道。他颇悔自己睡着，但也深怪他们不来招呼他。他又退一步想道：

"难道他们还没有知道我已经投降了革命党么？"

17. Highly decorative bronze censers were made during the Xuan De period (1426-35) of the Ming Dynasty.

The convent was as peaceful as it had been that spring, with its white wall and shining black gate, After a moment's reflection he knocked at the gate, whereupon a dog on the other side started barking. He hastily picked up some broken bricks, then went back again to knock more heavily, knocking until the black gate was pitted with pock-marks. At last he heard somone coming to open up.

Clutching a brick, Ah Q straddled there prepared to do battle with the black dog. The convent gate opened a crack, but no black dog rushed out. When he looked in all he could see was the old nun.

"What are you here for again?" she asked with a start.

"There's a revolution...didn't you know?" said Ah Q vaguely.

"Revolution, revolution...we've already had one." The old nun's eyes were red. "What more do you want to do to us?"

"What?" demanded Ah Q, dumbfounded.

Didn't you know? The revolutionaries have already been here!"

"Who?" demanded Ah Q, still more dumbfounded.

"The successful county candidate and the Foreign Devil."

"This completely took the wind out of Ah Q's sails. When the old nun saw there was no fight left in him she promptly shut the gate, so that when Ah Q pushed it again he could not budge it, and when he knocked again there was no answer.

It had happened that morning. The successful country candidate in the Zhao family was quick to learn the news. As soon as he heard that the revolutionaries had entered the town that night, he wound his queue up on his head and went out first thing to call on the Bogus Foreign Devil in the Qian family, with whom he had never been on very good terms. Because this was a time for all to work for reforms, they had a most satisfactory talk and on the spot became comrades who saw eye to eye and pledged themselves to make revolution.

After racking their brains for some time, they remembered that in the Convent of Quiet Self-Improvement there was an imperial tablet inscribed "Long live the Emperor" which ought to be done away with immediately. Thereupon they lost no time in going to the convent to carry out their revolutionary activities. Because the old nun tried to stop them and passed a few remarks, they considered her as the Qing government and gave her quite a few knocks on the head with a stick and with their knuckles. The nun, pulling herself together after they had gone, made an inspection. Naturally the imperial tablet had been smashed into fragments on the ground and the valuable Xuan De censer[17] before the shrine of Guanyin, the goddess of mercy, had also disappeared.

Ah Q only learned this later. He deeply regretted having been asleep at the time, and resented the fact that they had not come to call him. Then he said to himself. "Maybe they still don't know I have joined the revolutionaries."

第八章　不准革命

　　未庄的人心日见其安静了。据传来的消息，知道革命党虽然进了城，倒还没有什么大异样。知县大老爷还是原官，不过改称了什么，而且举人老爷也做了什么——这些名目，未庄人都说不明白——官，带兵的也还是先前的老把总。只有一件可怕的事是另有几个不好的革命党夹在里面捣乱，第二天便动手剪辫子，听说那邻村的航船七斤便着了道儿，弄得不像人样子了。但这却还不算大恐怖，因为未庄人本来少上城，即使偶有想进城的，也就立刻变了计，碰不着这危险。阿Q本也想进城去寻他的老朋友，一得这消息，也只得作罢了。

　　但未庄也不能说是无改革。几天之后，将辫子盘在顶上的逐渐增加起来了，早经说过，最先自然是茂才公，其次便是赵司晨和赵白眼，后来是阿Q。倘在夏天，大家将辫子盘在头顶上或者打一个结，本不算什么稀奇事，但现在是暮秋，所以这“秋行夏令”的情形，在盘辫家不能不说是万分的英断，而在未庄也不能说无关于改革了。

　　赵司晨脑后空荡荡的走来，看见的人大嚷说，

　　“嚄，革命党来了！”

　　阿Q听到了很羡慕。他虽然早知道秀才盘辫的大新闻，但总没有想到自己可以照样做，现在看见赵司晨也如此，才有了学样的意思，定下实行的决心。他用一支竹筷将辫子盘在头顶上，迟疑多时，这才放胆的走去。

　　他在街上走，人也看他，然而不说什么话，阿Q当初很不快，后来便很不平。他近来很容易闹脾气了；其实他的生活，倒也并不比造反之前反艰难，人见他也客气，店铺也不说要现钱。而阿Q总觉得自己太失意：既然革了命，不应该只是这样的。况且有一回看见小D，愈使他气

Chapter 8   Barred from the Revolution

The people of Weizhuang felt easier in their minds with each passing day. From the news brought they knew that although the revolutionaries had entered the town their coming had not made a great deal of difference. The magistrate was still the highest official, it was only his title that had changed; and the successful provincial cadidate also had some post — the Weizhuang villagers could not remember these clearly — some kind official post; while the head of the military was still the same old captain. The only cause for alarm was that, the day after their arrival, some bad revolutionaries made trouble by cutting off people's queues. It was said that the boatman Sevenpounder from the next village had fallen into their clutches, and that he no longer looked presentable. Still,the danger of this was not great, because the Weizhuang villagers seldom went to town to begin with, and those who had been considering a trip there at once changed their minds in order to avoid this risk. Ah Q had been thinkimg of going to town to look up his old friends, but as soon as he heard the news he gave up the idea.

It would be wrong, however, to say that there were no reforms in Weizhuang. During the next few days the number of people who coiled their queues on their heads gradually increased and, as has already been said, the first to do so was naturally the successful county candidate; the next were Zhao Sichen and Zhao Baiyan, and after them Ah Q. If it had been summer it would not have been considered strange if everybody had coiled their queues on their heads or tied them in knots; but this was late autumn, so that this autumn observance of a summer practice on the part of those who coiled their queues could be considered nothing short of a heroic decision, and as far as Weizhuang was concerned it could not be said to have had no connection with the reforms.

When Zhao Sichen approached with the nape of his neck bare, people who saw him remarked, "Ah! Here comes a revolutionary!"

When Ah Q heard this he was greatly impressed. Although he had long since heard how the successful county candidate had coiled his queue on his head, it had never occurred to him to do the same. Only now when he saw that Zhao Sichen had followed suit was he struck with the idea of doing the same himself. He made up his mind to copy them. He used a bamboo chopstick to twist his queue up on his head, and after some hesitation eventually summoned up the courage to go out.

As he walked along the street people looked at him, but without any comment. Ah Q, disgruntled at first, soon waxed indignant. Recently he had been losing his temper very easily. As a matter of fact he was no worse off than before the revolution, people treated him politely, and the shops no longer demanded payment in cash, yet Ah Q still

破肚皮了。

小D也将辫子盘在头顶上了，而且也居然用一支竹筷。阿Q万料不到他也敢这样做，自己也决不准他这样做！小D是什么东西呢？他很想即刻揪住他，拗断他的竹筷，放下他的辫子，并且批他几个嘴巴，聊且惩罚他忘了生辰八字，也敢来做革命党的罪。但他终于饶放了，单是怒目而视的吐一口唾沫道"呸！"

这几日里，进城去的只有一个假洋鬼子。赵秀才本也想靠着寄存箱子的渊源，亲身去拜访举人老爷的，但因为有剪辫的危险，所以也就中止了。他写了一封"黄伞格"的信，托假洋鬼子带上城，而且托他给自己介绍介绍，去进自由党。假洋鬼子回来时，向秀才讨还了四块洋钱，秀才便有一块银桃子挂在大襟上了；未庄人都惊服，说这是柿油党的顶子，抵得一个翰林；赵太爷因此也骤然大阔，远过于他儿子初隽秀才的时候，所以目空一切，见了阿Q，也就很有些不放在眼里了。

阿Q正在不平，又时时刻刻感着冷落，一听得这银桃子的传说，他立即悟出自己之所以冷落的原因了：要革命，单说投降，是不行的；盘上辫子，也不行的；第一着仍然要和革命党去结识。他生平所知道的革命党只有两个，城里的一个早已"嚓"的杀掉了，现在只剩了一个假洋鬼子。他除却赶紧去和假洋鬼子商量之外，再没有别的道路了。

钱府的大门正开着，阿Q便怯怯的蹩进去。他一到里面，很吃了惊，只见假洋鬼子正站在院子的中央，一身乌黑的大约是洋衣，身上也挂着一块银桃子，手里是阿Q曾经领教过的棍子，已经留到一尺多长的辫子都拆开了披在肩背上，蓬头散发的像一个刘海仙。对面挺直的站着赵白眼和三个闲人，正在必恭必敬的听说话。

阿Q轻轻地走近了，站在赵白眼的背后，心里想招

18. The Freedom Party was called Zi You Dang . The villagers, not understanding the word "freedom," turned Zi You into Shi You, which means persimmon oil.

19. Member of the Imperial Academy in the Qing Dynasty.

20. A figure in Chinese folk legend, portrayed with flowing hair.

felt dissatisfied. A revolution, he thought, should mean more than this. When he saw Young D, his anger boiled over.

Young D, had also coiled his queue up on his head and, what was more, had actually used a bamboo chopstick to do so too. Ah Q had never imagined that Young D would also have the courage to do this; he certainly could not tolerate such a thing! Who was Young D anyway? He was greatly tempted to seize him then and there, break his bamboo chopstick, let down his queue and slap his face several times into the bargain to punish him for forgetting his place and for his presumption in becoming a revolutioary. But in the end he let him off, simply fixing him with a furious glare, spitting, and exclaiming, "Pah!"

These last few days the only one to go to town was the Bogus Foreign Devil. The successful county candidate in the Zhao family had thought of using the deposited cases as a pretext to call on the successful provincial candidate, but the danger that he might have his queue cut off had made him defer his visit. He had written an extremely formal letter, and asked the Bogus Foreign Ddevil to take it to town; he had also asked the latter to introduce him to the Freedom Party. When the Bogus Foreign Devil came back he collected four dollars from the successful county candidate, after which the latter wore a silver peach on his chest. All the Weizhuang villagers were overawed, and said that this was the badge of the Persimmon Oil Party[18], equivalent to the rank of a Han Lin[19]. As a result, Mr. Zhao's prestige suddenly increased, far more so in fact than when his son first passed the official examination; consequently he started looking down on everyone else and when he saw Ah Q tended to ignore him a little.

Ah Q, disgruntled at finding himself cold -shoudered all the time, realized as soon as he heard of this silver peach why he was left out in the cold. Simply to say that you had gone over was not enough to make anyone a revolutionary; nor was it enough merely to wind your queue up on your head; the most important thing was to get into touch with the revolutionary party. In all his life he had known only two revolutionaries, one of whom had already lost his head in town, leaving only the things over with the Bogus Foreign Devil.

The front gate of the Qian house happened to be open, and Ah Q crept timidly in: Once inside he gave a start, for there was the Bogus Foreign Devil standing in the middle of the courtyard dressed entirely in black, no doubt in foreign dress, and also wearing a silver peach. In his hand he held the stick with which Ah Q was already acquainted to his cost, while the foot-long queue which he had grown again had been combed out to hang loosely over his shoulders, giving him a resemblance to the immortal Liu Hai[20]. Standing respectfully before him were Zhao Baiyan and three others, all of them listening with the utmost deference to what the Bogus Foreign Devil was saying.

Ah Q tiptoed inside and stood behind Zhao Baiyan, eager to pronounce some

呼，却不知道怎么说才好：叫他假洋鬼子固然是不行的了，洋人也不妥，革命党也不妥，或者就应该叫洋先生了罢。

洋先生却没有见他，因为白着眼睛讲得正起劲：

"我是性急的，所以我们见面，我总是说：洪哥！我们动手罢！他却总说道No！——这是洋话，你们不懂的。否则早已成功了。然而这正是他做事小心的地方。他再三再四的请我上湖北，我还没有肯。谁愿意在这小县城里做事情。……"

"唔，……这个……"阿Q候他略停，终于用十二分的勇气开口了，但不知道因为什么，又并不叫他洋先生。

听着说话的四个人都吃惊的回顾他。洋先生也才看见：

"什么？"

"我……"

"出去！"

"我要投……"

"滚出去！"洋先生扬起哭丧棒来了。

赵白眼和闲人们便都吆喝道："先生叫你滚出去，你还不听么！"

阿Q将手向头上一遮，不自觉的逃出门外；洋先生倒也没有追。他快跑了六十多步，这才慢慢的走，于是心里便涌起了忧愁：洋先生不准他革命，他再没有别的路；从此决不能望有白盔白甲的人来叫他，他所有的抱负，志向，希望，前程，全被一笔勾销了。至于闲人们传扬开去，给小D王胡等辈笑话，倒是还在其次的事。

他似乎从来没有经验过这样的无聊。他对于自己的盘辫子，仿佛也觉得无意味，要侮蔑；为报仇起见，很想立刻放下辫子来，但也没有竟放。他游到夜间，赊了两碗酒，喝下肚去，渐渐的高兴起来了，思想里才又出现白盔白甲的碎片。

greeting, but not knowing what to say. Obviously he could not call the man "Bogus Foreign Devil," and neither "Foreigner" nor "Revolutionary" seemed quite the thing. Perhaps the best form of address would be "Mr. Foreigner."

"I am so impetuous that when we met I kept urging, 'Old Hong, let's get down to business!' But he always answerd a '*Nein*!' — that's a foreign word which you wouldn't understand. Otherwise we should have succeeded long ago. This just goes to show how cautious he is. Time and again he asked me to go to Hubei, but I've yet agreed. Who wants to work in a small district town?..."

"Er — well — Ah Q waited for him to pause, then screwed up his courage to speak. But for some reason or other he still did not call him Mr. Foreigner.

The four men who had been listening gave a start and turned to stare at Ah Q. Mr. Foreigner too caught sight of him for the first time.

"What is it? "

"I...."

"Clear out!"

"I want to join...."

"Get out!" Mr. Foreigner raised the "mourner's stick."

Thereupon Zhao Baiyan and the others shouted, "Mr. Qian tells you to get out, don't you hear!"

Ah Q put up his hands to protect his head, and without knowing what he was doing fled through the gate; but this time Mr. Foreigner did not give chase. After running more than sixty steps Ah Q slowed down, and now his heart filled with dismay, because if Mr. Foreigner would not allow him to be a revolutionary, there was no other way open to him. In future he could never hope to have man in white helmets and white armour come to call him. All his ambitions, aims, hope and future had been blasted at one fell swoop. The fact that gossips might spread the news and make him a laughing-stock for the likes of Young D and Whiskers Wang was only a secondary consideration.

Never before had he felt so flat. Even coiling his queue on his head now struck him as pointless and ridiculous. As a form of revenge he was very tempted to let his queue down at once, but he did not do so. He wandered about till evening, when after drinking two bowls of wine on credit he began to feel in better spirits, and in his mind's eye saw fragmentary visions of white helmets and white armour once more.

有一天，他照例的混到夜深，待酒店要关门，才踱回土谷祠去。

拍，吧……！

他忽而听得一种异样的声音，又不是爆竹。阿Q本来是爱看热闹，爱管闲事的，便在暗中直寻过去。似乎前面有些脚步声；他正听，猛然间一个人从对面逃来了。阿Q一看见，便赶紧翻身跟着逃。那人转弯，阿Q也转弯，既转弯，那人站住了，阿Q也站住。他看后面并无什么，看那人便是小D。

"什么？"阿Q不平起来了。

"赵……赵家遭抢了！"小D气喘吁吁的说。

阿Q的心怦怦的跳了。小D说了便走；阿Q却逃而又停的两三回。但他究竟是做过"这路生意"的人，格外胆大，于是蹩出路角，仔细的听，似乎有些嚷嚷，又仔细的看，似乎许多白盔白甲的人，络绎的将箱子抬出了，器具抬出了，秀才娘子的宁式床也抬出了，但是不分明，他还想上前，两只脚却没有动。

这一夜没有月，未庄在黑暗里很寂静，寂静到像羲皇时候一般太平。阿Q站着看到自己发烦，也似乎还是先前一样，在那里来来往往的搬，箱子抬出了，器具抬出了，秀才娘子的宁式床也抬出了，……抬得他自己有些不信他的眼睛了。但他决计不再上前，却回到自己的祠里去了。

土谷祠里更漆黑；他关好大门，摸进自己的屋子里。他躺了好一会，这才定了神，而且发出关于自己的思想来：白盔白甲的人明明到了，并不来打招呼，搬了许多好东西，又没有自己的份，——这全是假洋鬼子可恶，不准我造反，否则，这次何至于没有我的份呢？阿Q越想越气，终于禁不住满心痛恨起来，毒毒的点一点头："不准我造反，只准你造反？妈妈的假洋鬼子，——好，你造反！造反是杀头的罪名呵，我总要告一状，看你抓进县里去杀头，——满门抄斩，——嚓！嚓！"

21. One of the earliest legendary monarchs in China.

One day he loafed about until late at night. Only when the tavern was about to close did he start to stroll back to the Tutelary God's Temple.

Crash-bang!

He suddenly heard an unusual sound, which could not have been firecrackers. Ah Q, always fond of excitement and of poking his nose into other people's business, headed straight for the noise in the darkness. He thought he heard footsteps ahead, and was listening carefully when a man fled past from the opposite direction. Ah Q instantly wheeled round to follow him. When that man turned, Ah Q turned too, and when having turned a corner that man stopped, Ah Q followed suit. He saw that there was no one after them and that the man was Young D.

"What's up?" demanded Ah Q resentfully.

"The Zhao... Zhao family has been robbed," panted Young D.

Ah Q's heart went pit-a-pat. After saying this, Young D went off. But Ah Q kept on running by fits and starts. However, having been in the business himself made him unusually bold. Rounding the corner of a lane, he listened carefully and thought he heard shouting; while by straining his eyes he thought he could see a troop of men in white helmets and white armour carrying off cases, carrying off furniture, even carrying off the Ningbo bed of the successful county candidate's wife. He could not, however, see them very clearly. He wanted to go nearer, but his feet were rooted to the ground.

There was no moon that night, and Weizhuang was very still in the pitch darkness, as quiet as in the peaceful days of Emperor Fu Xi.[21] Ah Q stood there until his patience ran out, yet there seemed no end to the business, distant figures kept moving to and fro, carrying off cases, carrying off furniture, carrying off the Ningbo bed of the successful county candidate's wife... carrying until he could hardly believe his own eyes. But he decided not to go any closer, and went back to the temple.

It was even darker in the Tutelary God's Temple. When he had closed the big gate he groped his way into his room, and only after he had been lying down for some time did he calm down sufficiently to begin thinking how this affected him. The men in white helmets and white armour had evidently arrived, but they had not come to call him; they had taken away fine things, but there was no share for him — this was all the fault of the Bogus Foreign Devil, who had barred him from the rebellion. Otherwise how could he have failed to have a share this time?

The more Ah Q thought of it the angrier he grew, until he was in a towering rage. "So no rebellion for me, only for you, eh?" he fumed, nodding furiously. "Curse you, you Bogus Foreign Devil — all right, be a rebel! That's a crime for which you get your head chopped off. I'll turn informer, then see you dragged off to town to have your head cut off — your whole family executed.... To hell with you!"

第九章　大团圆

　　赵家遭抢之后，未庄人大抵很快意而且恐慌，阿Q也很快意而且恐慌。但四天之后，阿Q在半夜里忽被抓进县城里去了。那时恰是暗夜，一队兵，一队团丁，一队警察，五个侦探，悄悄地到了未庄，乘昏暗围住土谷祠，正对门架好机关枪；然而阿Q不冲出。许多时没有动静，把总焦急起来了，悬了二十千的赏，才有两个团丁冒了险，逾垣进去，里应外合，一拥而入，将阿Q抓出来；直待擒出祠外面的机关枪左近，他才有些清醒了。

　　到进城，已经是正午，阿Q见自己被掮进一所破衙门，转了五六个弯，便推在一间小屋里。他刚刚一跄踉，那用整株的木料做成的栅栏门便跟着他的脚跟阖上了，其余的三面都是墙壁，仔细看时，屋角上还有两个人。

　　阿Q虽然有些忐忑，却并不很苦闷，因为他那土谷祠里的卧室，也并没有比这间屋子更高明。那两个也仿佛是乡下人，渐渐和他兜搭起来了，一个说是举人老爷要追他祖父欠下来的陈租，一个不知道为了什么事。他们问阿Q，阿Q爽利的答道，“因为我想造反。”

　　他下半天便又被抓出栅栏门去了，到得大堂，上面坐着一个满头剃得精光的老头子。阿Q疑心他是和尚，但看见下面站着一排兵，两旁又站着十几个长衫人物，也有满头剃得精光像这老头子的，也有将一尺来长的头发披在背后像那假洋鬼子的，都是一脸横肉，怒目而视的看他；他便知道这人一定有些来历，膝关节立刻自然而然的宽松，便跪了下去了。

　　“站着说！不要跪！”长衫人物都吆喝说。

　　阿Q虽然似乎懂得，但总觉得站不住，身不由己的蹲了下去，而且终于趁势改为跪下了。

　　“奴隶性！……”长衫人物又鄙夷似的说，但也没有叫他起来。

Chapter 9   The Grand Finale

After the Zhao family was robbed most of the people in Weizhuang felt pleased yet fearful, and Ah Q was no exception. But four days later Ah Q was suddenly dragged into town in the middle of the night. It happened to be a dark night. A squad of soldiers, a squad of militia, a squad of police, and five secret servicemen made their way quietly to Weizhuang and, after posting a machine-gun opposite the entrance, under cover of darkness surrounded the Tutelary God's Temple. But Ah Q did not bolt for it. For a long time nothing stirred till the captain, losing patience, offered a reward of twenty thousand cash. Only then did two militiamen summon up courage to jump over the wall and enter. With their co-operation, the others rushed in and dragged Ah Q out. But not until he had been carried out of the temple to somewhere near the machine-gun did he begin to wake up to what was happening.

It was already midday by the time they reached town, and Ah Q found himself carried to a dilapidated yamen where, after taking five or six turnings, he was pushed into a small room. No sooner had he stumbled inside than the door, in the form of a wooden grille, was slammed on his heels. The rest of the cell consisted of three blank walls, and when he looked carefully he saw two other men in a corner.

Although Ah Q was feeling rather uneasy, he was by no means depressed, because the room where he slept in the Tutelary God's Temple was in no way superior to this. The two other men also seemed to be villagers. They gradually fell into conversation with him, and one of them told him that the successful provincial candidate wanted to dun him for the rent owed by his grandfather; the other did not know why he was there. When they questioned Ah Q he answered quite frankly, "Because I wanted to revolt."

That afternoon he was dragged out through the grille and taken to a big hall, at the far end of which sat an old man with a cleanly shaven head. Ah Q took him for a monk at first, but when he saw soldiers standing guard and a dozen men in long coats on both sides, some with their heads clean-shaven like this old man and some with a foot or so of hair hanging over their shoulders like the Bogus Foreign Devil, all glaring furiously at him with grim faces, he knew that this man must be someone important. At once his knee-joints relaxed of their own accord, and he sank to his knees.

"Stand up to speak! Don't kneel!" shouted all the men in the long coats.

Although Ah Q understood, he felt quite incapable of standing up. He had involuntarily started squatting, improving on this finally to kneel down.

"Slave!" exclaimed the long-coated men contemptuously. They did not insist on his getting up, however.

"你从实招来罢，免得吃苦。我早都知道了。招了可以放你。"那光头的老头子看定了阿Q的脸，沉静的清楚的说。

"招罢！"长衫人物也大声说。

"我本来要……来投……"阿Q胡里胡涂的想了一通，这才断断续续的说。

"那么，为什么不来的呢？"老头子和气的问。

"假洋鬼子不准我！"

"胡说！此刻说，也迟了。现在你的同党在那里？"

"什么？……"

"那一晚打劫赵家的一伙人。"

"他们没有来叫我。他们自己搬走了。"阿Q提起来便愤愤。

"走到那里去了呢？说出来便放你了。"老头子更和气了。

"我不知道，……他们没有来叫我……"

然而老头子使了一个眼色，阿Q便又被抓进栅栏门里了。他第二次抓出栅栏门，是第二天的上午。

大堂的情形都照旧。上面仍然坐着光头的老头子，阿Q也仍然下了跪。

老头子和气的问道，"你还有什么话说么？"

阿Q一想，没有话，便回答说，"没有。"

于是一个长衫人物拿了一张纸，并一支笔送到阿Q的面前，要将笔塞在他手里。阿Q这时很吃惊，几乎"魂飞魄散"了：因为他的手和笔相关，这回是初次。他正不知怎样拿；那人却又指着一处地方教他画花押。

"我……我……不认得字。"阿Q一把抓住了笔，惶恐而且惭愧的说。

"那么，便宜你，画一个圆圈！"

阿Q要画圆圈了，那手捏着笔却只是抖。于是那人替他将纸铺在地上，阿Q伏下去，使尽了平生的力画圆圈。他生怕被人笑话，立志要画得圆，但这可恶的笔不但很沉重，并且不听话，刚刚一抖一抖的几乎要合缝，却又向外一耸，画成瓜子模样了。

"Tell the truth and you will receive a lighter sentence," said the old man with the shaven head in a low but clear voice, fixing his eyes on Ah Q. "We know everything already. When you have confessed, we will let you go."

"Confess!" repeated the long-coated men loudly.

"The fact is I wanted...to join..." muttered Ah Q disjointedly after a moment's confused thinking.

"In that case, why didn't you?" asked the old man gently.

"The Bogus Foreign Devil wouldn't let me. "

"Nonsense. It's too late to talk now. Where are your accomplices?"

"What?..."

"The gang who robbed the Zhao family that night."

"They didn't come to call me. They moved the things away themselves." Mention of this made Ah Q indignant.

"Where are they now? When you have told me I will let you go," repeated the old man even more gently.

"I don't know.... They didn't come to call me...."

Then, at a sign from the old man, Ah Q was dragged back through the grille. The following morning he was dragged out once more.

Everything was unchanged in the big hall. The old man with the clean-shaven head was still sitting there, and Ah Q knelt down again as before.

"Have you anything else to say?" asked the old man gently.

Ah Q thought, and decided there was nothing to say, so he answered, "Nothing."

Then a man in a long coat brought a sheet of paper and held a brush in front of Ah Q, which he wanted to thrust into his hand. Ah Q was now nearly frightened out of his wits, because this was the first time in his life that his hand had ever come into contact with a writing-brush. He was just wondering how to hold it when the man pointed out a place on the paper and told him to sign his name.

"I — I — can't write," said Ah Q, shamefaced, nervously holding the brush.

"In that case, to make it easy for you, draw a circle!"

Ah Q tried to draw a circle, but the hand with which he grasped the brush trembled, so the man spread the paper on the ground for him. Ah Q bent down and, as painstakingly as if his life depended on it, drew a circle. Afraid people would laugh at him, he determined to make the circle round; however, not only was that wretched brush very heavy, but it would not do his bidding. Instead it wobbled from side to side; and just as the line was about to close it swerved out again, making a shape like a melon-seed.

阿Q正羞愧自己画得不圆，那人却不计较，早已掣了纸笔去，许多人又将他第二次抓进栅栏门。

他第二次进了栅栏，倒也并不十分懊恼。他以为人生天地之间，大约本来有时要抓进抓出，有时要在纸上画圆圈的，惟有圈而不圆，却是他"行状"上的一个污点。但不多时也就释然了，他想：孙子才画得很圆的圆圈呢。于是他睡着了。

然而这一夜，举人老爷反而不能睡：他和把总呕了气了。举人老爷主张第一要追赃，把总主张第一要示众。把总近来很不将举人老爷放在眼里了，拍案打凳的说道，"惩一儆百！你看，我做革命党还不上二十天，抢案就是十几件，全不破案，我的面子在那里？破了案，你又来迂。不成！这是我管的！"举人老爷窘急了，然而还坚持，说是倘若不追赃，他便立刻辞了帮办民政的职务。而把总却道，"请便罢！"于是举人老爷在这一夜竟没有睡，但幸而第二天倒也没有辞。

阿Q第三次抓出栅栏门的时候，便是举人老爷睡不着的那一夜的明天的上午了。他到了大堂，上面还坐着照例的光头老头子；阿Q也照例的下了跪。

老头子很和气的问道，"你还有什么话么？"

阿Q一想，没有话，便回答说，"没有。"

许多长衫和短衫人物，忽然给他穿上一件洋布的白背心，上面有些黑字。阿Q很气苦：因为这很像是带孝，而带孝是晦气的。然而同时他的两手反缚了，同时又被一直抓出衙门外去了。

阿Q被抬上了一辆没有蓬的车，几个短衣人物也和他同坐在一处。这车立刻走动了，前面是一班背着洋炮的兵们和团丁，两旁是许多张着嘴的看客，后面怎样，阿Q没有见。但他突然觉到了：这岂不是去杀头么？他一急，两眼发黑，耳朵里喤的一声，似乎发昏了。然而他又没有全

While Ah Q was still feeling mortified by his failure to draw a circle, the man took back the paper and brush without any comment. A number of people then dragged him back for the third time through the grille.

By now he felt not too upset. He supposed that in this world it was fate of everybody at some time to be dragged in and out of prison and to have to draw circles on paper; it was only his circle not being round that he felt a blot on his escutcheon. Presently, however, he regained composure by thinking, "Only idiots can make perfect circles." And with this thought he fell asleep.

That night, however, the successful provincial candidate was unable to sleep, because he had quarrelled with the captain. The successful provincial candidate had insisted that the main thing was to recover the stolen goods, while the captain said the main thing was to make a public example. Recently the captain had come to treat the successful provincial candidate quite disdainfully. So banging his fist on the table he said, "Punish one to awe one hundred! See now, I have been a member of the revolutionary party for less than twenty days, but there have been a dozen cases of robbery, none of them yet solved; think how badly that reflects on me. Now this one has been solved, you come and haggle. It won't do. This is my affair."

The successful provincial candidate, most put out, insisted that if the stolen goods were not recovered he would resign immediately from his post as assistant civil administrator.

"As you please, "said the captain.

In consequence the successful provincial candidate did not sleep that night; but happily he did not hand in his resignation the next day after all.

The third time that Ah Q was dragged out of the grille-door was the morning following the night on which the successful provincial candidate had been unadle to sleep. When he reached the hall, the old man with the clean-shaven head was sitting there as usual. And Ah Q knelt down as usual.

Very gently the old man questioned him, "Have you anything more to say?"

Ah Q thought, and decided there was nothing to say, so he answered, "Nothing."

A number of men in long coats and short jackets put on him a white vest of foreign cloth with some black characters on it. Ah Q felt most disconcerted, because this was very like mourning dress and to wear mourning was unlucky. At the same time his hands were bound behind his back, and he was dragged out of the yamen.

Ah Q was lifted onto an uncovered cart, and several men in short jackets sat down beside him. The cart started off at once. In front were a number of soldiers and militiamen shouldering foreign rifles, and on both sides were crowds of gaping spectators, while what was behind Ah Q could not see. Suddenly it occurred to him — "Can I be going to have my head cut off?" Panic seized him and everything turned

发昏，有时虽然着急，有时却也泰然；他意思之间，似乎觉得人生天地间，大约本来有时也未免要杀头的。

他还认得路，于是有些诧异了：怎么不向着法场走呢？他不知道这是在游街，在示众。但即使知道也一样，他不过便以为人生天地间，大约本来有时也未免要游街要示众罢了。

他省悟了，这是绕到法场去的路，这一定是"嚓"的去杀头。他惘惘的向左右看，全跟着马蚁似的人，而在无意中，却在路旁的人丛中发见了一个吴妈。很久违，伊原来在城里做工了。阿Q忽然很羞愧自己没志气：竟没有唱几句戏。他的思想仿佛旋风似的在脑里一回旋：《小孤孀上坟》欠堂皇，《龙虎斗》里的"悔不该……"也太乏，还是"手执钢鞭将你打"罢。他同时想将手一扬，才记得这两手原来都捆着，于是"手执钢鞭"也不唱了。

"过了二十年又是一个……"阿Q在百忙中，"无师自通"的说出半句从来不说的话。

"好！！！"从人丛里，便发出豺狼的嗥叫一般的声音来。

车子不住的前行，阿Q在喝采声中，轮转眼睛去看吴妈，似乎伊一向并没有见他，却只是出神的看着兵们背上的洋炮。

阿Q于是再看那些喝采的人们。

这刹那中，他的思想又仿佛旋风似的在脑里一回旋了。四年之前，他曾在山脚下遇见一只饿狼，永是不近不远的跟定他，要吃他的肉。他那时吓得几乎要死，幸而手里有一柄斫柴刀，才得仗这壮了胆，支持到未庄；可是永远记得那狼眼睛，又凶又怯，闪闪的像两颗鬼火，似乎远远的来穿透了他的皮肉。而这回他又看见从来没有见过的更可怕的眼睛了，又钝又锋利，不但已经咀嚼了他的话，并且还要咀嚼他皮肉以外的东西，永是不远不近的跟他走。

这些眼睛们似乎连成一气，已经在那里咬他的灵魂。

"救命，……"

22. "In twenty years I shall be another stout young fellow" was a phrase often used by criminals before execution to show their scorn of death. Believing in transmigration, they thought that after death their souls would enter other living bodies.

dark before his eyes, while there was a humming in his ears as if he had fainted. But he did not really faint. Although he felt frightened some of the time, the rest of the time he was quite calm. It seemed to him that in this world probably it was the fate of everybody at some time to have his head cut off.

He still recognized the road and felt rather surprised: Why were they not going to the execution ground? He did not know that he was being paraded round the streets as a public example. But if he had known, it would have been the same: he would only have thought that in this world probably it was the fate of everybody at some time to be made a public example of.

Then he realized that they were making a detour to the execution ground, so after all he must be going to have his head cut off. He looked round him regretfully at the people swarming after him like ants, and unexpectedly in the crowd by the roadside he caught sight of Amah Wu. So that was why he had not seen her for so long: she was working in town.

Ah Q suddenly became ashamed of his lack of spirit, because he had not sung any lines from an opera. His thoughts revolved like a whirlwind: *The Youg Widow at Her Husband's Grave* was not heroic enough. The passage "Alas, in my cups" in *The Battle of the Dragon and the Tiger* was too feeble." Steel mace in hand I shall trounce you" was still the best. But when he wanted to raise his hands, he remembered that they were bound together; so he did not sing "Steel mace in hand" either.

"In twenty years I shall be another...."[22] In his agitation Ah Q uttered half a saying which he had picked up for himself but never used before. "Good!!!" The roar of the crowd sounded like the growl of a wolf.

The car moved steadily forward. During the shouting Ah Q's eyes turned in search of Amah Wu, but she did not seem to have seen him for she was looking intently at the foregn rifles carried by the soldiers.

So Ah Q took another look at the shouting crowd.

At that instant his thoughts revolved again like a whirlwind. Four years before, at the foot of the mountain, he had met a hungry wolf which had followed him at a set distance, wanting to eat him. He had nearly died of fright, but luckily he happened to have a knife in his hand which gave him the courage to get back to Weizhuang. He had never forgotten that wolf's eyes, fierce yet cowardly, gleaming like two will-o'-the-wisps, as if boring into him from a distance. Now he saw eyes more terrible even than the wolf's: dull yet penetrating eyes that having devoured his words still seemed eager to devour something beyond his flesh and blood. And these eyes kept following him at a set distance.

These eyes seemed to have merged into one, biting into his soul.

"Help, help!"

然而阿Q没有说。他早就两眼发黑，耳朵里嗡的一声，觉得全身仿佛微尘似的进散了。

至于当时的影响，最大的倒反在举人老爷，因为终于没有追赃，他全家都号咷了。其次是赵府，非特秀才因为上城去报官，被不好的革命党剪了辫子，而且又破费了二十千的赏钱，所以全家也号咷了。从这一天以来，他们便渐渐的都发生了遗老的气味。

至于舆论，在未庄是无异议，自然都说阿Q坏，被枪毙便是他的坏的证据；不坏又何至于被枪毙呢？而城里的舆论却不佳，他们多半不满足，以为枪毙并无杀头这般好看；而且那是怎样的一个可笑的死囚呵，游了那么久的街，竟没有唱一句戏：他们白跟一趟了。

一九二一年十二月。

But Ah Q never uttered these words. All had turned black before his eyes, there was a buzzing in his ears, and he felt as if his whole body were being scattered like so much light dust.

As for the after-effects of the robbery, the most affected was the successful provincial candidate, because the stolen goods were never recovered. All his family lamented bitterly. Next came the Zhao household; for when the successful county candidate went into town to report the robbery, not only did he have his queue cut off by bad revolutionaries, but he had to pay a reward of twenty thousand cash into the bargain; so all the Zhao family lamented bitterly too. From that day forward they gradually assumed the air of the survivors of a fallen dynasty.

As for any discussion of the event, no question was raised in Weizhuang. Naturally all agreed that Ah Q had been a bad man, the proof being that he had been shot; for if he had not been bad, how could he have been shot? But the consensus of opinion in town was unfavourable. Most people were dissatisfied, because a shooting was not such a fine spectacle as a decapitation; and what a ridiculous culprit he had been too, to pass through so many streets without singing a single line from an opera. They had followed him for nothing.

December 1921

方玄绰也没有说完话，将腰一伸，
咿咿呜呜的就念《尝试集》。
Fang Xuanchuo, not having had his say out either,
stretched and started intoning the poems in *An Experimental Collection*.

端午节

The Double Fifth Festival

方玄绰近来爱说"差不多"这一句话，几乎成了"口头禅"似的；而且不但说，的确也盘据在他脑里了。他最初说的是"都一样"，后来大约觉得欠稳当了，便改为"差不多"，一直使用到现在。

他自从发见了这一句平凡的警句以后，虽然引起了不少的新感慨，同时却也得到许多新慰安。譬如看见老辈威压青年，在先是要愤愤的，但现在却就转念道，将来这少年有了儿孙时，大抵也要摆这架子的罢，便再没有什么不平了。又如看见兵士打车夫，在先也要愤愤的，但现在也就转念道，倘使这车夫当了兵，这兵拉了车，大抵也就这么打，便再也不放在心上了。他这样想着的时候，有时也疑心是因为自己没有和恶社会奋斗的勇气，所以瞒心昧己的故意造出来的一条逃路，很近于"无是非之心"，远不如改正了好。然而这意见，总反而在他脑里生长起来。

他将这"差不多说"最初公表的时候是在北京首善学校的讲堂上，其时大概是提起关于历史上的事情来，于是说到"古今人不相远"，说到各色人等的"性相近"，终于牵扯到学生和官僚身上，大发其议论道：

"现在社会上时髦的都通行骂官僚，而学生骂得尤利害。然而官僚并不是天生的特别种族，就是平民变就的。现在学生出身的官僚就不少，和老官僚有什么两样呢？'易地则皆然'，思想言论举动丰采都没有什么大区别……便是学生团体新办的许多事业，不是也已经难免出弊病，大半烟消火灭了么？差不多的。但中国将来之可虑就在此……"

散坐在讲堂里的二十多个听讲者，有的怅然了，或者是以为这话对；有的勃然了，大约是以为侮辱了神圣的青年；有几个却对他微笑了，大约以为这是他替自己的辩解：因为方玄绰就是兼做官僚的。

而其实却是都错误。这不过是他的一种新不平；虽说不平，又只是他的一种安分的空论。他自己虽然不知道是因为懒，还是因为无用，总之觉得是一个不肯运动，十分

1. A quotation from *Mencius*.

2. A quotation from the *Analects of Confucius*.

3. A quotation from *Mencius*.

Recently the phrase "much of a muchness" had virtually become Fang Xuanchuo's watchword. Not only on his lips, it was indeed entrenched in his mind. At first he had said "all the same." Later, probably thinking this unreliable, he had switched to "much of a muchness" and used it right up till now.

Since his discovery of this commonplace dictum, although it had evoked not a few new emotions, at the same time he derived much comfort from it. For instance, when he saw the old domineering over the young, whereas once this had enraged him he now came round to thinking: When these youngsters have children and grandchildren themselves, they will probably throw their weight about like this too. Then it no longer seemed unjust. Or when he saw a soldier beating a rickshaw man, whereas once this had enraged him he now came round to thinking: If these two men were to change places, the rickshaw man would probably do the same. Then it no longer worried him. Sometimes, when such thoughts crossed his mind, he had misgivings, attributing his self-delusive escapism to his lack of courage to battle against social evils. It was akin to having "no sense of right and wrong,"[1] and fell far short of reform. None the less, this viewpoint grew on him.

He first made public this theory of "much of a muchness"in a classroom in Shoushan School in Beijing. At the time, doubtless referring to past history, he said, "the men of old and those of today are not far apart," whatever their colours "by nature they are akin,"[2] and finally he led up to students and officials, airing his views at some length.

"In our society today it's all the rage to inveigh against officials, and those who do this most harshly are students.But officials are not a race apart from birth; they come from the common people. Not a few of today's officials started as students, just like the old mandarins. 'If they changed places their conduct would be the same.'[3] There is not much to choose between them in outlook, speech, behaviour or appearance. As for many of the new activities launched by student bodies, didn't malpractices result, almost inevitably, so that most of them have now gone up in smoke? It's much of a muchness. But herein lies our concern over China's future...."

Of his twenty-odd auditors seated here and there in the classroom, some showed dismay, perhaps believing him right; some were angry, doubtless thinking this an insult to sacred youth; a few smiled at him, doubtless thinking this a self-justification — because Fang Xuanchuo also held an official post.

In fact, all of them were wrong. This was simply a new sense of injustice he had. Even so, it was just empty, law-abiding talk. Although not knowing himself whether owing to indolence, or because it was useless, at all events he refused to

安分守己的人。总长冤他有神经病，只要地位还不至于动
摇，他决不开一开口；教员的薪水欠到大半年了，只要别
有官俸支持，他也决不开一开口。不但不开口，当教员联
合索薪的时候，他还暗地里以为欠斟酌，太嚷嚷；直到听
得同寮过分的奚落他们了，这才略有些小感慨，后来一转
念，这或者因为自己正缺钱，而别的官并不兼做教员的缘
故罢，于是也就释然了。

他虽然也缺钱，但从没有加入教员的团体内，大家议
决罢课，可是不去上课了。政府说"上了课才给钱"，他
才略恨他们的类乎用果子耍猴子；一个大教育家说道"教
员一手挟书包一手要钱不高尚"，他才对于他的太太正式
的发牢骚了。

"喂，怎么只有两盘？"听了"不高尚说"这一日的
晚餐时候，他看着菜蔬说。

他们是没有受过新教育的，太太并无学名或雅号，所
以也就没有什么称呼了，照老例虽然也可以叫"太太"，
但他又不愿意太守旧，于是就发明了一个"喂"字。太太
对他却连"喂"字也没有，只要脸向着他说话，依据习惯
法，他就知道这话是对他而发的。

"可是上月领来的一成半都完了……昨天的米，也还
是好容易才赊来的呢。"伊站在桌旁，脸对着他说。

"你看，还说教书的要薪水是卑鄙哩。这种东西似乎
连人要吃饭，饭要米做，米要钱买这一点粗浅事情都不知
道……"

"对啦。没有钱怎么买米，没有米怎么煮……"

他两颊都鼓起来了，仿佛气恼这答案正和他的议论
"差不多"，近乎随声附和模样；接着便将头转向别一面
去了，依据习惯法，这是宣告讨论中止的表示。

待到凄风冷雨这一天，教员们因为向政府去索欠薪，
在新华门前烂泥里被国军打得头破血出之后，倒居然也发
了一点薪水。方玄绰不费一举手之劳的领了钱，酌还些旧
债，却还缺一大笔款，这是因为官俸也颇有些拖欠了。当

4. Fan Yuanlian, a former
Minister of Education,
was reported to have said
something to this effect in an
article "The Ideal Teacher" in
the Beijing weekly *The Tatler*
No.14.

5. On June 3,1921,over
ten thousand teachers
and students in Beijing
demonstrated against the
Northern Warlord government
headed by Xu Shichang to
demand payment. They were
suppressed and many of them
were injured. Xinhua Gate, on
Changan Boulevard, was the
entrance to the presidential
mansion.

take part in movements and regarded himself as thoroughly law-abiding. Accused by his superiors of being psychopathic, as long as this did not affect his position, he never protested. When his school salary was more than half a year in arrears, so long as he had his official pay to live on, he never protested either. He not only kept his mouth shut, when the teachers banded together to demand payment, he privately considered this imprudent and too vociferous; only when his colleagues ran them down too harshly did he feel slightly disturbed; but then it occurred to him that this might be because he himself was hard up and the other officials did not hold teaching posts, and so he overlooked it.

Although he, too, was hard up, he never joined the teachers' union; but when the others decided to go on strike he stayed away from class. The government ultimatum. "No pay till classes are resumed," annoyed him, because this seemed like tempting a monkey with fruit. However, not until an outstanding educationist[4] said, "It is in poor taste for teachers, a briefcase in one hand, to hold out the other for money," did he make any formal complaint to his wife.

"Hey, why are there only two dishes?" he asked, eyeing the suppper table, the evening after hearing this stricture on "poor taste."

They had not had a modern education, and as his wife had no school name or poetic name, he did not know what to call her. For although he could have used the old term "madam," he did not want to be too conservative and hence had invented this "Hey." His wife had not even a "Hey" for him. If she just faced him when talking, he knew from habit that she was speaking to him.

"But that fifteen per cent you got last month is all spent.... We had trouble getting yesterday's rice on credit." She stood beside the table confronting him.

"See here, they say teachers cheapen themselves by demanding payment. Apparently those creatures don't know the elementary fact that people need to eat, to eat you need rice, and to buy rice you need money."

"That's it. Without money how are we to buy rice, without rice...."

He puffed out his cheeks, as if angry because this answer was "much of a muchness" with what he had said, practically echoing it. Then he turned his head aside, this being his customary way to terminate a discussion.

One cold, wet, windy day, because teachers went to demand payment from the government, after they had been beaten over the head by troops, and their blood had dripped in the mud outside Xinhua Gate,[5] they unexpectedly got a little back pay. Without having lifted a finger, Fang Xuanchuo took his money, and with it settled some debts. But he was still very short, because of a serious delay in issuing his official

是时，便是廉吏清官们也渐以为薪之不可不索，而况兼做教员的方玄绰，自然更表同情于学界起来，所以大家主张继续罢课的时候，他虽然仍未到场，事后却尤其心悦诚服的确守了公共的决议。

然而政府竟又付钱，学校也就开课了。但在前几天，却有学生总会上一个呈文给政府，说"教员倘若不上课，便不要付欠薪。"这虽然并无效，而方玄绰却忽而记起前回政府所说的"上了课才给钱"的话来，"差不多"这一个影子在他眼前又一幌，而且并不消灭，于是他便在讲堂上公表了。

准此，可见如果将"差不多说"锻炼罗织起来，自然也可以判作一种挟带私心的不平，但总不能说是专为自己做官的辩解。只是每到这些时，他又常常喜欢拉上中国将来的命运之类的问题，一不小心，便连自己也以为是一个忧国的志士：人们是每苦于没有"自知之明"的。

但是"差不多"的事实又发生了，政府当初虽只不理那些招人头痛的教员，后来竟不理到无关痛痒的官吏，欠而又欠，终于逼得先前鄙薄教员要钱的好官，也很有几员化为索薪大会里的骁将了。惟有几种日报上却很发了些鄙薄讥笑他们的文字。方玄绰也毫不为奇，毫不介意，因为他根据了他的"差不多说"，知道这是新闻记者还未缺少润笔的缘故，万一政府或是阔人停了津贴，他们多半也要开大会的。

他既已表同情于教员的索薪，自然也赞成同寮的索俸，然而他仍然安坐在衙门中，照例的并不一同去讨债。至于有人疑心他孤高，那可也不过是一种误解罢了。他自己说，他是自从出世以来，只有人向他来要债，他从没有向人去讨过债，所以这一端是"非其所长"。而且他最不敢见手握经济之权的人物，这种人待到失了权势之后，捧着一本《大乘起信论》讲佛学的时候，固然也很是"蔼然可亲"的了，但还在宝座上时，却总是一副阎王脸，将别人都当奴才看，自以为手操着你们这些穷小子们的生杀之权。他因此不

salary. At this time, even those incorruptible officials were beginning to think a demand must be made for payment; and Fang Xuanchuo, as he was a teacher too, naturally felt even more sympathy for educational circles; thus when everybody proposed remaining on strike although he still did not attend the meeting he gladly abided later by the general decision.

Then, finally, the government resumed payment, and the schools started classes again. But a few days before this, the student union had petitioned the government, "If teachers still won't give classes, don't pay their arrears." Although this proved ineffectual, it suddenly reminded Fang Xuanchuo of the earlier government ultimatum, "No pay till classes are resumed." The reflection "much of a muchness" flashed before him, and did not fade away. Hence he had expounded it publicly in the classroom.

This being the case, obviously if the "much of a muchness" theory is hammered out, it can naturally be adjudged a sense of injustice combined with personal feeling, but not a justification for holding an official post oneself. However, at such times, he often liked to drag in such problems as China's future, and, unless careful, would even consider himself a high-minded man concerned for the country's future. It is a common failing, this lack of "self-knowledge."

But something "much of a muchness" happened again. The government, although at first it simply ignored those teachers who were such a headache, later ignored the innocuous officials, withholding their pay until finally quite a few of those good officials, who had despised the teachers for asking for money, boldly took the lead in a rally to demand payment. Only a few newspapers published articles deriding them. Fang Xuanchuo, no whit surprised, paid no attention, for according to his theory "much of a muchness," he knew this was because the journalists had not yet had their pay docked. If the government or the rich were by any chance to cut off their subsidies, most of them would hold a rally too.

As he had already expressed sympathy for the teachers demanding payment, he naturally approved of his colleagues doing the same; but he went on sitting in his yamen, still not accompanying the other duns. As for those who suspected him of holding aloof, that was just a misunderstanding. According to him, all his life, people had asked him to pay his debts but he had never dunned anyone else, so this was not something "he excelled in." Besides, he steered clear of those who wielded economic power. Certainly such people, once they lost their power and preached Buddhist scriptures, were also most "lovable"; but while still enthroned they behaved like the King of Hell, regarding the rest of mankind as their slaves, thinking they had the power

敢见，也不愿见他们。这种脾气，虽然有时连自己也觉得是孤高，但往往同时也疑心这其实是没本领。

大家左索右索，总算一节一节的挨过去了，但比起先前来，方玄绰究竟是万分的拮据，所以使用的小厮和交易的店家不消说，便是方太太对于他也渐渐的缺了敬意，只要看伊近来不很附和，而且常常提出独创的意见，有些唐突的举动，也就可以了然了。到了阴历五月初四的午前，他一回来，伊便将一叠账单塞在他的鼻子跟前，这也是往常所没有的。

"一总总得一百八十块钱才够开消……发了么？"伊并不对着他看的说。

"哼，我明天不做官了。钱的支票是领来的了，可是索薪大会的代表不发放，先说是没有同去的人都不发，后来又说是要到他们跟前去亲领。他们今天单捏着支票，就变了阎王脸，我实在怕看见……我钱也不要了，官也不做了，这样无限量的卑屈……"

方太太见了这少见的义愤，倒有些愕然了，但也就沉静下来。

"我想，还不如去亲领罢，这算什么呢。"伊看着他的脸说。

"我不去！这是官俸，不是赏钱，照例应该由会计科送来的。"

"可是不送来又怎么好呢……哦，昨夜忘记说了，孩子们说那学费，学校里已经催过好几次了，说是倘若再不缴……"

"胡说！做老子的办事教书都不给钱，儿子去念几句书倒要钱？"

伊觉得他已经不很顾忌道理，似乎就要将自己当作校长来出气，犯不上，便不再言语了。

两个默默的吃了午饭。他想了一会，又懊恼的出去了。

照旧例，近年是每逢节根或年关的前一天，他一定须在夜里的十二点钟才回家，一面走，一面掏着怀中，一面大声的叫道，"喂，领来了！"于是递给伊一叠簇新的中

of life and death over those paupers. This was why he steered clear of them. Although sometimes even he felt this showed a tendency to hold aloof, at the same time he often suspected it of actually being an incapacity.

With all these demands for payment right and left, they managed to get by somehow. But compared with the past he was in such desperate straits that, quite apart from his servant and the tradesmen with whom he dealt, even Mrs. Fang gradually lost her respect for him. You could tell this just from her recent lack of compliance, the way she often put forward her own views, and her rather brash behaviour. When he arrived home before noon on the fourth of the fifth lunar month, she thrust a pile of bills under his nose — somehing quite unprecedented.

"A hundred and eighty dollars in all are needed to settle these.... Have you been paid? She asked without looking at him.

"Huh, tomorrow I shall resign my official post. Cheques have been issued, but the representatives of the Demand Payment Rally are hanging on to them. First they said none would be given to those who didn't attend the rally, then said we must fetch them in person. Now that they've those cheques in their cluches, they've become like the King of Hell. I can't stand the sight.... I don't want the money, I shall quit my post, it's just too humiliating...."

Mrs. Fang was rather astonished by this unusual display of indignation, but she quieted down.

"I still think you'd better fetch it. What does it matter?" She asked, looking him in the face.

"Not I! My official stipent, not charity! By rights the accountants' office should send it over."

"But suppose they don't send it.... Oh, last night I forgot to tell you. The children say the school keeps prodding them for their school fees. If they aren't paid...."

"Rubbish! I'm not paid for my work or for my teaching, why should they charge my sons for a bit of schooling?"

She felt he was being unreasonable, taking out his anger on her instead of on the school head. It was not worth arguing with him.

They ate their lunch in silence. He thought things over, then went out in a temper.

It had been his rule in recent years, the day before New Year or a festival not to come home till midnight, when he would walk in, groping in his pocket, and announce loudly, "Hey, I've got it!" Then, a complacent look on his face, he would give her a wad of brand-new banknotes issued by the Bank of China or the Bank of Communications.

交票，脸上很有些得意的形色。谁知道初四这一天却破了例，他不到七点钟便回家来。方太太很惊疑，以为他竟已辞了职了，但暗暗地察看他脸上，却也并不见有什么格外倒运的神情。

"怎么了？……这样早？……"伊看定了他说。

"发不及了，领不出了，银行已经关了门，得等初八。"

"亲领？……"伊惴惴的问。

"亲领这一层，倒也已经取消了，听说仍旧由会计科分送。可是银行今天已经关了门，休息三天，得等到初八的上午。"他坐下，眼睛看着地面了，喝过一口茶，才又慢慢的开口说，"幸而衙门里也没有什么问题了，大约到初八就准有钱……向不相干的亲戚朋友去借钱，实在是一件烦难事。我午后硬着头皮去寻金永生，谈了一会，他先恭维我不去索薪，不肯亲领，非常之清高，一个人正应该这样做；待到知道我想要向他通融五十元，就像我在他嘴里塞了一大把盐似的，凡有脸上可以打皱的地方都打起皱来，说房租怎样的收不起，买卖怎样的赔本，在同事面前亲身领款，也不算什么的，即刻将我支使出来了。"

"这样紧急的节根，谁还肯借出钱去呢。"方太太却只淡淡的说，并没有什么慨然。

方玄绰低下头来了，觉得这也无怪其然的，况且自己和金永生本来很疏远。他接着就记起去年年关的事来，那时有一个同乡来借十块钱，他其时明明已经收到了衙门的领款凭单的了，因为恐怕这人将来未必会还钱，便装了一副为难的神色，说道衙门里既然领不到俸钱，学校里又不发薪水，实在"爱莫能助"，将他空手送走了。他虽然自己并不看见装了怎样的脸，但此时却觉得很局促，嘴唇微微一动，又摇一摇头。

然而不多久，他忽而恍然大悟似的发命令了：叫小厮即刻上街去赊一瓶莲花白。他知道店家希图明天多还账，大抵是不敢不赊的，假如不赊，则明天分文不还，正是他们应得的惩罚。

But today, the fourth, he broke his rule, arriving home before seven. Mrs. Fang was most dismayed, thinking he had resigned; but stealing a glance at his face, she could not see that he looked particularly down on his luck.

"What's up?... So early?..." she asked, eyeing him.

"Not issued, couldn't get it. The banks are closed, have to wait until the eighth."

"Did you go yourself?" She asked anxiously.

"That's no longer necessary, they say it will still be sent over by the accountants' office. But today the banks have already closed, for three days. Have to wait till the morning of the eighth." He sat down, his eyes on the floor. After a sip of tea he went on slowly, "Luckily there's no problem in the yamen, so I should be getting it for sure on the eighth....It's really troublesome trying to borrow from relatives and friends one's not on good terms with. After lunch I swallowed my pride and called on Jin Yongsheng. We chatted for a while. First he praised me for not going to demand payment and refusing to fetch my pay, calling me most high-minded, a fine example to others. When he learned that I wanted a short-term loan of fifty yuan, he looked as if I'd stuffed his mouth with salt — every wrinkle on his face crinkled. He said he hadn't been able to collect his rents, his business was losing money, and to go to fetch one's salary from a colleague was nothing to worry about. He sent me packing."

"In an emergency like this, who's willing to lend money?" said Mrs. Fang mildly and impassively.

Fang Xuanchuo hung his head, feeling hardly able to blame Jin Yongsheng, especially as they were not on terms. Then he recalled an incident last New Year's Eve, when a fellow provincial had asked for a loan of ten yuan. He had manifestly received his cheque from the yamen, but for fear this man might fail to pay him back he pretended to be in difficulties, saying that he could not get his official stipend and the school had not paid his salary, so much as he would like to help he could not. He sent him away empty-handed. Though he had not seen the expression he had assumed then, he now felt put out. His lips quivering, he shook his head.

Before long, however, as if suddenly seeing the light, he ordered the servant to go out at once and get him a bottle of Lotus-Flower White on credit. The storekeeper, he knew, was hoping he would settle his bills tomorrow, so probably wouldn't dare to refuse him credit. If he did, then not a cent would he get the next day — he deserved to be penalized.

莲花白竟赊来了，他喝了两杯，青白色的脸上泛了红，吃完饭，又颇有些高兴了。他点上一枝大号哈德门香烟，从桌上抓起一本《尝试集》来，躺在床上就要看。

"那么，明天怎么对付店家呢？"方太太追上去，站在床面前，看着他的脸说。

"店家？……教他们初八的下半天来。"

"我可不能这么说。他们不相信，不答应的。"

"有什么不相信。他们可以问去，全衙门里什么人也没有领到，都得初八！"他戟着第二个指头在帐子里的空中画了一个半圆，方太太跟着指头也看了一个半圆，只见这手便去翻开了《尝试集》。

方太太见他强横到出乎情理之外了，也暂时开不得口。

"我想，这模样是闹不下去的，将来总得想点法，做点什么别的事……"伊终于寻到了别的路，说。

"什么法呢？我'文不像誊录生，武不像救火兵'，别的做什么？"

"你不是给上海的书铺子做过文章么？"

"上海的书铺子？买稿要一个一个的算字，空格不算数。你看我做在那里的白话诗去，空白有多少，怕只值三百大钱一本罢。收版权税又半年六月没消息，'远水救不得近火'，谁耐烦。"

"那么，给这里的报馆里……"

"给报馆里？便在这里很大的报馆里，我靠着一个学生在那里做编辑的大情面，一千字也就是这几个钱，即使一早做到夜，能够养活你们么？况且我肚子里也没有这许多文章。"

"那么，过了节怎么办呢？"

"过了节么？——仍旧做官……明天店家来要钱，你只要说初八的下午。"

他又要看《尝试集》了。方太太怕失了机会，连忙吞吞吐吐的说：

"我想，过了节，到了初八，我们……倒不如去买一张彩票……"

6. A volume of poems in the vernacular by Hu Shi, published in March 1920 by the Yadong Library in Shanghai.

The Lotus-Flower White was duly bought on credit. After two cups his pallid face flushed, and after supper he was in fairly high spirits. He lit a Hademen cigarette, and picked up from the table a copy of *An Experimental Collection*,[6] then lay on the bed to read it.

"Well, how to cope with the tradesmen tomorrow?" Mrs. Fang, who had pursued him, was standing in front of the bed looking into his face.

"The tradesmen?... Tell them to come in the afternoon of the eighth."

"I can't do that. They wouldn't believe me, wouldn't be willing."

"Why shouldn't they believe you? They can ask around. Nobody in the yamen will be paid until the eighth." Under the mosquito net he sketched a semi-circle with his forefinger. Mrs. Fang saw the semi-circle, saw his hand continue leafing through the book.

Seeing him so unreasonably overbearing, she could say no more for the time being.

Finally, hitting on a different approach, she said, "I don't see how we can go on this wretched way. You must think of some way out in future, find something else to do."

"What way out? I can't be a copyist or join a fire-brigade. What else can I do?"

"Didn't you write for that bookshop in Shanghai?"

"That bookshop in Shanghai? They pay by the word, not by the page. Look at all the blank spaces in that volume of vernacular poems I wrote. I'm afraid it'll only fetch three hundred dollars. And for half a year I've had no word about royalties. 'Distant water can't put out a nearby fire.' Just have to lump it."

"Well then, write for the papers here."

"The papers? I've a student who edits one of the biggest of them. But even as a favour, he can't pay me more than a few dollars per thousand words. If I worked from morning till night, how could I keep you all? Besides, I haven't so much to write about."

"Well, after the festival, what then?"

"After the festival? — I'll go on being an official.... When the tradesmen ask for money tomorrow, just put them off till the afternoon of the eighth."

He picked up his book again. Afraid to miss this chance, Mrs. Fang faltered:

"I think, after the festival, on the eighth, we'd... better buy a lottery ticket...."

　　"胡说！会说出这样无教育的……"

　　这时候，他忽而又记起被金永生支使出来以后的事了。那时他惘惘的走过稻香村，看见店门口竖着许多斗大的字的广告道"头彩几万元"，仿佛记得心里也一动，或者也许放慢了脚步的罢，但似乎因为舍不得皮夹里仅存的六角钱，所以竟也毅然决然的走远了。他脸色一变，方太太料想他是在恼着伊的无教育，便赶紧退开，没有说完话。方玄绰也没有说完话，将腰一伸，咿咿呜呜的就念《尝试集》。

　　　　　　　　　　　　　　一九二二年六月。

"Rubbish! How can you talk in that uneducated way...."

This suddenly reminded him of what had happened after Jin Yongsheng had sent him packing. Dejectedly passing Dao Xiang Cun he noticed an advertisement in big characters on the shop door: "First Prize Tens of Thousands of Yuan." He had been tempted, he seemed to recall, and may have slowed down; but as if unwilling to part with the last sixty sents in his wallet, he had in the end gone resolutely on his way. His face changed colour. Mrs. Fang, supposing him annoyed by her lack of education, made haste to withdraw without having had her say out. Fang Xuanchuo, not having had his say out either, stretched and started intoning the poems in *An Experimental Collection*.

June 1922

而那下巴骨也便在他手里索索的动弹起来，
而且笑吟吟的显出笑影，
终于听得他开口道："这回又完了！"

He realized that it must be a jaw-bone twitched disconcertingly in
his hands and gaped as if with laughter.
Finally he heard it mutter: "Failed again!"

白光
The White Light

　　陈士成看过县考的榜，回到家里的时候，已经是下午了。他去得本很早，一见榜，便先在这上面寻陈字。陈字也不少，似乎也都争先恐后的跳进他眼睛里来，然而接着的却全不是士成这两个字。他于是重新再在十二张榜的圆图里细细地搜寻，看的人全已散尽了，而陈士成在榜上终于没有见，单站在试院的照壁的面前。

　　凉风虽然拂拂的吹动他斑白的短发，初冬的太阳却还是很温和的来晒他。但他似乎被太阳晒得头晕了，脸色越加变成灰白，从劳乏的红肿的两眼里，发出古怪的闪光。这时他其实早已不看到什么墙上的榜文了，只见有许多乌黑的圆圈，在眼前泛泛的游走。

　　隽了秀才，上省去乡试，一径联捷上去，……绅士们既然千方百计的来攀亲，人们又都像看见神明似的敬畏，深悔先前的轻薄，发昏，……赶走了租住在自己破宅门里的杂姓——那是不劳说赶，自己就搬的，——屋宇全新了，门口是旗竿和扁额，……要清高可以做京官，否则不如谋外放。……他平日安排停当的前程，这时候又像受潮的糖塔一般，刹时倒塌，只剩下一堆碎片了。他不自觉的旋转了觉得涣散了的身躯，惘惘的走向归家的路。

　　他刚到自己的房门口，七个学童便一齐放开喉咙，吱的念起书来。他大吃一惊，耳朵边似乎敲了一声磬，只见七个头拖了小辫子在眼前幌，幌得满房，黑圈子也夹着跳舞。他坐下了，他们送上晚课来，脸上都显出小觑他的神色。

　　“回去罢。”他迟疑了片时，这才悲惨的说。

　　他们胡乱的包了书包，挟着，一溜烟跑走了。

　　陈士成还看见许多小头夹着黑圆圈在眼前跳舞，有时杂乱，有时也排成异样的阵图，然而渐渐的减少，模胡了。

　　“这回又完了！”

　　他大吃一惊，直跳起来，分明就在耳朵边的话，回过头去却并没有什么人，仿佛又听得嗡的敲了一声磬，自己的嘴也说道：

It was afternoon before Chen Shicheng came back from seeing the results of the county examinations. He had gone very early, and the first thing he looked for on the list was the name Chen. Quite a few Chens leapt to meet his eye, but none followed by the characters Shicheng, thereupon, starting again, he made a careful search through all twelve lists. Even after everyone else had left, the name Chen Shicheng had not appeared on the list but the man was still standing there, a solitary figure before the front wall of the examination school.

A cool wind was ruffling his short greying hair and the early winter sun shone warmly on him, yet he felt dizzy as if from a touch of the sun. His pale face grew even paler; his tired eyes, puffy and red, glittering strangely. In fact, he had long stopped seeing the results on the wall, for countless black circles were swimming past his eyes.

He had won his first degree in the country examination and taken his second in the provincial capital, success following success.... The local gentry were trying by every means to ally with him by marriage; people were treating him like a god, cursing themselves for their former contempt and blindness. The other families renting his tumble-down house had been driven away — no need for that, they would move of their own accord — and the whold place was completely renovated with flagpoles and a placard at the gate.... If he wanted to keep his hands clean he could be an official in the capital, otherwise some post in the provinces would prove more lucrative.Once more the future mapped out so carefully had crashed in ruins like a wet sugar-candy pagoda, leaving nothing but debris behind.

Not knowing what he did, he turned with a strange sensation of disintegration, and shambled disconsolately home.

The moment he reached his door, seven small boys raised their voices to drone their lesson together. He started as if a chime had been struck by his ear, aware of seven heads with seven small queues bobbing in front of him, bobbing all over the room, with black circles dancing between. As he sat down they handed in their homework, contempt for him manifest on every face.

"You may go," he said painfully after a brief hesitation.

They snatched up their satchels, stuffed them under their arms, and were off like a streak of smoke.

Chen Shicheng could still see a host of small heads dotted with black circles dancing in front of him, now higgledy-piggledy, now in strange formation; but by degrees they grew fewer, hazier.

"Failed again!"

With a violent start he leapt to his feet, for undoubtedly the sound came from just beside him. When he turned his head there was no one there, yet he seemed to hear another muffled chime and his lips formed the words:

"这回又完了！"

他忽而举起一只手来，屈指计数着想，十一，十三回，连今年是十六回，竟没有一个考官懂得文章，有眼无珠，也是可怜的事，便不由嘻嘻的失了笑。然而他愤然了，蓦地从书包布底下抽出誊真的制艺和试帖来，拿着往外走，刚近房门，却看见满眼都明亮，连一群鸡也正在笑他，便禁不住心头突突的狂跳，只好缩回里面了。

他又就了坐，眼光格外的闪烁；他目睹着许多东西，然而很模胡，——是倒塌了的糖塔一般的前程躺在他面前，这前程又只是广大起来，阻住了他的一切路。

别家的炊烟早消歇了，碗筷也洗过了，而陈士成还不去做饭。寓在这里的杂姓是知道老例的，凡遇到县考的年头，看见发榜后的这样的眼光，不如及早关了门，不要多管事。最先就绝了人声，接着是陆续的熄了灯火，独有月亮，却缓缓的出现在寒夜的空中。

空中青碧到如一片海，略有些浮云，仿佛有谁将粉笔洗在笔洗里似的摇曳。月亮对着陈士成注下寒冷的光波来，当初也不过像是一面新磨的铁镜罢了，而这镜却诡秘的照透了陈士成的全身，就在他身上映出铁的月亮的影。

他还在房外的院子里徘徊，眼里颇清净了，四近也寂静。但这寂静忽又无端的纷扰起来，他耳边又确凿听到急促的低声说：

"左弯右弯……"

他耸然了，倾耳听时，那声音却又提高的复述道：

"右弯！"

他记得了。这院子，是他家还未如此雕零的时候，一到夏天的夜间，夜夜和他的祖母在此纳凉的院子。那时他不过十岁有零的孩子，躺在竹榻上，祖母便坐在榻旁边，讲给他有趣的故事听。伊说是曾经听得伊的祖母说，陈氏的祖宗是巨富的，这屋子便是祖基，祖宗埋着无数的银子，有福气的子孙一定会得到的罢，然而至今还没有现。至于处所，那是藏在一个谜语的中间：

"Failed again!"

Abruptly he raisd one hand and reckoned it up on his fingers: eleven, thirteen times, counting this year made sixteen, yet not a single examiner had been capable of appreciating good writing, all had been completely blind. It was so pathetic, in fact, that he had to snigger. In a fury he snatched his neatly copied examination essays and poems from their cloth wrapper and started out with them; but in the doorway he was dazzled by the bright light outside, where even the hens were making fun of him. Unable to still the wild pounding of his heart, he slunk back inside again.

He sat down once more, a strange glitter in his eyes. He could see many things, but hazily — his wrecked future, in ruins like a sugar-candy pagoda before him, was looming so large that it blocked all his ways out.

The neighbours' kitchen fires were long since out, their bowls and chopsticks washed, but Chen Shicheng had not started cooking a meal. His tenants knew from years of experience that after he had seen the results of the country examinations their best course was to close their doors early and mind their own business. First all voices were hushed, then one by one lamps were blown out, till nothing was left but the moon slowly climbing the cold night sky.

The deep blue of the sky was like an expanse of sea, while a few drifting clouds looked as if someone had dabbled a piece of chalk in a dish for washing brushes. The moon discharged cold rays of light down upon Chen Shicheng. At first the orb seemed no more than a newly polished iron mirror but by some mysterious means this mirror projected light through him until he reflected the shadow of the iron moon.

He paced up and down the yard outside his room, his vision clear now, all around him still. But this stillness was abruptly and rudely shattered as in his ear he distinctly heard the urgent whisper:

"Left turn, right turn...."

He pricked up his ears and listened intently as the voice repeated more loudly:

"Right turn!"

Now he remembered. This yard was the place, before his family fortunes declined, where he used to come with his grandmother on summer evenings to enjoy the cool. A boy of ten, he would lie on a bamboo couch while his grandmother sat beside him and told him interesting stories. She had it from her own grandmother, she said, that the founder of the Chen family was a man of great wealth who had built this house and buried a vast store of silver here, which some fortunate descendant was bound to find, although so far no one had discovered it. A clue to the hiding place was in this riddle:

"左弯右弯，前走后走，量金量银不论斗。"

对于这谜语，陈士成便在平时，本也常常暗地里加以揣测的，可惜大抵刚以为可通，却又立刻觉得不合了。有一回，他确有把握，知道这是在租给唐家的房底下的了，然而总没有前去发掘的勇气；过了几时，可又觉得太不相像了。至于他自己房子里的几个掘过的旧痕迹，那却全是先前几回下第以后的发了怔忡的举动，后来自己一看到，也还感到惭愧而且羞人。

但今天铁的光罩住了陈士成，又软软的来劝他了，他或者偶一迟疑，便给他正经的证明，又加上阴森的催逼，使他不得不又向自己的房里转过眼光去。

白光如一柄白团扇，摇摇摆摆的闪起在他房里了。

"也终于在这里！"

他说着，狮子似的赶快走进那房里去，但跨进里面的时候，便不见了白光的影踪，只有莽苍苍的一间旧房，和几个破书桌都没在昏暗里。他爽然的站着，慢慢的再定睛，然而白光却分明的又起来了，这回更广大，比硫黄火更白净，比朝雾更霏微，而且便在靠东墙的一张书桌下。

陈士成狮子似的奔到门后边，伸手去摸锄头，撞着一条黑影。他不知怎的有些怕了，张惶的点了灯，看锄头无非倚着。他移开桌子，用锄头一气掘起四块大方砖，蹲身一看，照例是黄澄澄的细沙，揎了袖爬开细沙，便露出下面的黑土来。他极小心的，幽静的，一锄一锄往下掘，然而深夜究竟太寂静了，尖铁触土的声音，总是钝重的不肯瞒人的发响。

土坑深到二尺多了，并不见有瓮口，陈士成正心焦，一声脆响，颇震得手腕痛，锄尖碰着什么坚硬的东西了；他急忙抛下锄头，摸索着看时，一块大方砖在下面。他的心抖得很利害，聚精会神的挖起那方砖来，下面也满是先前一样的黑土，爬松了许多土，下面似乎还无穷。但忽而又触着坚硬的小东西了，圆的，大约是一个锈铜钱；此外也还有几片破碎的磁片。

Left turn, right turn, forward, back!
Gold and silver by the sack!

Chen Shicheng often quietly cudgelled his brains to guess this riddle. Unfortunately he no sooner hit on a solution than he realized that it was wide of the mark. Once he was sure the treasure was under the room rented to the Tang family, but he lacked the courage to dig there and a little later it struck him as most unlikely. As for the vestiges of earlier excavations in his own room, these were signs of his depression over previous failures in the examination, and the sight of them later shamed and embarrsassed him.

But this iron light enfolding him today was gently persuasive. And when Chen Shicheng hesitated, the serious proofs it brought forward, backed up by some covert pressure, compelled him to cast his eyes towards his own room again.

A white light, like a round white fan, was flickering in his room.

"So it's here after all!"

With these words he charged like a lion into the room, but once across the threshold he saw no sign of white light, nothing but a dark, shabby room, with some rickety desks half swallowed up in the shadows. He stood there irrsolutely till by degrees his vision cleared and the white light reappeared beyond a doubt, broader this time, whiter than sulphurous flames and lighter than morning mist. It was underneath a desk by the east wall.

Chen Shicheng charged like a lion to the door, but when he put out his hand for the hoe behind it he bumped into a dark shadow. He gave an involuntary shiver and hastily lit the lamp, but there was nothing there except the hoe, he moved away the desk and hardly stopping for breath raised four square flagstones. Kneeling, he saw the usual fine yellow sand, and rolling up his sleeves he removed this sand to reveal black earth beneath. Very carefully and quietly he dug down, stroke by stroke. The night was so still, however, that the thudding of his sharp-bladed hoe against the earth was plainly audible.

The pit was over two feet deep yet still no crock had appeared and Chen Shicheng was beginning to lose heart when — *clang*! — he wrenched his wrist as the hoe struck something hard. He dropped his tool and scrabbled in the soil, discovering a large square brick beneath. His heart was throbbing painfully as with infinite care he prised up this brick, disclosing beneath it the same black earth as before. Although he loosened a great deal of earth, it apparently went down and down without end. All of a sudden, however, he struck a small hard object, something round, probably a rusty coin. There were some fragments of broken china too.

陈士成心里仿佛觉得空虚了，浑身流汗，急躁的只爬搔；这其间，心在空中一抖动，又触着一种古怪的小东西了，这似乎约略有些马掌形的，但触手很松脆。他又聚精会神的挖起那东西来，谨慎的撮着，就灯光下仔细的看时，那东西斑斑剥剥的像是烂骨头，上面还带着一排零落不全的牙齿。他已经悟到这许是下巴骨了，而那下巴骨也便在他手里索索的动弹起来，而且笑吟吟的显出笑影，终于听得他开口道：

"这回又完了！"

他栗然的发了大冷，同时也放了手，下巴骨轻飘飘的回到坑底里不多久，他也就逃到院子里了。他偷看房里面，灯火如此辉煌，下巴骨如此嘲笑，异乎寻常的怕人，便再不敢向那边看。他躲在远处的檐下的阴影里，觉得较为平安了；但在这平安中，忽而耳朵边又听得窃窃的低声说：

"这里没有……到山里去……"

陈士成似乎记得白天在街上也曾听得有人说这种话，他不待再听完，已经恍然大悟了。他突然仰面向天，月亮已向西高峰这方面隐去，远想离城三十五里的西高峰正在眼前，朝笏一般黑魆魆的挺立着，周围便放出浩大闪烁的白光来。

而且这白光又远远的就在前面了。

"是的，到山里去！"

他决定的想，惨然的奔出去了。几回的开门声之后，门里面便再不闻一些声息。灯火结了大灯花照着空屋和坑洞，毕毕剥剥的炸了几声之后，便渐渐的缩小以至于无有，那是残油已经烧尽了。

"开城门来……"

含着大希望的恐怖的悲声，游丝似的在西关门前的黎明中，战战兢兢的叫喊。

第二天的日中，有人在离西门十五里的万流湖里看见一个浮尸，当即传扬开去，终于传到地保的耳朵里了，便叫乡下人捞将上来。那是一个男尸，五十多岁，"身中面

Faint and soaked in sweat, Chen Shicheng burrowed desperately. His heart nearly turned over when he struck another strange object shaped somewhat like a horseshoe, but light and brittle in his hands. Having extracted it with infinite care, he picked it up cautiously and studied it intently by the lamp. Blotched and discoloured like a mouldering bone, it bore an incomplete row of teeth on the upper side. He realized that it must be a jaw-bone twitched disconcertingly in his hands and gaped as if with laughter. Finally he heard it mutter:

"Failed again!"

An icy shudder went through him. He let it go. The jawbone had barely dropped lightly back into the pit before he bounded out into the yard. He stole a glance at his room. The dazzling lamp and supercilious jaw-bone made it strangely terrifying. Averting his eyes in fear, he lay down in the shadows of the eaves some distance away, where he felt slightly safer. But another sly whisper sounded through the stillness in his ear:

"Not here.... Go to the hills...."

Chen Shicheng had a faint recollection of hearing this remark in the street that day, and at once light dawned on him. He threw back his head to look up at the sky. The moon was hiding itself behind West Peak, so that the peak a dozen miles from the town seemed immediately before him, upright, black, and awesome as the tablet carried by ministers to court, while from it pulsed great flickering beams of white light.

And this white light in the distance seemed just before him.

"Yes, to the hills!"

This decision taken, he rushed wildly out. Doors banged as he opened them, then all was still. The lamp, its wick heavily furred, lit up the empty room and the gaping pit. Presently it sputtered a few times and by degrees dwindled and died as the oil burned out.

"Open the gate!..."

In the dawn this cry, fearful and despairing yet fraught with infinite hope, throbbed and trembled like a floating thread before the West Gate of the town.

At noon the next day someone noticed a drowned man floating in the Wanliu Lake five miles from the West Gate. He lost no time in spreading the news till word reached the local bailiff, who got some villagers to recover the corpse. It was the body of a man in his fifties, "of medium height, pale and beardless," completely naked. It may have

白无须"，浑身也没有什么衣裤。或者说这就是陈士成。
但邻居懒得去看，也并无尸亲认领，于是经县委员相验之
后，便由地保抬埋了。至于死因，那当然是没有问题的，
剥取死尸的衣服本来是常有的事，够不上疑心到谋害去；
而且仵作也证明是生前的落水，因为他确凿曾在水底里挣
命，所以十个指甲里都满嵌着河底泥。

一九二二年六月

been Chen Shicheng. But since none of his neighbours could be troubled to go and look and no kinsmen went to identify and claim him, after the county authorities had held and inquest the bailiff buried him. The cause of death was beyond dispute and the theft of a dead man's clothes a common occurrence, insufficient grounds for suspicion of foul play. In fact, the post-mortem established that he had fallen in while still alive, for he had undoubtedly struggled under the water — embedded under all his nails was mud from the bottom of the lake.

June 1922

造物太胡闹，我不能不反抗他了，
虽然也许是倒帮他的忙……

The Creator goes too far. I cannot but oppose him,
although this may be abetting him instead.

兔和猫

The Rabbits and the Cat

住在我们后进院子里的三太太，在夏间买了一对白兔，是给伊的孩子们看的。

这一对白兔，似乎离娘并不久，虽然是异类，也可以看出他们的天真烂熳来。但也竖直了小小的通红的长耳朵，动着鼻子，眼睛里颇现些惊疑的神色，大约究竟觉得人地生疏，没有在老家时候的安心了。这种东西，倘到庙会日期自己出去买，每个至多不过两吊钱，而三太太却花了一元，因为是叫小使上店买来的。

孩子们自然大得意了，嚷着围住了看；大人也都围着看；还有一匹小狗名叫S的也跑来，闯过去一嗅，打了一个喷嚏，退了几步。三太太吆喝道，"S，听着，不准你咬他！"于是在他头上打了一掌，S便退开了，从此并不咬。

这一对兔总是关在后窗后面的小院子里的时候多，听说是因为太喜欢撕壁纸，也常常啃木器脚。这小院子里有一株野桑树，桑子落地，他们最爱吃，便连喂他们的波菜也不吃了。乌鸦喜鹊想要下来时，他们便躬着身子用后脚在地上使劲的一弹，砉的一声直跳上来，像飞起了一团雪，鸦鹊吓得赶紧走，这样的几回，再也不敢近来了。三太太说，鸦鹊倒不打紧，至多也不过抢吃一点食料，可恶的是一匹大黑猫，常在矮墙上恶狠狠的看，这却要防的，幸而S和猫是对头，或者还不至于有什么罢。

孩子们时时捉他们来玩耍；他们很和气，竖起耳朵，动着鼻子，驯良的站在小手的圈子里，但一有空，却也就溜开去了。他们夜里的卧榻是一个小木箱，里面铺些稻草，就在后窗的房檐下。

这样的几个月之后，他们忽而自己掘土了，掘得非常快，前脚一抓，后脚一踢，不到半天，已经掘成一个深洞。大家都奇怪，后来仔细看时，原来一个的肚子比别一个的大得多了。他们第二天便将干草和树叶衔进洞里去，忙了大半天。

大家都高兴，说又有小兔可看了；三太太便对孩子们

In summer, Third Mistress in our back courtyard bought a pair of white rabbits to amuse her children.

Apparently these two white rabbits had not left their mother long. Although a different species, their carefree innocence was evident. But they also raised their long, small crimson ears and wrinkled their noses, a very apprehensive look in their eyes. Probably, after all, they felt this place and the people here strange, and were less at ease here than in their old home. If you went to a temple fair yourself to buy creatures like these, they cost no more than two strings of cash apiece; but Third Mistress had spent a dollar, because she sent a servant to a shop to buy them.

The children, naturally, were overjoyed and crowded round boisterously to have a look. The grown-ups crowded round too. A puppy called S also came running over. Dashing up to sniff at them, he sneezed, then backed away a couple of paces. Third Mistress cried, "Listen, S! You're not to bite them!" Then she slapped his head, so that S ran off, and after that he never bit them.

These rabbits were kept most of the time in a small courtyard behind the back window. We were told this was because they were too fond of tearing the wall-paper and chewing the legs of furniture. In this little courtyard grew a wild mulberry tree. When the mulberries fell, these were what they liked eating most, and they would pass over the spinach given them. When crows and magpies wanted to fly down, they would hump their backs, stamp hard with their hind-legs on the ground and — whoosh! — bound straight up like flying snowballs. The frightened birds promptly took flight, and after several repetitions of this they no longer dared come near. Third Mistress said crows and magpies didn't matter, at most they would just steal a little food; the real menace was a big black cat, which often watched malevolently from the top of the low wall — they must be on their guard against it. Fortunately, S and the cat were enemies, so perhaps there would be no trouble after all.

The children often caught the rabbits to play with. They were very affable. Ears erect, their noses twitching, they stood meekly in the small hands encircling them; but as soon as they had a chance, they lolloped away. Their bed at night was a box, strewn with straw, under the eaves jutting over the back window.

After several months like this, they suddenly started burrowing, burrowing at top speed, fore-paws scrabbling, hind-legs kicking. In less than half a day they completed a deep burrow. Everybody marvelled, until a closer inspection revealed that one rabbit's stomach was much bigger than the other's. The next day, taking straw and leaves between their teeth, they busied themselves for hours moving these into the burrow.

Everybody was delighted, looking forward to another batch of small rabbits. Third

下了戒严令，从此不许再去捉。我的母亲也很喜欢他们家族的繁荣，还说待生下来的离了乳，也要去讨两匹养在自己的窗外面。

他们从此便住在自造的洞府里，有时也出来吃些食，后来不见了，可不知道他们是预先运粮存在里面呢还是竟不吃。过了十多天，三太太对我说，那两匹又出来了，大约小兔是生下来又都死掉了，因为雌的一匹的奶非常多，却并不见有进去哺养孩子的形迹。伊言语之间颇气愤，然而也没有法。

有一天，太阳很温暖，也没有风，树叶都不动，我忽听得许多人在那里笑，寻声看时，却见许多人都靠着三太太的后窗看：原来有一个小兔，在院子里跳跃了。这比他的父母买来的时候还小得远，但也已经能用后脚一弹地，逬跳起来了。孩子们争着告诉我说，还看见一个小兔到洞口来探一探头，但是即刻缩回去了，那该是他的弟弟罢。

那小的也检些草叶吃，然而大的似乎不许他，往往夹口的抢去了，而自己并不吃。孩子们笑得响，那小的终于吃惊了，便跳着钻进洞里去；大的也跟到洞门口，用前脚推着他的孩子的脊梁，推进之后，又爬开泥土来封了洞。

从此小院子里更热闹，窗口也时时有人窥探了。

然而竟又全不见了那小的和大的。这时是连日的阴天，三太太又虑到遭了那大黑猫的毒手的事去。我说不然，那是天气冷，当然都躲着，太阳一出，一定出来的。

太阳出来了，他们却都不见。于是大家就忘却了。

惟有三太太是常在那里喂他们波菜的，所以常想到。伊有一回走进窗后的小院子去，忽然在墙角上发见了一个别的洞，再看旧洞口，却依稀的还见有许多爪痕。这爪痕倘说是大兔的，爪该不会有这样大，伊又疑心到那常在墙上的大黑猫去了，伊于是也就不能不定下发掘的决心了。伊终于出来取了锄子，一路掘下去，虽然疑心，却也希望着意外的见了小白兔的，但是待到底，却只见一堆烂草夹些兔毛，怕还是临蓐时候所铺的罢，此外是冷清清的，全

Mistress strictly forbade the children to pick them up any more. My mother, too, was delighted by their family's flourishing and said, once the litter was weaned, she would ask for a couple to keep outside her own window.

After this they lived in the underground home they had made, sometimes coming out to eat. Then they disappeared. There was no knowing whether they had taken food inside in advance, or had really given up eating. More than ten days later, Third Mistress told me that the two rabbits had come out again. Most likely all their baby rabbits had died, because the doe had copious milk but showed no sign of going in to suckle her children. She sounded most indignant, but there was nothing she could do about it.

One warm, sunny day, when there was no wind and not a leaf stirred on the trees, I heard a sudden chorus of laughter. Thracking down the sound, I discovered quite a crowd leaning out of Third Mistress' back window to watch: a baby rabbit was frisking in the yard. He was much smaller than his parents had been when purchased. But already he could take off from the ground on his hind-legs and jump. The children eagerly told me that another little rabbit had peeked out of the burrow, but promptly drawn back his head. That must be his baby brother.

The little rabbit also nibbled at grass and leaves, but apparently this was not allowed by his parents, who kept snatching them out of his mouth, yet didn't eat them themselves. The children laughed so uproariously that finally the little rabbit took fright and hopped back to the burrow. The bigger ones followed him to the mouth of the burrow. With their fore-paws they pushed him inside, then scraped up earth to seal up the hole.

After that the little yard was livelier, there were often people at the window watching.

But then the rabbits, both small and big, disappeared. We were having a spell of dull weather. Once more Third Mistress worried that the malevolent black cat had done for them. I told her, no. Because it was cold, of course they were keeping under cover. Once the sun came out, they were sure to come out again.

The sun came out, but still no sign of them. Then everybody forgot them.

Only Third Mistress often thought of them, as she had been in the habit of feeding them spinach. Once, going into the small yard by the back window, she suddenly spotted another hole by the corner of the wall, and when she looked again at the old hole she saw a good many faint paw-prints round the entrance. Not even the big rabbits could have made such big prints. Once again her suspicion fell on the big black cat who was so often on the wall. Thereupon she felt impelled to dig up the burrow. She finally got out a hoe and dug down. Although fearing the worst, she hoped against hope to discover the small white rabbits; but a heap of mouldy grass and rabbit-fur, probably spread there for the doe's confinement. Apart from that the place was bare,

没有什么雪白的小兔的踪迹，以及他那只一探头未出洞外的弟弟了。

气愤和失望和凄凉，使伊不能不再掘那墙角上的新洞了。一动手，那大的两匹便先窜出洞外面。伊以为他们搬了家了，很高兴，然而仍然掘，待见底，那里面也铺着草叶和兔毛，而上面却睡着七个很小的兔，遍身肉红色，细看时，眼睛全都没有开。

一切都明白了，三太太先前的预料果不错。伊为预防危险起见，便将七个小的都装在木箱中，搬进自己的房里，又将大的也捺进箱里面，勒令伊去哺乳。

三太太从此不但深恨黑猫，而且颇不以大兔为然了。据说当初那两个被害之先，死掉的该还有，因为他们生一回，决不至于只两个，但为了哺乳不匀，不能争食的就先死了。这大概也不错的，现在七个之中，就有两个很瘦弱。所以三太太一有闲空，便捉住母兔，将小兔一个一个轮流的摆在肚子上来喝奶，不准有多少。

母亲对我说，那样麻烦的养兔法，伊历来连听也未曾听到过，恐怕是可以收入《无双谱》的。

白兔的家族更繁荣；大家也又都高兴了。

但自此之后，我总觉得凄凉。夜半在灯下坐着想，那两条小性命，竟是人不知鬼不觉的早在不知什么时候丧失了，生物史上不着一些痕迹，并S也不叫一声。我于是记起旧事来，先前我住在会馆里，清早起身，只见大槐树下一片散乱的鸽子毛，这明明是膏于鹰吻的了，上午长班来一打扫，便什么都不见，谁知道曾有一个生命断送在这里呢？我又曾路过西四牌楼，看见一匹小狗被马车轧得快死，待回来时，什么也不见了，搬掉了罢，过往行人憧憧的走着，谁知道曾有一个生命断送在这里呢？夏夜，窗外面，常听到苍蝇的悠长的吱吱的叫声，这一定是给蝇虎咬住了，然而我向来无所容心于其间，而别人并且不听到……

假使造物也可以责备，那么，我以为他实在将生命造得太滥，毁得太滥了。

1. By Jin Guliang of the Qing Dynasty. It comprises portraits of forty eccentrics from the Han to the Song Dynasty, with a poem on each.

with not a trace of the snow-white little rabbit, or of his baby brother who had peeped out not emerged from the burrow.

Anger, disappointment and grief impelled her to dig up the new burrow at the corner of the wall too. As soon as she started, out scuttled the two big rabbits. She was delighted, thinking they had moved house, but still she went on digging. When she reached the bottom, that too was strewn with grass, leaves and rabbit-fur, and on this were sleeping seven tiny rabbits, pink all over. A close look showed that they hadn't yet opened their eyes.

All became clear. Third Mistress' earlier guess had been correct. To forestall further danger, she put the litter of seven in a box, and moved it into her room. She put the doe in too, ordering her to suckle her little ones.

From that day on Third Mistress not only hated the black cat, but took a very dim view of the mother rabbit. She said, before the first two babies were killed, others must have died, because each litter was certainly more than two; but because of unequal suckling, those deprived of milk had starved. This sounded plausible, for two of the present litter of seven were very puny. So whenever Third Mistress had time, she would catch the mother rabbit and put the babies one by one on her belly to drink milk, no matter how long this took her.

My mother remarked to me that, in all her life, she had never so much as heard of so much trouble taken over raising rabbits. It deserved to be included in the *Register of Eccentrics*.[1]

The rabbit family was more flourishing than ever. Everybody was happy again.

But after that I kept feeling disconsolate. In the middle of the night, sitting under the lamp, I would think of those two little lives which had been lost none knows when, unnoticed by men or spirits, leaving no trace in the history of living creatures. Not even S had barked. This brought back old memories of when I was staying in our provincial hostel. Getting up early one day I saw beneath the big locust tree some scattered pigeon feathers, obviously let fall by a hawk. In the morning the attendant came to sweep up, and nothing was left of them. Who would have known that a life had been cut off here? Another time, passing the Xisi Archway, I saw a puppy dying, run over by a horse-cart. On my return it had gone, someone had removed it, and which of the passers-by would have known that a life had been cut off here? On summer nights, outside the window, I often heard the long-drawn-out drone of flies which must have been caught by a spider, but I never paid any attention, and other people did not even hear....

If it is possible to blame the Creator, then I think he really creates life too much at random, and destroys it too much at random.

嗥的一声，又是两条猫在窗外打起架来。

"迅儿！你又在那里打猫了？"

"不，他们自己咬。他那里会给我打呢。"

我的母亲是素来很不以我的虐待猫为然的，现在大约疑心我要替小兔抱不平，下什么辣手，便起来探问了。而我在全家的口碑上，却的确算一个猫敌。我曾经害过猫，平时也常打猫，尤其是在他们配合的时候。但我之所以打的原因并非因为他们配合，是因为他们嚷，嚷到使我睡不着，我以为配合是不必这样大嚷而特嚷的。

况且黑猫害了小兔，我更是"师出有名"的了。我觉得母亲实在太修善，于是不由的就说出模棱的近乎不以为然的答话来。

造物太胡闹，我不能不反抗他了，虽然也许是倒帮他的忙……

那黑猫是不能久在矮墙上高视阔步的了，我决定的想，于是又不由的一瞥那藏在书箱里面的一瓶青酸钾。

一九二二年十月

A yowl — two cats are fighting outside the window again.

"Xun! Are you beating cats again there?"

"No, they're biting each other. Why should I beat them?"

My mother has always disapproved of my cruelty to cats. Now doubtless suspecting me of employing sinister tactics to avenge the little rabbits, she had questioned me. Indeed, I was the byword of the whole household for my enmity to cats. I had killed cats, and often beat them, especially during the mating season. I beat them, however, not because they are mating, but because their caterwauling stops me from sleeping. I see no need for all that yowling when they mate.

Besides, since the black cat had killed the little rabbits, I had a more righteous cause for which to fight. Mother, I felt, was really too soft-hearted. That was why I made such an evasive, almost disapproving, answer.

The Creator goes too far. I cannot but oppose him, although this may be abetting him instead. That black cat must not be allowed to lord it much longer on the low wall, I resolved. Then, involuntarily, my eye fell on a bottle of potassium cyanide tucked away in my case of books.

October 1922

他独自靠在自己的卧榻上，
很高的眉棱在金黄色的长发之间微蹙了，
是在想他旧游之地的缅甸，缅甸的夏夜。

Eroshenko was resting alone on his couch,
his high brows slightly wrinkled under his long yellow hair as he thought
of his travels in Burma, of summer nights in Burma.

鸭的喜剧

The Comedy of the Ducks

俄国的盲诗人爱罗先珂君带了他那六弦琴到北京之后不多久，便向我诉苦说：

"寂寞呀，寂寞呀，在沙漠上似的寂寞呀！"

这应该是真实的，但在我却未曾感得；我住得久了，"入芝兰之室，久而不闻其香"，只以为很是嚷嚷罢了。然而我之所谓嚷嚷，或者也就是他之所谓寂寞罢。

我可是觉得在北京仿佛没有春和秋。老于北京的人说，地气北转了，这里在先是没有这么和暖。只是我总以为没有春和秋；冬末和夏初衔接起来，夏才去，冬又开始了。

一日就是这冬末夏初的时候，而且是夜间，我偶而得了闲暇，去访问爱罗先珂君。他一向寓在仲密君的家里；这时一家的人都睡了觉了，天下很安静。他独自靠在自己的卧榻上，很高的眉棱在金黄色的长发之间微蹙了，是在想他旧游之地的缅甸，缅甸的夏夜。

"这样的夜间，"他说，"在缅甸是遍地是音乐。房里，草间，树上，都有昆虫吟叫，各种声音，成为合奏，很神奇。其间时时夹着蛇鸣：'嘶嘶！'可是也与虫声相和协……"他沉思了，似乎想要追想起那时的情景来。

我开不得口。这样奇妙的音乐，我在北京确乎未曾听到过，所以即使如何爱国，也辩护不得，因为他虽然目无所见，耳朵是没有聋的。

"北京却连蛙鸣也没有……"他又叹息说。

"蛙鸣是有的！"这叹息，却使我勇猛起来了，于是抗议说，"到夏天，大雨之后，你便能听到许多虾蟆叫，那是都在沟里面的，因为北京到处都有沟。"

"哦……"

过了几天，我的话居然证实了，因为爱罗先珂君已经买到了十几个科斗子。他买来便放在他窗外的院子中央的小池里。那池的长有三尺，宽有二尺，是仲密所掘，以种荷花的荷池。从这荷池里，虽然从来没有见过养出半朵荷花来，然而养虾蟆却实在是一个极合式的处所。

1. V. Ia. Eroshenko (1889-1952) wrote poetry and children's stories. He lost his sight during a childhood illness, but travelled to Japan, Thailand, Burma and India. Expelled by the Japanese for taking part in a May Day parade in 1921, he travelled to China. In 1922 he went from Shanghai to Beijing, where he taught in Beijing University and the Esperanto School. He wrote in Japanese and Esperanto. Lu Xun translated his *Peach-Coloured Clouds* and a collection of his stories for children.

2. A quotation from *The Housebold Sayings of Confucius*.

Not long after the blind Russian poet Eroshenko[1] brought his six-stringed guitar to Beijing, he complained to me, "Lonely, lonely! Like the loneliness in a desert!"

This was no doubt his honest feeling, but not mine: I was an old resident. "Stay long in a room filled with iris and epidendrum, and you become oblivious of their scent."[2] I simply found the place noisy. But perhaps what I called noisy was what he called lonely.

It did seem to me though that Beijing had no spring or autumn. Old residents said that the warmth underground had shifted northward, making the climate milder. Still, in my opinion there was no spring or autumn; the end of winter merged with the start of summer; and as soon as summer ended, winter started.

One day, or rather one night, at this time when winter ended and summer began, happening to be free I called on Eroshenko. He stayed in Zhong Mi's home. By this hour the rest of the household was in bed, and the place was very quiet. Eroshenko was resting alone on his couch, his high brows slightly wrinkled under his long yellow hair as he thought of his travels in Burma, of summer nights in Burma.

"On a night like this," he said, "there is music all over Burma. Buildings, grass and trees, all have insects shrilling there. Those different sounds merge into a most extraordinary harmony. Now and then snakes hiss, but their hisses blend into the insects' shrilling...."

He fell silent, as if eager to recapture that scent.

There was nothing I could say. I had certainly never heard miraculous music of that kind in Beijing; so no matter how patriotic I was I could put up no defence, for although blind he was not deaf.

"You haven't even frogs in Beijing...." he sighed.

"Frogs? We do!" This sigh of his emboldened me to protest, "In summer, after the big rains, you can hear no end of frogs croaking in the gutters, because there are gutters all over Beijing."

"Oh...."

A few days later, sure enough, I was proved right, as Eroshenko bought a dozen or so tadpoles. He put them into a miniature pool in the middle of the yard outside his window. Three feet long and two feet wide, it had been dug by Zhong Mi to serve as a lotus pool. Although no one had ever seen even half a lotus growing there, it was a most appropriate place to raise frogs.

科斗成群结队的在水里游泳;爱罗先珂君也常常踱来访他们。有时候,孩子告诉他说,"爱罗先珂先生,他们生了脚了。"他便高兴的微笑道,"哦!"

然而养成池沼的音乐家却只是爱罗先珂君的一件事。他是向来主张自食其力的,常说女人可以畜牧,男人就应该种田。所以遇到很熟的友人,他便要劝诱他就在院子里种白菜;也屡次对仲密夫人劝告,劝伊养蜂,养鸡,养猪,养牛,养骆驼。后来仲密家里果然有了许多小鸡,满院飞跑,啄完了铺地锦的嫩叶,大约也许就是这劝告的结果了。

从此卖小鸡的乡下人也时常来,来一回便买几只,因为小鸡是容易积食,发痧,很难得长寿的;而且有一匹还成了爱罗先珂君在北京所作唯一的小说《小鸡的悲剧》里的主人公。有一天的上午,那乡下人竟意外的带了小鸭来了,咻咻的叫着;但是仲密夫人说不要。爱罗先珂君也跑出来,他们就放一个在他两手里,而小鸭便在他两手里咻咻的叫。他以为这也很可爱,于是又不能不买了,一共买了四个,每个八十文。

小鸭也诚然是可爱,遍身松花黄,放在地上,便蹒跚的走,互相招呼,总是在一处。大家都说好,明天去买泥鳅来喂他们罢。爱罗先珂君说,"这钱也可以归我出的。"

他于是教书去了;大家也走散。不一会,仲密夫人拿冷饭来喂他们时,在远处已听得泼水的声音,跑到一看,原来那四个小鸭都在荷池里洗澡了,而且还翻筋斗,吃东西呢。等到拦他们上了岸,全池已经是浑水,过了半天,澄清了,只见泥里露出几条细藕来;而且再也寻不出一个已经生了脚的科斗了。

"伊和希珂先,没有了,虾蟆的儿子。"傍晚时候,孩子们一见他回来,最小的一个便赶紧说。

"唔,虾蟆?"

仲密夫人也出来了,报告了小鸭吃完科斗的故事。

"唉,唉!……"他说。

3. Lu Xun translated this story in July 1922. It was published in Vol. 8, No.9 of the *Women's Magazine* in Shanghai that September, and later included in *Eroshenko's Tales for Children*.

Clustered tadpoles swam through the water, and Eroshenko often went over to visit them. Once, the children told him, "Mr. Eroshenko, they've grown legs." Then he smiled with pleasure and said, "Oh!"

But raising a poolful of musicians was only one of Eroshenko's projects. A great advocate of self-sufficiency, he was all in favour of women keeping livestock and of men tilling the land. So whenever he met a good friend, he would advise him to plant cabbages in his yard; and many a time he urged Mrs. Zhong Mi to keep bees, poultry, pigs, cows and camels. Subsequently, sure enough, many chicks appeared in the Zhong Mi household and flapped all over the yard, pecking it bare of the tender leaves on the ground. This was probably the outcome of his advice.

After that, the countryman selling chicks often called, and each time they bought a few, because chicks are prone to forage for themselves and fall ill — they are seldom very long-lived. One of them, moreover, became the central figure in *The Tragedy of the Chicks*,[3] the only story Eroshenko wrote in Beijing. One morning, unexpectedly, the countryman brought along some cheeping ducklings, but Mrs. Zhong Mi said she did not want them. Eroshenko hurried out too. They put a duckling in his hands, and it cheeped as he held it. He thought the little creature so lovable, he felt he had to buy it. He bought four in all, for eighty cash apiece.

And those ducklings were really lovable, covered with golden down. Set on the ground they waddled about, calling to each other and always keeping together. Everybody praised them and said they must buy some loaches the next day to feed them. Eroshenko said, "You must let me pay for it."

Then he went off to a class, and the others dispersed. When presently Mrs. Zhong Mi took out some left-over rice for the ducklings, she heard a distant splashing and, running over to look, saw the four of them having a bath in the lotus pool. They were turning somersaults too and eating something. By the time she shooed them ashore, the water in the pool was muddy. When eventually the mud settled, all that could be seen were a few thin lotus roots. Not a single tadpole that had grown legs was left.

"They've gone, Mr. Eroshenko, the baby frogs." The smallest child made haste to announce this as soon as he came back that evening.

"Eh? The frogs?"

Mrs. Zhong Mi came out too, to report how the ducklings had eaten all the tadpoles.

"Well, well!" he said.

待到小鸭褪了黄毛，爱罗先珂君却忽而渴念着他的
"俄罗斯母亲"了，便匆匆的向赤塔去。

待到四处蛙鸣的时候，小鸭也已经长成，两个白的，
两个花的，而且不复咻咻的叫，都是"鸭鸭"的叫了。荷
花池也早已容不下他们盘桓了，幸而仲密的住家的地势是
很低的，夏雨一降，院子里满积了水，他们便欣欣然，游
水，钻水，拍翅子，"鸭鸭"的叫。

现在又从夏末交了冬初，而爱罗先珂君还是绝无消
息，不知道究竟在那里了。

只有四个鸭，却还在沙漠上"鸭鸭"的叫。

一九二二年十月。

By the time the duckings shed their down, Eroshenko had suddenly become so homesick for "Mother Russia" that he hastily set off for Chita.

By the time frogs were croaking all around, the ducklings had grown into ducks, two white, two speckled, and they no longer cheeped but had started quacking. The lotus pool was too small for them to sport in; but luckily Zhong Mi's compound is so low-lying that each time it rained in summer it filled with water. Then they swam, dabbled in the water, flapped their wings and quacked joyfully.

Now the end of summer has once more merged with the start of winter, and still there is no news of Eroshenko. There is no knowing where he is.

Only four ducks are left, still quacking in the desert.

October 1922

在停船的匆忙中，
看见台上有一个黑的长胡子的背上插着四张旗，
捏着长枪，和一群赤膊的人正打仗。

While we hastily moored,
there appeared on the stage a man with a long black beard
and four pennons fixed to his back.
With a spear he fought a whole group of bare-armed men.

社戏
Village Opera

　　我在倒数上去的二十年中，只看过两回中国戏，前十年是绝不看，因为没有看戏的意思和机会，那两回全在后十年，然而都没有看出什么来就走了。

　　第一回是民国元年我初到北京的时候，当时一个朋友对我说，北京戏最好，你不去见见世面么？我想，看戏是有味的，而况在北京呢。于是都兴致勃勃的跑到什么园，戏文已经开场了，在外面也早听到冬冬地响。我们挨进门，几个红的绿的在我的眼前一闪烁，便又看见戏台下满是许多头，再定神四面看，却见中间也还有几个空座，挤过去要坐时，又有人对我发议论，我因为耳朵已经嗅嗅的响着了，用了心，才听到他是说"有人，不行！"

　　我们退到后面，一个辫子很光的却来领我们到了侧面，指出一个地位来。这所谓地位者，原来是一条长凳，然而他那坐板比我的上腿要狭到四分之三，他的脚比我的下腿要长过三分之二。我先是没有爬上去的勇气，接着便联想到私刑拷打的刑具，不由的毛骨悚然的走出了。

　　走了许多路，忽听得我的朋友的声音道，"究竟怎的？"我回过脸去，原来他也被我带出去了。他很诧异的说，"怎么总是走，不答应？"我说，"朋友，对不起，我耳朵只在冬冬嗅嗅的响，并没有听到你的话。"

　　后来我每一想到，便很以为奇怪，似乎这戏太不好，——否则便是我近来在戏台下不适于生存了。

　　第二回忘记了那一年，总之是募集湖北水灾捐而谭叫天还没有死。捐法是两元钱买一张戏票，可以到第一舞台去看戏，扮演的多是名角，其一就是小叫天。我买了一张票，本是对于劝募人聊以塞责的，然而似乎又有好事家乘机对我说了些叫天不可不看的大法要了。我于是忘了前几年的冬冬嗅嗅之灾，竟到第一舞台去了，但大约一半也因为重价购来的宝票，总得使用了才舒服。我打听得叫天出台是迟的，而第一舞台却是新式构造，用不着争座位，便放了心，延宕到九点钟才出去，谁料照例，人都满了，连立足也难，我只得挤在远处的人丛中看一个老旦在台上唱。那老旦嘴边插着两

1. A famous Beijing opera actor who played old men's roles.

In the past twenty years only twice have I been to see Chinese opera. During the first ten years I saw none, lacking both the wish and the opportunity. The two occasions on which I went were in the last ten years, but each time I left without seeing anything in it.

The first time was in 1912 when I was new to Beijing. A friend told me Beijing had the best opera and that seeing it was an experience not to be missed. I thought it might be interesting to see an opera, especially in Beijing, and hurried in high spirits to some theatre, the name of which escapes me. The performance had already started. Even outside I could hear the beat of the drums. As we squeezed in, gaudy colours flashed into view, then I saw many heads in the auditorium; but when I collected myself to look around there were still a few empty seats in the middle. As I squeezed my way in to sit down, someone addressed me. Already there was such a buzzing in my ears that I had to listen hard to catch what he was saying — "Sorry, these seats are taken!"

We withdrew to the back, but then a man with a glossy queue led us to one side and indicated an unoccupied place. This was a bench only a quarter the width of my thighs, but with legs two-thirds longer than mine. To begin with I hadn't the courage to get up there. Then, being reminded of some instrument of torture, with an involuntary shudder I fled.

I had gone some way when suddenly I heard my friend's voice asking, "Well, what's the matter?" Looking over my shoulder I saw he had followed me out. "Why are you marching along without a word?" he inquired in great surprise.

"I'm sorry," I told him. "There's such a ding-dong skirling in my ears, I didn't hear you."

Whenever I thought back to this it struck me as most strange and I supposed that the opera had been a very poor one — or else a theatre was no place for me.

I forget in what year I made the second venture, but funds were being raised for flood victims in Hubei and Tan Xinpei[1] was still alive. By paying two dollars for a ticket, you contributed money and could go to the Number One Theatre to see an opera with a cast made up for the most part of famous actors, one being Tan Xinpei himself. I bought a ticket primarily to satisfy the collector, but then some busybody seized the chance to tell me why Tan Xinpei simply had to be seen. At that, I forgot the disastrous ding-dong skirling of a few years before and went to the theatre — probably half because that precious ticket had cost so much that I would feel uncomfortable unless I used it. I learned that Tan Xinpei made his appearance late in the evening, and the Number One Theatre was a modern one where you did not have to fight for your seat. That reassured me, and I waited till nine o'clock before setting out. To my surprise, just as before, it was full. There was hardly any standing-room and I had to squeeze into

个点火的纸捻子，旁边有一个鬼卒，我费尽思量，才疑心他或者是目连的母亲，因为后来又出来了一个和尚。然而我又不知道那名角是谁，就去问挤小在我左边的一位胖绅士。他很看不起似的斜瞥了我一眼，说道，"龚云甫！"我深愧浅陋而且粗疏，脸上一热，同时脑里也制出了决不再问的定章，于是看小旦唱，看花旦唱，看老生唱，看不知什么角色唱，看一大班人乱打，看两三个人互打，从九点多到十点，从十点到十一点，从十一点到十一点半，从十一点半到十二点，——然而叫天竟还没有来。

我向来没有这样忍耐的等候过什么事物，而况这身边的胖绅士的吁吁的喘气，这台上的冬冬喤喤的敲打，红红绿绿的晃荡，加之以十二点，忽而使我省悟到在这里不适于生存了。我同时便机械的拧转身子，用力往外只一挤，觉得背后便已满满的，大约那弹性的胖绅士早在我的空处胖开了他的右半身了。我后无回路，自然挤而又挤，终于出了大门。街上除了专等看客的车辆之外，几乎没有什么行人了，大门口却还有十几个人昂着头看戏目，别有一堆人站着并不看什么，我想：他们大概是看散戏之后出来的女人们的，而叫天却还没有来……

然而夜气很清爽，真所谓"沁人心脾"，我在北京遇着这样的好空气，仿佛这是第一遭了。

这一夜，就是我对于中国戏告了别的一夜，此后再没有想到他，即使偶而经过戏园，我们也漠不相关，精神上早已一在天之南一在地之北了。

但是前几天，我忽在无意之中看到一本日本文的书，可惜忘记了书名和著者，总之是关于中国戏的。其中有一篇，大意仿佛说，中国戏是大敲，大叫，大跳，使看客头昏脑眩，很不适于剧场，但若在野外散漫的所在，远远的看起来，也自有他的风致。我当时觉着这正是说了在我意中而未曾想到的话，因为我确记得在野外看过很好的好戏，到北京以后的连进两回戏园去，也许还是受了那时的影响哩。可惜我不知道怎么一来，竟将书名忘却了。

1. Maudgalyayana was a disciple of Sakyamuni Buddha. Legend has it that his mother went to hell for her sins and he rescued her.

2. Well-known Beijing opera actor who played old women's roles.

the crowd at the rear to watch an actor singing an old woman's part. He had a paper spill burning at each corner of his mouth and there was a devil-soldier beside him. After racking my brains I guessed that this might be Maudgalyayana's[2] mother, because the next to come on was a monk. Not recognizing the actor, I asked a fat gentleman squeezed in on my left who he was. "Gong Yunfu!"[3] he said, throwing me a withering sidelong glance. My face burned with shame over my ignorant blunder, and I mentally resolved at all costs to ask no more questions. Then I watched a heroine and her maid sing, next an old man and some other characters I could not identify. After that, I watched a whole group fight a free-for-all, and after that two or three people fighting together — from after nine till ten, from ten till eleven, from eleven till eleven-thirty, from eleven-thirty till twelve — but still there was no sign of Tan Xinpei.

Never in my life have I waited so patiently for anything. But the wheezes of the fat gentleman next to me, the ding-dong skirling, gonging and drumming on the stage, the whirling of gaudy colours, combined with the lateness of the hour, suddenly made me realize that this was no place for me. Mechanically turning round, I tried with might and main to shove my way out and felt the place behind me fill up at once — no doubt the elastic fat gentleman had expanded his right side into the space I vacated. With my retreat cut off, naturally there was nothing to do but push and push till at last I was out of the door. Apart from the rickshaws waiting for playgoers, there were practically no pedestrians in the street; but there were still a dozen or so people by the gate looking up at the programme, and another group not looking at anything who must, I thought, be waiting to watch the women come out after the show ended. And still no sign of Tan Xinpei....

But the night air was so crisp, it really "seeped into my heart." This seemed to be the first time I had known such good air in Beijing.

I said goodbye to Chinese opera that night, never thinking about it again, and if by any chance I passed a theatre it meant nothing to me for in spirit we were long since poles apart.

A few days ago, however, I happened to read a Japanese book — unfortunately I have forgotten the title and author, but it was about Chinese opera. One chapter made the point that Chinese opera is so full of gongs and cymbals, shouting and leaping, that it makes the spectators' heads swim and is quite unsuited for a theatre; but if performed in the open and watched from a distance, it has its charm. I felt that this put into words what had remained unformulated in my mind, because as a matter of fact I clearly remembered seeing a really good opera in the country and it was under its influence, perhaps, that after coming to Beijing I went twice to the theatre. It is a pity that, somehow or other, the name of that book escapes me.

至于我看那好戏的时候，却实在已经是"远哉遥遥"的了，其时恐怕我还不过十一二岁。我们鲁镇的习惯，本来是凡有出嫁的女儿，倘自己还未当家，夏间便大抵回到母家去消夏。那时我的祖母虽然还康健，但母亲也已分担了些家务，所以夏期便不能多日的归省了，只得在扫墓完毕之后，抽空去住几天，这时我便每年跟了我的母亲住在外祖母的家里。那地方叫平桥村，是一个离海边不远，极偏僻的，临河的小村庄；住户不满三十家，都种田，打鱼，只有一家很小的杂货店。但在我是乐土：因为我在这里不但得到优待，又可以免念"秩秩斯干幽幽南山"了。

和我一同玩的是许多小朋友，因为有了远客，他们也都从父母那里得了减少工作的许可，伴我来游戏。在小村里，一家的客，几乎也就是公共的。我们年纪都相仿，但论起行辈来，却至少是叔子，有几个还是太公，因为他们合村都同姓，是本家。然而我们是朋友，即使偶而吵闹起来，打了太公，一村的老老小小，也决没有一个会想出"犯上"这两个字来，而他们也百分之九十九不识字。

我们每天的事情大概是掘蚯蚓，掘来穿在铜丝做的小钩上，伏在河沿上去钓虾。虾是水世界里的呆子，决不惮用了自己的两个钳捧着钩尖送到嘴里去的，所以不半天便可以钓到一大碗。这虾照例是归我吃的。其次便是一同去放牛，但或者因为高等动物了的缘故罢，黄牛水牛都欺生，敢于欺侮我，因此我也总不敢走近身，只好远远地跟着，站着。这时候，小朋友们便不再原谅我会读"秩秩斯干"，却全都嘲笑起来了。

至于我在那里所第一盼望的，却在到赵庄去看戏。赵庄是离平桥村五里的较大的村庄；平桥村太小，自己演不起戏，每年总付给赵庄多少钱，算作合做的。当时我并不想到他们为什么年年要演戏。现在想，那或者是春赛，是社戏了。

就在我十一二岁时候的这一年，这日期也看看等到了。不料这一年真可惜，在早上就叫不到船。平桥村只有

4. The earliest anthology of poetry in China and part of every school curriculum.

As to when I saw that good opera, it was really "long, long ago," when I could not have been much more than eleven or twelve. It was the custom in Luzhen where we lived for married women not yet in charge of the household to go back to their parents' home for the summer. Although my father's mother was then still quite strong, my mother had quite a few domestic duties which made it impossible for her to spend many days at her old home during the summer. All she could spare was a few days after visiting the ancestral graves, and at such times I always went with her to stay in her parents' house. That was in Pingqiao Village not far from the sea, a very remote little village on a river with less than thirty households of peasants and fishermen, and just one tiny grocery. To me, however, it was heaven, for not only was I treated as a guest of honour but here I could skip reading the *Book of Songs*.[4]

There were many children for me to play with. For with the arrival of a visitor from such a distance they got leave from their parents to do less work in order to play with me. In a small village, the guest of one family is virtually the guest of the whole community. We were all about the same age, but when it came to determining seniority many were at least my uncles or granduncles, since everybody in the village had the same family name and belonged to one clan. But we were all good friends, and if by some chance we fell out and I hit one of my granduncles, it never occurred to any child or grown-up in the village to call me "insubordinate." Ninety-nine out of a hundred of them could neither read nor write.

We spent most of our days digging up earthworms, putting them on little hooks made of copper wire, and lying on the river bank to catch prawns. The silliest of water creatures, prawns willingly use their own pincers to push the point of the hook into their mouths; so in a few hours we could catch a big bowlful. It was the custom to give these prawns to me. Another thing we did was to graze buffaloes together. But, maybe because they are animals of a higher order, oxen and buffaloes are hostile to strangers, and they treated me with such contempt that I never dared get too close. I could only follow at a distance and stand there. At such times my small friends, no longer impressed by my ability to recite classical poetry, would all start hooting with laughter.

What I looked forward to most was going to Zhaozhuang to see the opera. Zhaozhuang was a slightly larger village five li away. Since Pingqiao was too small to afford to put on operas, every year it chipped in towards a performance at Zhaozhuang. At the time, it never occurred to me to wonder why they should put on operas every year. Thinking back to it now, I dare say it may have been a ritual drama for the late spring festival.

The year that I was eleven or twelve, this long-awaited day came round again. But as ill luck would have it, there was no boat for hire that morning. Pingqiao Village had

一只早出晚归的航船是大船，决没有留用的道理。其余的
都是小船，不合用；央人到邻村去问，也没有，早都给别
人定下了。外祖母很气恼，怪家里的人不早定，絮叨起
来。母亲便宽慰伊，说我们鲁镇的戏比小村里的好得多，
一年看几回，今天就算了。只有我急得要哭，母亲却竭力
的嘱咐我，说万不能装模装样，怕又招外祖母生气，又不
准和别人一同去，说是怕外祖母要担心。

总之，是完了。到下午，我的朋友都去了，戏已经开
场了，我似乎听到锣鼓的声音，而且知道他们在戏台下买
豆浆喝。

这一天我不钓虾，东西也少吃。母亲很为难，没有法
子想。到晚饭时候，外祖母也终于觉察了，并且说我应当不
高兴，他们太怠慢，是待客的礼数里从来所没有的。吃饭之
后，看过戏的少年们也都聚拢来了，高高兴兴的来讲戏。只
有我不开口；他们都叹息而且表同情。忽然间，一个最聪明
的双喜大悟似的提议了，他说，"大船？八叔的航船不是回
来了么？"十几个别的少年也大悟，立刻撺掇起来，说可以
坐了这航船和我一同去。我高兴了。然而外祖母又怕都是孩
子们，不可靠；母亲又说是若叫大人一去，他们白天全有工
作，要他熬夜，是不合情理的。在这迟疑之中，双喜可又看
出底细来了，便又大声的说道，"我写包票！船又大；迅哥
儿向来不乱跑；我们又都是识水性的！"

诚然！这十多个少年，委实没有一个不会凫水的，而
且两三个还是弄潮的好手。

外祖母和母亲也相信，便不再驳回，都微笑了。我们
立刻一哄的出了门。

我的很重的心忽而轻松了，身体也似乎舒展到说不
出的大。一出门，便望见月下的平桥内泊着一只白篷的航
船，大家跳下船，双喜拔前篙，阿发拔后篙，年幼的都陪
我坐在舱中，较大的聚在船尾。母亲送出来吩咐"要小
心"的时候，我们已经点开船，在桥石上一磕，退后几
尺，即又上前出了桥。于是架起两支橹，一支两人，一里

only one big ferry-boat, which put out in the morning and came back in the evening, and it was out of the question to use this. All the other boats were unsuitable, being too small. And the neighbouring villages, when people were sent to ask, had no boats either — they had all been hired already. My grandmother, very vexed, blamed the family for not hiring one earlier and started nagging. To console her, Mother said that our operas at Luzhen were much better than in these little villages, and as we saw several a year there was no need to go today. But I was nearly in tears from chagrin, and Mother did her best to impress on me on no account to make a scene, because it would upset my grandmother; nor must I go with other people either, or Grandmother might worry.

In a word, it had fallen through. In the afternoon, when all my friends had left and the opera had started, I imagined I could hear the sound of gongs and drums and knew they were in front of the stage buying soyabean milk to drink.

I caught no prawns that day, did not eat much either. Mother was very upset but could not think what to do. By supper time Grandmother too had finally caught on and she said I was right to be cross, they had been too remiss, and never before had guests been treated so badly. After the meal, youngsters back from the opera gathered round and gaily described it to us. I was the only one silent. They all sighed and said how sorry they were for me. Suddenly one of the brightest, Shuangxi, had an inspiration and asked, "A big boat? Hasn't Eighth Granduncle's ferry-boat come back?" A dozen other boys cottoned on and at once started agitating to take the boat and go with me. I cheered up. But Grandmother was nervous, thinking we were all children and undependable. And Mother said it would not be fair to ask grown-ups to stay up all night and go with us, as they all had to work the next day. While our fate hung in the balance, Shuangxi went to the root of the problem, declaring loudly, "I guarantee it'll be all right! It's a big boat, Brother Xun never jumps around, and all of us can swim!"

It was true. Not a boy in the dozen but could swim, and two or three of them were first-rate swimmers in the sea.

Grandmother and Mother, convinced, raised no further objections. Both smiled. We immediately rushed out.

My heart after being so heavy was suddenly light, and I felt as though floating on air. Once outside, I saw in the moonlight a ferry-boat with a white awning moored at the bridge. We all jumped aboard, Shuangxi seizing the front pole and Afa the back one, while the younger boys sat down with me in the middle and those a little older went to the stern. By the time Mother followed us out to warn "Be careful!" we had already cast off. We pushed off from the bridge, floated back a few feet, then moved forward under the bridge, Two oars were set up, each manned by two boys who changed shifts every li. Chatter,

一换，有说笑的，有嚷的，夹着潺潺的船头激水的声音，在左右都是碧绿的豆麦田地的河流中，飞一般径向赵庄前进了。

两岸的豆麦和河底的水草所发散出来的清香，夹杂在水气中扑面的吹来；月色便朦胧在这水气里。淡黑的起伏的连山，仿佛是踊跃的铁的兽脊似的，都远远地向船尾跑去了，但我却还以为船慢。他们换了四回手，渐望见依稀的赵庄，而且似乎听到歌吹了，还有几点火，料想便是戏台，但或者也许是渔火。

那声音大概是横笛，宛转，悠扬，使我的心也沉静，然而又自失起来，觉得要和他弥散在含着豆麦蕴藻之香的夜气里。

那火接近了，果然是渔火；我才记得先前望见的也不是赵庄。那是正对船头的一丛松柏林，我去年也曾经去游玩过，还看见破的石马倒在地下，一个石羊蹲在草里呢。过了那林，船便弯进了叉港，于是赵庄便真在眼前了。

最惹眼的是屹立在庄外临河的空地上的一座戏台，模胡在远处的月夜中，和空间几乎分不出界限，我疑心画上见过的仙境，就在这里出现了。这时船走得更快，不多时，在台上显出人物来，红红绿绿的动，近台的河里一望乌黑的是看戏的人家的船篷。

"近台没有什么空了，我们远远的看罢。"阿发说。

这时船慢了，不久就到，果然近不得台旁，大家只能下了篙，比那正对戏台的神棚还要远。其实我们这白篷的航船，本也不愿意和乌篷的船在一处，而况并没有空地呢……

在停船的匆忙中，看见台上有一个黑的长胡子的背上插着四张旗，捏着长枪，和一群赤膊的人正打仗。双喜说，那就是有名的铁头老生，能连翻八十四个筋斗，他日里亲自数过的。

我们便都挤在船头上看打仗，但那铁头老生却又并不翻筋斗，只有几个赤膊的人翻，翻了一阵，都进去了，接着走出一个小旦来，咿咿呀呀的唱。双喜说，"晚上看客

laughter and shouts mingled with the lapping of water against our bow; to our right and left stretched emerald green fields of beans and wheat, as we flew forward towards Zhaozhuang.

The scent of beans, wheat and river-weeds wafted towards us through the mist, and the moonlight shone faintly through it. Distant grey hills, undulating like the backs of some leaping iron beasts, seemed to be racing past the stern of our boat; but I still felt our progress was slow. When the oarsmen had changed shifts, four times, we began to make out the faint outline of Zhaozhuang and to catch the sound of singing and music. There were several lights too, which we guessed must be on the stage unless they were fishermen's lights.

The music was probably fluting. Eddying round and round and up and down, it soothed me and set me dreaming at the same time, till I felt as though I was about to drift far away with it through the night air heavy with the scent of beans, wheat and river-weeds.

As we approached the lights, they proved to be fishermen's lights and I realized it was not Zhaozhuang that I had been looking at. Directly ahead of us was a pine-wood where I had played the year before and seen a broken stone horse, fallen on its side, as well as a stone sheep couched in the grass. Once past the wood, our boat rounded a bend into a cove, and Zhaozhuang was really before us.

Our eyes were drawn to the stage standing in a plot of empty ground by the river outside the village, hazy in the distant moonlight, barely distinguishable from its surroundings. It seemed that the fairyland I had seen in pictures had come alive here. The boat was moving faster now, and presently we could make out figures on the stage and a blaze of gaudy colours. The river close to the stage was black with the boat awnings of the spectators.

"There's no room near the stage, let's watch from a distance," suggested Afa.

The boat had slowed down now, and soon we arrived. True enough, it was impossible to get close to the stage. We had to make fast even further away from it than the shrine opposite. But, in any case, we did not want our boat with its white awning to mix with those black ones and, besides, there was no room....

While we hastily moored, there appeared on the stage a man with a long black beard and four pennons fixed to his back. With a spear he fought a whole group of bare-armed men. Shuangxi told us this was a famous acrobat who could turn eighty-four somersaults one after the other. He had counted for himself earlier in the day.

We all crowded to the bow to watch the fighting, but the acrobat did not turn any somersaults. Only a few of the bare-armed men turned head over heels a few times, then trooped off. Then a girl came out and sang in a shrill falsetto. "There aren't many

少，铁头老生也懈了，谁肯显本领给白地看呢？"我相信这话对，因为其时台下已经不很有人，乡下人为了明天的工作，熬不得夜，早都睡觉去了，疏疏朗朗的站着的不过是几十个本村和邻村的闲汉。乌篷船里的那些土财主的家眷固然在，然而他们也不在乎看戏，多半是专到戏台下来吃糕饼水果和瓜子的。所以简直可以算白地。

然而我的意思却也并不在乎看翻筋斗。我最愿意看的是一个人蒙了白布，两手在头上捧着一支棒似的蛇头的蛇精，其次是套了黄布衣跳老虎。但是等了许多时都不见，小旦虽然进去了，立刻又出来了一个很老的小生。我有些疲倦了，托桂生买豆浆去。他去了一刻，回来说，"没有。卖豆浆的聋子也回去了。日里倒有，我还喝了两碗呢。现在去舀一瓢水来给你喝罢。"

我不喝水，支撑着仍然看，也说不出见了些什么，只觉得戏子的脸都渐渐的有些稀奇了，那五官渐不明显，似乎融成一片的再没有什么高低。年纪小的几个多打呵欠了，大的也各管自己谈话。忽而一个红衫的小丑被绑在台柱子上，给一个花白胡子的用马鞭打起来了，大家才又振作精神的笑着看。在这一夜里，我以为这实在要算是最好的一折。

然而老旦终于出台了。老旦本来是我所最怕的东西，尤其是怕他坐下了唱。这时候，看见大家也都很扫兴，才知道他们的意见是和我一致的。那老旦当初还只是踱来踱去的唱，后来竟在中间的一把交椅上坐下了。我很担心；双喜他们却就破口喃喃的骂。我忍耐的等着，许多工夫，只见那老旦将手一抬，我以为就要站起来了，不料他却又慢慢的放下在原地方，仍旧唱。全船里几个人不住的吁气，其余的也打起呵欠来。双喜终于熬不住了，说道，怕他会唱到天明还不完，还是我们走的好罢。大家立刻都赞成，和开船时候一样踊跃，三四人径奔船尾，拔了篙，点退几丈，回转船头，架起橹，骂着老旦，又向那松柏林前进了。

月还没有落，仿佛看戏也并不很久似的，而一离赵庄，月光又显得格外的皎洁。回望戏台在灯火光中，却又

watching in the evening," said Shuangxi, "and the acrobat's taking it easy. Who wants to show off to an empty house?" That made sense to me, because by then there were not many spectators. The country folk, having work to do the next day, could not stay up all night and had gone home to bed. Standing there still were just a scattering of a few dozen idlers from Zhaozhuang and the villages around. The families of the local rich remained in the boats with black awnings, but they were not really interested in the opera. Most of them had come to the opera to eat cakes, fruit or melon-seeds. So it could really be reckoned an empty house.

As a matter of fact, I was not too keen on somersaults either. What I wanted most to see was a snake spirit swathed in white, its two hands clasping above it a wand-like snake's head, and next a leaping tiger dressed in yellow. But I waited a long time in vain. As soon as the girl left, out came a very old man acting the part of a young one. Feeling tired, I asked Guisheng to buy me some soyabean milk. He came back presently to say, "There isn't any. The deaf man who sells it has gone. There was some in the daytime, I drank two bowls then. I'll get you a dipperful of water to drink."

Instead of drinking the water, I stuck it out as best I could. I cannot say what I saw, but by degrees something strange seemed to happen to the faces of the players, whose features blurred as if melting into one flattened surface. Most of the younger boys yawned, while the older ones chatted among themselves. It was only when a clown in a red shirt was fastened to a pillar on the stage, and a greybeard started horsewhipping him, that we roused ourselves to watch again and laughed. I really think that was the best scene of the evening.

But then the old woman came out. This was the character I dreaded most, especially when she sat down to sing. Now I saw by everybody's disappointment that they felt just as I did. To start with, the old woman simply walked to and fro singing, then she sat on a chair in the middle of the stage. I felt most dismayed, and Shuangxi and the rest started swearing. I waited patiently till, after a long time, the old woman raised her hand. I thought she was going to stand up. But dashing my hopes she lowered her hand slowly again just as before, and went on singing. Some of the boys in the boat could not help groaning; the rest began to yawn again. Finally Shuangxi, when he could stand it no longer, said he was afraid she might go on singing till dawn and we had better leave. We all promptly agreed, becoming as eager as when we had set out. Three or four boys ran to the stern, seized the poles to punt back several yards, then headed the boat around. Cursing the old woman, they set up the oars and started back for the pine-wood.

Judging by the position of the moon we had not been watching very long, and once we left Zhaozhuang the moonlight seemed unusually bright. When we turned back

　　如初来未到时候一般，又漂渺得像一座仙山楼阁，满被红霞罩着了。吹到耳边来的又是横笛，很悠扬；我疑心老旦已经进去了，但也不好意思说再回去看。

　　不多久，松柏林早在船后了，船行也并不慢，但周围的黑暗只是浓，可知已经到了深夜。他们一面议论着戏子，或骂，或笑，一面加紧的摇船。这一次船头的激水声更其响亮了，那航船，就像一条大白鱼背着一群孩子在浪花里蹿，连夜渔的几个老渔父，也停了艇子看着喝采起来。

　　离平桥村还有一里模样，船行却慢了，摇船的都说很疲乏，因为太用力，而且许久没有东西吃。这回想出来的是桂生，说是罗汉豆正旺相，柴火又现成，我们可以偷一点来煮吃的。大家都赞成，立刻近岸停了船；岸上的田里，乌油油的便都是结实的罗汉豆。

　　"阿阿，阿发，这边是你家的，这边是老六一家的，我们偷那一边的呢？"双喜先跳下去了，在岸上说。

　　我们也都跳上岸。阿发一面跳，一面说道，"且慢，让我来看一看罢，"他于是往来的摸了一回，直起身来说道，"偷我们的罢，我们的大得多呢。"一声答应，大家便散开在阿发家的豆田里，各摘了一大捧，抛入船舱中。双喜以为再多偷，倘给阿发的娘知道是要哭骂的，于是各人便到六一公公的田里又各自偷了一大捧。

　　我们中间几个年长的仍然慢慢的摇着船，几个到后舱去生火，年幼的和我都剥豆。不久豆熟了，便任凭航船浮在水面上，都围起来用手撮着吃。吃完豆，又开船，一面洗器具，豆荚豆壳全抛在河水里，什么痕迹也没有了。双喜所虑的是用了八公公船上的盐和柴，这老头子很细心，一定要知道，会骂的。然而大家议论之后，归结是不怕。他如果骂，我们便要他归还去年在岸边拾去的一枝枯柏树，而且当面叫他"八癞子"。

　　"都回来了！那里会错。我原说过写包票的！"双喜在船头上忽而大声的说。

　　我向船头一望，前面已经是平桥。桥脚上站着一个

to look at the lantern-lit stage, it appeared just as it had been when we came, hazy as a fairy pavilion, covered in a rosy mist. Once again the flutes sounded melodiously in our ears. I suspected that the old woman must have finished, but could hardly suggest going back again to see.

Soon the pine-wood was behind us. Our boat was moving fairly fast, but there was such thick darkness all around you could tell it was very late. As they discussed the players, laughing and swearing, the rowers pulled harder on the oars. Now the plash of water against our bow was even more distinct. The ferry-boat seemed like a great white fish carrying a freight of children through the foam. Some old fishermen who fished all night stopped their punts to cheer at the sight.

We were still about one li from Pingqiao when our boat slowed down, the oarsmen saying that they were tired after rowing so hard, with nothing to eat for hours. It was Guisheng who had a bright idea this time. He said the broad beans were just ripe, and there was fuel on the boat — we could filch some beans and cook them. Everybody approving, we promptly drew alongside the bank and stopped. The pitch-black fields were filled with plump broad beans.

"Hey, Afa! They're your family's over here, and Old Liu Yi's over there. Which shall we take?" Shuangxi, the first to leap ashore, called from the bank.

As we all jumped ashore too Afa said, "Wait a bit and I'll have a look." He walked up and down feeling the beans, then straightened up to say, "Take ours, they're much bigger." With a shout we scattered through his family's bean field, each picking a big handful of beans and throwing them into the boat. Shuangxi thought that if we took any more and Afa's mother found out, she would make a scene, so we all went to Old Liu Yi's field to pick another handful each.

Then a few of the older boys started rowing slowly again, while others lit a fire in the stern and the younger boys and I shelled the beans. Soon they were cooked, and we let the boat drift while we gathered round and ate them with our fingers. When the beans were finished we went on again, washing the pot and throwing the pods into the river, to destroy all traces. What worried Shuangxi now was that we had used the salt and firewood on Eighth Granduncle's boat, and being a canny old man he was sure to find out and berate us. But after some discussion we decided that we had nothing to fear. If he swore at us, we would ask him to return the tallow branch he had taken the previous year from the river bank, and to his face call him "Old Scabby."

"We're all back! How could anything go wrong? Didn't I guarantee that?" Shuangxi's voice suddenly rang out from the bow.

Looking past him, I saw we were already at Pingqiao and someone was standing at

人，却是我的母亲，双喜便是对伊说着话。我走出前舱去，船也就进了平桥了，停了船，我们纷纷都上岸。母亲颇有些生气，说是过了三更了，怎么回来得这样迟，但也就高兴了，笑着邀大家去吃炒米。

大家都说已经吃了点心，又渴睡，不如及早睡的好，各自回去了。

第二天，我向午才起来，并没有听到什么关系八公公盐柴事件的纠葛，下午仍然去钓虾。

"双喜，你们这班小鬼，昨天偷了我的豆了罢？又不肯好好的摘，踏坏了不少。"我抬头看时，是六一公公棹着小船，卖了豆回来了，船肚里还有剩下的一堆豆。

"是的。我们请客。我们当初还不要你的呢。你看，你把我的虾吓跑了！"双喜说。

六一公公看见我，便停了楫，笑道，"请客？——这是应该的。"于是对我说，"迅哥儿，昨天的戏可好么？"

我点一点头，说道，"好。"

"豆可中吃呢？"

我又点一点头，说道，"很好。"

不料六一公公竟非常感激起来，将大拇指一翘，得意的说道，"这真是大市镇里出来的读过书的人才识货！我的豆种是粒粒挑选过的，乡下人不识好歹，还说我的豆比不上别人的呢。我今天也要送些给我们的姑奶奶尝尝去……"他于是打着楫子过去了。

待到母亲叫我回去吃晚饭的时候，桌上便有一大碗煮熟了的罗汉豆，就是六一公公送给母亲和我吃的。听说他还对母亲极口夸奖我，说"小小年纪便有见识，将来一定要中状元。姑奶奶，你的福气是可以写包票的了。"但我吃了豆，却并没有昨夜的豆那么好。

真的，一直到现在，我实在再没有吃到那夜似的好豆，——也不再看到那夜似的好戏了。

一九二二年十月。

the foot of the bridge — it was my mother to whom Shuangxi had called. As I walked up to the bow the boat passed under the bridge, then stopped, and we all went ashore. Mother was rather angry. She asked why we had come back so late — it was after midnight. But she was pleased to see us too and smilingly invited everyone to go and have some puffed rice.

They told her we had all had a snack to eat and were sleepy, so we had better get to bed at once, and off we all went to our different homes.

I did not get up till noon the next day, and there was no word of any trouble with Eighth Granduncle over the salt or firewood. That afternoon we went to catch prawns as usual.

"Shuangxi, you little devils stole my beans yesterday! And instead of picking them properly you trampled down quite a few." I looked up and saw Old Liu Yi on a punt, coming back from selling beans. There was still a heap of left-over beans at the bottom of the punt.

"Yes, we were treating a visitor. We didn't mean to take yours to begin with," said Shuangxi. "Look! You've frightened away my prawn!"

When the old man saw me, he stopped punting and chuckled. "Treating a visitor? So you should." Then he asked me, "Was yesterday's opera good, Brother Xun?"

I nodded. "Yes, it was."

"Did you enjoy the beans?"

I nodded again. "Very much."

To my surprise, that gratified Old Liu Yi enormously. Sticking up one thumb he said complacently, "People from big towns who have studied really know what's good! I select my bean seeds one by one, yet country folk who can't tell good from bad say my beans aren't up to other people's. I'll give some to your mother today for her to try...." With that he punted off.

When Mother called me home for supper, on the table there was a large bowl of boiled beans which Old Liu Yi had brought for the two of us. And I heard he had praised me highly to Mother, saying, "He's so young, yet he knows what's what. He's sure to come first in the official examinations in future. Your fortune's as good as made, ma'am." But when I ate the beans, they did not taste as good as those of the night before.

It is a fact, right up till now, I have really never eaten such good beans or seen such a good opera as I did that night.

October 1922

图书在版编目（CIP）数据

呐喊：汉英对照 / 鲁迅著；杨宪益，戴乃迭译
—北京：外文出版社，2010
（经典回声）
ISBN 978-7-119-06680-6

Ⅰ.①呐... Ⅱ.①鲁... ②杨... ③戴...
Ⅲ.①英语—汉语—对照读物②鲁迅小说—选集 Ⅳ.①H319.4：I

中国版本图书馆CIP数据核字(2010)第176835号

策　　划：胡开敏
责任编辑：杨春燕　杨　璐
装帧设计：圙圙吾昱设计工作室
印刷监制：冯　浩

经典回声　呐喊

鲁　迅　著

杨宪益　戴乃迭　译

裘　沙　王伟君　插图

©2010外文出版社
出 版 人：呼宝民
总 编 辑：李振国
出版发行：外文出版社
地　　址：中国北京西城区百万庄大街24号
邮政编码：100037
网　　址：http://www.flp.com.cn
电　　话：（010）68320579/68996067（总编室）
　　　　　（010）68995844/68995852（发行部）
　　　　　（010）68327750/68996164（版权部）
印　　制：外文印刷厂
经　　销：新华书店 / 外文书店
开　　本：720mm×1020mm 1/16
印　　张：18.375
字　　数：140千字
装　　别：平装
版　　次：2010年9月第1版　210年9月第1版第1次印刷
书　　号：ISBN 978-7-119-06680-6
定　　价：34.00元　　　　　　　　建议上架：双语学习